Liz, the Neighbour

Hea Sook Jung

Copyright © 2021 Hea Sook Jung All rights reserved

The characters and events portrayed in this book are fictitious. Any similarity to real persons, living or dead, is coincidental and not intended by the author.

No part of this book may be reproduced, or stored in a retrieval system, or transmitted in any form or by any means, electronic, mechanical, photocopying, recording, or otherwise, without express written permission of the publisher.

ISBN-13: 9798722072795
ISBN-10: 1477123456

Cover design by: Art Painter
Library of Congress Control Number: 2018675309
Printed in the United States of America

Liz, the Neighbour

The Liz Knight Trilogy #2

1

FRIDAY, NOVEMBER 22

A stranger had been quietly watching a 2-storey single-family home on a dimly lit street called Culnan Avenue from his 2012 Chevrolet Malibu while patiently waiting for the city to fall asleep.

The street was located in the southwest corner of the great city of Toronto. It wasn't an opulent neighbourhood by any measure, but it had a contented, tranquil feel to it. The street featured well-kept single-family homes with neatly trimmed lawns.

Every now and then, somebody appeared on the street, walking hurriedly along the street and then darting into one of the homes.

Some cars drove through with their headlights on, flushing out the odd stray cat or squirrel. Every now and then, one of these cars finished its journey here on

Culnan Avenue. Its driver quickly popped out of the vehicle and made haste to the comfort and warmth of their home.

Minus the man in the Chevrolet Malibu, this was a typical night scene in late November on Culnan Avenue. The brave residents of Culnan Avenue deserted the street in the early hours of the evening for only one reason – the cold weather.

The residents went about their day just like any other day, oblivious to the man in the Malibu.

The man in the parked car wore khaki canvas cargo pants, a black leather jacket and military-style black boots. His strawberry blond hair was neatly styled with a little longer hair on top short on the sides. A clean-shaven face revealed him as a white man in his late 20s or early 30s.

He had shown up for work early, so he could park his car in this particular spot on the street. This parking spot gave him two advantageous positions – one, quick access to his target and two, a good cover that would explain his presence here.

From this spot, he not only had quick access to the house and a clear view of the comings and goings of its residents but best of all, he could remain inconspicuous because of a full-on renovation one house down. Construction made strangers and strange cars a familiar part of the everyday scene. When the police came to investigate the murder, no one would even bother to mention the car that had been parked there for a good part of the last few days.

In the house lived a 74-year-old black gentleman named Ed Jamieson and his 27-year-old gorgeous granddaughter, Madison Cooper. He knew that

Madison's room was upstairs directly left of the staircase. He knew that because he'd been in her room just a couple of days ago while they'd been out grocery-shopping as part of his reconnaissance.

He liked her room very much. It wasn't too clean as to make him feel bad about making such a mess tonight and not so messy that he might trip on something. *Oh yes,* it was a nice, small bedroom with a single bed covered with a crisp indigo ocean striped duvet, a desk with a chair, and a closet full of business suits as well as some strictly-for-fun dresses hung on a rod, and neatly folded casual clothes placed on shelves.

A thigh-high slit, V-neck, red dress had caught his eye. He didn't have to see it to know it. She would look like a sexy goddess in that dress. Her big, dark black eyes, her full lips and prominent cheeks would be so intensified in the dress that it would make her look vulnerable to the touch. As she sashayed, her long, flawless chocolate silky smooth legs would appear and disappear through the slit and tease any man's heart.

She was totally his type. He bet he was hers. Why wouldn't he be? He wasn't tall, being 5 feet and 10 inches, but was still considered a very handsome man. A lot of women had told him so. He was sure that Madison and he would totally go on a date if they had met under different circumstances. So, that was that – no date.

Ed had a slightly bigger bedroom at the end of the hallway. He wouldn't call it a master bedroom. It just didn't feel right to call it that. Ed's room had similar items to Madison's – a bed, a side table with a lamp, a desk with a chair, a closet full of clothes. He hadn't stayed in Ed's room for long because the only thing that mattered to him was its layout.

Once Madison and Ed retired to their bedrooms tonight, he would walk into the house, up the stairs, into Madison's room and kill her first and then move quickly into Ed's room to finish him off. That would be all.

He just needed to patiently wait for the perfect time to strike. When it was time to strike, he would make a perfect hole in her heart and then Ed's just like he'd done so many times before. He felt the Glock in his waistband through the jacket.

Although he had no plan to carry out his mission before midnight, he had to be here at this early hour for one reason only – To prepare for the unexpected, just as his military training had taught him. He really had to give it to the military, especially when he saw Madison suddenly appear on the front porch in her 4-inch red stiletto heels out of nowhere.

Shit! He let out a muffled howl in fury.

He took one long, slow breath. That was all it required to slow his heart rate and get focused back on the mission. He asked himself as he hovered his hand over the Glock in his waistband, *Retreat or Advance?* And the Glock answered, *Advance.*

That meant he had to do it before she reached her car parked on the driveway. That gave him less than a minute: *tick-tock, tick-tock.*

His current position was no longer advantageous to make the best use of his Glock. He needed to put himself at closer range. That meant he now had less than thirty seconds: *tick-tock, tick-tock.*

Liz, the Neighbour

As he put the key in the ignition, he quickly searched the street to assess his new operational environment and saw two old ladies coming out of the house next door to Madison's. Then, he knew his Glock was wrong – *retreat, not advance, you idiot.*

In surrender, he just sat in the car and watched Madison's careful maneuver from the front door to the porch steps. Suddenly, *bang!* She fell, slid down the rest of the steps landing hard on the pavement.

Women! He shook his head.

For the next long moment, he enjoyed the show as it unfolded.

The old woman was almost hopping as if trying to make up for her short strides to rush to Madison, and then the other old lady followed the first one on her cane: *click, click, clicking frantically.*

The two old ladies hovered over Madison making a fuss. He couldn't make out the words they were spitting out, so he made his own words and dubbed their conversation as if it were a foreign film:

Old lady #1: Damn, your heels are so sexy. Can I borrow them?

Madison: Not even in your dreams, you wrinkly old fart.

Old lady #2: That's a very slinky dress. Shake it baby, shake it.

Madison: Buzz off you useless old hags. I'll shake it when I'm with my man.

Old lady #1: Do you have a boyfriend? Is he handsome?

Madison: Of course, I have a boyfriend. He's watching me right there across the street. Isn't he handsome?

The wailing sound of an ambulance that rose and descended and rose again, drew him out of his own little movie making. He then saw Ed come out of his house and quickly run to Madison in a panic.

Two paramedics came out of the ambulance and scooped her up onto a gurney. As they were whisking her away into the ambulance, she waved her hands as if to say that they shouldn't come to the hospital with her. The ambulance doors were closed and they drove away.

The man remained at the scene for a few seconds to see if anyone was going to follow Madison to the hospital. When he saw the three oldies walk towards Ed's home, he slowly drove out of the parking spot and followed the ambulance.

The man in Chevrolet Malibu took out his cellphone and clicked 'Sir' as he parked the car in the parking lot of the Mississauga Hospital.

"The mission is at halt. '*Operation Plan A*' aborted and improvising as circumstances unfold. Eve broke her ankle and possibly her hip."

The man pressed his cellphone hard to his ear to better hear his boss's muffled voice.

"I gave the codename Eve for my target. Adam and Eve, I thought it had a nice ring to it."

There was a bout of silence from the other end of the call.

"Sir, are you there?"

He then heard his boss asking his whereabouts.

"I'm at the Mississauga Hospital."

He listened for a bit and then he said, "Negative, sir. It wasn't my doing. Eve fell and slipped all on her own."

He listened for another moment and then assured his boss. "It'll be done before sunrise."

• • •

Seventeen miles away from the man in the Chevrolet Malibu, another man stood on a path in a ravine, squeezing his grip on his cellphone tighter and tighter in anger and frustration.

Damn it, Adam!

He didn't like improvising, especially when things were improvised by *Adam Doyle*. The last time Adam Doyle had improvised, the army had handed them both dishonourable discharges. He had once been a soldier doing thug stuff. Now, he was just a thug, doing his thug job day in, day out. He really didn't like it.

Eve... Mission... He just shook his head in annoyance mixed with anger. *Who the fuck needs a codename? And this is just a job, not a mission. We're two ex-military who don't get to use codenames or go on missions anywhere. Got it?*

He shouldn't be so riled up by Adam or him improvising. He knew two things about Adam Doyle. One, Adam always got lucky when a woman was involved – whether it was a mission or not. That was why he had given Adam, Madison. Two, Adam wouldn't stop until the mission was successfully completed or he got caught. He just hoped like hell that it was the former.

For camouflage, he was dressed almost all in black – black canvas cargo pants, a black field jacket and military-style black boots. The back of his jacket was emblazoned with a tiger's head with white fur that framed its ferocious snarl. His dark brown hair was cut short military style. He was a 32-year-old white man which put him senior to Adam Doyle by two full years.

The man resumed his walk. Although it was completely dark, every step was effortlessly agile. For the last few days, he'd carried out his ISTAR practice - Intelligence, Surveillance, Target Acquisition and Reconnaissance, and as a part of the practice, he had put himself through his reconnaissance training mission once in the daytime and once at night, for the last few days to make himself familiar with the route to his target acquisition.

When he finally made it to the thick trees bordering the backyard of Adam Brooks' house, he took a few seconds before proceeding.

From here to Brooks' house, he was in sight of anyone with watchful eyes. Right now, luck was with him. The house on the right side of Brooks' place wasn't occupied, and the house on the left side was occupied by a crazy old man and his caregiver. So really, there was no one with watchful eyes to watch him, but it was his second nature checking and double-checking between checkpoints.

Shit! He hissed under his breath in astonishment, stopping himself in his tracks. In the brightly lit kitchen, his target was cooking... for somebody... no, no, not for somebody. His target appeared to be cooking for two people while humourlessly conversing away with his guests.

He wasn't a fan of improvising, but here he was, contemplating the idea of eliminating three instead of one. It was totally doable with his Glock 18 – one person or three persons actually didn't make much of a difference as long as he could position himself inside the house without being seen.

As he was searching for a new entry point, his cellphone vibrated. He saw Adam Doyle's number on the screen, causing him to frown involuntarily. *What now?*

Putting his irritation aside, he took the call. He patiently listened while breathing in and out at regular intervals trying to control his anger as Adam Doyle was briefing him on the situation.

"Let me summarize what you just said. You and Madison—"

What the... Did you just cut me off to correct her name? He held back a breath as his frustration was building up to an explosion. He breathed out a long breath under his lips before he continued. "You're telling me that you and Eve, somehow, struck up a conversation and now you're going to give her a ride home when she's done at the hospital. And you'll kill her in your car after CCTVs at the hospital have caught you cozying up to Ma... I mean *Eve*, and *Eve* getting into your car. At least, tell me the car is registered to your *codename*."

After waiting a bit for a response, when none came, he continued. "Don't do anything. Do you hear—" Before he had a chance to finish, something finished him dropping him to the ground.

What the hell!

He didn't know what had hit him or who had hit him. He had become so frustrated with Doyle that he had lost sight of his surroundings. All he knew was that he had been knocked to the ground and his head was bleeding. He then heard an old man threatening him with his shaky but loud voice.

"Piss off, you dirty trash hunting cat!!!"

Then Brooks' concerned voice came, "What is it, Gerald? Are you okay?"

Oh shit! Next thing he knew, everyone was coming out of the woodwork having the time of their lives.

Now, Brooks' guests were joining in the conversation.

He knew then that his mission had been foiled big time and a hasty retreat was his only way out.

He retreated down the ravine as quickly and quietly as he could. When he managed to put a good distance between himself and Adam Brooks, he hid under a stand of trees and took out his phone. Once connected, he debriefed the situation. He could hear his boss breathing hard out of anger and then the hard breathing stopped. There was just complete silence. He was about to disconnect the call, thinking that he had lost cell service when he heard the voice again.

"Yes, it sounds like she took quite an interest in him."

He was then asked a second question.

"What else would she call him besides Adam?"

Again, dead silence, then he received a new order. He disconnected the call and then called Adam Doyle to relay the order – *Drive your Eve home safely and let her live for now.*

2

TUESDAY, NOVEMBER 26

It was early in the morning in late November, and Liz Knight was driving down the road in a yellow Porsche 718 Boxster at full speed, top down. Her long, sunflower-blond hair was elegantly wrapped in a silk headscarf like a movie starlet. Huge black Channel sunglasses covered half her face making her full red lips appear even more delicious than usual. The car slowed as she entered a school safety zone finally coming to a full stop in the half-moon designated children drop zone.

She climbed out of the vehicle in a red spandex dress that revealed her perfect hourglass body, 36-24-36. Everybody dropped whatever they were doing and looked at her – women with jealous eyes, men with lustful hearts. Secretly enjoying all the attention she was receiving, she circled around to the other side, reached into a girl in the backseat.

"Did you enjoy the ride, Em?" Liz said, looking at her perfect 4-year-old daughter strapped into her car seat. She freed her from her safety straps and hoisted her into her arms.

"Of course, mommy." Emma squeezed Liz with her tiny hands. Emma's curly blond hair, like Liz's, flowed in the wind. "Achoo!" Emma sneezed.

"Oh my sweetie pie, did you catch a cold? I'm sorry. I should've closed the top."

Emma tightened her lips while shaking her head disapprovingly. "You can't drive a sports car top closed mommy." Emma's nose suddenly wrinkled up for a second and then, "Aaah... Aaah… Achoo!"

The image of her imaginary daughter sneezing made Liz smile. In reality, Liz didn't have a sports car let alone a daughter in real life. This was just what Liz Knight had envisioned her life would be like by the time she hit 32.

Another daydream she'd indulged in various forms, back when she'd been in her early 20s, was that of her dazzling husband trying to put their twin boys to bed early so that he could make love to her in their cheap rental apartment. Her breath-takingly gorgeous-looking husband only had eyes for her. Working hard to build a beautiful world for her and their children, he could've had any girl he'd wanted but he'd chosen her simply because his heart beat only for her.

So much for misdirected fairy tale daydreams. In reality, she had no husband, no boyfriend, and no child. She was just a woman, feeling generally unfulfilled in her life, still desperately wishing to have someone special in her life even after all the painful heartaches and numerous breakups. She'd had 6 relationships since high school and had been the one that got dumped every single time.

The worst boyfriend out of the six? Without a shred of doubt, that would have to be her second to last ex-boyfriend, the one and only Ken Steele. He was a pathological liar who had put her through a living hell for 6 years: *Son of a bitch!*

The worst breakup? That was definitely the one with her last boyfriend, Al DeStefano. He'd sent his lawyer to do the breaking up for him: *Son of a bitch!* The worst part of it all though was that she'd been accused of the murder of his new girlfriend. At that time, she'd had to move into her brother's home as part of her bail conditions. Although she'd cleared her name, she'd stayed there and was still mooching off her brother and his wife to this day.

Did that make her feel bad about herself? No. She felt no shame. Quite frankly, she enjoyed her current living arrangement. She had no boyfriend to have over for a hot, steamy night or some dark secret to be accidentally revealed by a roommate.

You know what else she didn't have? A job. That wasn't actually entirely true. Since she had proven her innocence with the help of her family and friends, she'd become a private investigator. She didn't want to call it a job yet because she hadn't made a penny doing it. Today, she hoped that she could change that.

She sat by the window of a little dessert place called Delights located in uptown Toronto, waiting for her first client to show. She was dressed in a black business suit, just like her associate Ella Seo who was sitting across from her.

The sky was blue and 11°C cold. The street was full of restaurants, bars, cafes, beauty spas and boutique shops. Although it was just two o'clock in the afternoon on a Tuesday, the street was already buzzing with young people. They were out on the street in groups, trying to find the next hot spot to hang. Some were dressed in a low-cut top, a skirt that barely covered their butt, a trench coat on top and knee-high boots. Some wore jeans and a hoodie. Others wrapped themselves up in a Canada Goose winter parka and Ugg winter boots.

The road was congested with heavy traffic, but who really cared about traffic when you were tucked away inside a warm cafe that was filled with aroma, right?

Liz tucked her long, wavy, blonde hair behind her ear and sipped a coffee while watching Ella with alarm.

Ella Seo was Korean through and through. At age eight, she had immigrated to Canada with her family. Mocked, teased and bullied during her elementary school years, she'd entirely closed herself off from other people, and her family had become her entire world.

At age twenty-one, murder had stolen her whole world from her, and she'd lost her way. She'd got hooked on drugs and finally kicked her bad habit when she'd re-connected with Yuul Kwon, her brother's best friend from back home. They'd become sisters by bond. When Yuul had married Jeffrey Knight, Liz's brother, Ella had gotten herself an even bigger family.

A few months ago, at age twenty-seven, Ella had met a man and they'd been dating ever since. One of the few good things that had actually come out of Liz's arrest for murder. It was evident that Ella loved everything about him. She'd had no social life since the age of eight, and she was trying to change that.

Ella looked frightened, her face pale and tense. Her distress was palpable. Liz knew why – she was having one of those panic attacks she used to get back in the day. Liz knew she had to do something to take Ella's mind off things, and then it came to her. She stared at Ella shaking her head.

"What?" Ella asked.

"I hate you."

"What did I do?" Ella's eyebrows arched.

"You over there drinking that super fatty Caramel Frappuccino in front of me is what you did."

Ella smiled. "Guilty."

"I've lost just 3 lbs in the last three months by watching everything I put into my body. I don't know why I even bother."

"I hate you," Ella said, shaking her head disapprovingly.

"What did I do?"

"You have a body that most women would die for, and you're complaining about it to me – me short and skinny."

"I'm 135 lbs."

"Yes, 135 lbs in a 5'6" body frame." Ella shook her head in disgust. "How more perfect do you want to be?"

"117 lbs."

"Why?"

"I'd just like to be skinny for a change. Who knows? I might even get lucky with a man."

"I don't think guys are really into skinny girls. Charlie's on a secret mission to make me fat. Our last date, we ate before the movie, during the movie, and after the movie. And then he sent me home with a super fatty dessert. Then, he called me at night to make sure I've eaten the dessert."

"That's adorable."

"He is. I just don't think he understands what he's getting himself into. At this rate, in 6 months I'll be a block, and in a year from now, he'll have turned me into an exercise ball. Let's see how he feels about me then." Ella smiled weakly.

"Who would've ever thought that that arrogant jerk could be turned into such a lovey-dovey marshmallow?" Liz shook her head in astonishment, recalling what Charlie had been like until just a few months ago.

Charlie Khoury was 33-year-old, 6'2" tall. His clean-shaven face honed his classic good looks and made him look sharp and professional. He had a short blowout haircut tapered at the sides. Before Ella had entered his life, his eyes had beamed with an intensity that would've made people think twice before approaching him. Through his whole life, every move Charlie made had been a shrewd and calculating one, right down to his hairstyle choice. He hadn't done anything on a whim, and his every move had been fueled by his ambitions. He'd been a ruthless opportunist. That had been back before he'd met Ella. Nowadays, Liz barely recognized him. He'd changed a lot. His eyes had softened. He could just hang out with people shooting the breeze and laughing, no agenda. *Who knew? No one!*

"He's a lovey-dovey hottie," Ella added, blushing.

"Haha. That's true. I only saw him in social settings a handful of times." Liz leaned towards Ella. "I've got to tell you. Women drooled when he walked into the room undressing him with their eyes. They whispered about the nasty things they would do to him and with him." Liz paused and smiled a mischievous smile for a moment. She then raised her right eyebrow up slightly. She said almost in a whisper, "So, you lucky girl, what kind of nasty things have you done with him, or to him for that matter?"

Ella sucked her burning cheeks in while fixing her stare at her coffee mug.

"Don't tell me you haven't slept with him yet?"

Ella didn't say a word but her burning cheeks said it all.

"Hmm…" Liz wrinkled her nose. "I know as a fact that he's into girls… and I heard he's fantastic in the bed. So—"

"Are we really talking about this now?" Ella hissed, darting a glance around the café to remind Liz they were not alone.

"Now is as good a time as any." Liz raised her right eyebrow slightly, wearing a smile. "Or, we can talk about it with Yuul and Jeffrey."

"You're horrible."

"We all know that. So, tell me. Don't you see him in that way?"

Ella bit her lower lip and chewed on it for a bit. Then she dropped her gaze to her coffee mug and kept it there. "I do wonder… you know… what it'd be like. The thought of him and me… you know… makes me… uh… feverish." Ella slowly rubbed her forehead.

"But at the same time, I'm scared he might be disappointed at what he sees. Skinny girls don't have much to show off when the clothes come off and the lights are still on."

"Hahaha. You *waant* him. You want him *baad*," Liz spoke in a singsong.

"Shh." Ella hushed Liz and looked around to see if anyone was listening. When she saw no judgmental stares from patrons of the cafe, she said, "And I don't really know much about that stuff."

Liz's face broke into a grin. "Rip his clothes off with your teeth and then you kiss every inch of his skin, then work your way down—."

"Liz," Ella hissed, glancing around the café again.

Liz smiled roguishly. "Have I embarrassed you?"

"A little. You can't say things like that in public."

"Hahaha. Okay, later but we've got to have the sex talk. We can have the talk that I had with my mom, or talks I had with Cheryl when we were in high school. Your choice."

"Both."

"What? Okay, when we get home…" Liz paused and lifted her chin up a little bit to point out to a man who'd just walked through the door. "I think that's him."

Ella followed Liz's direction and found a middle-aged, short, stocky man wearing a baseball cap.

• • •

The man in the baseball cap stood by the entrance door of Delights, slowly scanning patron's faces in the half-emptied café. Finally, his eyes settled on a woman with long blonde hair smiling directly at him. He knew that she had to be the one, or at least one of them. The Asian woman who sat at the table with the blondie was also looking in his direction, smiling.

With one quick glance, he knew that they were younger than him. He never trusted anyone younger than him, and they were definitely younger than his forty-five years. Worse yet, they didn't even look tough enough to chase down a bar shot let alone a murderer or a kidnapper. He looked at the doorknob for a minute as he contemplated slipping back out the door he'd just entered through.

He'd phoned every PI agency in town and now he knew why KSK Private Investigative Services had the best price – Inexperience.

How naïve was I to believe that I got lucky, finding a top-notch agency at a bargain basement price! He silently wallowed in self-pity. He should've asked them what kind of experience they had in this finding missing persons business before he'd set up the meeting, but he hadn't. It was on him. With that thought in mind, he turned and walked over to the table where the two young women sat.

"KSK Private Investigative Services?" He asked politely, still hoping they weren't.

The blondie stood up and extended her hand. "Jonas Fischer?"

Jonas then knew for sure that he had gotten the right people, the wrong choice but the right people. He reluctantly grasped the fingertips of her hand in his just for a second and let go. With trepidation, he slowly took off his green canvas backpack and put it on the floor next to the empty chair and sat down.

Everyone sat in awkward silence for a long moment until the blondie swallowed hard and said, "I'm Liz Knight." She smiled and turned to the Asian girl. "This is Ella Seo."

Ella nodded at him with an awkward smile.

"I'll cut right to the chase," Liz spoke plainly. "Here's the deal. After you tell us the details about your missing aunt, we'll tell you how long it'll take, and if we can't locate your aunt within the agreed upon time, we won't charge you a dime. You can go find another agency. No hard feelings."

Jonas thought it over, drumming his fingers on the table for a moment. He concluded that he had nothing to lose. He extended his hand. "You've got yourself a deal."

Liz shook his hand, and he could see on her face that this deal almost caused her to jump out of her chair. Enthusiasm. He liked it.

Liz said, interest sharp in her emerald green eyes, "Now, tell us everything you can about your aunt and the circumstances surrounding her disappearance."

Jonas smiled for a couple of seconds. As the smile faded on his face, he heaved a big sigh. "The missing aunt is my father's 75-year-old sister, Agnes Winter. She and her husband, Hans Winter, never had children of their own. Sadly, Hans died a couple of years ago from cancer, leaving Agnes all on her own. So it was that several months ago, she decided to move into a retirement home in Grimsby."

Ella pulled her chair closer to the table.

Jonas liked that – an attentive audience. He glanced at Ella and gave her a warm nod. "This is how it all started. I called Agnes one day just to say hi, but her cellphone was out of service. So, I called the retirement home. The receptionist there was like, *Agnes who?*" He felt a wave of fury flow through him. His nostrils flared, he hissed, "And then that nasty piece of work hung up on me." His voice shook with anger, his face as red as a beet.

"How unbelievably thoughtless and rude!" Liz said almost in a shout, her brow furrowed.

Ella nodded vigorously.

"Right?" Jonas said, excited to have his anger validated. He took several deep breaths, trying to regain control again. Then he continued in a more controlled tone. "I called up my sisters and cousins, and we all went down to the retirement home together. We met up with a big shot at the home – the office manager. He was rude and totally uncooperative. He said that the home wasn't a prison and that she had walked out one day and never came back. The staff gave us boxes with all her stuff that she'd left behind and shooed us out the door. I came back home in total frustration. Not knowing what else to do I called all her friends. No one had heard from her or knew where she was." He again stopped himself and drew in a deep breath.

He was troubled with the next part of the story. He thought for a moment and decided to stick with his original plan: *No great detail, just get through it quick and give them the bare bones.*

Jonas swallowed. "One day, out of the blue, she called and told me some crazy ass things. Her final remark was not to come looking for her and that it might put her in more danger than she was already in."

Liz held up a finger. "Tell us more about the crazy things she told you were going on."

Jonas stared at Liz in shock, his eyes wide. He felt like he had been caught red-handed. He looked off into space while mulling over how much he really wanted to tell them.

"Jonas?" Liz said.

Jonas turned his attention back to Liz and Ella. He let out a sigh in resignation. "She said that people were being killed at the retirement home, and that the place was up to no good."

Liz frowned. "That sounds terrifying. You should be taking this to the police, not us."

"Here's the thing." Jonas rubbed his forehead for a while before he continued. "Before she moved into the retirement home, she said she saw dead people." He paused and faked a little chuckle. "Just like the movie, the Sixth Sense. We all saw her talking to herself. She said she wasn't talking to herself and that she was actually talking to ghosts. One day, she said she needed to get out of her place and needed to start living with the living again, not stuck here with the dead."

Liz and Ella just blinked hard.

Jonas heaved another big sigh. "Mental illness runs deep through our family line. Considering her age and our family history, she's probably lost it… just like my father." The memory of his deranged father sent a shiver down his spine and at the same time made him very sad. He shook his head to stop himself from going down the rabbit hole.

"What's the name of the retirement home?" Liz asked.

"Wild Peach Estate."

"Did you bring any pictures with you?" Ella asked.

Jonas picked up his backpack and sat it down on the table. "I brought albums of them."

He took out one of the albums and flipped it open. "These pictures here are the most recent ones. I don't know most of the people in the albums, but I do know a few of them."

As Jonas put names to faces to the people in the pictures, using an app on her cellphone, Ella took pictures of the pictures and attached names and any relevant info Jonas offered to the images.

"That's it. That's everything," Jonas said with a pang of guilt. "I should've been more involved in her life."

They sat silently, a sombre air hanging over them, until Jonas cleared his throat. "Anyway, what's your assessment? How long do you think it'll take for you to find her?"

"Give us two weeks from tomorrow. If we can't find her by then, you move on."

3

TUESDAY, NOVEMBER 26

Yuul Kwon had stayed at home to finally get things ready for the move this coming Saturday. Her long, black hair tied in a ponytail was swinging side to side as she packed the clothes from her bedroom closet into a heavy, black moving bag.

The television was blasting away from the living room with the volume cranked. Liz and Ella had forgotten to turn it off before they'd left home to meet with their first client. Yuul was simply too lazy to walk over to the living room and turn it off.

While packing, Yuul half caught the pieces of a news report about a shooting that had taken place in the city last night. Yuul shook her head in disgust. *Another one...*

Thirty-four-year-old Yuul Kwon had been born into a rich family in Korea. At age fourteen, she was kidnapped, and almost raped by her abductors but managed to survive. In the aftermath of the kidnapping, her brother had hired the best people money could buy, from martial artists to ex-green berets to train her to be unbreakable.

Growing up, she had only one friend – Hayden Seo. They did everything together – a lot of stupid things, brave things and more stupid things. Before she turned sixteen, Hayden had moved to Canada with his family and left her friendless.

At age twenty-eight, her wedding ceremony was hijacked by her ex-boyfriend, and she left Korea to search for Hayden in Canada. After two years of fruitless searching, just as she was ready to give up and go back home, she happened to stumble upon Hayden's younger sister, Ella, on her last breaths in a very dark corner of the city. It was in that very same fateful spot where she had met the love of her life, Jeffery Knight, and with his help, she saved Ella. Since then, there had always been just Yuul, Jeffrey and Ella.

A few months ago, Jeffrey's sister had been accused of murder. Yuul had joined "the innocence project for Liz" and helped get the charges against her dropped. After Liz was cleared and free to live her life again, Liz and Ella had decided to start a private investigation business together, and Yuul had hopped on the train with them. From there on in, it had been Yuul, Jeffrey, Ella and Liz in a condo located on Yonge and Finch.

The last few months proved that condo-living had no longer suited her or anyone else in her household for that matter and hence the house searching had begun. When she'd come across this old house on York Ridge Road, it had felt lucky, so she bought it.

Yuul was in the living room removing the many books that lined their bookcases when Liz and Ella came home. Tons of books and plastic moving boxes covered the floor. The house was a mess as one might expect a place to look in the middle of a move.

Liz and Ella manoeuvred their way right passed all the mess and beelined it straight to the comfy couches where they flopped themselves down.

"I didn't think you had that much stuff to pack," Liz said, glancing at the disarray of containers and books on the floor.

"Life's a mystery, isn't it?" Yuul said in slightly accented English. "You never think you have enough stuff right up until the moment you have to start packing it up,"

"What can we do?" Ella asked.

"You guys go change and make dinner. I'm starved, and Jeffrey should be coming home anytime soon."

"Can we order in?" Ella asked mischievously. "I want to use the company card."

"Didn't you just use it at a coffee shop?" Yuul asked, loading containers.

"Liz did. I haven't had a chance to use it." Ella pouted her lips.

"Okay. But remember once you guys go over on the entertainment budget, I'm garnishing your paycheques."

"We get paid?" Ella asked in surprise.

"Of course," Yuul said

"How much?" Liz wanted to know.

"$500."

"$500 a day or $500 a week?" Liz asked.

"$500 a month. Until you guys start generating a profit, trust me, I'll work you hard to get my money's worth from snow shovelling to cleaning up around the house."

"That's labour exploitation," Ella claimed.

"Say whatever you want to say in your fancy English. But it won't change a thing."

"We protest!" Liz said.

"$450 per month," Yuul said.

"$450 per month?" Ella cried.

"$400 per month" Yuul said.

"You're the worst employer ever," Ella declared.

"$350."

"Okay, okay, we'll take the $500," Liz said, putting her hands up in surrender.

Yuul flashed her lopsided smile. "$500 every two weeks, that's my final offer."

"When do we get our first paycheque?" Ella asked excitedly.

"This Friday."

"*Whaaat?*" Ella cried with joy.

"Remember, just like the company name says, we are all owners of the company. However, since I'm also an investor, my cut is bigger than yours. Sign the papers on the dining table."

"What papers?" Liz said, staring Yuul down.

Yuul did not respond.

Liz and Ella stood there for several seconds in silence and then walked over to the table. They picked up the contracts and started nodding as they read it.

"It looks good," Liz said, rolling her eyes when she finally flipped the last page.

"If we do it right, we'll have a multi-million dollar business on our hands. If we don't, we've got to find a place to live and a job to make ends meet."

"That sounds scary," Ella said.

"Go big or go home?" Liz said, smiling.

"Yes," Yuul flashed out her lopsided smile again. "Now, what about dinner?"

"I'm on it!" Ella took her cellphone out. "Okay, what do you feel like?"

"Let's do Greek," Liz said.

"That sounds good," Ella said. After taking Yuul and Liz's order, Ella phoned it in. When she disconnected the call, Ella announced, "I've got to go pee!"

"TMI!" Liz said.

• • •

Ella smirked in satisfaction that she'd fooled them. *Hohoho! Now you think you know where I'm gonna be and what I'm up to. Hoho, the truth is you'll never know what I am REALLY up to.* With that happy thought, she snuck out of the living room and quietly made it to her bedroom. She didn't need to pee. What she needed to do was to brag about her first paycheque to Charlie. Once in her room, she carefully closed the door, and then excitedly called Charlie.

"Hi Charlie," Ella whispered.

"What's wrong?" Charlie said in a concerned voice.

"Nothing's wrong."

"Why are you whispering then?"

"Uh that? I've got something to tell you."

"What is it?" Charlie whispered.

"I want to take you out for dinner this Friday."

"What's the occasion?"
"My first payday."
"Your payday?"
"Yes, so I want to take you out for dinner."
"So, why are you whispering?"
"They don't know I'm on the phone with you."
"Who are they and why not?"
"Liz and Yuul, that's who they are. I just don't want them to know that I'm calling you right after I found out that I'm getting paid this Friday."

Charlie laughed.

"I wanted to look cool," Ella said.
"Okay, but no can do."
"Are you busy?"
"Yes. As a matter of fact, I'm going out on a blind date this Friday."

That took Ella's breath away. Her heart just dropped to the ground.

"Ella, are you there?"

Ella didn't know what to say. *Did I imagine it all – me and Charlie? Did I take it the wrong way? Maybe he was just being nice to me? Did I fill all the blanks in my head with fantasies?* She was confused and hurt. To top it off, she felt embarrassed about misunderstanding his feelings and telling everyone that he was her boyfriend.

"My mom thinks you don't exist, and that I made you up."

What about his mom? Why is he saying about his mom? His mom… me… He told his mom about me!

"Are you there, Ella?"
"Yes. Yes, I am."
"Good. I have to marry the woman I'm meeting on Friday, unless…"

"Unless what?"

"Unless you tell my mom I'm yours."

"Tell your mom you're mine?"

"Unless I'm not."

Oh my god, he's mine. She danced to a song in her mind. Then, the reality hit her.

"I don't think your mom's going to approve of me."

"Why not?"

"You're a corporate lawyer who makes a lot more than $500 every two weeks. That's why."

"$500 every two weeks, that's what you'll be making?"

"Yes," Ella sucked in her cheeks embarrassed.

"Is it after taxes or before taxes? If it's before taxes, that'd be a deal breaker."

"Uh, I don't know. I have to ask Yuul."

"If it's before taxes, you've got to demand more."

"It won't happen. Liz and I already put up a fight, which we lost miserably."

"Hahaha."

"At least, I have 30% of the company shares."

"Why didn't you say so? 30%, that's a game changer."

"She said that it'll be a multi-million-dollar business in a few years, or we'll be bankrupt and lose everything."

"I'm praying for the former."

"Me too."

"So, what's it going to be? Will you meet my mom or should I marry the woman I'm meeting on Friday?"

"I'll meet your mom."

"What are you gonna tell her?"

"You're mine." Ella blushed in embarrassment and couldn't stop grinning.

"Very good."

4

WEDNESDAY, NOVEMBER 27

Liz revved her red 2016 Mazda along Highway 401, Highway 407 and the Queen Elizabeth Way/QEW, music blasting away on the radio, daydreaming Ella in the passenger seat, well on their way to Wild Peach Estate on Thirty Road in Grimsby, Ontario.

Located just 30 minutes from the Canada US border, Grimsby was a small town on Lake Ontario originally known for its many fruit orchards, but more recently as the gateway to the Niagara region and its many wineries.

Liz made it to Thirty Road in Grimsby before 11:00 a.m. It had only taken an hour and fifteen minutes. It wasn't a record-breaking time; nonetheless, it was still a record for her.

Wild Peach Estates was lined with mature trees and shrubbery that acted as a natural barrier to block the view of the property from the roadside.

Liz almost passed the entrance to the place but managed to catch it at the last second. Braking hard, she made a quick right turn into the drive that led to the parking area below. Surprisingly the parking lot looked fairly new with the blacktop clearly marked out with crisp neat bright white lines. The row on her left was taken up by a variety of company vehicles. There was a thirty-passenger, mid-range sized bus and a couple of heavy duty, shiny black, pick-up trucks. After the pick-up trucks there were a few SUVs and a couple of 4-door sedans.

In the opposite row on her right, the row was mostly empty with only a few random passenger cars parked here and there. The entrance sign had indicated visitor and staff parking on the right, and she was more than happy to help try and fill the empty visitor parking.

Liz and Ella, who were dressed like twins again in dress shirts, dress pants and stretched down duffle coats, got out of the car and stretched their stiff bodies while inspecting the two buildings. One was a bungalow that was stretched out in the southwest corner of the parking lot, and the other was a 5-storey apartment building to the north.

The grey apartment building looked old, overused and industrial. A paved walkway bridged the parking lot and the apartment building across the manicured lawn. A 1' x 5' white plastic banner reading: **Welcome to Wild Peach** hung at the entrance door to the apartment building.

The banner was blowing in the wind, making a flop, flop noise. It looked just downright sad and made the cloudy sky seem more ominous than it already was.

Liz and Ella had stayed up all night, brainstorming on an investigation strategy but to no avail. By sunrise, they'd decided that their best bet was to start with the retirement home and then they'd just have to wing it from there. So here they were, about to wing it.

The receptionist, sitting at the front desk, greeted them with a nice smile as they approached her. The name tag on her chest read: Nora.

"Hi, I'm Liz Knight, and this is my associate, Ella Seo."

"Associate?" Nora asked confused.

"Yes, we're with KSK Private Investigative Services." Liz handed her their business card.

The receptionist examined it carefully before handing it back to Liz.

"What can I do for you?" Nora pursed her lips.

"We're looking for Agnes Winter," Liz said.

"Agnes Winter?" Nora raised her eyebrows.

"Yes," Liz said, gazing at Nora.

Nora frowned. "As I told her nephew, everything was fine and then she just up and left one day. That's all I know."

"Do you have any idea where she went or why she left in such a rush?" Liz asked.

"No, I have no idea where she went or why she left. As I said earlier, she just up and left without a word to anyone."

"Can we speak to any residents here who Agnes was close to?" Ella asked, looking down the hallway where the murmuring noise of people and the smell of food were coming from.

"No one here was close to her. Do you know why? I'll tell you why. She was paranoid that everyone was out to get her."

"That's not true." A woman in her 50s appeared out of thin air. "She was close to Tom. Remember?"

"Do you work here?" Liz asked.

"Yes, I do. I'm Lilibeth Valentia. I'm a nurse here." Lilibeth flashed a bright smile and gave a short nod to Liz and then Ella.

"He doesn't count," Nora protested. "He's dead. Dead men don't count."

"True." Lilibeth chortled for a moment. Then, she suddenly stopped laughing and clapped her hands. "There was another one. What's her name? She got kicked out of here. It must've been a few months ago. Seriously, what was her name?" Lilibeth asked, looking at Nora, constantly snapping her fingers fast. "It's right on the tip of my tongue. Give me a minute. It'll come to me."

"Out of curiosity, why did she get kicked out?" Liz asked.

"I guess birds of a feather flock together," Nora said, her upper lip curling into a disdainful look.

"Haha... Nora might have put it a little too bluntly. Sadly though, that doesn't make her wrong. Nancy believed..." Lilibeth snapped her fingers again. "I knew it would come to me. Agnes's friend, her name is Nancy, Nancy Drew, just like the old TV show."

"Why did Nancy get kicked out?" Liz asked again as she wrote down the name in her notepad.

Lilibeth smiled. "She was another conspiracy theorist. Don't believe what you see. Woooo! There's a lot of that going on these days all over the world."

"Do you think they still keep in touch?" Liz asked, looking at Lilibeth.

"I would think so. They seemed to be very close, whispering at each other all the time." Lilibeth paused and smiled as if she remembered something funny. "Maybe they were plotting a prison escape, I mean the retirement home walk-out." Lilibeth winked. "They seemed to be very comfortable with each other." She paused, tilting her head to the right side. "Now that I think of it, they had the air of an old married couple who's spent the last 50 years together. You know what I mean?"

"Are you saying they knew each other even before they came here?" Liz asked.

Lilibeth shrugged. "I don't know. Maybe." A pause. "They just looked like really old pals. Even if they weren't bosom pals, I believe they'd built a really good friendship while they were staying here." She suddenly narrowed her eyes and snorted, "Huh!"

"What is it? Do you remember something?" Liz said hastily, her eyes wide open with expectations.

"Do I remember something?" Lilibeth said slowly, enunciating each word while staring at Liz as if she was about to eat Liz alive. "Didn't you just see me remembering so much about Nancy Drew?"

"Uh… Yees." Liz said in confusion.

Lilibeth said, "Good!" Slowly her long face widened into a smile. "I haven't been able to remember much since a car accident I had not too long ago. This is something to celebrate!"

"Congratulations?" Liz rolled her eyes and then turned to Nora. "Would it be possible for you to give us her contact info?"

"That's personal information. We can't release it to you," Nora said.

"Come on, Nora. What harm can it do?" Lilibeth said, still wearing the goofy smile.

"I can't make a decision of this magnitude. I have to call management." Nora picked up the phone. She explained the situation over the phone and listened intensely while nodding.

"While you're at it, can you ask "management" if we can have a copy of the facility's CCTV footage from the day that Agnes disappeared?" Liz said.

Nora asked the person on the other end of the phone about the CCTV footage and listened a little more before hanging up. "You can have both things, under one condition though. You have to let us know her whereabouts when you find her. Her nephews and nieces stampeded in here like a herd of elephants and threatened to sue us and all. We don't think they will, but you just never know. As my boss said, we'll give you something but we've got to get something in return."

"I guess that's only fair," Liz said.

Fifteen minutes after, Liz and Ella walked out of the building and rushed back to their car with a printout of Nancy's phone number and home address and a copy of the CCTV stored in their SSD.

"Whew! It's cold," Ella said, shivering.

"Tell me about it." Liz turned ignition. "It's unseasonably cold even for November."

Ella unfolded the printout. "We've got a lead to follow up."

"And it's a good lead," Liz said.

"Let's make a call to Nancy now. I'm so excited."

"Why not?" Liz agreed.

Ella punched in the number. "Hello? May I speak to Nancy Drew?"

Ella listened for a second and then yelled into the phone, "NAANCY DREWW!"

Again, crickets, so Ella yelled one more time, "NAAAANCY..."

Ella listened again and said, "Uh, wrong number? GOT IT! GOODBYE!" Ella coughed as she disconnected the call. She turned to Liz and said, "It's the wrong number."

"You're telling me because you thought I couldn't hear you?" Liz laughed. "I guess it's time to meet Nancy Drew, the great PI, in person."

"Can we have lunch first? I don't think I can make it to Toronto."

Liz nodded as they left Wild Peach Estate behind in their rearview mirror.

• • •

Adam Brooks parked his car on York Ridge Road, glancing at the digital clock on the dash. 3:41 p.m. – that was what it said, and he didn't like it. Feeling anxious, he hurriedly got out of his car almost slamming the door. He wasn't himself today. He didn't normally get anxious. He'd never slammed any door. Unfortunately, today wasn't just like any other day. Today, Anya was leaving him again.

Standing at the front door, he fixed his tie and took a very deep breath before opening it. He walked in, looking uninterested. Although his mind was anxiously looking for Anya, he didn't show it.

"You came," Anya Orlove-Brooks said, smiling.

Hearing her voice almost made him let out a sigh of relief, but he managed not to. He saw her sashaying towards him.

A yellow, 50s swing dress, and her short and curly blond hair made her look like she just walked out of a 50s magazine. She might not have looked like a fashion model to anyone else but she did to him. To him, she was prettier than anyone who had ever made it to the list of The Most Beautiful Women in the World.

When she placed her cool, fresh lips lightly on his left cheek, he just wanted to drop down on his knees and beg her not to leave him, but he didn't. He just squinted at the wall.

"I thought you already left," Adam said, looking unimpressed.

"Are you happy that I've waited for you?" Anya gave him an inquisitive look.

"Yes," Adam said in resignation.

Anya gazed at him and her lips curved upwards in a satisfied smile. "You just earned another kiss." She kissed him on his right cheek. "I'll be with Harley in Paris. We'll walk on the same streets you and I used to roam and eat the croissants and éclairs that you and I once ate. Or, we might just stay in bed all day."

Adam gazed at her without a word. Anya met his gaze. A silence fell between them. The silence was eventually broken by Harley.

"We're ready to go," Harley shouted while taking the last step of the staircase, suitcase in hand.

"Travelling light?" Adam said in a cold voice.

"You don't go to Paris full of packed bags. You come home from Paris full of packed bags." Anya smiled.

Adam smiled, too, thinking about her dad, Viktor Orlov.

Viktor spoiled Anya like there was no tomorrow. He adored her. He worshiped her. At their wedding, Viktor stood at the end of the aisle, holding her hand tighter and tighter. He didn't release her hand for a really, really long time, asking her if she was sure she wanted to marry Adam over and over again. She eventually had to unlock his fingers one at a time.

Good old times, Adam thought.

"Thank you for coming to see me off," Anya said. "Harley, can you carry our luggage out please?"

"Of course," Harley said, steering the suitcase along.

Adam silently watched Harley as he walked out the entrance door. Although Harley closed the door behind him and was long gone, Adam just stood there stoically, burning a hole right through the front door with his laser glare.

"You don't like him much, do you?"

"No," Adam said without looking at her.

"Good." Anya smiled. "I love you in that painting." She pointed at the painting that she had hung over the fireplace in the middle of their living room.

"I like that one, too. It puts a smile on my face every time I look at it." Adam looked at the painting that looked more geometric shapes than a portrait.

"If you're willing to fly to New York in January, you can buy another one before my dad buys them all. You know he never gives anyone else a chance to buy my paintings." Anya pouted.

Adam thought about Viktor again. He always went the extra mile to see that his daughter was never disappointed. Viktor always bought all of her ridiculously high-priced paintings just because no one else would. She wouldn't even be able to have an exhibition if it wasn't for her father's money and influence. Anya wasn't a gifted painter to put it mildly; nonetheless, her paintings relaxed him and made him happy. If he had the kind of money Viktor had, he'd buy them all, too.

"I will, only if you get rid of him," Adam said.

"I will, only if you stop working all those crazy hours and stay home with me."

"I always came home for dinner."

"If you call having a meal at 12 midnight a family dinner, yes you were always home for dinner."

"Why him?"

"Don't you know?"

"Know what?"

Anya smiled. "He looks like you. I can just look at him whenever I miss you. When he doesn't do it for me, I can just drop by here to see the real deal."

"Come home, honey. I promise I'll come home early."

"Not good enough."

"You can paint while I work." Adam begged.

"I knew that that was the only reason you liked me painting," Anya said teasingly.

"I like your paintings because they speak to me."

"True art does that to people." Anya let out a laugh.

Her laugh always made him want to hug her, touch her.

"I have to be inspired to paint something. Inspiration doesn't come just because my husband needs to work late."

"I'll—"

"The airport limousine's here," Harley informed her poking his head slightly inside the door.

"Figure it out – me or your job, which one you can't live without. No, you can't have it all," Anya whispered in Adam's ear and kissed his cheek again before she walked away.

Adam followed her outside and silently watched her get into the limousine. Even long after she'd left, he stood on the driveway, looking longingly down the path on which the limousine had disappeared on.

While the street was devoid of any human life other than Adam Brooks, there were a couple of people hidden behind drawn curtains watching Adam intensely with smug little looks on their faces.

5

WEDNESDAY, NOVEMBER 27

With the help of Google Maps, Liz and Ella found Nancy's bungalow on Baldwin Road in Mississauga, no sweat. The exterior featured Pella windows and a beautiful wood front door with sidelights. White clapboard siding with a roof extension over the front porch added a cottage-style-meets-colonial-charm to the house.

Liz and Ella walked up onto the concrete stamped front porch and knocked twice on the beautiful front door. They immediately heard a boy's voice yelling, "Mom, somebody's at the door."

They heard a noise half-running, half-skiing, and then the same boy's voice yelling, "Mom, Nathan is going to get the door." Then they heard a heavy stomping noise. A woman's voice followed in a rushed tone. "No, Nathan!"

The door was already wide open and a pre-teen's face appeared. Within a second or two, a woman, assumedly Nathan's mother, now stood behind him.

"How many times do I have to tell you that you can't open the door to strangers?" The woman in her late 30s said in an exhausted combined with frustrated voice.

"Five hundred times!" Nathan declared, showing his two missing front teeth.

"Go inside," The woman said, shaking her head in surrender.

"No! I want to stay. I'll protect you against these zombies." Nathan put his hands up, making a cross.

"I need protection from you. Go inside. Otherwise, there won't be any dessert for you later."

Nathan glared at Liz and then Ella in silence for a moment and then said in a serious tone, "Don't eat my mom."

Liz stared at Nathan. "We won't, I promise."

The woman shook her head and smiled. "Yes, he's adorable, isn't he? Now, what can I do for you?"

"He absolutely is," Liz said. "We're looking for Nancy Drew."

"Who?"

"Nancy Drew?"

"We're the Sokolovs. There's no one by that name living here."

Liz sighed, realizing that Nancy Drew got them again.

"What brings you to our place, looking for Nancy Drew?" The woman asked.

Ella took out her business card and handed it to the woman. "We're private detectives."

The woman studied it closely. "I didn't think private detectives were actually a real thing. I thought that they were all made-up characters on TV shows." She gave it back to Ella and said, "Anyway, why are you looking for her? And why are you looking for her here?"

"We're actually looking for Agnes Winter, a 75-year-old widow. She's gone missing, and her nephew hired us to find her. During our investigation—"

"Agnes Winter?" The woman interjected.

"Do you know her?" Liz asked.

"I think that's the name of the previous owner of this house."

Ella took out her cellphone and found one of Agnes's pictures. She zoomed in and enlarged Agnes in the picture. "Is this her?"

"I can't believe it. Yes, that's her. When we came here to see the house, she was sitting in a rocking chair on the front porch. She was so nice to my two boys. What's happened to her?"

There was a moment of silence. Liz just stood there, stunned.

Ella looked up at Liz for several seconds and then cleared her throat. "Agnes Winter has gone missing. We went to the retirement home that she disappeared from and were told—."

"Do you remember," Liz said excitedly, interrupting Ella, "what Lilibeth said about Agnes and Nancy's relationship?"

Ella looked up at Liz, looking a little annoyed by the sudden interruption. But she said nothing.

"Agnes and Nancy looked like an old couple who's spent a half century together. That's what Lilibeth said. It turns out Lilibeth might have been right on the money."

Ella cocked her head for a few seconds, and then her face slowly brightened up. "Oh My God!"

Liz slowly nodded, smiling smugly.

"Does that mean you'll be able to find Agnes?" The woman asked.

"I think so," Liz said with a smile.

"That's good." The woman smiled as well.

"Thank you for your help," Liz said.

"I'm glad I could. I really liked her."

They walked briskly back to their car, shivering from the cold but both smiling excitedly. Liz fired up the car and let it idle so they could warm up a bit.

"We're definitely dealing with a conspiracist," Ella said, thinking aloud about the old lady called Nancy Drew. "Now, we need to find out who Agnes's BFF really is."

"Let me call the person who might have the answer for us." Liz took out her cellphone and put him on speaker.

"Hi Jonas, it's Liz Knight from KSK Private Investigative Services."

"Good," Jonas said. "It'll be even better if this call is about you already locating my aunt."

"We're one step closer. Anyway, we're trying to locate Agnes's best friend. Let me start with the name, Nancy Drew. Does that name ring a bell?"

"Nancy Drew? The only Nancy Drew I know is a character on TV that my daughters watch."

"Same with us," Liz said. "Who would you say is Agnes's best friend?"

"Birdie Pemberton," Jonas said without hesitation.

"How long have they been friends?" Liz asked

"I don't know. Is it even relevant?"

"Just humour me. How long would you say? Five months? One year? Ten years?"

"All their lives, as in they've been friends their whole lives."

"Do you have Birdie's home address?" Ella asked.

"No, I don't." Annoyance was evident in his voice.

"No worries," Liz said. "You gave us her phone number already. We'll start from there. We'll get back to you when we know more. Have a good night, Jonas."

"Wait!" Jonas shouted, irritation strong in his voice. "I already called Birdie, and she doesn't know where Agnes is. I've already told you all of this."

"Yes, you did. We'll be in touch. Have a good night!" Liz disconnected the call and covered her mouth with her fist while looking over at Ella.

Ella covered her mouth with her hand, too, her eyes wide with disbelief.

They looked over at each other for a brief moment and then burst out laughing.

Wiping tears from the corner of her eyes, Ella said, "Did you just hang up on him?"

"I guess I did."

"He sounded very angry at us."

"Yes, he did, but let's put that aside, so we can get on with the real question."

"What are you thinking?" Ella asked as she put her phone away.

"Nancy Drew used Agnes Winter's old address, which means their friendship goes way back. How did Lilibeth put it?"

"Like an old couple that's spent 50 years together," Ella said, enjoying the view of children playing in nearby Westacres Park. With a sudden realization she whipsawed her head around to Liz causing her to jolt her neck. While applying pressure to the crick in her neck, she said, "Are you saying what I think you're saying? That Birdie Pemberton is our Nancy Drew?"

Liz nodded her head.

"Okay Liz, but why would Birdie use a fake name to get into the retirement home?"

"Agnes might've told Birdie the same thing she told Jonas – People were being killed at the retirement home, and the home was up to no good. That might've intrigued Birdie, and she decided to go there undercover."

Ella slowly nodded her head in agreement. "Being paranoid and all, Birdie provided Wild Peach with all false information, like a fake name, fake phone number and fake home address. That makes sense."

"If it's not Birdie, Birdie will have a good idea who Nancy Drew might be."

"That's great news. We can show Nora and Lilibeth the pictures of Agnes's friends. They'll probably be able to point out which one is Nancy."

"A good idea, but let's not take anything to the home just yet, in case Agnes is right. We both know that Nancy Drew is paranoid. So, let's play on her paranoia a bit and see if we can flush her out. Give me her phone number?"

"Put it on speaker," Ella said.

"Of course," Liz said.

As Ella read out the phone number, Liz punched it in. After a couple of rings, the call was answered.

"Hello, may I speak with Birdie Pemberton?" Liz said.

"You've got the wrong number," an elderly woman replied and was just about to hang up.

"Jonas Fischer, Agnes's nephew, hired us to find Agnes Winter. If you hang up, we'll have no choice but to go to Wild Peach with pictures of you and Agnes together."

"I really don't know what you're talking about. I'm—"

"Nancy Drew? Is that the name you were about to say?"

"Who?"

"Just let me finish what I need to say, and then you can hang up."

"I really don't know what you want from me but go ahead."

"My name is Liz Knight, and I'm with my associate, Ella Seo right now. We're private investigators. We went to Wild Peach and talked to Nora the receptionist and Lilibeth the nurse, and we were able to obtain Agnes's good friend, Nancy Drew's phone number and her home address. Can you guess where we are right now?"

"At a strip bar?"

"Haha! You're funny. We're sitting in the car across from supposedly Nancy Drew's home."

"Good for you."

"It was good for us. Do you know why?"

"I'm done with this game."

"Don't hang up! I'll get straight to it. Where was I? Oh, yeah. We talked to the owner of that house, and she confirmed that the house was previously owned by Agnes Winter. Nancy Drew used Agnes's old home address. So, we're thinking Agnes and Nancy must go way back. Jonas confirmed that Birdie Pemberton is Agnes' BFF, Best Friend Forever. So, here is the main point of this whole mumbo jumbo. If we can't find Agnes or Nancy Drew tonight, we're going back to Wild Peach tomorrow to show the pictures we have of Agnes with her friends. We have the friends' phone numbers to go with their faces.

"Just one more thing, Wild Peach gave us Nancy's information as well as all the CCTV footage from the day Agnes disappeared but under one condition. They want us to keep them updated on our progress. We don't have any intention of doing so at this point, but we might change our minds, depending on the outcome of this phone conversation. So, now you tell me if I've got the wrong number."

"Yes, you did." The elderly woman abruptly hung up.

Liz looked at her cellphone blankly for a moment and then put it back in the dash mounted holder.

"I guess Jonas had the wrong number for her," Ella said.

"Or, we got the right number. If we did, what do you think it means?" Liz said.

"Why would she lie about it?" Ella said, looking puzzled. After a moment of silence, she snapped her fingers. "Birdie would lie about it because she was as paranoid as Nancy Drew. It means we've found our Nancy Drew."

"Yes. You're exactly right."

"What do you want to do?"

Liz tapped her index finger on the steering wheel for a bit and then said, "Just to be on the safe side, let's double-check the phone number with Jonas."

"That sounds like a plan." Ella said excitedly.

"Let's not get ahead of ourselves just yet. We'll go home first. If we've got the wrong number, we can always make a few more calls before dinner from our comfy home." Liz slowly pulled out of her parking spot and merged onto the road.

It was just a little after 4 p.m., but the sky was already losing light, and the highway was getting crowded with commuters. Liz tried her best to manoeuvre her way through traffic, so they could get home fast, but really wasn't making much progress when her phone rang.

"I think it's Birdie's number," Ella said.

"Put it on speaker."

Ella answered the call and hit the speakerphone icon.

"Liz here."

"We checked you out, and we find you to be legit."

"Legit is good, right?" Liz asked.

"We'd like to meet."

"We'd like that, too."

"Under one condition."

"Name it."

"Can you swear on your mother's grave that you won't say a word about us to Wild Peach?"

"Oh My God! No! My parents are alive! Don't kill them."

"Ha!"

"Ella here. I swear over my parents' graves that we won't tell Wild Peach anything about you."

"Oh…", Birdie mumbled, evident in her voice that she wasn't expecting that response.

"It's okay. Now, you tell us where and when, and we'll be there."

"There's a café called 'Just Baked' on the ground floor of Union Station. You think you can find it?"

"Yes. When?"

"Tomorrow at 12 noon."

"We'll, see you at Just Baked for 12 noon"

"Since you have our pictures, we need yours. Send them to us asap."

"We're driving right now. We'll send them to you as soon as we get home."

"Make sure you don't have a tail."

"A tail?"

"Yes, make sure you're not being followed."

Liz instinctively checked her rearview mirror as well as the two side mirrors to see if there was, in fact, a tail. There were too many cars on the road, so she couldn't tell if she was being tailed or not.

"I don't think we're being followed, but we'll be vigilant all the way home and tomorrow as well."

"Good. Don't be late."

"You don't be late," Liz said jokingly.

"Old people are never late."

"Uh, okay."

With that, Birdie was gone.

"I think we hit the jack pot," Liz said, smiling.

6

THURSDAY, NOVEMBER 28

It was 11:45 a.m. and despite the cold weather, there was still a good number of tourists strolling around on Front Street, appreciating the grand scale and classical details of the limestone façade of Union Station.

After parking the car close to Union Station, Liz and Ella paid no attention to anything except their mission, making sure they weren't being followed as they hurriedly walked down the street. Once inside the station, they quickly looked around and started walking purposefully towards their final destination – Just Baked. They'd looked it up on the website and had a pretty good idea where it was located.

Although rush hour was over, the station was still crowded with people. After passing by a group of tourists and others just strolling about, they arrived at Just Baked.

Just Baked was a tiny cafe that didn't offer any inside seating. While Liz was grabbing a table right in front of the bakery, Ella ordered two coffees and a butterscotch pie topped with a golden French meringue and a coconut pie topped with whip cream. The smell of freshly baked goods filled the shop. Feeling heavenly, Ella brought over the tray of coffees and pie to the table.

The first 15 minutes of waiting, they were very forgiving and grinned happy-go-lucky grins. The second 15 minutes, the grins were gone. Liz pouted while Ella tapped the floor impatiently with her foot. After 30 minutes of waiting, they thought that they had been played for fools by the old lady.

"Let's go to Wild Peach," Ella said in annoyance.

"You swore you wouldn't do that." An old lady's voice chirped behind Ella.

Ella quickly turned around and saw two old ladies standing there.

Both ladies had silver hair, which made them look their 70 plus years. The lady in the pastel pink hooded puffer jacket was leaning on her cane. The other one in the dark grey bomber jacket stood legs spread shoulder width her arms folded across her chest. Even though they both were short and skinny, they emitted a strong presence.

Liz and Ella figured that they were looking at Agnes and Birdie. The one with the cane was Agnes, and the other had to be Birdie.

"We need chairs," Birdie said, looking at Liz.

Liz stood up to go and get more chairs.

Birdie looked at Ella. "Can you get us two Earl Grey teas and a Danish for her and a raspberry scone for me,"

"I'll get them for you only if you promise you won't start without me."

"I promise," Birdie said.

Agnes slouched into Ella's chair and let out a weary sigh. "I'm getting old, Birdie. Everything tires me out."

Birdie flopped herself down into Liz's chair and started rubbing her knees. "We're not getting old. We just need a vacay. Once it's all over, let's go down to Mexico and drink Margaritas all day long on some white sand beach in our sexy swimming suits."

Agnes giggled. "I want a couple of silver foxes in my arms."

Birdie winked at Agnes. "Why not?"

"What's this about silver foxes?" Liz asked, pulling over two chairs.

Birdie widened her eyes and said, "What about silver foxes?"

"You guys said something about silver foxes, didn't you?" Liz looked back and forth between the two retirees.

Birdie shrugged her shoulders. "I don't think so. Did we, Agnes?"

"Don't make her feel bad, Birdie." Agnes turned to Liz, her head nodding up and down, "Yes, we did."

Liz couldn't tell if they were being playful or condescending. However, Liz quickly realized that either way, she needed Ella. Two on one, they were going to drive her insane in a matter of minutes. Two on two, she might be able to keep her sanity. So, she decided to play it safe until Ella joined them again. She dropped the subject and picked a new one. "You must be Agnes," Liz said, looking at Agnes and then turning to Birdie, "and you must be Birdie, a.k.a. Nancy Drew."

"Yes." Agnes nodded her head with an approving smile. "Jonas told me that he hired you just a few days ago, and you already found us. That's great detective work."

"Thank you, but really we just got lucky. If it wasn't for Lilibeth, and the new owner of your old house, we wouldn't be meeting you in person today."

"All in all, it's still not bad," Birdie said.

"You started without me…" Ella pouted her lips and put the tray down on the table.

Agnes smiled. "We didn't. It was more like a long greeting."

"Didn't you say old people are never late?" Liz asked, looking at Birdie.

Birdie stirred her tea with a grin on her face. "We weren't late. We just needed to make sure you weren't followed."

"What?" Liz and Ella said in unison.

"We were watching you from over there." Agnes pointed at a clothing store not too far from where they sat.

"Uh, okay," Liz said.

Birdie squinted at Liz. "I know what you're thinking."

Liz shook her head rapidly. "I wasn't thinking anything." She denied hard.

"It's okay," Agnes said with a smile. "We've been getting it a lot recently – two oldies with the onset of dementia or something like that."

Liz, the Neighbour

Liz racked her brain to come up with a polite and convincing excuse, but she had nothing. So, she decided to change the subject. "What made you run?"

The two retirees didn't bite. They just stared at Liz, their eyes hardened.

Liz rolled her eyes, trying to avoid their stares.

After a moment, Agnes let out a laugh. She turned to Birdie and gave her a nod.

Birdie hesitated for three seconds and then finally replied, "Too many suspicious deaths – that's what."

"Suspicious, how?" Liz asked.

Birdie said, "Healthy people one day, dead the next."

Liz looked at Birdie with eyes like saucers. "That's terrible. Did you report it to the police?"

"Of course, I did." Birdie frowned. "But no one listened. They were like, old people die all the time. That's called the cycle of life, no cause for suspicion there."

"Old people, meaning?" Ella asked with caution.

"Residents of Wild Peach," Birdie said. "Yes, they were old but they were healthy."

"What did they die of?" Liz asked.

"Heart attacks" Birdie said.

"Did the police say anything else?" Liz asked.

"What police? That's what Wild Peach said. Didn't you hear me? The police did nothing, so they've got nothing to say." Birdie suddenly fell silent for a bit and then continued. "I guess I shouldn't say that. Actually, there was one sweet detective. Although he didn't think much of the deaths of the residents just like the other cops, at least he looked into the deaths of the three staff members for me."

"Three staff members?" Totally intrigued, Liz hurried Birdie to continue on with the story.

"Yes, they were three nurses that worked at the home. They died as well, but in the end, the detective said that all three deaths were unrelated to each other. There was no link. No link my ass," Birdie snuffled. After another bout of silence, Birdie said. "I shouldn't have said that. He was a really nice man. He promised he would look into it some more."

Liz looked at Agnes, then back to Birdie. "These deaths happened at Wild Peach. Agnes left Wild Peach. That should've been enough to keep her out of harm's way, and yet, she is still in hiding. Why?"

Birdie picked up her tea cup and took a sip. "She saw her friend murdered after he made a fuss over another resident's death."

Liz held the look of disbelief combined with anger on her face. "She witnessed a murder, and the police still didn't do anything?"

Birdie and Agnes exchanged a look, and Agnes picked it up from there. "I didn't witness a murder per se. Officially, the cause of death was a heart attack, but I know he was murdered."

"How do you know?" Liz asked.

"He was as healthy as a horse when he went to bed. The next morning, they pronounced him dead." Agnes paused. She could tell what Liz and Ella were thinking. "You don't think that's much of an earth-shattering lead, do you?"

Liz didn't think what they had was damning evidence but didn't want to say it out loud. She gave a quick glance at Ella who was looking at Liz as if to say that the question was only directed to Liz. So, Liz pretended to think it over. Then she said slowly as she was putting a positive spin on her answer, "It's probably not an earth-shattering lead." A pause. "But too many seemingly random things," a pause again, "can pile up to be something."

"A very diplomatic answer." Agnes smiled. "It's okay. Birdie has a special nose for this kind of stuff. Since we were little, whatever we lost, she always found it for us. That's why we called her Nancy Drew." Agnes looked at her lifetime friend with a warm smile. "She said the home is a dangerous place and told me to leave right away. That's why I left. I trust her with my life."

"It still doesn't explain why you had to go into hiding," Liz said to Agnes.

Birdie and Agnes exchanged a look, and Birdie gave a nod to Agnes. With the nod, Agnes said, "It's because we're not done yet."

"You mean..."

"Yes," Agnes said, "we're still in pursuit of the truth. We're in hiding just in case they find out what we're up to. When it happens, we don't want to make it easy for them to find us."

"Is there anything we can help you with?" Ella asked.

Birdie and Agnes looked at each other in silence for a moment and shook their heads.

"We're good," Birdie said. "Everything's under control."

"Whew," Ella let out a sigh of relief.

Agnes smiled wide and nodded to Ella and Liz. "You two are alright," "I don't know about Birdie but I actually had a good time." Agnes winked at Birdie.

"Hmm… Definitely more fun than going to a funeral to see another dead friend." Birdie smiled. "Now, we should get going."

"Uh…" Ella looked at Agnes.

"What is it, dear?" Agnes said to Ella.

Ella rubbed her forehead. "Can you really see dead people?"

Agnes arched her eyebrows. "Huh?"

"Jonas said you saw dead people."

Agnes let out a laugh. "I did. It was more like I saw a dead person, as in one, my husband, Hans. But what fun is there in saying you see your dead husband's ghost? So, I exaggerated a little," Agnes said, holding her thumb and forefinger an inch a part.

Ella looked at Agnes, her eyes wide in terror. She said, a tremor in her voice, "You can see ghosts…"

"Hoho. My Dear. It happens when you lose someone you lived with forever. It's just a matter of recalling the familiar images from your memory."

Ella let out a big sigh of relief and there were a few laughs at the table.

Her eyes still smiling, Liz asked, "Does Jonas know you're staying with Birdie?"

Agnes and Birdie exchanged another look. Then, Birdie fielded the question. "He's probably figured that out by now. Still, don't tell him unless he asks. If he does, you can tell him but make him swear he won't tell another living soul about where she's staying."

Looking at Agnes, Ella said, "Can I take a selfie with you and send it to Jonas?"

"I don't see why not." Agnes leaned closer to Ella.

"Make sure you delete the picture after you send it to Jonas and tell Jonas to do the same," Birdie said.

"Yes, ma'am," Ella said cheerfully.

"Do you need a ride home?" Liz asked.

Agnes nodded. "That'd be nice. It was too much the first time. I don't think I can go through it all over again without breaking a few bones."

"Not so fast." Birdie interjected. "What are you going to tell Wild Peach?"

Liz didn't need to think about it. So, almost immediately, Liz said, "Nothing. We go off the grid just like you have. If they call us, then we'll tell them we didn't get anywhere, and Jonas took the case to another agency."

"Swear?" Birdie asked.

"Yes, I swear." Liz confirmed.

When they got to Birdie's house on Culnan Avenue, Liz turned back and handed her business card to Birdie. "If you need anything, call us."

"I don't think—"

Agnes hijacked the card. "You never know, Birdie. I'll keep it with me just in case." Agnes tucked it away in her purse before she got out of the car.

Driving again, Liz asked Ella, "What do you think?"

"I don't know. It sounds crazy, but they don't look crazy. I'm just hoping they are crazy."

"Me too, my friend. Me too…"

They drove on, passing by a few blocks in silence until Liz saw a woman walking on the sidewalk holding a box of cake in her hand. "Ella?" Liz called out. A big grin grew on her face.

"What is it?"

"We did it!" Liz squealed in delight without taking her eyes off the road. "We solved our first case.

"Oh My God!" Ella screamed in joy. "You are right!"

"You know what that means?"

"What does it mean?"

"KSK's future is looking so bright we're gonna have to wear shades."

· · ·

A man loaded dirty dishes into the dishwasher and gave a quick wipe to his kitchen countertop. He didn't have to do it. After all, he was the superior officer or simply put, the boss, in this civilian world, but years of military training had instilled it in him, he'd always tidied up after himself. He put on his black field jacket and black boots and took a quick look around the place to make sure everything was in its proper place before he walked out of his residence on Thirty Road in Grimsby.

He got into his 2019 Jeep Wrangler Rubicon JL Sting Ray that was waiting out in the parking lot and drove off. D-Day was tomorrow, and he didn't like leaving things to the last minute. But more than anything, he hated getting stuck in rush hour traffic.

The drive to Dunkinfield Crescent in Toronto was smooth and uneventful, and he liked that. Cruising along Dunkinfield, he gathered intelligence on the neighbours making sure nothing was out of the ordinary. He was well aware that he was being paranoid to a certain extent, but that's what had saved him more times than he could count. For that, he was constantly on alert at all times, even when it wasn't an operational area.

Both sides of the street were adorned with well-kept houses on decent sized lots, and most of these houses were occupied by young families with one or two children. At this hour of the day, you barely saw people on this quiet street, as the hard working residents of this neighbourhood were somewhere else in the city busy putting in their day's work.

Once the man in the Jeep was pleased with what he'd seen, he drove up to the driveway of a detached, single-storey home and parked the car. He liked this house because the trees and the shrubs planted alongside the front porch kept the Peeping Toms and nosy neighbours out. He walked up to the front door, unlocked it and walked inside.

After hanging his jacket in the hallway closet, he walked over to the kitchen and helped himself to a beer. It was a cold day, and the cold beer warmed him up almost instantly. He took out his cellphone and called his ex-subordinate and comrade, Adam Doyle.

As the phone rang, he prayed to God that Adam didn't annoy him too much today. It had been a while for him, turning to God for help. If his prayers weren't answered, he thought he might have to resort to shooting him in the head once this job was over. The image of a big chunk of his face blown off, pieces of it all over the floor calmed him down. The image even put a little smile on his face.

"Bring me up to speed," he said.

He listened.

"Good. Now, read me through the battle plan."

He nodded as he listened.

"She didn't have any problem meeting you so late?"

He listened in amusement. He once again realized that when it came to women, Adam had the magic touch. Anything and everything was possible.

"Good. We rendezvous at the parking lot of the Strange Bookstore—" He couldn't finish as Adam had cut him off. He said through his teeth, "No, I don't know any girls working at the Strange Bookstore. The location was convenient for Operation Sommer just like it will be for this one. Can we—" He was cut off again.

As he listened, he made a mental note to talk to a shrink as soon as this job was done or to kill him.

"No, I don't know what's so strange about the bookstore. Now, do not interrupt me again."

As he heard Adam say yes, he moved on. "Again, we rendezvous at the parking lot of Strange Bookstore at nineteen thirty hours. Show up early just in case. Keep your gloves on at all times. Make sure you leave no trace of you anywhere or on anyone. Do you think you can manage to do so?"

He listened and said, "Out."

He opened the fridge door and stared at an open package of dried out ham and cheese just as dry as the ham in another open package. He saw some eggs but didn't think it was wise to eat them. He moved on to the cupboards but had no luck there, either. He punched numbers on his cellphone.

"Are you on a diet? Where's the food at?"

He listened, shaking his head.

"I'm telling mom."

He listened more and burst into laughter. "Bwahaha! Okay, no mom, but let me introduce you to some real food tonight." A pause. "See you soon." He put his phone in his pants pocket while walking over to the closet. He took out his jacket and left to go shopping.

7

FRIDAY, NOVEMBER 29

It was 11:30 a.m. on Friday, November 29. The sky was clear, and the air was crispy cold. In a European-style condo building on the northeast corner of Yonge Street and Finch Avenue in Toronto, Yuul sat at the dining table having breakfast while Liz slouched on the couch watching Ella pace back and forth in the living room, skillfully weaving her way between all the boxes and furniture. Ella had two hours before she had to meet Charlie's mother – Hala Khoury. She was too anxious and too stressed to sit still.

"Everything's going to be okay," Liz said.

"How?" Ella asked defiantly.

"Just be yourself," Liz said in a gentle voice. "She'll love you."

"Oh My God! Do you even know what it means to be myself? I'm a high school-graduate, ex-drug addict who's never had a job. I slept through the last 6 years while other people my age busied themselves being mature and all, making something out of themselves. And who can even say I won't fall through the cracks again."

"You now have a job," Yuul interjected blithely.

"Yup, you hired me out of pity for my brother's sake."

Yuul put the chopsticks down on the table and looked at Liz. "Do you think I hired you because of your brother, too?"

"Yes." Liz shrugged.

"I don't think you remember how this investigative business came about. Ella, you suggested it, and Liz seconded it. I've never hired either of you. I decided to invest in this business because I saw an opportunity for it to grow. Your wages and 30% of the company stock are for the partnership. It's nothing to do with either of your brothers. I thought that 40:30:30 would be fair for everyone. I guess I sold myself short and it sounds like you feel the same way. That's wonderful news. I'll have the agreement changed to 80:10:10."

"No, no." Liz waved her finger at Yuul. "I'm keeping my 30%. Take Ella's since she's the one who has the big problem with it."

"Don't you dare! I have a lawyer," Ella said, looking at Yuul.

Yuul shrugged. "I'll have my lawyer talk to your lawyer then."

"Am I the only one without a lawyer?" Liz asked.

"Looks that way," Yuul said.

They let out a laugh in unison. Once the laughter came out, they couldn't stop laughing until their cheeks ached.

As silence fell, Ella said, "I'm short and ugly."

Yuul cocked her head and asked Ella, "I thought that you're short, but I didn't think you're ugly. Are you on the ugly end of the beauty spectrum?"

"You can't say that," Liz hurriedly interjected. "And she's definitely not on the ugly end of any spectrum. She's cute and adorable in anyone's eyes but her own. That's what it is."

"What about me? Am I cute and adorable, too?" Yuul asked in a more serious tone than usual.

Liz and Ella looked at their feet and kept their silence.

Yuul squinted at them shaking her head. "Definitely changing it to 80:10:10."

"Of course, you are!" Liz said.

They let out a laugh again.

"Seriously, where is this all insecure talk coming from?" Liz asked Ella.

"Meeting his mom is forcing me to get real. He's got it all and I've got nothing."

"He doesn't have it all until he has you," said Yuul.

"*Wooooo, so romantic!*" Liz said wickedly. "Our no-nonsense, straight shooter speaks the eloquent language of love."

"That's what your brother once said to me."

"Of course, he did," Liz nodded as it made sense. "Ella, it's time to go and show him what it really means to have it all. That is, if it's what you want."

"Ok this is getting too heavy," Ella said now beaming a little. "Is this too conservative for my age?"

Ella asked, pointing at her business suit outfit. "Should I change into something more vibrant?"

"You look beautiful just as you are," Liz said as she pushed Ella to the foyer and to the underground parking level 2.

Liz drove out of the underground parking lot with Ella in the passenger seat and slowly merged into the south bound traffic. After 20 minutes of driving down Yonge Street in silence, Liz turned to the right and drove along Bloor Street West.

Bloor Street West was full of interesting shops everything from your mom-and-pop shops to franchises to one-and-only boutiques to department stores to murder mystery dinner theatres to movie theatres to you name it, it had it all.

Liz began to enthusiastically offer her thoughts on what had gone wrong in this world as they drove along.

Ella couldn't understand a word Liz was saying. It was nothing more than white noise. Her mind was preoccupied with one hundred different ways she might humiliate herself in front of Hala, and those thoughts made her sick to her stomach. She felt the sour taste in her mouth when it occurred to her that Liz was slowing down the car to pull over to the side of the road. She looked out through the window and saw a cute, Instagrammable café called Café Byblos.

"We're here," Liz said.

Ella gave Liz a weak smile and then slowly climbed out of the car. With her shaky legs, she managed to walk over to the Lebanese bakery, through the front door and seat herself at a table.

She kept telling herself that no one would laugh at her and even if they did, it wasn't a big deal. Her little pep talk wasn't working at all until she spotted Liz grabbing a table not far from where she sat. She caught Liz's eye and mouthed thanks.

Ella didn't have to wait long for Charlie's mom, Hala. Ella recognized Hala immediately as Charlie had sent her many pictures of his mom. Ella waved at Hala as she stood up to greet her.

"Hi, I'm Ella. Nice to meet you," Ella tried to hug Hala awkwardly.

Hala swiftly turned her body to avoid the hug and pulled a chair out to sit.

Ella blushed and sat down in her chair.

"You are not anything that I expected," Hala said in a heavy accent.

Ella blinked her eyes, not understanding what Hala had meant by it and not knowing how to respond to it, either.

"Since Charlie told me about you, I've watched Korean shows to learn about my..." Hala stopped in the mid-sentence.

"To learn about your," Ella repeated in an attempt to encourage Hala to finish it, but it didn't seem to work.

Hala ignored Ella and just looked at the menu that was placed in front of her until a young, pleasant waitress came.

"Do you know what you want to get?" Hala asked.

"This one," Ella pointed a picture on the menu, "with a coffee"

"Maamoul Madd Bi Ashta, a good choice. I will have Osmaliyeh with zhourat."

Liz, the Neighbour

The waitress took the orders and disappeared.

Ella wanted to show Hala that she was paying full attention to her by continuing what Hala had said earlier. "You watched Korean shows to learn—"

"Let it go. Nagging is a bad quality in a woman," Hala said curtly.

"Sorry," Ella said.

"Are you Muslim?"

"No, I'm not."

"Are you planning to convert?"

"I'm sorry. I haven't thought about it." Ella just wanted to cry. It felt like Grade School all over again.

"What did you think when you came here to meet me?"

"Um… uh… well I worried so much that you wouldn't like me because I didn't finish university, because I don't have a great job like Charlie does and because I'm short and ugly, I didn't have time to get to the religion part."

"You didn't finish university? That's a big no, no. You don't have a great job? That's not a deal breaker. You are short and ugly? That, I didn't notice. Actually, I thought that you used your pretty face to seduce my son."

"You thought I was pretty? Thank you so much!"

"Don't be cute with me. You're still no good for my Charlie. Education's very important."

They stopped talking as the waitress came back with their orders.

Once the waitress was gone, Ella said, "I've been thinking about going back to school to get my bachelor's degree. I'm only short of a few credits."

"Then you should do it for your own good, but religion is what defines us. We can't have a non-Muslim as a family member." Hala slid a white envelope to Ella.

"What's this?"

"As I said earlier, I watched enough Korean shows to know how Koreans handle a situation like this. Take it and go away."

Ella opened the white envelope and found ten $5 bills. "That happened in the 70s, and… and people usually put in a lot more."

"You like money?" Hala said in a serious tone.

Ella hung her head in shame.

"Me too!" Hala said. "Anyway, at least I tried to learn about your culture. Tell me what you've learned about Lebanese culture."

"Why Lebanese?"

"You didn't even know Charlie is Lebanese?"

Ella put her head down in embarrassment.

"What did you think he was?"

"Canadian?"

"Are you running for a political position?"

"Uh? Oh. Sorry. Honestly, I never thought about it."

"Do you know anything about Lebanon or the Lebanese?"

"No, but I'm willing to learn. Are there any Lebanese shows on Netflix?"

"Why are you sweating so much? Are you sick?"

"No, no," Ella waved her hand vehemently while mopping the sweat off her neck. "I'm not sick. I'm very nervous. I talked myself into thinking that I might… I might win you over. Who was I kidding? How could I? Look at Charlie and look at me."

"What does this mean?"

"Charlie's perfect." Ella sniffed.

"He's not perfect. He's pretty close; nonetheless, he's not perfect. Love blinds you. That's okay, but you shouldn't put anyone including Charlie on a pedestal. You have to stand on an equal footing."

Ella stared at Hala mystified.

"You can blink now," Hala said.

Ella blinked her eyes a few times as her eyes were really sore.

"Don't marry him at least for a year or two. You might change your mind about how perfect Charlie is. When that happens, you might lose your love for him, or you might be okay with his imperfections. See how you feel about it before marriage. Somehow, if you two end up marrying each other, I want my grandchildren to be raised as Muslim. Is it okay?"

"Yes!"

"Don't you want to think about it first?"

"Uh… Yes. Actually, I'd like to take some time to think about it."

"Good. You think about it. This is the most important part. So, listen carefully. Until Charlie is married to you, keep in mind that I always have a pull on him. So, make sure you do lots of things to please me. I love those Korean cosmetics. I am not saying you should buy them for me, but if you do, I won't say no."

"Any brand you like more than another?"

"I don't have one yet. I have to use it to know which one works on my skin."

"Anything else?"

"Send me a list of good Korean shows to watch. Here is my phone number."

Ella saved Hala's phone number in her cellphone.

"Does it mean you're gonna stop sending Charlie on blind dates?"

"What blind date?"

"Charlie said you're setting him up on a blind date."

"Huh? That's interesting."

"You didn't?"

Hala said nothing but just looked at Ella.

"He lied?" Ella asked

"I guess he really wanted you to meet me." Hala slowly shook her head as if she was disappointed by her son, but her smiley eyes betrayed her.

"About school, go back to school and get the degree for your mom. I know she would love that."

What Hala said didn't register in Ella's brain right away. When it eventually did, tears ran down her cheeks.

• • •

At night, season's greetings were sent to everyone along Bloor Street West. Christmas lights twinkled and blinked everywhere lifting people's spirits and lighting up the street. Overhead, light canopies stretched for miles floating magically above the street. Storefronts and streetlamps were draped with lights and adorned with Christmas décor of every manner. This time of year, the street looked more like a galaxy of twinkling stars and wonderment than just a tiny spot on planet earth.

The Strange Bookstore was located on Bloor Street West, and it was no exception although maybe a little understated as it had only a few white and blue strings of light decking it out. Its parking lot was located at the back of the store tucked off a dimly lit street called Brock Crescent.

Adam Doyle showed up early at the parking lot of the Strange Bookstore as instructed. The bookstore was literally within walking distance from his home, but his wary superior officer had concocted a getaway plan that required him to drive.

In so many ways, his boss reminded him of his dad. Like his boss, his father had drilled into him the importance of punctuality and for them, punctuality meant showing up earlier than the agreed upon time, not just showing up on time. More importantly, both men had let him in on their little secrets and because of that trust, they'd both lost something very dear to them – for his boss, it had been the premature loss of his military career and all the perks and prestige that went with it and as for his father, the cost was his freedom as he'd been locked up for life. Sadly, both men could never forgive him for his mistakes. He wanted their forgiveness more than anything else in his life.

He'd written many, many letters to his father asking for his forgiveness. The most recent one said:

> To my dear dad:
> It's been a while since the last time I wrote you a letter.
> How are you?

Liz, the Neighbour

I understand that you still can't find it in your teeny-weeny heart to forgive me for what I did. I wish you learned your lesson and let it go. *What lesson?* You ask. I'll tell you. Don't let anyone in on your secrets if you want it to stay a secret. I'm into this multiplayer virtual reality game with a smart dude and he told me about another smart dude by the name of Benjamin Franklin. Whoever this Benjamin dude is, I've got to say he's dead smart. He said, 'three can keep a secret only if two of them are dead.' *How true is that?*

I thought about you when I heard it. All these years, I thought that it was my fault that you're locked up in the Pen. But I was wrong. The truth is that you did it to yourself. Why did you tell me you were a treasure hunter, hunting for jewelry? Why did you share all those trophies, memorabilia or whatever you want to call, with me?

I didn't ask any of it. If you really wanted to let me in on your dirty secrets, you should've at least had the courtesy to be honest with me from the get-go. Then, I would've understood the magnitude of your secrets and I wouldn't have tried to sell your stuff online to make some extra cash.

> You should've just come out and told me you were a serial killer and that all your trophies were the belongings of all those women you killed.
> Anyhow, I miss you, dad, and I hope you find it in your teeny-weeny heart to forgive me.
> Love,
> Xoxo

He didn't actually write it and send it to his father because his father scared him. Something about his dad's eyes, slightly crossed, it scared the hell out of him. Like so many other letters, he carried with him in his head, never putting them to pen and paper or email or whatever. One day, he thought, he would actually write that one down on paper though, and mail it to his father courtesy of Millhaven, maximum security prison.

The incident between him and his superior officer was very similar but an entirely different story. As he started thinking about what happened, he saw his superior officer driving up.

His boss was getting out of a 2019 Audi A6, so he got out of his car as well. "Sir." Adam gave the man a short salute.

"You've got to lose the military stuff. That life is long gone."

"How should I address you then, sir?"

"Troy."

"Will do, sir!"

"Here's the fob." Troy extended the car fob for Adam to take.

Adam put the fob in his pocket and took out the key to his Malibu. As he gave the car key to Troy, Adam asked, "Did you have any trouble securing the car?"

"No. You should learn how to do it. Everything you need to know is on YouTube. I can't be stealing a car and dropping it off for you on every job."

"I'll pass, sir."

Troy looked at Adam for a long moment and then shook his head. "I'll wait for you at our next rendezvous point. Gloves?"

Adam took out his gloves from his jacket pocket and put them on.

"Do it at the pre-determined location. When it's done, drive the car to our next rendezvous point. We'll switch cars again there."

"You drilled the mission into my brain. Trust me. I won't screw it up."

"No, you won't. You've never screwed up any mission that involved a woman. It's just my habit to go over the mission over and over until the very last second."

"I appreciate your faith in me." Adam smiled widely.

"Enjoy the date." Troy showed a half smile.

Adam walked over to the Audi, slid himself in and drove away.

As Adam Doyle drove onto Culnan Avenue, the familiarity washed over him. Those days he had spent on the street carrying out ISTAR even made him feel somewhat nostalgic. It was only a week ago.

Like a week ago, the street was dimly lit. Cars occasionally drove through, and people were rarely seen on the street.

Good old times, Adam thought smiling. He slowed down as he saw Madison waiting for him on the sidewalk. Madison looked gorgeous mixed with cuteness in her long black wool coat over her knee-length red dress with one foot in a running shoe and the other in a cast. He wished for a very brief moment that this was the real deal, not a charade.

"Maddie," Adam called out through the open window, waving at her.

Madison scoured the street as if she couldn't pinpoint where the voice had come from.

"Maddie," Adam yelled again, flashing the headlights this time.

Madison looked at the car and saw Adam. She flashed a smile at him as she took her first step towards the car.

"Where are you going so late?" An old lady appeared out of the darkness.

Madison glanced quickly over at Adam before she said, "Meeting a friend."

The old lady inspected Madison smiling teasingly. "That's got to be one lucky friend. Don't let me hold you up. Go have fun."

"Have a good night," Madison said.

As Madison got into the car, Adam yelled through the open window, "She's going on a date with Adam."

The old lady yelled back, "Tell Adam he is one lucky fella."

8

SATURDAY, NOVEMBER 30

The move had gone as smoothly as it could. It was just 11 o'clock in the morning, and everything was now moved out of their condo, thanks to the fact that they didn't have much stuff to begin with and also because Yuul had booked 4 movers and a truck.

Yuul, Ella and Liz were already at their new home located on York Ridge Road waiting for the movers to arrive. Jeffrey Knight had stayed behind to help the movers and to return their keys to the superintendent of the building.

As Jeffrey looked around at his home sweet home one last time, he felt his phone vibrate just before he heard the ring. He was irritated by the name on the screen: *captain*. It was definitely a bad sign getting a call from the captain on his day off.

Liz, the Neighbour

"Hey captain,"

He listened intensely without saying one word until the end of the call.

"I'll be there."

He pressed Yuul's phone number as he walked over to the closet in the master bedroom where he had left his black jacket and grabbed it hurriedly.

"Hi sweetie," Jeffrey said.

Jeffrey smiled. He didn't know why, but Yuul's no-frill response always made him smile.

"I was about to but I just got called into a case."

He let out a short laugh. "No! Swear to God I'm not lying." A pause. "Yes ma'am. I'm on it!" He disconnected the call and quickly scanned every corner of the place looking for any forgotten items and then locked the door for the last time. He went down to the superintendent's place to return the keys and say a last good-bye. He hustled his way out and grabbed his ride from the visitor's parking.

As soon as he drove past the gatehouse, he flipped his siren on and blazed south down Yonge Street until he hit the Gardiner Expressway and headed west for about 3 kilometers. He took the Lakeshore Shore Boulevard exit and then turned right, he wound his way north on Royal York Road for five minutes then took a quick left on Hillside Avenue and suddenly there he was, at the crime scene.

Jeffrey parked the car on the street and approached the crime scene on foot. Despite the cold weather, a good number of spectators were out, watching on in curiosity. Walking through the spectators, he showed his badge to one of the uniformed officers and walked past the road barrier.

He continued along a walkway and saw portable barrier posts with yellow police tape placed around the bench where the victim was found. Forensic identification officers were busy photographing and taking video of the crime scene and the victim, and collecting fingerprints as well as other forensic evidence on around the scene.

He saw, Philip Seward, a 67-year-old coroner, examining the body. He saw his new partner, Wylie Townsend, standing next to Philip.

Since the retirement of his old partner, Neil Armstrong, almost three months ago, Jeffrey hadn't had a permanent partner until very recently.

Wylie was a 29-year-old, 5'10" tall Caucasian male. He seemed to be easy-going and eager to learn. Jeffrey liked those qualities in people, but what he really liked about Wylie was that he was younger and in better shape. With Neil, he'd had to do most of the chasing and leg work as he had been the one who was younger and in better shape. Now, it was payback time.

"How's your morning been?" Wylie asked.

"Can't complain in front of the dead. What do we know?"

"The victim is Madison Cooper. At the time of her death, she was 27 years old, working for a local radio station as a news reporter."

"You already IDed the victim?"

"The forensic team found her wallet and her lipstick not far from the body. It looks like the perpetrator dropped her purse as he was running away with it. In the dark and in a rush, he collected whatever he could see and ran off."

"How did you know that she was a news reporter?"

Liz, the Neighbour

"I got her name from her driver's license. I googled her name and found her."

"Lived close by?"

"Close enough, but not that close. According to her license, she lived on Culnan Avenue. That's roughly 10 minutes away from here by car."

"So, she got here by car. Did you find her car?"

"No, not yet. I sent out some officers to search the neighbourhood. If she drove here by herself, she should've parked the car close by."

"Good job."

"I tried to think like you."

"Think like me?"

"Yup. Thought about what you would look for."

"Am I that predictable?"

"I'm just that good."

"A modest man."

"A man can only try, right?"

Jeffrey laughed thinking Wylie could really shoot the shit.

"What time was the body discovered?" Jeffrey asked.

"9:37 this morning. The first 911 caller was logged when she called it in."

"Did Dr. Philip call the time of death?"

"No, not yet." Wylie turned to the side and said in a whisper, "The man is too meticulous. We'll probably be dead before he concludes his findings."

"I heard that's happened."

That drew a chuckle from Wylie.

"You two," Dr. Philip said stretching his body.

Jeffrey and Wylie turned towards Dr. Philip.

"Unfortunately, I can't tell you the exact time of death yet. There are too many variables to be taken into consideration to give a precise determination. What I can tell you though is that it took place between 10:00 p.m. last night and 4:00 a.m. this morning. Now, look at the amount of blood found on her clothes, on the bench and the ground below where the victim sat. This was definitely the kill-site. Look here." Dr. Philip pointed at the front of the victim's neck.

"There are two ways to die from a deep, long slit like this one: damage to the trachea or the carotid arteries. By the look of it, arterial damage is much more likely, but I'll probe both possibilities. The blood spatter indicates the perp was sitting on her right side. Let me show you something." Doctor Philip walked over to Wylie's right side.

"The perp sits next to her on her right, holds her head like this and then slits her throat."

Wylie quickly twitched his head and moved his upper body backward to get out of the Doc's reach. Jeffrey curled his lips upwards.

"It explains the blood spatter and proves that the perp is right-handed. Now, look at the posture of the body."

As instructed, Jeffrey and Wylie looked at the body.

"Considering the body was found sitting-up, and how the blood spread over the ground, it shows that the perp sat next to her keeping her upright until she was completely dead. Now, I'm going to take the body to the lab and do a more thorough examination."

"Thank you, Doc," Jeffrey said to the Doc who was already walking over to the forensic team. Jeffrey turned to Wylie. "Why do you think she was killed here?"

"What do you mean?"

"Why did the perp choose this spot?"

"Maybe, the perp saw an opportunity and cashed in on it."

"Then why leave the body here in this playground? It's a residential area. I get it. It's winter. There wouldn't be many people out, but people still come out to do stuff. Why leave the body upright? The body is more likely to be seen than if it was lying prone on the bench or stuck under it for that matter. It looks like the perp wanted the body to be found as soon as possible. Why?"

As Wylie tried to come up with something to say to Jeffrey, a uniformed officer approached them.

"All the cars are accounted for," the uniform said. "Nothing here seems to belong to the victim."

"For now, we'll work on the assumption that she got a ride. Can you collect all the CCTV footage and dash footage you can get within a 15-kilometre radius? We'll contact the TOC (Traffic Operations Centre) and then the MTO (Ministry of Transportation of Ontario)."

"You got it." The uniform left.

"We're done here. Let's go to the vic's home. Send me her home address," Jeffrey said to Wylie.

As Jeffrey walked past the crime barricade, he was bombarded by reporters.

"What can you tell us?" As the reporter tried to put the mic close to Jeffrey, she poked him in his left eye with it. "I'm sorry," The reporter said profusely.

"It's okay." Jeffrey gently rubbed his eye for a minute and then kept on walking, ignoring the reporters.

"Who's the victim?" A reporter from CTC put his microphone to Jeffrey.

"Are you in charge of the investigation?" A reporter from CBC asked, putting her microphone to Jeffrey.

"What's the cause of death?" A reporter from 365 News put her microphone to Jeffrey as well.

Jeffrey stopped and turned to the mics. "No comment at this time, but there'll be a news conference to address the case once we know more."

Just like Wylie said, it took a little over 10 minutes to get to the victim's home on Culnan Avenue from the crime scene. Jeffrey parked his car on the street and waited in his car for his partner to arrive. He debated in his mind whether or not he would have a quick puff of a smoke before going in. Breaking the news to loved ones that a family member had been murdered was hard enough. But asking questions to those who had just lost their loved one was definitely worse.

When he saw Wylie's car going into the park position, he took it as a sign not to smoke. He got out of his car and started walking over to the front door of the 2-storey, detached house with the faded white brick exterior.

"Sweet Jesus!" Jeffrey exclaimed while flailing his arms to keep his balance before he reached the stair railing just in time to save himself from a fall. Letting out a sigh of relief, he said, "Watch out. It's very slippery here." He studied the ground to see what had caused the slip. There wasn't any ice on the ground.

He couldn't tell whether the paved stairs were somehow too polished or too worn out. He gave up on this slip and fall case and kept on walking.

"Thanks for the heads-up," Wylie said, catching up to Jeffrey.

Jeffrey stepped aside so that Wylie could knock on the door. He liked having a young partner.

Wylie stood in front of the wooden door and knocked. Waiting for a few seconds, Wylie knocked on the door again but this time, he did it a little harder. He then heard a shuffling sound approaching the door.

"Put your hands up where I can see them and state your business. I'll shoot you if you even breathe one tempo faster." An old, high pitched voice came from the other side of the door.

Jeffrey and Wylie looked at each other startled by the threat.

"Ma'am, we're the police. Don't do anything you're gonna regret later. Okay?" Jeffrey said.

"No time for regrets when you hit my age. And I'm letting you know that I'm not alone."

"What's all the noise?" An old man's voice came through the door. "Can you guys step aside?"

"You can't open the door to just anyone," The same old woman's voice came.

"We're not just anyone. We're the police," Wylie said at the door, raising his voice an octave.

"Agnes, Birdie, step aside," The old man said in a gentle but stern voice. After a moment, the door was wide open, and there stood an old black man in his 70s. He was tall and still in great shape for his age.

The old man studied Wylie for a moment and then asked, "Why are the police here? Show me your ID."

Wylie took out his ID from his pocket inside of his jacket. "I'm Wylie Townsend, a detective with the Toronto Police."

The old man turned to Jeffrey. "You?"

Jeffrey took out his badge and showed it to the old man. "Can we come in?"

"What's this all about?" The very same high pitched white woman asked, standing next to the old man.

Jeffrey scanned the woman but saw she was unarmed. "Where's your gun?"

"Didn't your mom tell you that you shouldn't believe everything you hear?" the old woman said, staring at Jeffrey hard. "State your business."

Looking at her determined eyes, Jeffrey realized that she wasn't going to let him in unless he played by her rules. He let out a deep sigh of resignation. "This concerns Madison Cooper. Now, how are you related to Ms. Cooper?"

"Something… happened to… her?" the old man said.

"Let's go inside," Jeffrey said.

The old man stared at Jeffrey before he slowly turned to his right. The two old women followed the old man in silence.

The two ladies looked to be in their mid 70s. Both had short, silver hair. They looked to be the same height, somewhere close to 5'2" tall, and the same weight, less than 100 lbs. Considering that they even looked like they had the same number of facial wrinkles, Jeffrey wondered if they were twins.

Jeffrey and Wylie followed the old women in. The old man sat down in his armchair and the two women sat on a 3-seater sofa. There was no sofa or chair for

Liz, the Neighbour

Jeffrey or Wylie to sit on unless they wanted to squeeze themselves onto the couch with the ladies, which they didn't.

"Follow me," the same high pitched woman said, standing up.

Jeffrey and Wylie stood up and followed her. As Jeffrey neared the fireplace, he saw pictures displayed on the mantle. He then knew that they had the right place. He followed Wylie to the kitchen and grabbed a chair and took it with him.

As he sat, he heard the old man saying, "What happened to Maddie?"

Wylie cleared his throat. "We found her dead this—"

"What did you say?" the old man said in the thunder of his booming voice, staring at Wylie.

"Madison Cooper was found dead," Wylie said.

The old man jumped at Wylie. He held his shirt collar tight. "You got it wrong! You got it wrong!"

Jeffrey walked over to the old man and gently pulled him off of Wylie. He held the old man upright. "I am sorry."

The old man looked at Jeffrey and shook his head. "It can't be Maddie. It cannot be..."

Jeffrey felt the old man's body muscles go lax and worried that he was about to collapse to the floor, but he didn't let him. He held the old man tight in his arms and took him to his armchair.

"How did she die?" the old man asked.

"She was murdered," Wylie said matter-of-factly.

"No!" the old man wailed. This time he did fall to the floor.

The two old women gathered around him on the floor and cried with him.

Jeffrey walked over to them and patted them on the back. "We're really sorry for your loss."

"Do you know who did it?" the old man asked, sniffling.

"We don't know yet, but we'll find the person who's responsible for this," Jeffrey said in his determined voice.

"You have questions?" the old man said.

"Yes," Jeffrey continued. "Can I have your names and how you're related to Madison Cooper?"

"I'm Ed Jamieson. Maddie is my granddaughter. She's my daughter's daughter. Since my daughter moved to the States, Maddie's been living here with me."

"I'm Birdie Pemberton. I live next door to him. We've been friends for the last 50 years," the old woman who'd threatened them with a gun said.

"I'm Agnes Winter. I'm a friend as well," the old woman with the cane said.

"When was the last time you saw Madison?" Jeffrey asked, looking at Ed.

"It was right before 8 o'clock last night. I know it because her friend was supposed to pick her up at 8." Ed stopped as his voice trembled harder. He closed his eyes, trying to fight back tears.

Birdie understood what Ed was going through as she'd lost her own child a long time ago. She swallowed tears and picked up where Ed had left off. "I saw her last night outside my home. She was actually going out on a date."

"How did you know she was on a date?" Jeffrey asked.

"When I saw her outside, I asked her where she was going. At first she said that she was going to meet up with her friend. Then the guy inside the car that was picking her up, yelled out his name to me. To be precise he said, "She's going on a date with Adam.""

"Did you see his face?" Jeffrey asked.

"No. He said it as he drove off."

"Do you remember the plate number or the make of the car?" Jeffrey asked.

"No, I wasn't looking. Even if I did, I don't think I could. It was too dark. But it was a black or dark blue 4-door sedan."

"Was there anybody else in Madison's life we should be looking into?" Jeffrey asked.

Ed, Birdie and Agnes took a moment to consider it, but in the end, they just shook their heads.

Jeffrey looked at Ed in silence for a moment and said, "I'm so sorry for your loss." He stood up, reaching his wallet for his business card, but Wylie beat him to it.

"If you remember anything else, please call us." Wylie extended his business card to Birdie.

Jeffrey walked over to the front door with Wylie on his tail.

Wylie quietly followed Jeffrey down the staircase to the curb and stopped. "I'm sorry about what happened earlier. I just wanted to move things along. I was such an inconsiderate jerk."

"Don't worry about it. There's no good or bad way to deliver the news about a loved one's death." Jeffrey shrugged.

"Where to next?" Wylie said in a more cheerful tone.

"I don't know about you but I'm starved. Let's eat and then we go to the station to see what Santa brought us for Christmas. If we're lucky, one of the footages will show Madison arriving at the playground in a car. Who knows? Maybe, one of the videos might've even captured the license plate number and then we go to TOC."

"If you want, you can go home and help your wife with the move. I'm not sure how many cam footages our officers were able to collect, but I think I can get started on my own."

"Hmm… You're setting the bar way too high for yourself. Once you spoil me, I can't and won't go back."

"Ha-ha. I'll try my very best to keep the bar where I set it today."

Jeffrey drove north on Yonge Street and turned right at York Mills and then left shortly after on to York Ridge Road and suddenly, there it was, his new home quietly sitting under the cloudy sky. His new place came with a huge backyard that was bordered by a ravine. Although his home was located in the heart of Toronto, it felt like he was in the countryside, which really pleased Jeffrey.

As he couldn't find a parking spot at or next to his house, he drove past the place and went up a couple of more houses to park his car. It wasn't as cold as it should've been; nonetheless, it definitely wasn't hot, sticky summer weather.

While tracking back to his place, he casually scanned the houses on the street. As far as he could tell, all the houses were built in either a Colonial or a Victorian Style, all on very big lots with natural fencing on either side– fences made of stone or flowering trees, or natural shrubbery and big oak trees defined the property lines. None of the 'fences' were too high or too thick to block outsider's peeping eyes. Those eye-pleasing fences were there to claim ownership of the land, nothing more and nothing less.

The street appeared tranquil in every sense. At 3:00 p.m. on a little cloudy day, the street revealed a close to picture perfect neighbourhood.

Jeffrey saw a couple watching him through an opening in the curtains of the house right across from his. He casually waved at them, and they waved back at him. It put a smile on him. Nice neighbours, he thought. At that moment, he knew that he was really going to love his new place. He waved at them one more time before he turned around and opened his front door.

"Honey, I'm home," Jeffrey said as closing the door behind him.

"Oh, is it my Jeffrey honey?" Ajay said in a woman's voice.

Jeffrey heard a sea of laughter as he took off his shoes in the foyer. He knew that there were very few things that bothered Yuul but one of them was people walking around her house in their shoes.

"Jeffrey, keep your shoes on. I haven't had a chance to wipe the floor yet."

"Okay honey."

As he proceeded his walk into the living room, he found Yuul, Liz, Ella, Charlie and Ajay sitting on the couches, eating pizza and chicken wings.

"What timing! You came home just as we finished the move," Liz said, frowning.

"A man can only try." Jeffrey sat next to Yuul. "Hmm…" He squinted at Ajay. "I didn't expect to see you again."

"Why not? I'm showing up here anytime I want. You guys owe me. Your sister's walking around free, thanks to me."

"You met another girl at a wedding where my sister took you to as her date, and then you left the wedding with that girl."

"Your sister told me to."

Liz dismissively waved her hand at Jeffrey. "Leave him alone. You didn't even want me to see him to begin with, and you've got to see them together. They're truly a match made in heaven."

"Still, I don't like it."

"Do you want me to break his legs?" Yuul asked Jeffrey.

"Let me see how he does today and then we decide one leg or both."

Yuul slowly nodded in agreement.

• • •

After Jeffrey had disappeared into his house, the couple who'd made Jeffrey fall in love with the neighbourhood had just stood there, grinning ear to ear. They had been watching the street and the neighbours intensely over the last few weeks. Today, they'd been watching the street just like any other day, when they spotted Jeffrey walking along it and then pop into the house across from them. They didn't know what to think of it – Could it be pure luck or the result of all their hard work? Either way, they felt lucky and watched Jeffrey with undeniable interest.

"Is he the guy we saw on TV today?" the bald man asked. He knew it was him but wanted it to be confirmed by his lovely wife, Doreen.

"I think so. This calls for a little celebration. Do you want some tea and a piece of chocolate cake?"

"You've got to give me a big slice," the man said closing the curtains all the way.

"Hmm…" Doreen stared at him, her eyes frowned for a few seconds. Then her frown turned into a smile. "Okay. After all, this is a celebration." Doreen sashayed to the kitchen.

"And I want steak for dinner," the man yelled.

"Rob, you don't have to yell," Doreen said from the kitchen. "I'm not deaf."

Wearing a big smile, Rob marched into the kitchen. "I got too excited." He kissed her on her cheek.

She kissed him back. "Steak for dinner, it is." She started humming the song, Sweet Caroline, while boiling the water for tea. Her short, wavy, blond hair swayed as she moved to the rhythm. Her white face had pink colour on her cheeks as if to show her contentment.

Rob Ryan had seen many beautiful women in his 67 years of life, but he'd never seen a woman like Doreen. He'd met Doreen Pelletier 20 some years ago. When he'd met her, he'd been down on his luck as had she.

Doreen's first husband hadn't been a poor man but had been as stingy as Scrooge. Being cheap and all, she'd never suspected him of being a cheater. Carrying on with a mistress cost money. How shocking it had been when she'd found out about his many affairs. It'd probably hit her harder because of the timing. When she'd found out about his affairs, she'd just had another miscarriage.

During those tough days, she'd buried herself in her work. She'd refused to think about her loss and the betrayal. She'd worked three jobs – as a cleaner, waitress and cashier.

When Rob Ryan had met Doreen Pelletier, he'd had to leave everything behind and move up to Canada from the United States. He'd had some cash but not much. He'd lost his way. He'd met her at the grocery store where she'd worked as a cashier. It hadn't been love at first sight, but it'd been close.

He watched her, observed her and stalked her before he'd asked her out on a date. At that time, she'd just turned 40 but something about her caught his attention.

She hadn't just been a hard working woman with a pretty face, she was also smart with a great sense of humour. More strikingly, she'd always known what he'd needed. She'd been like a psychic when it'd come to his needs.

Now at age 64, her body had changed and was getting heavier and wrinklier every day but in his eyes she hadn't aged a day since he'd met her. Rob himself was 5'10" tall and his big beer belly wasn't getting any smaller. His extra fat just said how happy and contended he'd been with his life.

Doreen sipped her tea and said, "I guess I've got to make a welcome basket tomorrow morning. You should call Mike and Abigail to go with us."

"No one says hello like them," Rob said scooping another piece of the cake.

9

SUNDAY, DECEMBER 1

Jeffrey woke up to find his entire body sore and all of his muscles aching from having wiped the entire floor on his hands and knees for hours last night. A hot shower helped ease the pain a little. A greasy breakfast washed down with tons of coffee helped ease the pain a little more. By the time he was ready to leave home, he felt as fresh as a new born baby.

Since it was just 9:30 in the morning on a Sunday, the road was wide open like the autobahn in Germany. While enjoying the drive on the open road, his mind drifted to the case. The name 'Adam' had been bothering him. It felt like it had been a clumsy attempt to make his name known.

Why? Because he didn't know that he was going to kill her? Does that mean it was a crime of passion? Is that why he revealed his name? Is there even such a thing "as a crime of passion" on a first date? Can't be… unless… unless you are a serial killer who is passionate about killing. If her date was a serial killer, then he knew he was going to kill her. Then, why the hell would he shout out his real name to Birdie?

Jeffrey stopped at the red light. While waiting for the signal to change, he impatiently tapped his index finger on the steering wheel. The answer was on the tip of his tongue. By the time the light had changed to green he knew: *Adam isn't his real name. It can't be.* He was sure of it.

He was excited that he'd figured it out, but his excitement was short lived as this meant they had nothing to go on. He let out a sigh of disappointment as he parked the car at the police station.

When Jeffrey arrived at the homicide squad, he was surprised to see Wylie already at his desk, morning coffee in hand, working away.

"I didn't expect to see you in this early," Wylie said.

"You took the words right out of my mouth." Jeffrey chuckled.

"How was the move?"

"It was a battle, but I lived to tell the tale."

"Good! Now, get ready for the best day of your life." Wylie exclaimed with a big shit eating grin on his face.

"What've you got?"

"I found the car. Seeing is believing, right? I've got it all cued up. You're gonna love me for this. Here's the car." Wylie pointed at a car with his index finger on his computer screen, and then played the footage. "Did you catch that? The car turned onto Hillside Avenue from Royal York Road?"

"No, I missed it."

Liz, the Neighbour

"Don't feel bad. I watched it a thousand times at different speeds to track it." Wylie played it again, but in slow motion this time, tracing the car with his finger. "Did you see it get off at Hillside Avenue now?"

"It's impossible to miss with your big fat finger pointing right at it."

"You're welcome. This is the last part of the movie. Spoiler alert! This one has a happy ending, for us anyway." Wylie played more footage, his finger still on the car. "Here, Madison and the perp go into the playground at 10:52 p.m., *aaand* wait for it..." Wylie leaned over to the keyboard: Click, click. "Here! Look, it's the suspect returning to his car, alone, at 11:47 p.m. and then him pulling back onto Royal York Road again.

Jeffrey blew out a whistle. "I can't believe you pieced that all together. Good work!"

"Playing around with all that video, I feel like I need an eye massage or something.

"I don't care what kind of massage it is, don't look at me for it, eh? Did you end up pulling an all-nighter?"

"Yup. That's the only way to make the magic happen, right?"

"Now, you're just bragging."

"I'll show you bragging rights. I've got the first two letters of the license plate – a B and a Y."

"You're a goddamn overachiever!" Jeffrey exclaimed as gave Wylie a good slap on the back.

"I think I earned my breakfast today."

"What are you waiting for? Lead the way. It's on me"

It couldn't have gone any smoother or quicker at TOC. Based on the time and the location Wylie had provided, TOC almost instantly located the car. Also, luck was with the good guys for a change.

First off, because the crime took place very late at night during winter, there had been almost no other cars on Royal York Road. That had expedited the tracking process enormously.

Secondly, considering the fact that TOC had only 297 cameras to monitor traffic city-wide, they could've easily lost track of the suspect right after he pulled off Royal York. All he had to do was stick to the side streets. But he didn't do that. Instead, the perp had taken one main road after another all of which had CCTV cameras installed, right up to York Ridge Road where they finally lost him.

People say good things come in threes, right? The third was that they even picked up the rest of the plate number along the way.

Jeffrey was amused by the route the perp had taken – Royal York Road to Lakeshore Boulevard to Gardener Expressway to Yonge Street to York Mills to York Ridge Road.

"What is it?" Wylie asked.

"That would be the exact route I would take if I've come home from the crime scene yesterday."

"Is this a confession?" Wylie asked, cocking his head.

"Yeah, yeah, sure, whatever bro. Let's go run the plate."

. . .

Liz, the Neighbour

Liz, Ella and Yuul were relaxing on their couches enjoying a late brunch while discussing their detective business. The business talk was all light and casual as Yuul was the one taking care of the serious part of the actual running of the business end. As they were just about to wrap up the discussion, they heard a woman's voice, "Yoo-hoo" followed by a knock on the door.

"Who can that be?" Yuul said.

"Charlie said his mom was going to drop by today. Maybe it's her," Liz said.

"Really?" Ella whispered. "Oh, shoot!" Ella let out a cry, looking up and down at her T-shirt and jeans. "Should I change into something classier?"

"She would be way more appreciative if you don't keep her waiting outside in the cold," Liz said.

Ella looked at Liz and then the front door, back to Liz. "Shoot." She ran to the door.

"Too easy," Liz said, shaking her head smiling.

Ella opened the door and yelled, "Welcome..." Ella stopped herself and stared at the people crowding up the front door. It was two older couples and it couldn't have been more obvious that they were not Hala or anyone related to Charlie as Charlie didn't have any white relatives.

Ella figured that both ladies had to be around 5'4" tall as they stood a little taller than herself, and that both men had a few inches on the ladies. Ella thought that the man and woman on the left must be at least in their 70s considering the fact that they looked a lot older than Liz's parents. The other two looked closer to Liz's parents' age which put them somewhere in their sixties. Both ladies wore ankle length skirts below winter jackets, and the gentlemen wore pants way too high above the waistline. The two women held serving dishes in their arms.

Ella looked at them, confused. "Who are you?"

The lady in her 70s said, "We're here to see your master... Kekekeke" She covered her mouth with her hand, giggling. The man in his 70s laughed along with the lady.

Ella didn't know what they were laughing about and she had no interest in finding out. She suddenly felt tired and yawned. "I'm sorry. What can I do for you?"

"We're here to see your employer," the lady in her 70s said. She then pushed Ella aside and marched on in. On cue, the other three waddled after her.

Ella was bound to the ground dumbstruck. When she finally realized what had just happened, she quickly hightailed it back to the living room.

"Who are you?" Liz asked as dumbstruck as Ella.

"I'm Abigail Kelly," the lady in her 70s said. She pointed to the man beside her. "This is my husband, Mike Kelly." She then gestured towards the woman in her 60s. "She's Doreen Ryan and he's Rob Ryan, Doreen's husband. They live right across from you, and we live next to them. We're the welcoming committee. I brought a Shepherd's Pie, and Doreen made some cookies." Abigail turned to Yuul and said, "Can you bring some plates and silverware?"

"Do you want some coffee to go with it?" Yuul asked.

"Do you have tea?" Abigail said.

"We have Earl Grey."

"That sounds lovely," Doreen said.

Yuul stood up from the couch and walked over to the kitchen. Doreen followed Yuul to the kitchen.

"You can go back to work." Abigail waved at Ella as Ella was about to sit down on the couch.

Ella looked at Abigail in confusion.

Abigail turned to Liz and said, "You've got to teach these girls some manners."

"What girls?" Liz asked in confusion.

Abigail pointed at Ella and then pointed to the kitchen with her chin. "Anyway, where did you get them?"

Liz frowned as she finally understood what Abigail meant.

"She got us from Korea," Yuul shouted from the kitchen. "Don't ruin it, Liz."

Abigail shook her head in damnation, "This is exactly what I'm talking about. You can't just expect them to know their place. You have to tell them. Anyway, you're Liz?"

"Yes," Liz said. Sometimes, she really couldn't understand Yuul. *How can she find this funny?* She shook her head slightly.

"Huh, Korea?" Mike said looking at Ella. "I know the country well. The Rocket Man, right? That's your leader, isn't he? How did you make it over here anyway?"

"We walked," Yuul said, coming out of the kitchen with a tea set. "It took us some time, but we finally made it to Canada."

"Walked?" Mike arched his eyebrows in shock. "It must be one heck of a walk."

While placing the teacups and saucers on the coffee table, Yuul shook her head. "It wasn't that bad."

"You must be shocked to see all the stuff we have here," Mike said, pointing around the house with his index finger. "Which one impressed you the most? The toilet? It has to be the indoor plumbing. Isn't it awesome? You do your business and then flush it down. It's all gone. It's like magic."

"Can you imagine what happened until I learnt about the flushing part?" Yuul said.

"Yuck!" everybody screamed in unison including Liz and Ella.

"Who wants Shepherd's Pie?' Yuul said.

"Not me," Abigail said vehemently shaking her head.

Yuul looked at Liz and said, "May I sit, ma'am?"

"Yes, you may," Liz said, swallowing down her laughter.

"What does your husband do for a living?" Abigail asked, looking at Liz.

"I'm not married."

"What about the good-looking man we saw last night?" Doreen asked.

"You must be talking about my brother."

"Your brother? What does he do for a living?" Doreen asked.

"He's a detective," Liz said.

Rob got excited quickly. "I thought so." A goofy smile on his face. "I saw him on the news about some murder case yesterday."

"Oh yeah?" Liz said.

"On a detective's salary, he could afford to buy a house here?" Mike said in surprise.

Liz shrugged, looking at Yuul. "He's got a rich wife."

"Where is she?" Mike asked.

Liz pointed at Yuul. "Meet my sister-in-law."

Mike and Abigail looked lost at first, and then disappointed... devastatingly.

Yuul looked at Mike, her lips pursed very tightly as if to fight back a laugh for a few seconds. Then a boisterous laugh actually did come out. She laughed for a long moment, taking no notice of all the eyes watching her. When she finally stopped, she said almost in a crying voice, "You... need to... get out more."

10

SUNDAY, DECEMBER 1

Jeffrey Knight and Wylie Townsend drove back to the station and ran the license plate number. With a few more clicks, they got everything they needed to know about the car and its owner.

Are you kidding me? Looking at the owner's name displayed on the computer, Jeffrey leaned in, his nose almost touching the screen, to make sure he wasn't seeing things.

Adam Brooks? It can't be. No matter how close or far away Jeffrey got to the screen, it didn't change a thing, it still read that the car was registered to Adam Brooks.

Who would ever think that the perp would actually broadcast his real name before killing someone? Jeffrey just shook his head slowly in disbelief.

Liz, the Neighbour

"A Crown Prosecutor? What the hell, man!" Wylie said, pointing at the screen.

"A Crown Prosecutor who happens to live next door to me." Jeffrey slowly shook his head.

"For real?"

"Yup."

"Do you know the guy?"

"No, I haven't had the pleasure of meeting the neighbours yet."

"What do you want to do?"

"Let's go over what we have first. What do we know about the victim?"

Wylie took out his notepad from the inside pocket of his jacket. "The vic's name is Madison Cooper, 27-years old, black. She worked for a local radio station as a news reporter. The last person who saw Madison alive was her neighbour, Birdie Pemberton. Birdie saw Madison leave to go on a date with Adam Brooks at 8:00 p.m. on the day that she was murdered."

"Birdie didn't see Madison with Adam Brooks," Jeffrey corrected. "Birdie heard a man identify himself as Adam from inside his car."

"If he's not Adam, why would he say to Birdie his name was Adam?"

"I'm wondering the same thing. Okay, for now, let's move on."

Wylie looked at Jeffrey for a moment and then went on. "Birdie saw the car that Madison got into and confirmed that it was a black or dark navy sedan, just like Adam Brooks'."

"Tell me about the crime scene."

"The body was found in a sitting position on a bench in a playground located on Hillside Avenue on

Liz, the Neighbour

Saturday, November 30 at 9:37 a.m. We found the vic's wallet and lipstick at the crime scene. A video feed shows that the perp and the vic got there at 11 p.m. on Friday. The feed also shows the perp leaving the playground alone at 11:47 p.m. that same night and then getting into his car and driving away on Royal York Avenue. All the video feeds that we have show no other visitors entering the playground until the first 911 caller called it in."

"What do we know about the murder?"

Wylie quickly flipped through his notepad until he found the page. "Based on the video, we can conclude that the vic was killed sometime on Friday, November 29 between 10:52 p.m. and 11:47 p.m., which falls within the timeline the coroner estimated earlier. The coroner has confirmed that the findings were compatible with the vic's throat being slit by a right handed person sitting next to her, her head firmly restrained."

"Tell me how you identified the car and its owner."

"We first identified the car from a video feed collected close to the crime scene. It captured the vic and the perp getting out of the car and later, the perp leaving the crime scene in that same car alone. The video at the crime scene also captured the first two letters of the license plate. We were able to get the complete plate number from TOC as well as the route the perp took after leaving the crime scene. The car belongs to a Crown Prosecutor by the name of Adam Brooks."

"The location and the time of when the car was last seen travelling on the road?"

"The car turned onto York Ridge Road from York Mills at 12:34 a.m."

"Hmm..." Jeffrey rubbed his forehead, his eyes closed.

"What is it? Did I miss something?"

"No, you haven't missed a thing. You, indeed, got all of it in fact. I just can't decide if he's the most arrogant guy or the stupidest guy on this planct."

"What makes you say that?"

"He didn't try to cover his tracks at all. In fact, he even told Birdie Pemberton his real name. Why would he do that? Is it because he's one arrogant SOB or just another dumb fuck?"

"Hmm..."

"Let me call my wife and then we'll talk to the captain."

"Trouble in paradise?"

"Haha. I'm calling my wife to keep an eye on Adam for us. We don't want to lose him, do we?"

"Ah."

Jeffrey made a call to Yuul and asked her to go out and see if there was a black Audi A6 parked either in the next door neighbour's driveway or on the street. Yuul said nothing, but her footsteps could be heard over the phone. A few minutes later, she reported that she did in fact see a black car parked in the driveway next door.

He asked her to keep an eye on it and told her to call him if the car moved. Yuul said she would and then hung up. That was it. This was why he had called Yuul, not Liz or Ella. Yuul asked questions later if she felt like she needed to know.

Jeffrey then called the captain and put her on speaker phone. He gave Wylie the go ahead to brief her. Wylie started filling her in. Jeffrey could hear the captain gasp as Wylie was wrapping it up.

"Good job, boys!" the captain said with a hint of pride.

"I can't take credit for this one, captain. It's all Wylie. Superman reborn."

"Wylie, you did real good," the captain said.

"Thank you, ma'am."

"What's next?" the captain asked.

"We'll get a search warrant for the car and have it towed to the forensic facility and we'll bring Adam in for questioning," Wylie said.

"Keep me apprised." The captain ended the call.

• • •

Liz, Ella and Yuul hung by the window facing the street and watched in excitement as all the cop cars began silently pouring onto York Ridge Road in excitement. They watched as Jeffrey got out of the passenger side of one of the cars. A man in his late 20s, approximately 5'10" tall, physically very fit with curly, brown hair got out of the same car from the driver's side.

"$10 says he's Wylie," Liz said confidently.

"Me, too," Yuul said.

"Me, too," Ella said at last.

They looked at each other, slowly shaking their heads, eyes narrowing for a moment. When they turned their attention back to the window again, Jeffrey and Wylie were nowhere to be seen. They could guess where they were though.

They lowered their bodies and quickly tiptoed over to the other window that faced the next door neighbours. When they poked their heads out ever so slightly, they saw Jeffrey standing beside Wylie at the neighbour's front door.

It didn't take long, before they saw their neighbour for the very first time. The neighbour had a serious look and a hairstyle similar to a crew cut but with more volume on the top and sides. They thought that he was cute in his own right, especially when he adjusted his silver framed round eyeglasses with his thumb and index finger.

Although they were more than 20 feet away, they could see the surprised look on his clean-shaven face after opening the front door and finding two strange men at his door holding up police badges. Probably, seeing his car being towed away added to his shock as well.

The neighbour disappeared into his house and came out again with a jacket in his hand. As he was being escorted to Wylie's car, he suddenly stopped and turned to the window where the three amigos were watching. The three amigos dropped to the floor, feeling like they'd been caught stealing.

• • •

Jeffrey Knight stood in a dimly lit room, looking at Adam Brooks sitting in the brightly lit interrogation room through a one-way mirror.

"What are you waiting for?" Wylie asked Jeffrey, standing next to him.

"I'm waiting for him to rattle."

"Rattle?"

"A guilty man always rattles after a period of isolation, unless he's a psychopath. Does he look like a psychopath to you?"

"What does a psychopath look like?"

"Looks like you, looks like me."

"Then he's definitely a psychopath."

"Haha. Let's go."

Jeffrey entered the interrogation room with Wylie hot on his tail. Adam Brooks looked up at Jeffrey who was showing no emotion. Jeffrey sat across from Adam while Wylie stood, leaning against the wall.

"Where were you on Friday, November 29th from 7:30 p.m. to Saturday, November 30th 1:00 am?"

Adam stared at Jeffrey looking lost, his head cocked to the right as if asking Jeffrey to elaborate. When Jeffrey stared straight back at him in silence, Adam he said, "I was at home."

"Is there anyone who can corroborate your statement?" Jeffrey asked.

"No, I have no one to confirm my whereabouts. What's the name of the woman who was found dead on the playground early Saturday?"

That startled Jeffrey a little. Shit! Jeffrey cursed inside. He didn't want to react but he knew that his surprise showed on his face.

Adam's upper lip curled slightly upward. "I guess I impressed you. In that case, you're in for a big disappointment." Adam paused and stared at Jeffrey's left eye.

Jeffrey frowned.

"How's your eye? Did you go get it checked?" Adam said. Then he pursed his lips really tight to fight a smile, but his eyes betrayed his efforts.

The memory of the news reporter poking his left eye with a mic came back to Jeffrey. "Was that aired?"

Adam nodded, still pursing his lips.

Jeffrey slammed his fists on the table. "What channel was that? I will sue the crap out of that TV station."

Adam leaned closer. "Anyway, the news said that you're the lead detective on the case. What's the woman's name?"

Jeffrey shook his head. "We're the ones asking the questions around here right now pal. When we're done, you can ask all the questions you want. What about your neighbours? Did you see anyone doing anything in their houses or yards? Have you talked to anyone at all since Friday night?"

"No, I didn't see anyone. I didn't talk to anyone. You're the first people I've talked to since Friday night."

"For almost two days?" Jeffrey asked.

"Yes. I was wrapped up in a case that started off as nothing, more like a conspiracy theory. But it's taking me—"

"Ooh-kay, that's enough," Wylie interjected, sitting down next to Jeffrey. "You're trying to sidetrack us here. You're here as a suspect for the murder of Madison Cooper. Did you know her?"

As Wylie said the victim's name out loud, Jeffrey caught something flash past Adam's face although he wasn't sure if it was guilt or shame, but it was definitely one of the two or both. *Interesting,* Jeffrey thought.

Adam closed his eyes and kept them closed for a long moment. When he finally said, yes, his voice cracked.

"How did you know her?" Wylie asked.

"We are, I mean we were friends. As you know, she was a crime reporter with WHT. That was how we met and became friends. Later, she became a good friend of my wife's."

"You have a wife?" Jeffrey asked.

"Yes," Adam said.

"Where was your wife last Friday?" Jeffrey asked.

"She was, and probably still is in Paris."

"You don't know where your wife is?" Jeffrey raised his right eyebrow.

"We're separated. She left for Paris last Wednesday. We talked once, she was checking in to a different hotel the next day and I haven't heard from her since then."

"When was the last time you saw Madison Cooper?" Jeffrey asked.

"A little over 3 weeks ago, that was the last time I saw her."

Jeffrey caught that little something flash across Adam's face again. He couldn't help but wonder what had caused Adam to crack – *The shame of having been caught so soon or the guilt he had from killing her?*

"Knowing that I'm a Crown Prosecutor, you wouldn't have brought me down here on a Sunday to interrogate me unless you have very strong evidence linking me to her death. Level up the playing field and let's hear what you have."

Jeffrey felt that it was the right time to show his hand a little. So, he told Adam what they had on him so far and the fact that his car was being searched for Madison's fingerprints and whatever else they could find as they spoke.

Liz, the Neighbour

The colour had drained out of Adam's face, leaving him ashen.

The shock on his face was clearly discernible to Jeffrey. The pain on his face looked real.

"Why would I kill her?" Adam said, looking a little angry, even a little frightened. "What's my motive?"

"Maybe, she was blackmailing you?" Wylie said.

"Blackmailing me with what?"

"Maybe, you slept with her. She wanted to come clean to your wife about the affair. You went mad. You killed her."

Adam snorted out a smile.

"Is something funny?" Wylie said, animated.

With a smile on his face, Adam said, not particularly to anyone, "The last time I saw Maddie, she accused me of cheating on Anya, Anya is my wife, with some woman. Maddie got me all wrong then, and today," turning to Wylie, "you've got me wrong. Yes, I did see the humour in it. And no, I never slept with Maddie. Again, we were never more than friends."

Jeffrey felt his cellphone vibrate in his pants pocket. "Let's take a break. I need a coffee. Do you want one?"

"Lots of cream and sugar if you don't mind," Adam said nonchalantly.

Jeffrey connected the call as soon as he was out of the interview room. "What do you have? Hmm..." He didn't know what to think about what he'd just heard. But again, he shouldn't have expected to hear anything else. He ended the call.

"What is it?" Wylie asked.

"It's the forensic team. They found the vic's fingerprints as well as Adam's in the car."

"That's good news, no?"

"The forensic team also confirmed that there are smudged fingerprints on the steering wheel at the 10 and 2 o'clock positions."

"So?"

"Exactly. What do you think it means?" Jeffrey squinted. "I have one more thing to check with Adam." Jeffrey opened the door to the interrogation room and asked Adam, "Have you ever given Cooper a ride in your Audi?"

After a moment of silence, Adam said no.

Jeffrey closed the door behind him. Standing by the door, Jeffrey tried to decide if Adam was a criminal mastermind or just another dumb criminal. *Which one are you?*

Jeffrey applauded Adam's performance in the interrogation room. It was simply brilliant if he was the killer. It was a brilliant way of planting doubt in any reasonable person's mind showing off his deduction and inference skills to arrive at why he'd been brought down here in such a short time, Jeffrey had to admit.

Are you playing me, Adam? Are you singing and dancing in the interrogation room right now, savouring how you fooled me? "You see, Jeffrey, I'm too smart to kill someone and leave behind all the clues to catch me." Is this how you're going to get away with the murder? Or, are you innocent? Were you set up?

Jeffrey couldn't tell which one he was, but he knew that there was one more stone to turnover. He couldn't wait to see what he would find underneath that stone.

"Get a search warrant for Adam's house," Jeffrey said.

"Why?' Wylie almost cried in surprise.

"We don't have any piece of evidence that directly links our Adam here as the driver. Let's hope Adam didn't throw out the jacket and shoes he wore during the murder. Who knows he may even have kept the murder weapon in his house?"

"What jacket? What shoes?"

"The jacket and shoes that the killer wore in the video"

"He's not stupid. He probably already threw them out."

"He's done every stupid thing I can think of so far. Why would he change now? That goes against his character, don't you think?"

"It won't be easy to get a search warrant this time of the night, especially considering it's a Sunday."

"Holy! It's already a quarter to six. You're right. Let's do it first thing tomorrow morning."

11

SUNDAY, DECEMBER 1

Yuul massaged her stiff neck in the study room that she had turned into her office. It had been an intense couple of weeks, working on the business plan and the investment details for KSK Private Investigative Services as well as keeping up with her regular job for her brother.

As she was standing up to do some stretching, the silhouette of a person walking up from the ravine towards her backyard caught her eye through the window: *Thief!* She narrowed her eyes to discern if the assailant had a gun, but it was almost impossible to tell from her office.

Let's find out, she thought while grabbing a golf club that she kept in the room. She quietly walked out through the side door that led to their outdoor swimming pool instead of using the back door so that the outdoor sensor light didn't come on. She needed to have the element of surprise in case he was armed. She quickly but quietly circled a quarter of the way around the house to get to a spot where she could cut across her backyard towards the approximately 3' high by 40' long stretch of stone fence that worked as a border between her estate and Adam Brooks'.

She hid in the dark, waiting for the assailant to close the distance between them first. She needed to be at the right distance to utilize the golf club.

Although the ground was icy and the sky was dark, the assailant moved quietly and deftly as if he'd done it a million times. Yuul didn't like that. When she saw that the assailant was close enough, she started moving towards him. It hit her that the regular running shoes she was wearing didn't have the same grip as the military grade boots that the intruder wore. She made a mental note to buy at least one pair as she approached him.

She had come within a few feet but before she was able to position herself to strike, he saw her. She knew what he was thinking in his little brain: *Take her down or run away*. She couldn't help but let out a lopsided smile. *He thinks he has a choice.*

Right before she was about to swing her golf club upward, he swung his arms forward and over his head as he leapt upward. In that instant, she dropped her golf club and kicked into the air. She extended her right leg with all her mighty power and swung it to the left, trying to connect with his leg. He avoided her foot by a split second. He leapt backwards as his arms swung, drawing an arc. He landed on the ground, completing his full backflip.

She started running. She just needed to hit the ground a few times to propel her speed when she slid. The downhill to the ravine was pretty steep at this point. She knew that she couldn't catch him by running but she had a good chance if she slid down the hill at full strength. As it turned out, her stride was too aggressive, and she had underestimated the icy ground. She had made no more than two strides when she slip and fell.

Damn shoes. Sitting on the ground, she saw him running back to the ravine faster than a cat. He really was very deft. She really didn't like this. He was the first one to ever get away. After watching his back completely disappear into the shadows of the ravine, she slowly stood up and dusted herself off.

• • •

When Jeffrey found Yuul sitting at the dining table at 8:00 a.m., and not in bed sleeping, it worried him. He'd seen Yuul awake before 10:00 a.m. only a handful of times throughout his marriage to her, and each and every one of those times something had been up.

"What's wrong?" Jeffrey asked without even the slightest attempt to hide his worry.

Yuul looked at Jeffrey with a confused look.

"Why are you up so early?" Jeffrey asked.

"Oh, that." She smiled. "A new business idea came when I saw a burglar late last night or early this morning, depending on how you look at it. I'm trying to think if—"

"Stop! Back up a bit and start from the burglar part again."

"Oh that. Unlike what was advertised, this neighbourhood it turns out is not that safe."

"What time of the night did you see the burglar? Why didn't you wake me up?"

"It was sometime before 1:30 a.m."

"Don't tell me you ran after him?" Jeffrey said, his nostrils flaring.

Yuul dropped her gaze to the table and rolled her eyes.

"Did something happen while we were sleeping?" Liz asked, walking over to the dining table.

"Mom, Dad, please don't fight," Ella said, walking behind Liz.

"You guys are up. That's great. I've got a business idea I'd like to run by you."

"Yuul, don't change the subject. Why didn't you wake me up? Which way did he get in?"

"He didn't break into our home. I saw him walking towards our home from the ravine. I went out. He saw me and ran off. That's it. I have got to say though he was damn good, and I don't like that even a bit."

"Why didn't you wake me?" Jeffrey asked again in desperation.

"He was gone. I didn't see the point of waking you in the middle of the night. I was going to tell you this morning, which I'm doing right now."

"What were you thinking going out there alone? He could've had a gun," Jeffrey said, throwing his hands up in the air.

"That was exactly what I was thinking as well. We think alike." Yuul put her hand up for the high five.

Her hand was up in the air for a long time but didn't get the high five. She slowly put her hand down. "I watched him from a safe distance and made a move. Anyhow, it gave me a business idea."

Liz sent Ella telepathy: *This is not the place for kids like us. Retreat to our haven.*

Ella gave Liz an almost imperceptible nod, and they started walking backwards.

"I'll wake you next time, I promise." Yuul looked at him with the sweetest eyes she could muster.

"Okay stop. I don't know what you're trying to tell me with your eyes, but they're down-right terrifying."

"Terrifying?"

"Yes."

"Hmm." Yuul shrugged. "I was going for more of a cute look. I guess I need more practice."

"I don't want you to be any cuter than you already are. You staying alive and safe, that's all I want."

"You got it." Yuul winked.

"Good. Focus on the growing old together thing, okay?"

"Okay, can I now talk about the business idea from last night?"

"Yes," Jeffrey said, letting out a sigh of resignation.

"Liz, Ella! You can come back down now," Yuul yelled.

Liz and Ella appeared from thin air.

"That was fast," Jeffrey said.

"Ha-ha. We were just around the corner. We knew that it was just a matter of time before you'd wave the white flag," Liz said.

"I guess you were too far away to see that I won this round."

"You really think so?" Liz asked.

"Yes. Yuul promised she won't do that ever again."

"My sweet, sweet brother." Liz gently patted his back.

"I hope Charlie is as easy as Jeffrey," Ella added.

"What am I missing here?" Jeffrey narrowed his eyes.

"Brother, don't try to understand everything. You'll just get hurt. Okay, what's your business idea?" Liz asked.

"We provide personal protection services as well," Yuul saw Jeffrey's jaw dropping. "Or not..."

"I told you," Liz smiled at Jeffrey.

"Let me explain. This is not what you think. I'm talking about data protection, more specifically memory protection. It's an online safe deposit box in which wonderful moments or tragic events of people's lives can be stored. Some people might want to use it to re-live their happy moments. Some people might use it, so they don't have to carry around horrific memories with them all the time. Knowing that you stored the memory in a very safe but secret place, you might be able to convince yourself that you don't have to think about it all the time because it's locked away safely and you can access it any time but only if you want to.

"We'll implement the currently available virtual reality equipment to have users interact with their memories. Of course, we'll develop a computer algorithm to screen the information people want to store in our cyber space. No matter what, we can't have a serial killer re-living their happy moments in our space. We're gonna call it Memory Lane. What do you think?"

All three listeners dropped their jaws slightly, but no one said a word.

Jeffrey was speechless because he was simply in awe of Yuul's idea. When Jeffrey finally got over his awe, he broke the silence. "Didn't you say you got the idea from your encounter with the burglar?"

"Yes." Yuul shrugged nonchalantly.

Although a long time ago Jeffrey had accepted that Yuul's thought process was something way beyond his grasp, she still managed to shock him here and there like today.

"I understand that there are many details we need to work on, but I think the idea has some potential," Yuul added.

"What about the detective agency?" Ella wanted to know.

"We'll change the name to KSK Private Investigation and Protection Services. We'll call it KSK PIPS for short. Our main focus will be to continue to promote our detective services to individuals, insurance companies and other corporations. I think that this Memory Lane branch will come in handy. As the name says, I want to promote it for personal use although I can think about a few reasons why corporations would like to use it as well. Anyway, we'll brainstorm on how to promote this new business after figuring out all the logistics and the costs."

"Anyone hungry?" Jeffrey asked, looking around the table. "The real detective who actually goes out to catch murderers will make some breakfast for the rest of you wannabes."

"Nothing for me. The real business mind needs to catch up on her sleep." Yuul stood up and walked over to her bedroom.

Ella asked for omelettes, pancakes, fried eggs, fried potatoes, grilled tomatoes.

In the midst of taking Liz's order, Jeffrey heard Yuul yelling to the kitchen: "Jeffrey, you've got company,"

"Who?" Jeffrey yelled back.

"Wylie."

"Tell him to come in."

Yuul walked over to the front door and opened it. "Come in," she said loudly.

"Me?" Wylie said, pointing his index finger at himself in surprise.

"Aren't you Wylie, Jeffrey's new partner?"

"Uh, yes."

"Jeffrey wants you to come in."

"Uh, okay." Wylie just stood on the sidewalk for one second.

"Wylie, your trunk is open."

Wylie hastily walked around to the back of the car and closed the trunk. "How did you know I'm Wylie?" Wylie asked as he entered the front door.

"We saw you with Jeffrey yesterday."

"That's my wife, Yuul. She wouldn't introduce herself unless you specifically asked her to," Jeffrey yelled from the kitchen, waving a spatula in the air.

"Oh, nice to meet you," Wylie said, extending his hand to her.

"Nice to meet you as well," Yuul said, taking his hand. "For the record, I was going to introduce myself to you."

"Me, too." Wylie smiled.

"I'm sorry but I was about to go to bed. Let's have a proper visit next time."

"Let's do that." Wylie smiled again and walked over to the kitchen.

"What's up and how did you know where to find me?" Jeffrey asked.

"You told me yesterday that you live next door to Adam Brooks. I've got the search warrant."

"You did?" Jeffrey said surprised.

"Yup."

"Let's go," Jeffrey said, turning off the stove.

"The forensic team is not here yet. We have an hour or so."

"That's great news. I don't like to start my day hungry. Have a seat, partner. You're in for a big surprise. I make a killer breakfast."

"I wouldn't expect anything less from you," Wylie chuckled, "you being a homicide detective and all."

"Isn't he great?" Jeffrey let out a long, contented laugh. "Meet my two sisters. That's Liz. That's Ella."

"Nice to meet you," Wylie said to Liz and then Ella with a nod of recognition to each.

"Likewise," Liz said, "though we aren't quite ready for the party yet." Liz pointed to her messy hair with her eyes. "It's not that there's anything wrong with how we look."

"Absolutely not!" Wylie said. "Don't let anyone say otherwise."

• • •

Jeffrey opened the front door and almost in the same instant, he shut it. He turned around, his back leaned against the door. "Sorry, buddy. We can't go out there right now, at least not through the front door."

"Why not?" Wylie wanted to know.

"There's press. It's just unbelievable. It's bad enough to have the press on us before we even have all the facts, but you know what's even worse than that?"

"No."

"The press somehow got a line on who we're looking into and where our suspect lives. But you know what's even worse than that?"

"No."

"The press is about to find out where I live."

"What do you want to do?"

"Liz!" Jeffrey yelled to the kitchen. "Ella!"

12

MONDAY, DECEMBER 2

Liz and Ella pleaded with Jeffrey for some time to change into something decent before they made their TV debut nationwide, but their pleas were ignored by merciless Jeffrey. They were pushed out the door in the clothes they had slept in.

They stood awkwardly by the door feeling naked. Liz's long, wavy, disheveled blonde hair was blowing in the wind and it tangoed with Ella's shoulder-length, straight, greasy black hair.

They were frozen to the spot when the door flung open again. Through the opening, two winter jackets flew out and the door closed again. Right before their eyes, the jackets dropped to the ground. Realizing that there was no alternative but to carry on with the mission, they put on the jackets and began walking along the sidewalk towards the crowds.

Feeling the stares upon them from everyone on the street, Liz said in a trembling voice, pointing her index finger at Adam Brooks' house, "I cannot believe he…"

"Me, either. Isn't he the guy you used to…" Ella's voice came out all squeaky as she tried to raise her voice a few octaves.

"Yes, we used to…" Liz cried out.

"Are you saying you used to date Adam Brooks?" A reporter from TBC asked as he put a mic to Liz.

"Isn't he the guy who did that unspeakable thing to you?" Ella shouted.

"What did he do to you?" A reporter from ONN asked, poking her mic at Liz.

"How long did you date him?" A reporter from CBC asked jockeying his mic for position.

"Did you get any kind of vibe that he might be a killer?" A reporter from a newspaper put her mic to Liz as well.

• • •

In the meantime, Jeffrey and Wylie went out to the back door and walked along, keeping themselves as close to the wall of the house as possible. Jeffrey held his hand up, giving Wylie a signal to stop. He poked his head out to the alley that lay between his house and Adam Brooks' to scan the street. Then he quickly moved his body backward as he almost met the searching eyes of the reporters. "Shit. They are not in position yet." He thought about his next move and quickly made the decision. "Let's hang back here until they do their job."

"This house is huge!" Wylie said, looking around the backyard. "It must be expensive as hell. What kind of offer did you put in to get this place?"

Jeffrey just shrugged.

Wylie raised an eyebrow, his lips curled upward in a smile. With it, he said almost in a whisper, "Let me in on whatever you have going on?"

Jeffrey scanned around the backyard, moving his head left to right back to left as if to make sure no rats were listening in on their conversation. Then he turned his attention back to Wylie with intense eyes. "Can you keep a secret?"

Wylie nodded animatedly.

Jeffrey winced, like he didn't want to say it.

"Come on," Wylie said almost in a begging tone.

"Okay." Jeffrey leaned closer to Wylie. "I sold a product to," a pause while scanning the area with searching eyes, "a very powerful organization."

Wylie's face lit up in excitement.

Jeffrey slowly nodded, giving Wylie a knowing smile, but no word was spoken.

"What's the product?" Wylie said.

Again, Jeffrey turned his head back and forth and then up in the sky for a drone. "I created an app that controls the weather."

Wylie stared, mouth agape, at Jeffrey for a moment. Then he slowly heaved his shoulders, clearly showing his annoyance.

With a wide smile on his face, Jeffrey gently punched Wylie on his arm. "I got you, didn't I?"

Wylie shrugged, still looking slightly annoyed.

"This time for real," Jeffrey said, "my wife came from money,

"Huh. I was expecting something interesting," Wylie said, the disappointment obvious in his voice.

"That was why I got creative," Jeffrey said. "Let's check the street." Jeffrey once again poked his head out to the alley. Satisfied that his plan had worked, he smiled. "Look at that." He pointed over at Liz and Ella who were standing at the centre of the media scrum.

Wylie said in awe, "I don't know how they're doing it, but they're sure doing one hell of a job."

"Who cares how? This is our chance. Let's run for it."

• • •

Liz saw Jeffrey and Wylie sneak inside Adam's place from a passing glance.

"Ken! Kenny!" Liz shouted, waving at one of the police officers in uniform guarding Adam's house.

The police officer pointed at himself, mouthing, "Me?"

Liz nodded. "Yes, you rascal! It's me!"

The police officer walked over to Liz still pointing his index finger at his chest.

"You don't have to pretend you don't know me. I forgive you," Liz said.

"You're mistaking me for someone else. I'm Omar, not Kenny."

Liz checked out the officer left to right, up and down. "My bad. Definitely, you're not my scumbag ex-boyfriend, Ken Steele."

"Is Ken Steele the boyfriend you had before Adam Brooks or after?" The reporter from CNBC asked.

With an innocent look, Liz said, "Who's Adam Brooks?"

"The guy you used to date, the guy who did the unspeakable thing to you."

"That's Ken Steele," Liz said without batting an eye. "By the way, who's Adam Brooks?"

The reporters looked at Liz and Ella blankly for a while, then slowly turned their backs on them.

Liz and Ella quietly moved back and to the side, creating some distance from the reporters.

"How are you?" Liz said.

"Strangely, exhilarating is the word that I've found suitable to describe how I feel right now. I'm still blushing and uncontrollably shaking from being in the spotlight. But I did it and survived it. Even only a few months ago, I would never have dared to do something like this.

Liz looked at Ella with a bright smile and pointed at her hand below her waistline with her head.

Ella smiled dazzlingly and gave Liz a down-low five with her shaking hand.

"Shall we go home?" Liz said.

Ella nodded.

They were about to turn to leave when they heard a man clearing his throat. That startled them. They turned in the direction where the voice came from and found a middle-aged man about Liz's height standing there.

"Who are you?" Liz said, furrowing her brow. She wondered if he was a reporter and if he was pissed off at their stunt.

"I'm Gabriel. I live right there with Gerald McKellen." The man pointed to the house beside Adam Brooks' on the right. "I'm his live-in caregiver. Are you the new residents of the Evan's old house?"

Liz cracked a smile and said, "I thought that you were one of the pissed-off reporters." She took a pause and smiled some more. "Yes, we're the new residents on the other side of Adam Brooks' place. I'm Liz." Liz extended her hand.

Gabriel burst out laughing and unable to talk. Finally after ten seconds, he managed to shake his head and said, "A pissed-off reporter? I was a happy audience to that."

"I'm Ella." Ella held out her hand.

"Why did you do it?" Gabriel asked, shaking Ella's hand.

"Uh?" Liz and Ella said in unison.

"Ken, Kenny," Gabriel whispered covering his mouth.

"Oh," Liz said. She looked at Ella and Ella gave her a shrug. Taking the shrug as a green light, Liz motioned for Gabriel to follow her.

When they were far enough from the reporters and the spectators, Liz told Gabriel about her brother and what they had been asked to do.

Gabriel laughed even harder this time and had to cover his mouth to subdue the sound of his laughs. After another ten seconds, he suddenly stopped and cocked his head to the right for a moment and then cocked his head to the left.

"What is it?" Liz asked.

"Actually, I could use the help of a detective right now."

"Why is that?" Liz asked.

"It doesn't sound like your brother would be the type to take on a silly job, would he?"

"Let's start with what kind of silly job it is that you have in mind." Liz said.

"Here's the thing. Poor Gerald is suffering from the early on-set of Alzheimer's. That's why his son, Jerry, hired me to look after his father. Gerald has some good days and bad days. When he has a good day, he's sharp. When he has a bad day," Gabriel shrugged, "he gets pretty confused. Recently, Gerald lost his book and he's been frantically looking for it on his good days. Jerry told me that Gerald was an avid reader and collector. Losing the book is driving Gerald nuts. Do you see the irony?" Gabriel laughed for a bit and then stopped laughing. Then he started laughing again.

Liz thought that Gabriel's sense of humour could only match Yuul's.

"Did you search the house?" Liz asked.

"Yes, we did. Whenever it's a good day, that's what we do. In fact, he's searching for the book right now. I just snuck out to check and see what all the commotion's about." Gabriel gestured towards all the reporters and onlookers.

"When did he lose the book?" Ella asked.

"I don't know. To be honest, I'm not even sure if he lost a book at all."

"Hmm... When did he start looking for the book?" Liz asked.

"I guess about 10 days ago or so."

"Did you have any guests over?" Ella asked.

"The only person that's come over was Jerry, and Jerry swears he hasn't taken any books from his dad."

"Has Gerald gone anywhere?" Liz asked.

"We did go out for a walk, but he's never taken any books outside the home."

"Can't you just replace the book with a new one?" Liz asked.

"Haha. Jerry tried that, but Gerald knew right away that it wasn't his book. By the way, you guys sound like detective yourselves."

"We're private detectives," Liz said.

"Are you saying that you guys are like Magnum P.I.?" Gabriel said in surprise.

Liz and Ella nodded.

Gabriel smiled ear to ear. "Could you please solve the case of the missing book for us, so we can get Gerald to stop obsessing about it?"

Liz and Ella looked at each other for a bit and nodded.

"Let me talk to Jerry first since he'll be the one doing the hiring and firing." Gabriel took out his cellphone and moved off to the side. A few minutes later, Gabriel came back. "What's your price?

"How much?" Liz said, looking at Ella.

"It's a book." Ella shrugged. "How much can you charge for locating a book?"

Liz turned to Gabriel. "Tell him someone from KSK agency will contact him this afternoon regarding the fee. Tell him not to worry too much about the fee. It'll be very reasonable since we're neighbours and all. If he doesn't like it, he doesn't have to hire us."

Gabriel walked away from them while relaying the information over the phone and returned back to them shortly with a smile on his face. "Jerry said yes."

"Awesome!" Ella exclaimed.

"How's Gerald today? Can we talk to him now?" Liz asked.

"As much as that sounds good, why don't you come and see him after you've dressed up a little." Gabriel smiled.

• • •

His scrawny, 6' tall body frame drew a long shadow in the study as Gerald McKellen stood in front of a bookcase looking annoyed as hell.

"Gerald, you have guests. Come on out," Gabriel said, standing at the entrance to the study.

Gerald didn't move an inch and didn't look any happier than a moment ago. He just stood there.

"Gerald, are you looking for a book?" Gabriel said.

"How did you know that I lost a book?" Gerald slowly turned around with eyes that could bring lightning.

"Come on out. We have two detectives here that are going to help look for your book."

"Detectives?" Gerald cocked his head and then slowly curled the corners of his lips upwards. He slowly moved his fragile body to follow Gabriel but stopped short when he saw Liz and Ella on the couch.

"Girls?" Gerald cried out. "For God's Sake!!!"

Liz said, "We're a special task force that specializes in locating missing books. Our task force consists of women only. Can you guess why that is, Gerald?"

"Why?"

"It is because the task requires delicate fingers that can get their way into any little crack to fish out even the smallest book without causing damage, sharp eyes that do not miss any detail, no matter how small it may be, and a tenacious mindset that keeps going until the job is done. Who do you think has all these characteristics – men or women?"

Gerald seemed to think the question over for a moment. Finally he said, his voice unsure, "Women?"

"Correct! You're just as sharp as we were told. Tell us about the book you lost. What's the name of the book? What does the cover look like?"

"To Have and Have Not by Ernest Hemingway, it's got a brown cover."

"When was the last time you saw the book and what do you remember about that day?"

"Gabriel, when was it I saw the wild cat?"

"That would be two nights ago, but you lost your book at least a week ago."

"Maybe, I'm losing my mind."

"You don't say." Gabriel laughed and laughed all alone.

Everyone else in the living room, in contrast, remained silent, until Gabriel suddenly smacked his forehead with the palm of his hand. "My bad!" Gabriel leaned forward and said animatedly, "You're right, Gerald. There was another time you saw the wild cat ever since you've been looking for the book. That was Friday night, not the Friday just passed but a week before. I remember because Jerry always brings dinner for us on Fridays. You had a really good day that day. You and Jerry even played chess. After Jerry left, you fell asleep on the couch and I went to the kitchen to make some late night snacks. The next thing I knew, I heard you screaming Wild Cat. I followed your voice and found you on the deck. When I got to you, you forgot about why you were out on the deck, and I forgot about the whole incident until now."

Gerald glanced at Gabriel, confused. "I don't remember that."

Gabriel smiled. "It's okay. I forgot about it, too. We remember some and we forget some." He turned to Liz to say something. Then, it came to him. He snapped his fingers. "What about Anya? Do you remember seeing your favourite girl?"

"Anya?" Gerald said cocking his head. "Oh yes, Anya." A big smile spread across his face.

"Yes, Anya. You remembered." Gabriel smiled a lovely smile, looking at Gerald. "Your favourite girl was out on the deck with Adam and some stranger. That was Friday, November 22."

"Where's the deck?" Liz asked.

Gabriel turned around and pointed to the far end of the house. "Do you see the door over there? That's the door to the deck overlooking the ravine. Jerry had the railings replaced with higher ones after Gerald fell off the deck a while back."

"We'll go get our gear and a helper, and come back to search the backyard. Is that okay?" Liz asked Gerald.

Gerald stared at Liz with inquisitive eyes for a moment and then slowly nodded.

・・・

Yuul rested her head on the dining table, feeling miserable and groggy. She was dragged out of bed before she'd had her 8-hour beauty sleep.

"At least, feed me before you drag me out to work," Yuul said in a gravelly voice.

"Don't say another word," Liz said, placing a plate in front of Yuul.

Yuul turned her head to eye the plate without actually lifting her head and then dragged a fried egg around on her plate with a fork. "It looks sad."

"What's sad?" Ella wanted to know.

"The fried egg."

"Searching for a lost book in a big backyard is way too much for just two people. We need an extra pair of hands and eyes," Ella said.

"Own up to your words. You said we are all employees, and we are all owners," Liz said.

"I'm eating."

"Oh, by the way, you have to call Jerry about our fee. We didn't know how much we should charge him for the case of the missing book," Liz said.

"Oh, and we need a metal detector of some sort," Ella said, a twinkle in her eye.

When Liz, Ella and Yuul came out of the house all geared up, the cop cars, TV station vans and all the other vehicles were gone, and the street was dead quiet.

They marched over to Gerald's backyard, Liz cradling a broom on her shoulder, Ella holding an umbrella tight to her chest and Yuul dragging a golf club across the ground. The cold winter fresh air slapped their faces all the way to Gerald's backyard. When they got there, they came together in a circle, put their hands in the middle, and chanted their cheer before they fired up.

Liz swept the lawn with her broom. Ella combed it with her umbrella, and Yuul raked it with her golf club. They went on for over an hour combing, sweeping and raking back and forth, and still they came up with nothing.

"It has to be here," Ella said, massaging her back.

"Are you sure the inside was searched, like every inch?" Yuul asked, stretching.

"Yes, we're sure," Ella said.

"What about extending the perimeter in the direction that Gerald was looking toward?" Liz said, rubbing her neck.

"Which way was that?" Yuul said, looking at Liz.

"I guess we should go ask Gabriel," Liz said, dropping her broom to the ground.

"Good idea," Ella said, dropping her umbrella on the ground as well.

Liz stopped in her tracks and turned to Yuul. "Aren't you coming?"

"Somebody has to keep an eye on our equipment."

When Liz and Ella came back, the search was extended over to Adam's backyard. It was 4:00 p.m. and night had already started to fall. They could hear their bones cracking and their muscles aching like never before. It was hard work, but they kept on going.

"Eureka!" Ella shrieked with joy, dropping to her knees. She let go of the umbrella, picked up the book and hoisted the book triumphantly up in the air.

"Perfect timing. I was about to give up," Yuul said, leaning her weary body on the golf club.

"I was this close, too." Liz put her thumb and index almost together.

They joyfully walked over to Gerald's.

They walked into the living room and found Gerald nodding off in his recliner and Gabriel nodding off on the couch.

Liz mouthed "Let's go home," pointing her index finger to the front door.

"We've got the book," Yuul shouted.

Startled awake, Gabriel said, "That was quick."

Ella presented the book to Gerald.

Gerald stared at the book in disgust.

"What's wrong?" Ella asked.

"What do you mean, what's wrong? You can't see that? The book has dog shit on it. Are you trying to tell me you can't see it?"

"Shit?" Ella pulled the book in as if she might smell it. After closer inspection, she noticed a reddish stain at the top of the spine. "I don't think it's shit." She passed the book to Liz.

"I know what that is, it's shit alright? You ravaged my book," Gerald yelled at Ella.

"We found it in this condition," Ella defended.

"It's definitely not shit," Liz declared.

"Prove it," Gerald said.

Liz looked at Gabriel for advice and saw him slowly shaking his head as if to say, 'stop'.

Gabriel motioned for them to follow him and led the way to the front door. "It's probably best if you guys leave for now. Make something up that proves it's something other than shit and come back later with it." Then, he closed the door on them.

As soon as the door shut completely, Ella looked to Liz and Yuul and sighed. "How are we gonna do that?"

Yuul shrugged.

Liz closed her eyes and focused. She was racking her brain to devise the perfect plan and it didn't take long for the lightbulb to suddenly go off. "Jeffrey!"

Liz, the Neighbour

They all smiled a devilish smile.

• • •

That night, Liz, Ella and Yuul sat on the couch and waited for Jeffrey to come home. When the front door finally slung open, they held their breath in excitement. They exchanged a look when they heard Jeffrey trudging. Heavy, exhausted footsteps.

Without breathing a word, Jeffrey flopped down onto the couch next to Yuul.

"How did it go with the search?" Liz asked, trying to appear as nonchalant as possible.

"I don't want to talk about it," Jeffrey said, looking crestfallen.

"It might make you feel better if you talk about it," Liz said.

"It's all bullshit. The captain's pressuring me to close the case. Am I not the lead detective on this case? Well guess what? I sure as hell am! So, why is she butting her nose in where it doesn't damn well belong and trying to tell me what to do and how to do it? Right now, she really needs to back off and let me do my job before I lose it!!"

Ella looked carefully at Jeffrey's face. "I really don't understand a word of what you're talking about right now. Can you give us some background on it so we can put it all into context?"

Jeffrey shook his head with a sigh. "Why not. Did you hear about the news reporter who was murdered a couple of nights ago?"

The three amigos nodded.

"I might have to charge Adam Brooks, our neighbour, for that very same murder." Jeffrey paused and let out another sigh. "We have overwhelming evidence all of which points to him."

"What's the problem then?" Liz asked in confusion.

"A motive. I can't figure out a motive." A pause. "Today's search came up with nothing. Actually, it's probably a good thing that we didn't find anything in his house. If we had found even one more piece of evidence that points to Brooks for the murder, it would have been game over," Jeffrey paused and sighed more deeply now, his shoulders slumped all the way down. "Actually, it is game over for me. The captain wants us to charge Adam tomorrow any away and pass the case over to the prosecutors."

Ella fiddled with the book that lay on her lap for a moment and then hesitantly presented it to Jeffrey. "I guess this is not a good time to give you this then."

"What's this?" Jeffrey was confused, and he wasn't hiding it.

"We found it in Adam's backyard today. Look here," Ella pointed at the red stain on the edges of the book.

"Is this blood?" Jeffrey said, squinting at the stain.

"What else can it be?" Ella said nervously, unsure if he might explode or burst into angry flames at any moment.

"You should have it DNA-tested," Liz said. "Although I wouldn't go as far as to say this might be the key evidence to your case, whatever does come out of the DNA test certainly can't hurt your case."

"Are you telling me that this is Adam Brooks' book?" Jeffrey asked, his eyebrows arched in a questioning look.

"Could be," Liz answered it carefully, "considering this book was found on Adam's property."

"Hmm…" Jeffrey narrowed his eyes, first at Liz, then Ella and then Yuul. His lips pursed. "I thought that I had no choice but to charge Adam first thing tomorrow morning since I've got nothing else to keep the investigation going…" There was a pregnant pause before his mouth slowly morphed into a smile, "until now." He took the book from Ella and held it tightly to his chest.

13

TUESDAY, DECEMBER 3

The first knock on the door was ignored and the second knock was also ignored. A series of loud bangs on the door followed and that was definitely heard. Jeffrey opened the door and found Wylie standing there.

"Hey, what's up?" Jeffrey couldn't hide the surprise on his face.

"I want breakfast." Wylie had the look of a 5-year-old asking his mom for an ice cream cone.

Jeffrey let out a smile and stepped aside.

"You really do make one killer breakfast. What's your secret?" Wylie said in a serious tone.

"Love," Jeffrey said proudly.

"GACK!"

"Bwahaha..."

Wylie walked over to the kitchen and gave the cook top a once-over as well as all the stuff that was laid out on the countertop.

"What's on the menu for today?" Wylie asked.

"Omelettes"

"Hmm..." Wylie let the disappointment show on his face.

"Don't judge until you taste it."

"OK then, what's on the schedule for today?" Wylie asked, pulling a chair out.

"I was handed some new evidence last night and am planning to drop it off at the crime lab for analysis on my way into work."

"What kind of evidence? Where'd you get it?"

"My wife and my sisters found a book in Adam's backyard last night."

"Huh."

"It might be nothing, but it's my last ditch attempt. I'm grasping at straws now, trying to keep this case open."

"Let's attack the enemy on both flanks," Wylie said cheerfully.

"What do you mean by that?"

"I'll go drop off the evidence while you try and convince the captain. You should get there early just in case she has one of her meetings to attend."

"Hmm..." Jeffrey stared at Wylie for a long moment.

"What?"

"I like it." Jeffrey nodded. "One thing I'm sure of, there's a lot more to this than meets the eye."

• • •

Liz, the Neighbour

Across the street from Jeffrey's, Doreen Ryan was on the phone. This was the third call that she had made this morning. Her voice was crackling, but she didn't mind. "This is a classic case of protecting their own. Think about it. Why do you think they haven't arrested him?"

She's too easy, Doreen thought, shaking her head, a smile on her face.

"Exactly! It's because he's a prosecutor. If he was a regular citizen like you or me, he would've already been charged and put behind bars. I just want to live in an equal society, at least in the eyes of the law. Is that too much to ask?"

She could sense that she just needed to give the reporter one last push to seal the deal.

"What do you think your job is all about? You have to fight inequality and right the injustices for the people who don't have the power to do it themselves." A pause. "You have a good day." She disconnected the call with a big smile on her face.

Three major TV stations down and two more to go. After that, she was going to move onto the newspapers. It was going to be a busy day, but she didn't mind.

It wasn't her first time calling the press about Adam Brooks. She was the one who had leaked it to the press about the police searching Brooks' property. Adam Brooks had to go. There was no doubt about that in her mind. It was the only way for her to get her peaceful neighbourhood back. She didn't want her work hitting too close to home.

• • •

It turned out that Wylie had psychic powers. Jeffrey walked into the captain's office, just as she was grabbing her jacket off her chair.

"Go away," the captain said while putting her jacket on.

"I've found new evidence."

"New evidence?" the captain paused.

"Yes, I've found a book in the suspect's backyard with a blood stain on it. Just one more week, that's all I'm asking."

"Don't care."

"Please do care. If it's the vic's blood, I'll charge Adam Brooks with 1st degree murder, I promise."

"I don't need your promises. Tell me what's really bothering you."

Jeffrey stared at the captain with his deep green eyes for a long moment and said, "Its all just a little too neat, don't you think? The whole thing seems like it came specially gift wrapped for us with a great big red bow, and one thing I do know for sure is that it ain't Christmas morning. How many times have you ever seen the killer actually shout his real name before the kill to a potential witness? And think about how the body was found. The vic's body was positioned sitting up on a park bench for everyone to see. If the murderer had left her lying on the ground, it sure as hell would've taken longer for the body to be found. Then to top it all off, the killer took all the major roads so his getaway could be captured by CCTVs every step of the way. It's like the killer couldn't wait to get caught."

"If the blood is not the vic's, then what?" the captain said.

"Then…"

"Exactly!" The captain stared at him. "Do you have any other suspects you're looking into?"

"No."

"I've got to run to a meeting. Let me know what you find out when I come back."

"What do you mean?" Jeffrey asked.

"You've just earned a little more time. That's what it means." The captain pushed him away.

"You're the best!"

The captain marched out, shaking her head but smiling.

• • •

Jeffrey sat in the interview room, his eyes dissecting Adam Brooks, the man who now sat directly across the table from him. Adam was of average height, on the skinny side of the scale, with fair skin. He had some stubble on his face. He looked pretty much like just your average Joe – a normal guy you would have a beer with at your local neighbourhood backyard barbecue. He appeared to be as calm as a mill pond. If he was rattled or unnerved inside, he wasn't showing it on the outside. His breathing was calm and steady as if he was relaxing on the beach, enjoying a nice, summer breeze. Looking at Adam, Jeffrey finally said, "You look awfully calm for a guy who's about to go down for murder in the first degree."

"Do I?" Adam gave him an easy shrug. "I guess mind-control works." A pause. "Or, it's simply because I accepted the grim reality of my situation and made peace with it. Based on what you have on me, I don't expect you'll be letting me go anytime soon."

Another pause. "Actually, I should've already been charged the day you brought me here. So, the real question is why haven't you charged me yet?"

Jeffrey met Adam's stare head-on. Jeffrey laughed a little inside. He was the stare master. He would win. Adam wasn't bad himself but he would eventually fold. The loser always talked first. Jeffrey needed Adam to talk because he still couldn't figure Adam out – was he an evil mastermind who had devised a sophisticated murder plan, or an innocent who was set up to take the fall?

As expected, Adam blinked first and broke the long silence. "It's just too perfect. That's what bothers you, isn't it? You might want to believe that I'm an evil genius, but I'm not."

Jeffrey was so close to asking Adam how he'd known that. Luckily, he stopped himself just in time.

Adam continued. "In the same breath, I'm not an idiot, either. If I were the killer, I would've covered my tracks a hell of a lot better than most."

Jeffrey shrugged. "Maybe, you did it just to say that. At the time of the crime, you accepted the fact that you would be arrested sooner or later, so why hide it, right? You decided to incorporate reverse psychology in a sense. You see I am too smart to make obvious mistakes like this."

"If that's the case, how's that working out for me so far?"

Not well at all, Jeffrey thought.

Adam smiled a little. "Exactly, it isn't."

Jeffrey raised his right eyebrow. *What the… Are you… a mind reader? No way! Or, are you?*

"The perp did more than cry out my name. So, there's no doubt that somebody framed me for this murder. What I'm trying to figure out is who set me up and why. I don't know yet. It's not easy to see all the pieces or the big picture when you're locked up. But I'm trying. This is how I keep myself calm. There's one more thing that keeps me calm."

"What's that?"

"I don't have a motive."

"Love gone bad?"

"Haha. I loved her but not in a way that would cause one to commit a crime of passion."

"Your neighbour Gerald McKellen lost a book 10 days ago. The book was found in your backyard with a bloodstain on it. He keeps saying something about a wild cat. Do you remember anything about a wild cat?"

The question threw Adam off guard. He didn't know what Jeffrey was driving at.

Jeffrey smiled a bit. "I'm grasping at straws here."

"It was the day my wife and her boyfriend came by before their trip to Paris. I was making spinach pasta for her in the kitchen when I heard Gerald yelling something about a wild cat. He sounded so upset. We all went out and saw Gerald shouting and shooing."

"Did you see who or what Gerald was yelling at?"

"It was Gerald who got my attention. You have to understand that he has Alzheimer's. He seems to see wild cats a lot lately. As much as I would like that to mean something, I don't think it does. Last Saturday, very early morning, I heard him yelling about a wild cat this time from his front porch."

"Do you mean the day that Madison's body found?"

Adam took a moment to think about it and then nodded. "Indeed, it was the same day."

"Do you remember what time it was?"

"Not the exact time. Basically, it was between midnight and 1:00 a.m."

"Did you go out to talk to Gerald?"

"If I had been a good neighbour, I wouldn't be in this predicament." Adam rubbed his forehead smiling a sad smile. "I remember thinking it's just Gerald being Gerald. He has Alzheimer's and I didn't even think about checking on him. Anyway, shortly after I heard him yelling, the yelling stopped. I figured that Gabriel took him inside. Gabriel Cruz is Gerald's caregiver."

"Look at that." Jeffrey smiled. "Your case may not be all that hopeless after all."

Adam frowned as if asking him to elaborate.

"I'll go check with Gabriel. If Gabriel corroborates your story, you might have an alibi."

"Thank you. Your brilliance as a detective is finally working in my favour."

"What do you mean?"

"Frankly, it's unfortunate for me that you are too good of a detective. I'll bet whoever set me up for the murder is very impressed with your detective skills as well. You found everything you needed to find *in a day*. It just wouldn't be possible unless you knew where to look and what to look for, and *that* makes you a great detective. Even if this alibi thingy doesn't pan out, no hard feelings."

Liz, the Neighbour

Am I really that good a detective? Jeffrey thought as he watched the officer take Adam back to the holding cell. Remaining in his chair in the interview room, he organized his thoughts. *What's next if Gabriel corroborates all this?* He flipped through his notepad and found exactly what he was looking for: The vic got into the car around 8:00 p.m., and then flipped through his notepad again and found what he was looking for: The suspect parked the car near the playground at 10:52 p.m.

They wouldn't have just stayed in the car for almost 3 hours. They must've been somewhere else before they hit their final destination. Jeffrey wrote in his notepad: Check the car navigation system. *What else? Hmm...* Jeffrey tapped his finger on the table. *Yes, the vic's neighbourhood. Begin at the beginning.*

Jeffrey felt he was on a roll and was feeling upbeat when he answered an incoming call. "What's up, partner?"

"Where are you?" Wylie let out a muffled yell. "You've got to come back to the office right away. The captain wants to see us."

"Why?"

"Don't know. FYI, she's with Grayson Laskaris."

"The Chief?"

"Who else?"

"Okay, I'll be right there."

Jeffrey followed Wylie over to the captain's office and as advertised, he found Grayson Laskaris, Chief of Police, in the office looking unhappy.

"Sir," Jeffrey addressed Grayson.

"Why the hell aren't you charging Adam Brooks for the murder?" Grayson screamed.

"We don't have all the facts yet, sir," Jeffrey said.

"What do you mean by that? What more could there be?" Grayson demanded.

"There's a new development."

"What the hell is it now?"

"Brooks might have an alibi." Jeffrey dropped the mic.

Everyone seemed frozen in time that you could've heard a pin drop. After the pregnant pause, Grayson composed himself and continued in a somewhat calmer tone, "Elaborate."

"Gerald McKelleb lives next door to Adam Brooks along with his caregiver. On the night of the murder, Brooks heard McKelleb screaming something about a wild cat. If Gabriel Cruz, McKelleb's caregiver, can corroborate Brooks' statement, it could prove that he was home at the time the murder was committed."

Grayson stared at Jeffrey for a long moment before he calmly asked, "What time did Brooks hear his neighbour's scream?"

"Between late Friday night and early Saturday morning."

"Huh," Grayson said in a huff. "You're telling me that Adam Brooks is innocent because he heard a noise the night of the murder. Did I get that right?"

"Yes."

"So then, the neighbour can unequivocally testify that Adam had been at home all night until such time that he heard his neighbour creating a commotion outside from the inside of his house? Isn't it possible that it was Brooks the old man was yelling at as he was coming home after killing the poor girl?"

Liz, the Neighbour

Jeffrey had gone over the conversation he'd had with Adam in his mind over and over again and bottom line, he truly believed Adam was innocent, but here and now, bottom line was that the answer to the Chief's questions was that there was *no* corroboration period. He realized how stupid he had been. He hadn't thought it all the way through. The Chief saw through it right away – IT MEANT NOTHING.

Staring at Jeffrey, Grayson said, "Now, do you get it? It's been over 24 hours. We're wasting time on useless what if's when we already have all the evidence that we need. Do you even have one single shred of evidence to that would cast doubt on the airtight case we have against Brooks?"

"Yes," Jeffrey said spiritlessly.

"What did you say?" Grayson asked, seething.

"I've recovered a book with blood stains on it from Adam Brooks' property. I sent it to the lab for a DNA test." Jeffrey said monotonously.

"What the hell could that have to do with anything?"

"Maybe it'll prove nothing, but we don't know for sure. Let me get the results from the DNA test. If it turns out it's nothing then it's a wrap."

"Where did you find the book?"

"In Adam Brooks' backyard,"

"Where did the victim get murdered? Did it occur in his backyard?"

"No."

"Do we have enough evidence right now to confidently charge him with first degree murder?"

"Yes."

"So, I want you to do exactly that. If I hear one more reporter say that we're not charging him because he's one of our own, I'll send all of you to such a remote out of the way place. The only way you'll be able to find your way home is by horse or cow or whatever. I have a press conference at 12:00 p.m. and I will be telling the press that Adam Brooks has been charged. Do not make a liar out of me, Knight!" Grayson stomped out pissed.

"You heard the man." The captain pointed her index finger at the door. "You know the way. Get out."

• • •

Jeffrey flopped into his chair feeling totally defeated.

"What do you want to do?" Wylie asked, waiting for instructions.

Jeffrey had the same question for himself, *What do you want to do, Jeffrey?* Jeffrey rubbed his forehead, trying to come up with an earth-shattering idea that would buy more time to fully investigate the case but came up short. Standing he said, "You heard the Chief. We've got a man to arrest."

14

TUESDAY, DECEMBER 3

34,000 feet up in the sky, an airplane flying at 926 km per hour was carrying William Pemberton. He was a Hollywood star, who looked like a Hollywood star. At age 32, his hazel eyes and golden locks still made him look like a pretty boy from a boy band. His fairytale-prince-like gorgeous face and tall slender physique made anything he wore look like a designer brand and made him one of the most beloved stars on this planet. He lived a life like the world was rightfully his. He was never burdened by it or shied away from it. Today though, he had kept his sunglasses on as he didn't want to be recognized. He needed privacy. His eyes were blood-shot, not from drugs or a hangover, but from him crying his heart out. *Maddie, oh my angel!* Tears poured down again.

Liz, the Neighbour

• • •

32 years ago, 18-year-old Chloe Pemberton gave birth to a lovely boy and named him William Pemberton. Her little boy's father had no idea that he became a father that day. The last she'd seen of him, he was being dragged off to another rehab clinic by his father. Holding her baby in her arms, she cried with overwhelming joy and promised herself that she'd never do drugs again and turn over a new leaf. Sadly, it wasn't long after she'd made that promise that her old habits dragged her back to her old ways eventually ending in a fatal overdose. All in less than two years after William's birth.

Chloe's father died from a heart attack shortly after Chloe passed and so it was that Birdie Pemberton, after suffering the loss of the two great loves of her life, her husband and her daughter, was about to let go of everything and follow them to heaven when seemingly out of nowhere the sound of a baby's cries penetrated her catatonic state. She wondered whose baby was crying so sadly. The crying grew louder and louder, and then she felt tiny, sweaty hands touching hers. She barely managed to open her eyes but when she did, Birdie saw a crying baby boy standing on his toes at her bedside. His face was damp with tears and snot. She realized who that crying baby was: her grandson. *How did I forget all about Will?*

Photos of Will's mom revealed a beautiful girl with a brilliant smile. He'd wanted to see her brilliant smile for real. Looking at her pictures, he'd often wondered what it would've felt like to have been held and hugged by her. His mother being an only child, Will didn't even have a cousin. His grandmother had been a rock; nonetheless, he'd felt so alone until Madison Cooper entered his life.

Maddie was the granddaughter of Ed Jamieson, who lived next door to his grandma's. Maddie's mom, Tina Cooper, brought Maddie to Ed's when she was just a few months old. Will was on the couch at Ed's with his grandma. He was mesmerized by what Tina was doing with her baby – Gently holding the tiny baby in her arms, Tina moved her body slowly and rhythmically side to side. As he was heedlessly watching the mother and the daughter, Tina asked if he wanted to hold the baby. When he nodded, Tina carefully placed Maddie in his arms and held Maddie and him in her arms. *It's so very nice*, he thought. He felt Maddie's tiny fingers crawling on his arm and clenching his wrist. The warmth from her tiny fingers spread through every vein in his body like an electric charge flies through water when a live power cord is dropped into it. At that moment, Maddie opened her tiny mouth as if she was about to yawn. She started twitching and stretching her arms and legs for a minute. The next minute, he heard *poop* and then his hands got warmer and warmer. *Ew!* He had never been more disgusted and at the same time happier.

On her 5th birthday, Maddie clapped her hands in excited anticipation as she watched her mother bringing out her birthday cake with the 5 lit candles mounted on top. Everybody in the room started chanting, "Make a wish. Make a wish." She didn't know what she would like to wish for. She looked around the room and saw Will. "I want to marry Will!"

she yelled. She then drew a long and deep breath and blew it out long and hard, spitting everywhere.

Before the divorce proceedings were finalized, Maddie's parents had grown further and further apart from each other. The home no longer felt like a home to anyone living there. Maddie was sad, upset and jittery. During those dark days, Will sometimes sang songs for her over the phone.

"Twinkle, twinkle, little star…"

"I'm not a baby anymore," Maddie protested.

"Yes, you are. You're just two years old, right?"

"Your jokes are seriously *infantile*," Maddie said, acting all cool.

"*Infantile?* Wow! Big word! You must be all grown-up."

Maddie giggled. "Yes, I am. I'm like ten years old now.

"In two years"

"In one year and 9 months," Maddie corrected proudly.

"I've got another song for you. I've practiced it for a very long time. So, you'd better love it."

"I'll try," Maddie said.

"Fighting evil by moonlight, winning love by daylight…" Will sang the Sailor Moon theme song, getting the melody all wrong. God gave Will good-looks, a warm heart and even blessed him with a well-functioning brain. One gift Will didn't get though was even a hint of musical talent. He was tone-deaf.

"Hahahahahaha…." Maddie laughed crying.

"Okay, now go to bed."

"Read me a bedtime story."

"Somebody just told me she's not a baby anymore."

"Grown-ups love bedtime stories, too."
"No, they don't."
"Yes, they do, too."
"Hahaha. I'll read you a bedtime story tomorrow. You go to bed now."
"Okay. Good night, Will!"
"Good night, Maddie!"

He read her bedtime stories until she fell asleep the next day, and the next, next day.

When Maddie turned 10, her parents officially divorced. Before she turned 12, both of her parents had remarried. When her stepfather accepted a job offer from a company in America, Maddie moved in with her grandfather, Ed Jamieson. She liked her stepfather and stepmother. They were all nice people. She just didn't want to move to America or South America where her father lived with his new wife. Ever since then, Maddie and Will had lived next door to each other until he moved to Hollywood.

• • •

It pained Will to remember how happy she'd sounded when she'd talked about Adam and going out on a date with him. He held his right wrist with his left hand, trying to feel Maddie's touch, the same touch that he had felt when he was only five. Tears came down again.

Oh Maddie, my little sister.

15

WEDNESDAY, DECEM BER 4

The hustle and bustle in the house woke Will. He draped his right arm over his forehead to subdue the throbbing headache from last night's hangover.

As soon as his airplane had touched ground, he'd gone straight to Ed's spending the night there with Ed, Maddie's parents, his grandma and her friend, Agnes Winter, talking, crying and drinking.

Through a gap between the curtains that were hung over the living room window, he saw the dark cloudy sky. It felt right to him. It wouldn't have been right to wake up to a bright sunny morning. He felt like even heaven above was mourning Maddie's death. *It should*, he thought.

His body ached from sleeping on the 100 years old crappy couch and the chills he'd had to embrace coming through every wall, window and door in the house that were even older than the couch. He got the couch because his old bedroom was occupied by his grandma's friend, Agnes Winter.

His grandma and Agnes were already up and at 'em. Why all old people got up so early? He didn't know. He thought to himself that when he got old, he would sleep through at least until 10:00 a.m. He had flipped his body to the other side in an attempt to easy his body aches when he heard his grandma yelling, "Get up!", from the kitchen.

He thought about getting up but opted not to. Instead, he made a boisterous snoring sound that could rattle the shingles. "Chrrr… Shshshsh… Chrrr… Shshshsh…"

"Stop faking it," Birdie yelled from the kitchen. "I can tell that's a fake snore from miles away. I don't know how you make a living as an actor."

Will pulled the blanket over his head to block the noise and gave another go at a fake snore. "Hurr… Shshsh… Hurr…"

"Get up!" Birdie yelled again. "We've got to go to Ed's now."

"Grandma, it's really rude to visit anyone before noon even on the best of days," Will yelled from under his blanket.

"That's why we're going now," Birdie shouted.

"What are you talking about? What time is it?"

"One o'clock," Birdie yelled.

"I'm not falling for your old jokes."

He heard no reply after that. The house fell into silence for a moment and then was filled with a series of clicking noises: *click, click, click*. Before he even had a

Liz, the Neighbour

chance to make out what the clicking noise was, his blanket got yanked. Startled by the sudden attack, he turned to face his aggressor. Instead, he was met by a cellphone jammed in his face displaying 1:07 p.m. It took one long minute for him to process the information in his brain: *Shoot!* "Give me like 5 minutes. I just need to brush my teeth." He leapt off the couch and ran upstairs.

• • •

As Will was coming down the stairs, he saw his grandma and Agnes sitting on the couch leaning into the TV as close as they could.

"Why don't—"

"Shh!" they said almost in unison as they urgently waved him over to join them, never once breaking their focus on the TV.

Will rushed over and saw a news reporter relaying the superior court's decision on Adam Brooks, a Crown Prosecutor, who had been charged in the first degree murder of Madison Cooper. Adam Brooks was to remain in police custody until the trial.

"Uh… Ahh… Uhm…" Will pointed his index finger at the TV.

Whack, Birdie smacked him in the back of his head.

"Oww! That hurts, Grandma!" Will cried, rubbing the back of his head sorely.

"Look at you. Words are no longer stuck in your throat. So, what was it that you were going to say?" Birdie said.

"He's the suspect?"

"He must be the killer," Birdie said. "His name is Adam. Maddie went on a date with Adam and never came home."

"That's not the Adam she went on a date with."

"What do you mean?" Birdie said, furrowing her brow.

Agnes just stared at him without blinking, and that scared Will a little.

"Do you remember the day she broke her ankle?"

"Yes," Birdie and Agnes said in unison.

"Do you remember that she went to the Mississauga Hospital that day?"

"Yes, we remember. Stop playing 20 questions and just spit it out," Birdie said impatiently.

"They met there. They started talking and hit it off. He asked her out on a first date that Friday night."

"So, how do you know that man," Birdie pointed at Adam Brooks on TV, "isn't the man Madison went out with that night?"

Will jabbed his finger at the TV. "That man has been friends with Maddie for a long time."

"How do you know they were friends? Have you ever met him?" Agnes asked.

"No, but she told me all about her friends, Crown Prosecutor Adam and his wife."

"You're 100 percent sure that the guy she went out on a date with that night wasn't the prosecutor?" Birdie asked, narrowing her eyes at him.

"Yes."

As far as Will remembered, there hadn't been many times when his grandma was at a loss for words, but he could tell this was one of those rare moments.

They all sat in silence until Birdie stood up and walked over to the closet next to the foyer. She took her jacket out and rummaged through a pocket and fished out a business card.

"What is that, Grandma?"

"One of the two detectives who are investigating Maddie's death gave me his business card."

"What are you going to do?" Will wanted to know.

Birdie grabbed her cellphone off the coffee table and called the number on the card. "We have to let them know that, just in case they haven't checked into the other Adam."

"Put him on speaker," Agnes said.

Birdie did as asked. After the fourth ring, the phone was finally answered.

"Detective Wylie Townsend here. How can I help you?"

"I'm Birdie Pemberton, a neighbour of Ed Jamieson, Madison Cooper's grandfather. Do you remember me?"

"Yes. How can I help you?"

"My grandson has something to tell you about the guy you just arrested. Will, tell him what you know."

Will cleared his throat first and then said, "The Prosecutor you just arrested is *not* the guy Maddie went out with on the night she was … uhh you know what I'm trying to say. Prosecutor Adam was Maddie's long time friend. Maddie went on a date with that guy she had just met at the Mississauga Hospital on… Hold on." Will clicked on the phone and opened Calendar. "Friday, November 22."

Birdie shouted into the cellphone, "Check the CCTV from the Mississauga Hospital Emergency. I think he's worth looking into."

There was a long silence.

"HELLO? ARE YOU THERE?' Agnes shouted.

"Yes, yes, I'm here. I'll definitely do that. Thank you!"

Still shaken by Agnes' sudden blast, Birdie whispered to Agnes, "What's that all about?"

Agnes smiled an innocent smile and whispered, "Once in awhile, I like to shout it out."

Birdie shook her head disapprovingly while looking at Agnes. After a moment of head shaking, Birdie said to the phone, "Let us know what you've found out. By the way, are you on College Street?"

"Yes. How did you know?"

"I was there not long ago for another case. I'll drop by sometime next week. I hope you've found something by then."

"It's too cold to be out and about. I'll call you when I find something."

"It's not just about your case. I have the Wild Peach case to talk about with Detective Tim Johnson and Sam O'Hara at your station."

"What?" Wylie said. "I just lost you. Wild what?"

"Oh, never mind. It's a retirement home case I asked Detective Johnson to look into."

"Did you already make an appointment to see him next week?" Wylie asked.

"Oh no, I haven't. I don't have his business card. Do you have his phone number?"

"I don't know it off the top of my head. I'll call you later with his phone number," Wylie said.

"I might be too busy with Maddie's funeral. Just tell Detective Johnson I'll drop by sometime next week."

"I can do that. When is the funeral?"

"This Saturday,"

"Hope everything goes as well as it can," Wylie said.

"It will. Have a good night."

"You too, ma'am."

Birdie put her cellphone into her skirt pocket. "Don't say a word to Ed or Tina about the other Adam."

"I'm not stupid, Grandma."

"I know that." Birdie paused and gazed at Will for a moment. "Though, you sometimes make me wonder." Her mouth slowly morphed into a smile.

• • •

It was a dark and dreary day outside, but Ed's house was even darker than it was outside. Ed let them in without a word and shuffled back to his Lazy Boy recliner.

"Go make plates," Birdie said to Will.

Will walked through the house to the kitchen with trays of food in his arms.

Birdie sat down on the couch with Agnes. Looking at Ed, Birdie said, "Are Tina and Ned back yet?"

Ed was about to say something when they heard the door squeak open and closed, locks flipped. A few seconds later, Ned and Tina entered the living room, offering a tired little smile and a nod to Birdie and Agnes. Tina moved to the couch and sagged low next to Birdie while Nate walked into the kitchen.

Birdie silently rubbed Tina's back. Birdie knew how Tina and Ned were feeling. She had been through it herself years ago – making funeral arrangements for her own child.

The little gesture from one mother to another who had been through the same grief broke Tina. Tears welled up in her eyes. The thought that she would never be able to hold her beautiful daughter again broke her even deeper. This time, she let out a wail of grief. Madison was gone just like Chloe, her best friend. Tina missed her best friend and she ached for her daughter.

Ned took Tina upstairs to Madison's bedroom – the bedroom that had been Tina's before Madison's.

16

WEDNESDAY, DECEMBER 4

While Jeffrey chopped cucumber, he told himself not to think about the case. While he chopped tomatoes, he reminded himself not to think about the case. While he chopped onion, he admonished himself for thinking about the case. *Damn it!* He muttered out under his breath.

"You'd better put the knife down. Is this about you having to make dinner?" Liz said, shuffling into the kitchen.

"Go away. The kitchen is a man's sanctuary."

"Even if you beg me to stay, I won't."

As soon as Jeffrey saw Liz disappear from the kitchen, he started slicing the beef into the right sized pieces and his mind drifted back to the case. As Adam

Brooks had pointed out, he'd just followed the evidence, which had taken him to Adam Brooks.

What evidence? A video that showed everything I needed to see. If I had gone through all the CCTV footage and dash cam feeds myself, would I have seen something that Wylie didn't see?

It hit Jeffrey what had been bothering him all this time. He put the knife down on the cutting board realizing that this was the first case that he ever worked on where he hadn't put in any of the legwork in himself.

Huh! Who knew I have a god complex? Maybe, other people did. It wasn't a nagging feeling about putting away the wrong guy. It was me not liking the fact that the case was solved by the other guy. I couldn't accept the fact that the newbie did a better job than I've ever done with any case. He did it in a quick and clean way. I just hoped that he might have missed something, but he didn't.

The realization took some weight off his chest. *That's all there is to it*, he said to himself as grabbing a knife on the cutting board.

"I think that's enough cutting," Ella said, holding out her hand. "Give it to me."

"Yikes!" Jeffrey nearly jumped out of his skin. "Make some noise. You almost gave me a heart attack. How long have you been here?"

"I did. I waltzed in singing."

"Really?" Jeffrey felt bad. "I'm sorry."

"Don't be. I lied." Ella pointed at the knife and said, "Give it to me."

"I don't want to," Jeffrey whined, pulling the knife closer to his chest.

"I'll give you something better." Ella opened the top drawer next to the sink and took out a wooden mallet. "Remember this is for garlic, not for your fingers."

Jeffrey took it, studied it and slowly nodded his head with a grin on his face. He liked it. He liked it a lot. "This is exactly what I needed."

"I know." Ella waltzed out of the kitchen.

Jeffrey started smashing garlic while thinking about the case. Whatever he'd said to himself didn't help him let it go. Rather, he found himself even more obsessed with the case.

Why am I forcing myself not to think about the case? Why am I trying to convince myself to let it go? A god complex or not, I need to walk through it myself. With that thought, Jeffrey bashed the last clove of garlic.

"Still deep in your thoughts?" Yuul asked, standing a few feet away from him.

"Yikes" Jeffrey said, rubbing his heart. "You've got to make some noise when you walk into Hell's Kitchen."

Yuul cocked her head, eyes narrowed.

Looking at Yuul's serious look, Jeffrey smiled. "I was, but I'm done thinking. What do you need?"

"Dinner. Should I order?"

"No, no! It'll be ready in 20 minutes."

After looking at Jeffrey for a moment, Yuul said, "Do you need a hug?"

"Yes! Yes, I do." Jeffrey hugged Yuul.

Exhilarated by his new found energy and happiness, Jeffrey suddenly had a burning desire to cook teppanyaki style, grilling the beef and prepared veggies over an open flame and to wow the three amigos. An image quickly flashed through his mind – an image of one big bang explosion, and himself and the three amigos covered in soot and ash with singed hair watching from the street as their house burned to the ground. *If I get a teeny-weeny propane gas tank—*

"DINNER!!!" the three amigos yelled, sitting at the dining table tapping the table with a fork in one hand and a knife in the other.

"Be patient," Jeffrey said, turning off the stove. He removed a beef noodle stir fry from the heated pan onto four plates and some fruit salad in a mixing bowl into four smaller serving bowls. "Dinner's ready. Come and get it!!"

• • •

By the time Jeffrey sat at the table with his plate and bowl, the three amigos had already devoured half of the noodle dish.

"Why are you in such a foul mood?" Liz said, gobbling down another big forkful of the noodle dish.

"I was but I'm not anymore," Jeffrey said, having his first bite.

"You know that you're totally in a safe place to spill the tea," Ella said.

Jeffrey saw three sets of eyes staring at him waiting. "Something bothered me about this date killer case, and I finally found out what it was just now." Jeffrey told them about his god complex.

"It's not a god complex. A god can't have a god complex," Yuul said.

Jeffrey turned to Yuul and looked at her with his eyes moist. He then hugged her, hugged her tight.

"Rule number 1: No hugs at the dinner table," Ella said.

"You're despicable," Liz said, squinting at Yuul and then at Jeffrey.

"Get a boyfriend," Jeffrey said, smiling.

Liz shook her head. "So, you're all good now?"

"Yes, I AM. God complex or not, I'm going over the case again."

"But isn't the case closed already?" Ella asked.

"In the traditional sense, yes, it is since the case is now awaiting trial. However, it doesn't mean that I can't continue on."

"You should if you think there's more to it than meets the eye. Don't leave any stone unturned," Liz said, thinking about the time when she'd been accused of murder.

"I've got a question for you guys. Let's say, you're on a date. Would you stay in the car for three hours with him on your first date?"

"You mean like seriously being inside the car for three hours?" Liz asked.

"Yes," Jeffrey said.

They all thought about the question for a moment and shook their heads to say no.

"What can you do in a car for three hours?" Ella said. "It's way too uncomfortable and boring."

"You can talk," Jeffrey said.

"True if you're on a clandestine operation, not on a date," Liz said. "You don't want to be seen, so you pick a secretive spot and talk about secretive stuff inside the car. Still, you have to have a lot of secrets to fill three hours."

Ella said, "Jeffrey, however you want to look at it, sitting in a car for three hours is just not romantic."

"What about inside a moving vehicle?" Jeffrey said. "Would you stay inside a car for three hours?"

"I might if we were travelling to a final destination that takes three hours to get to, but the place would really have to be worth the drive, oh…" Ella paused. After a moment of silence, Ella cautiously added, "It would have to be someone I'd feel comfortable with." After giving some more thought to it, Ella shook her head. "Still, I would have to get out at least once just to pee."

That made Jeffrey happy. "That's what I thought."

"What are you getting at?" Liz asked.

"Since you said it's a safe place to spill my guts," Jeffrey looked around the house, squinting his eyes as if to see the unseen and then said, "I'll tell you all about it."

The three women moved their chairs closer to eliminate any unnecessary gap between them and Jeffrey.

"We know that the victim was picked up at 8:00 p.m. by our suspect who clearly identified himself as Adam. We also know that the victim got out of the car and entered the playground at 10:52 p.m. with the suspect. However, we don't know where they were from 8:00 p.m. to 10:52 p.m. Now, I'm almost sure that they had to be somewhere for those three hours and if they were somewhere other than the car, somebody might have seen them. I intend to find an eye witness who saw the victim with the suspect. I also want to see the video footage that captured the suspect and the victim at the playground. I want to see the video before it captured them and after. I want to talk to the first 911 caller. I want to do it all!"

The three amigos clapped enthusiastically.

"Yay, way to go, Jeffrey!" Ella said.

"Respect, my brother!" Liz said.

"It's not done until you say it's done," Yuul said.

"It's not done until I say it's done," Jeffrey declared.

17

THURSDAY, DECEMBER 5

As Jeffrey walked into the homicide squad, people in the squad slowly stood up one by one clapping and cheering. That slowed him down causing him to look around. He caught a glimpse of Wylie standing next to Chief Laskaris, who was wearing an ear to ear smile, yet somehow managing not to reveal any of his pearly whites.

Jeffrey saw himself teleported into that perfect moment of happiness like in a movie where the sun was shining a brilliant golden colour, flowering trees full of green leaves on every stem were blossoming right before your eyes, and children were running through sprays of water spouting from fountains under the clearest blue sky – the Perfect Moment, the moment right before everything shatters into pieces.

Jeffrey just knew how this story was going to end for him.

In the blink of an eye, teleported back to the squad-room, Jeffrey saw impatient Laskaris beckoning him over. He slowly walked over and stood next to Wylie.

Laskaris began loudly commanding everyone's attention, "Jeffrey and Wylie showed the people of this city two important things throughout this high-profile investigation. First and foremost, that all people are equal in the eyes of the law. Secondly, that the citizens of this good city can have complete confidence in us as guardians of law and order. Their work was textbook exemplary of an efficient and effective investigation. To match their exemplary work, the captain and I have decided to reward Jeffrey and Wylie with some well deserved time off, effective immediately."

Everyone in the squad-room clapped and cheered enthusiastically.

Jeffrey looked at the captain to rescue him, but she just gave him a nod.

Laskaris continued on. "Take the rest of the week off and I want you to report to work Monday morning and be ready for a mind blowing surprise."

"Sir, I'm perfectly happy with continuing—" Jeffrey couldn't finish it.

"This is not up for discussion. This is an order. Go home. Spend quality time with the family while you can." Laskaris shooed Jeffrey and Wylie.

Jeffrey stayed in protest for a moment, but Laskaris' unwavering stare wore him down. He stomped out of the room like a little child. Wylie chased him out. Jeffrey sulked all the way out to the parking lot and stopped next to his car.

Standing next to Jeffrey, Wylie said, "I don't understand why you look all pissed. Can't you use some time off, especially considering the fact that you just moved into a new house? Is there trouble in paradise?"

"No trouble in paradise. It's just that Grayson just ruined all my plans."

"What plans?"

"I had a plan to still go over a few things on the date killer case."

"Why?"

"It's just a hunch I wanted to follow up on."

"What do you want me to do?"

The light switch turned on in Jeffrey's brain "Can I borrow the murder book on the case?"

"I already put it away."

Jeffrey's breaker tripped and the light went out

Looking at the disappointment on Jeffrey's face, Wylie said, "You can have it on Monday. It's only a few days away."

Jeffrey thought about it and nodded. "Thanks."

"I'm gonna go home and catch up on some sleep. What about you?"

"I guess I'll do the same."

Jeffrey drove up Yonge Street in frustration. Songs played on the radio, but he didn't nod his head or tap the steering wheel to the beat. His plan had been ruined. It squashed his upbeat mood from earlier in the morning. He didn't want to wait until Monday. He needed to figure out what to do next and how to reopen the case *NOW*.

He thought and thought, but eventually accepted the fact that there was nothing else left for him to do, at least at this point, but go home. *Home…* he thought. Then, it hit him. There was something he could do for his family. *At least, I can go home bearing a gift*, he thought. With that thought, he changed direction and headed to the Toronto Police Forensic Identification Services.

• • •

One thing for sure that was apparent to Jeffrey was this just wasn't his day. He stood in the parking lot of the forensic facility, holding his phone so tight that the bones in his fingers were about to break. Thick, white steams of anger were now pouring out of his head.

"Where is the book?" Jeffrey gritted through his phone. His anger flashed like a lightning strike on the darkest night.

"What book?" Wylie asked, sounding perplexed.

"The book I gave you to run the DNA test on."

"Oh, that book."

"What do you mean *oh that book*?"

"I'm sorry. There was an accident."

"Do tell."

"On my way to the lab, I bought a coffee. I'm telling you right now I've never spilled a coffee before in my whole life."

That stupefied Jeffrey.

"Are you there?" Wylie's voice ratcheted up an octave.

"I'm here," Jeffrey finally said.

"I'm sorry."

Liz, the Neighbour

Breathing hard, Jeffrey said, "You spilled coffee. I get that. It still doesn't explain why you didn't take the book to the lab. The book got some spills. The lab could still do testing."

"I'm sorry. It wasn't just some drips that got on the book. Coffee got all over the book."

"How the hell did coffee get all over the book? I gave you the book in a plastic bag, didn't I?"

"You did, but you didn't seal the bag."

"Are you trying to blame this on me?"

"No, no. That's not what I'm saying."

"What exactly are you telling me then? I still don't get it."

"Jeffrey, I really *am* sorry about the book. But I don't understand why you've got your panties in a knot. At the end of the day, you know and I know that book has nothing to do with the case."

"What makes you so sure?"

"The book was found in the suspect's backyard. Meanwhile the vic had her throat slit in a playground miles and miles away from Brooks' backyard."

"Still, we don't know what evidence we could have got from the book."

"Yes, we do. You and I *both* know that there was nothing to be found. Did you ask Adam about the book? Is it even his book?"

"Hey, if that's what you were thinking the whole time, then why the hell did you volunteer to take it to the lab for me?"

"You wanted to keep the case open and you believed that the book would give you that. I'm your partner. I'm on your side. I was just trying to do whatever I could to support you. That's why I volunteered. Plus, I really didn't think you actually cared if we ran a DNA-test on it or not. I thought the only thing that mattered was to make the captain to think that we had something else to follow up on.

"When did you get so smart?" Jeffrey softened in acquiescence.

"I was born this way." Wylie chuckled. "You know what, Jeffrey? I was and am still very embarrassed by it. Fake evidence or not, it should've never happened. I still can't believe I did that."

"Why didn't you tell me when it happened?"

"I honestly forgot all about it until now. You know, so many things were happening at the speed of light."

Jeffrey understood exactly what Wylie meant. He'd felt like he'd been caught in a whirlpool himself. "Are you at home? I still need the book back. I've got to return it to its rightful owner."

"It's *really* in bad condition."

"It's okay. It wasn't in good condition to begin with. Text me your home address."

"I'm not home yet. Why don't I meet you at the gas station at York Mills and Young in 30 minutes?"

"Just come to my house."

"Unlike you, I have a life besides work."

"I don't believe you." Jeffrey paused for a bit and cleared his throat. "I was pissed off about the Chief putting the kibosh on my plan, and I guess I was trying to take it out on you. Did I say sorry?"

"No, but don't worry about it. That's what partners are for."

. . .

Liz, the Neighbour

Liz and Ella were melted into the couch, half heartedly watching a show when they heard the *click* of the front door. Everyone at home was already accounted for, and no one should have been entering without their express welcome. Simultaneously recalling Yuul's encounter with the thief from a few nights ago, Liz and Ella exchanged looks. Reading each other's mind, they sprang over to Yuul's bedroom, jumped in the bed and dove under the covers.

"Intruder," Ella whispered, shaking Yuul by the hand.

"Stay here." Yuul quietly crawled out of bed. She pulled open a drawer from underneath the bed and took out an 11" steel baton. Within the blink of an eye, she rotated her wrist and flicked it in a downward motion: *Snap, snap*. The baton extended to 31" down the side of her leg.

Yuul raised the baton up and ready to strike and walked lightly on her tiptoes to the bedroom door. She slowly opened it a little, scanning the space through the crack in the door and spied their intruder sitting comfortably on the couch. She shook her head in disbelief and collapsed the baton. "It's Jeffrey."

"Jeffrey? Why is he home so early?" Ella asked.

"Let's go interrogate the hell out of him," Liz said, jumping out of the bed.

"Yup, let's totally do that," Ella said, following Liz.

Yuul put the baton back in the drawer shaking her head and followed them out of the bedroom.

"What's up, Brother?" Liz said, flopping down on the couch beside him. "Why are you home so early? Did you get suspended from work?"

"Yes, I did and I don't want to talk about it."

"Huh?" The three amigos all eyed him.

"By the way, there's your book." Jeffrey pointed to a plastic bag lying on the coffee table. "Something bad happened to it, and now it's beyond repair."

Ella hurriedly grabbed the plastic bag and took the book out of it.

The three amigos simultaneously gasped when they saw it. It wasn't just beyond repair; it was beyond recognition. It looked like some sort of paper mache cake.

Liz grabbed the book. "What happened to it?"

"I can't talk about it right now. It'll get me going again. Let me eat something first and then maybe I can talk about it." Jeffrey stood up.

"No, no. You stay. We'll make something." Ella grabbed Liz by the arm.

"What is it?" Yuul said moving in close to Jeffrey.

"It's a long story."

"They usually are."

"I need a hug."

"Do you want to go to the bedroom?" Yuul asked, fluttering her eyelashes.

"Do you have something in your eye?" Jeffrey extended his hand to see what had gotten into her eyes.

"Stop! You're gonna scratch my eye. I guess I still need more practice. I saw a girl doing it on TV. All the guys collapsed to the floor holding their chests. I want to reach that level."

"Bwahaha." Jeffrey threw himself at her and held her tight. "I really can't figure out what planet you're from, but I love your planet. Do you know what I mean, Jelly Bean?"

Liz made Kraft Dinner while Ella made tuna melts with cheddar cheese knowing that they were Jeffrey's comfort food.

"Lunch's ready," Liz called out.

Jeffrey and Yuul walked over to the dining table and sat down smiling away.

"Tell us about your long story," Yuul said.

"You know how excited I was about continuing the investigation again?"

The three amigos nodded.

"That's not happening. Chief Laskaris killed it. He put me and Wylie on vacation for a job well done." Jeffrey shook his head in disbelief. "It really pissed me off, and then I found out about the book." Jeffrey told them about the coffee incident.

"That's a short story. I expected something a lot longer," Yuul said.

"You should thank me for my concise account. I could've told you all the bits and pieces and bored you to death."

"How did Wylie end up with the book? I thought that you were going to take it to the testing lab that morning," Liz said.

"That's simple. Wylie dropped by here for my killer breakfast that morning and ended up with the book."

"Your breakfast is good but it's not that good," Ella chimed in.

"Yes, it is," Jeffrey protested.

"Yes, it is," Yuul said, shooting Ella a sharp look.

"Yes, it is." Ella averted her eyes downward. After brief silence, Ella snapped her fingers. "Then, how come you never get up for his breakfast? You don't even have to go outside to have it."

Yuul slowly tapped her index finger on the table for a bit and said, "No more Lebanese shows."

"I would totally drive for miles for Jeffrey's amazing breakfast," Ella said.

"That's what I thought." Jeffrey smiled.

"What are we gonna tell Gerald about the book?" Ella said.

Liz smiled a devilish smile. "The truth – The police did it."

"I like it." Ella nodded.

"We should get him a new copy," Liz said.

"Who's gonna pay for it?" Yuul asked.

"Don't do the crime if you can't do the time. Who committed the crime?" Liz asked.

Ella raised her hand.

Liz gave her a nod to go ahead.

"The police?" Ella said.

"Exactly!"

"I love it!" Ella screamed.

"You know what else we would all love?" Jeffrey said.

"Hmm… I'll pass on this one. What's the answer?" Ella asked.

"A housewarming party," Jeffrey said.

"That's actually a great idea. Mr. Sandhu's been asking me about it every day," Liz said.

"When do you want to throw the party?" Ella asked.

"Tomorrow," Jeffrey said.

"Tomorrow?" Ella slammed the table with her palms.

"Yes. Since I have some time on my hands, I might as well make the best of it."

With a concerned look, Ella said, "What about Saturday? I don't want to just throw *a* party. I want it to be the best party ever."

"Do it for me," Jeffrey said, slowly nodding his head prodding them to say yes. "I need a reason to get hammered. I can't make it to Monday sober."

"Tomorrow, it is then," Yuul said.

"Mr. Sandhu, Charlie and who else are we inviting?" Ella asked.

"Ajay and his girlfriend and our little brother Tejas," Liz said.

"I'll invite a couple of my friends," Jeffrey said.

The girls arched their eyes in a questioning look almost in unison thinking, *a couple of friends?*

"Should I invite Charlie's mom?" Ella asked, looking all serious.

"Once she meets us, you won't have a chance at winning her heart," Jeffrey said.

Ella thought about it and then nodded in agreement.

"Let's go shopping," Jeffrey suggested.

"Let's make a list first," Ella said, running to her room to grab a pen and paper. She loved making lists. She loved itemizing and organizing.

• • •

Walking down the veggie & fruit aisle pushing a cart, Jeffrey wondered if he was being paranoid. Liz, Ella and Yuul were busy talking away and picking up stuff for the party.

What's the big deal about Wylie showing up at my home for breakfast on a weekday? Partners do that all the time, don't they?

He'd never done it. Then again, his ex-partner had lived way too far out of his way to just drop by for breakfast. He wondered where Wylie lived. He didn't know.

Somewhere close to the crime scene, he thought remembering that Wylie had been at the crime scene already leading the team, way before he got there.

A little too far to drive just for breakfast, he thought. If it hadn't been for breakfast, he didn't know for what else.

The book? How did he know I had the book? More importantly what would he have wanted with it?

He didn't know the answers to these questions. *What else then? It had to be for my breakfast.*

In the meat & fish aisle, he thought about his forced vacation. It still pissed him off. The timing was just too perfect as if someone had listened in on his conversation from the night before.

I'm going too far down the rabbit hole. He shook his head.

The forced vacation thingy couldn't have had anything to do with Wylie. He was sure of that. It had to be pure coincidence unless Wylie had superpowers to make people do his bidding.

Or, does he? He wondered for a moment before he laughed it off.

Separately the incidents could be chalked up to coincidence but when he put them altogether, let's just say, there was just way too much coincidence going around. That reassured him that it did need to be checked out for peace of mind if nothing else.

On the way out of the grocery store, he said, "We need to talk." He pointed to a coffee shop a couple of stores down. "I'll meet you there after I put the groceries in the car."

• • •

At the coffee shop, Jeffrey talked away about Wylie, the breakfast, the book, the investigation and the forced vacation. "There are way too many coincidences which leads me to believe that someone has been listening in on our conversations. Since I don't have access to a bug detector, I've asked Tim and Sam to come by tomorrow and swipe the house during the housewarming party."

"There's a hole in your theory though," Liz said. "When did Wylie ever have the chance to plant a bug? Monday, he came to our home for the first time. Do you remember Ella and I were there with him the whole time? We gave you the book that same night."

"I know I sound like I'm losing my mind and believe me I almost feel like I am, but something doesn't add up here and I need to know what it is. Until everything's clear, we just talk about nonsense at home," Jeffrey said.

"That's what we do best," Ella said.

"I don't think our house is bugged, but there's definitely something off about Wylie," Liz said.

"What do you mean?" Jeffrey said, furrowing his brow.

"Honestly, did you see the book? Even if we give him all the benefit of the doubt, it still doesn't explain the condition that the book is in. The book was in a plastic bag. Let's say, you think the book is totally useless, but you just take it with you to show support for your partner. You get into your car with the book. Where would you put the book?"

"The front passenger seat?" Ella said with caution.

"Bingo! Would you take the book out of the bag?"

"No. Why would I?" Ella said.

Liz snapped her fingers. "Exactly! You put the book down on the front passenger seat or maybe even in the trunk. How could that much coffee get inside the bag and turn the book into that? Even if the book wasn't in a bag, it just couldn't be damaged like it is. Every page is pasted together and turned into paper mache. Even the front, the back and the spine of the book are all smeared and streaked. It looks like it took a lot of effort to get it to look like that."

"Why would he do that?" Jeffrey asked.

"Maybe, he hates you," Ella said. "When people did awful things to me in school, I thought about doing things *just* like that, petty stuff, back to them."

"But I didn't do anything wrong."

"You probably did but just forgot," Liz said: her mouth tipped into a smile – a devilish smile.

"Hmm…" Jeffrey pursed his lips.

18

FRIDAY, DECEMBER 6

It had been a long wait. The clouds had finally hit their climax and snow began to pour out of them at a steady pace. While the others were busy in the kitchen preparing for the best housewarming party ever, Liz snuck out to the living room to gaze at the snow covered street.

She hated everything about winter except for a fresh blanket of snow. Something about it made her believe that everything was going to turn into something magical. Then again, she loved everything about summer except for rain. Something about the rain annoyed her.

While enjoying the tranquility of the snow-covered scene before her, she saw a tall white man dressed only in a T-shirt and ripped jeans walk by. *HA-ha! The village idiot*, she pointed her imaginary finger at the man laughing to herself, just as her mom had taught her. She was laughing so hard inside her head that she almost missed the knock on the door. While walking over to the door, she was still laughing at the village idiot. Upon opening the door, her laughing stopped. There he was, the village idiot, standing right there on her doorstep. "HELLO!" Liz flashed her trademark mega-volt smile.

The village idiot furrowed his brow for a split second before he could wipe it off.

She wasn't sure if he'd heard her. She was about to say 'hello' again but stopped after she finally heard him reply, "Hello."

His voice was deep and calm. His face was rugged and hard but handsome. He looked somewhere close to 6'4, she figured. His brown dark hair was cut short in a crew cut style. His face tanned, he looked like an instant tech millionaire who had just come back from a month-long vacation in a tropical country. But she quickly scratched that thought as his physical presence screamed danger to her – the intense gaze, serious body muscles, and the scars on his arms. *Definitely not the village idiot*, she thought. She said, toning down her voice level, "What can I do for you?"

The stranger fixed his gaze on her, and her heart skipped a beat. "Hi, can I speak to Detective Jeffrey Knight?" the stranger said.

She'd watched too many movies to just let a stranger like him into their home. "Who are you?"

"I'm sorry. I should've introduced myself to you first," the stranger said as if he could sense her concern. "My name is Caleb Brooks. I'm the brother of your neighbour Adam Brooks. I would really like to speak to Detective Jeffrey."

Arms crossed over her chest, she stood in silence, her eyes dissecting the stranger named Caleb Brooks. Although he looked a little rough around the edges, she couldn't discern any trace of evil. Then again, she wasn't exactly known for being the best judge of character.

"I really am sorry to disturb him at home, but it'd be much appreciated if he could find some time to speak with me." Caleb involuntarily stepped back a couple of steps as he saw the woman stepping outside. She scared him. Her earlier ear-bursting hello and the crazy toothy smile still made him shiver.

Moving closer to him, Liz spoke in a whisper, "He's not home."

Caleb stepped back even further from her. The woman standing in front of him scared the piss out of him, not the other way around, which had never happened to him before. He rationalized that she wasn't afraid of him because crazies, more often than not, couldn't spot danger if their lives depended on it, even when it was standing there right in front of them. His mental alarm screamed at him to turn around and run away from her as fast as he could, and that her craziness, her innocent look, the fearless look were all too dangerous even for him. But the thought of Adam kept his feet in place. To hide the uneasiness in his mind, he cleared his throat. "With all due respect, ma'am, please don't lie to me. I know he's home."

Ma'am? How dare he? How old do you think I am? Liz gave him an angry look, but he didn't budge. "How do you know he's home?"

"I saw his car parked in the driveway."

"Were you watching him?"

"Yes."

His candor surprised her. She didn't know what to make of it. Once again, she noticed his T-shirt and ripped jeans. "Aren't you cold?"

"Yes, I am. I didn't expect to be interrogated on the doorstep. Wrong calculation on my part." He chuckled.

"Are you staying at your brother's?"

"*Yesss...*" He answered hesitantly.

"Go home. I'll send him over to you shortly." Liz turned abruptly and went inside the house.

• • •

Jeffrey was perplexed when Liz gave him a beckoning gesture but he obliged. In the backyard, Jeffrey listened to what Liz had to say while studying the man who was in turn watching them through the window of Adam Brooks' house. Jeffrey thought that the man called Caleb Brooks probably didn't even blink once so as not to miss a thing.

When Liz was done explaining the situation, Jeffrey walked over to Adam's back door and walked straight in as Caleb was already there, holding the door open for him. Jeffrey gave a quick glance around the house. "I'm Detective Jeffrey Knight. My sister said you wanted to see me."

"I'm Caleb Brooks. I'm sorry I showed up at your place unannounced. Since I couldn't get a line on you at work, I got caught up in the heat of the moment and took advantage of the geographical convenience."

"The geographical convenience?"

Liz, the Neighbour

"You being the next door neighbour," Caleb said in a more good-natured than smart-ass tone.

"What are all those scars on your arms?"

"Oh these? Well now, that might explain why your sister didn't want to let me in." Caleb let out a short chuckle.

Jeffrey just stared down at the scars in silence.

"Come on, they're not that bad," Caleb replied casually. "You should see the other guys."

"I just hope the other guys were all bad guys," Jeffrey said in a serious, almost accusatory manner. It was the cop in him. He couldn't help it.

"Affirmative."

Jeffrey narrowed his eyes a little more.

By way of explanation, Caleb said, "I'm in the army. They come with the territory."

Jeffrey noticed the relaxed nature of the man. It was very much like that of his brother Adam Brooks. "Good to know. What did you want to talk to me about?"

"Have you made any headway on the case since the last time you saw Adam?"

"The case is closed as far as the police are concerned."

Caleb frowned but just for a split second. "Does that mean you're no longer looking into the case?"

"Yes."

"How can you stop when you know he's innocent?"

"I don't know if he's innocent. What I know is that we have overwhelming evidence that all points to your brother."

"Evidence or not, I know he didn't do it just like you knew that your sister was innocent when she got accused of murder."

"I do *not* take kindly to a suspect's family member talking about my family," Jeffrey said his body visibly tensing up.

Caleb let out a heavy sigh. "That didn't come out right. Please let me start over."

Jeffrey said nothing, keeping a hard gaze on Caleb.

Caleb took his silence as a green light and continued. "I went to see Adam yesterday. He told me about the last time you interviewed him. You told him that he might have an alibi and that his case may not be hopeless after all. That lessened my fears, to be honest. I know he didn't do it, but I don't count when it comes to the legal system. I know that, but you count. You're a cop. After the visit with Adam, I looked into you and happened to find out about your sister. I didn't bring her up for any other reason than the fact that I just wanted to tell you that I believe in my brother just like you believed in your sister, although I don't count."

"What do you want to know?" Jeffrey said.

"Were you able to verify his alibi?" Caleb said.

"No. Sorry."

Caleb moved one step back from Jeffrey, creating physical and emotional distance from the guy, he thought, might be his brother's saviour. He'd put too much importance on Jeffrey since Adam had mentioned him. "No worries. You were just my plan A."

"What's your plan B?"

"Prison break."

Liz, the Neighbour

Jeffrey chuckled. "Talk to Adam's lawyer."

"I already did. Let's just say I don't have any high hopes. Just out of curiosity, how did you prove her innocence?"

"I didn't. Because I'm her brother, they, the police, didn't even let me take part in the investigation."

"Then, how did her charges get dropped? Was it her lawyer? Can I have that lawyer's number?"

"She did it herself although she did have the help of others who believed in her as well."

"How did she do it?"

"She investigated her own case and found the real killer."

No way! Caleb shook his head in astonishment. He still couldn't get passed her ear deafening hello and her wacky smile.

Jeffrey glanced sideways. "Why are you shaking your head? You don't think she is some kind of halfwit, do you?"

"No, no. Of course not." Caleb waved his hands vehemently. "I just thought... I... I meant..."

Jeffrey sized Caleb up. Caleb looked indestructible. There was only one way he could hurt Caleb physically – Kick him right between the legs. Yes, it was a slime ball move, but he didn't see any other way.

"Is she for hire?" Caleb said jokingly.

Jeffrey started to see some light at the end of the tunnel. He couldn't believe he hadn't thought of it before. "I've got to go. I have a party to throw tonight." Jeffrey put his index finger on his lips and signalled Caleb to follow him. Standing on the deck, Jeffrey cracked a smile. "She actually is."

"Why am I wasting my time here with you? Let's go."

"No, you can't come over to my house."

"Why not?"

"Until I'm sure my house isn't being tapped, I don't want anyone talking about Adam's case inside my place. That's why she didn't let you come in."

"This is not good."

"Maybe I'm just being paranoid, but I need to know. Before we talk about Adam's case, I'd like to sweep your house as well."

"When are you going to do it?"

"Tonight. I'll come by around 8 with a couple of other detectives. Let us in and don't say a word until we know your house is clean."

"This must be how people feel when they meet their secret lover in a cheap motel for a rendezvous. I'll wait for you by the door, my love," Caleb winked and disappeared into the house.

• • •

Lots of food and lots of drinks were placed out buffet style and the housewarming party was all set to go. The guests came in one by one. Tim and Sam came with a bottle of wine. Charlie brought a bouquet of flowers in a matching vase. Mr. Ramesh Sandhu brought a barbeque grill set. Ajay brought a bottle of Champagne and his 27-year-old girlfriend, Rani Malik.

She wore traditional Indian clothing – a pinkish purple choli top and a long skirt that elegantly emphasized her feminine figure. A choli scarf put an exclamation point on her fashion sense. Her long, wavy hair came down to her waist and created hypnotic waves whenever she sashayed by. She was the definition of beauty, everybody thought. From this beauty queen, there were people who expected some kind of attitude or ignorance, but Rani's personality truly matched her beauty.

Tim felt his throat go dry and had to clear it whenever he tried to converse with Rani. Rani worried that he might have caught a fever.

Sam cracked jokes to show off his wonderful sense of humour to Rani. Unfortunately, all of his jokes came out slightly more on the creepy side than funny. Rani quietly backed off a couple of steps from Sam.

Charlie laughed showing his bright teeth all night, which nobody ever thought he was capable of, even when the most mundane things were said. He chortled long and hard as if it was the funniest thing he'd ever heard when Rani said, "This is the best spinach salad I've ever had." He roared with laughter when Rani said, "The night seems to fall earlier every day this time of year, doesn't it?" Rani wasn't sure if Charlie had all his faculties.

Jeffrey started every sentence with her name and his face blushed. His cheeks turning red, he said, "Rani said I'm a famous detective." His face flaming red, he passed the salad bowl to Rani, as he said, "Rani wants more salad." Rani suspected that Jeffrey might be an alcoholic.

The girls wanted to hate this beauty purely out of their inferiority, but Rani made that impossible with her cheerful, infectious smile.

After dinner, Tim and Sam walked around the house with a hand-held bug detector. Jeffrey walked along with them ready to mark the spot if a listening device was found. The rest talked and laughed, and they even sang when they ran out of things to talk about.

When the search was over, they had found 3 eavesdropping transmitters – one under the coffee table, another under the kitchen sink and the other placed on the underside of the dining table.

Jeffrey took Tim and Sam over to Adam's house.

As promised, Caleb was waiting for them by the door, and welcomed them in with a nod.

They searched the house, but the detectors didn't beep even once.

"3 to 0. I lose. See ya at your place tomorrow, let's say, 12 noon."

"Let's do it first thing tomorrow morning. Why wait?"

"Happy wife, happy life. See you at noon."

"Happy wife?" Caleb cocked his head to one side.

"A story for another day. Have a good night."

19

SATURDAY, DECEMBER 7

Jeffrey turned the TV on and put the volume up on high before leaving home with Liz, Ella and Yuul. As discussed, Caleb was already there, waiting at his door to let them in.

"I don't get it. Why can't we just remove the bugs and go back to our normal lives?" Liz whimpered as she was making her way towards the living room couch.

Jeffrey hooked the neck of Liz's T-shirt from behind and stopped her in her tracks.

"What now?" Liz said, irritation clearly showing in her voice.

Jeffrey pointed to the stools around the kitchen island. "This is where we stay."

"See?" Liz pointed her finger at the window closest to her and then moved it clockwise from one window to the next. "The curtains are drawn closed over every window."

"Was I right about the bugs?" Jeffrey said in a smart-ass tone.

"Okay, okay. Where do you want me to sit?" Liz said.

"Any one of these stools."

"What do you want to talk about?" Yuul said, placing her head on the island.

Jeffrey smiled. "Let me introduce you to your next client."

"A client?" All three said, their heads up, their eyes wide open and a big smile on everyone's lips.

"Meet your new client, Caleb Brooks. He's Adam Brooks' brother."

"Caleb? Isn't he your village idiot?" Yuul said, looking at Liz.

Her cheeks blushed. "First of all, I never said he's *my* village idiot. Second of all, you can't say those things out loud. Lastly, I thought that he *was* the village... Once I talked to him, I knew he wasn't. Do you remember *that part*?"

"I do." Turning to Caleb, Yuul said, "She also said you were sort of cute. Can I have a coffee?"

Caleb stood slack-jawed.

"That's my wife, Yuul. And this is Ella."

Ella nodded at Caleb, her mouth quivering from her effort not to burst out a laugh.

"And this is Liz who thought—"

"*JEFFREY!*" Liz shrieked.

Jeffrey put his hands up in surrender. "I'll have a coffee as well."

"You yelled hello at me because you thought I was the village idiot?" Caleb spoke with a tone of astonishment.

Hardly holding back his laughter, Jeffrey said, "And then she thought—"

"JEFFREY!" Liz's cheeks got redder than a rose kissed by the morning dew.

"Let me get this straight. You thought that I was the village idiot. That was why you said hello like that. It means you're not crazy." Caleb put his fist on his lips as if he was trying not to cry from joy.

"You thought Liz was touched in the head?" Jeffrey narrowed his eyes. Again, he contemplated kicking Caleb right between his legs.

"A coffee please!" Yuul said.

"What about you two?" Caleb asked, eyeing Liz and Ella.

"Water please," Ella said.

"Water for me as well," Liz said as casually as she could muster.

After Caleb served everyone their drinks, Jeffrey placed both hands down on the countertop and leaned in a bit with a serious look on his face. "All jokes aside, I need you to take this case and be my eyes and ears on it."

"Are you using us?" Liz said, narrowing her eyes at Jeffrey.

"Yes," Jeffrey said, no shame. He then gestured towards Caleb with a quick nod of his head and a flash of his eyes. "But he'll be the one picking up the tab for it."

Caleb nodded.

Yuul quickly went over the numbers in her head. "Your brother's case will take up a lot of our resources. Since Jeffrey wants this case, we'll give you a discount and charge you $200 per work hour."

Caleb extended a hand. "I look forward to the work you'll do. And I am also hoping to come on board and help you with whatever I can."

Yuul saw Liz, Ella and Jeffrey nodding. Yuul shook his hand. "Well, welcome on board then. You've got our full attention on the case, we'll send you an invoice after the case is closed," Yuul said.

"Now that you guys are done talking business, can we start talking about the case?" Ella said excitedly.

"Yes," Yuul said, sipping the coffee.

"Let's start with Wylie," Jeffrey said. "Wylie Townsend is my partner."

"Hmm... It means he's a cop. I don't like where it begins," Caleb said.

Jeffrey crossed his arms over his chest. "This is deeply disturbing to me, both personally and professionally, but that's where we're gonna start."

Jeffrey gave Caleb a quick rundown of Wylie and the book. Jeffrey couldn't tell if Caleb had been shocked by any of the things he'd said. If so, Caleb hadn't shown it. Jeffrey wrapped up his account with a question: "How did Wylie know about the book?"

After a bout of silence, Liz slowly smiled. "He had an accomplice."

"Aha!" Everybody exclaimed.

Resting her chin on her palm, Ella said, "Who could it be though? It has to be someone who came into our house between moving day and last Monday. There was only Charlie, Ajay and the movers."

"Don't forget about our charming neighbours," Liz said.

"Oh, My, My!" Ella exclaimed, her eyes growing bigger and bigger. "I can't believe I actually managed to block them out. What were their names again?"

"Mike, Abigail, Rob and Doreen," Liz said.

"Doreen followed me into the kitchen, opening the cupboards," Yuul said.

"Shut the front door!" Ella exclaimed.

Jeffrey shook his head in disbelief. "Our neighbour Doreen is Wylie's accomplice? That's crazy. On the other hand, at this point, I guess anything's possible."

"And Rob," Liz added with a smile.

"Who's Rob?" Jeffrey asked.

"Doreen's husband," Liz said.

"What do you know about them?" Jeffrey said.

"They're racist," Ella said, shaking a little in anger. "That's all we know."

"That means they've been listening to us since Sunday afternoon," Liz said.

Ella couldn't remember how many silly things she'd said between Sunday and Thursday. She just hoped not too, too many.

Liz said, "What has that book got to do with Wylie? It's Gerald's book. He threw it at a wild cat."

"I wouldn't call it a wild cat but go on," Yuul interjected.

"What do you mean?" Ella wanted to know.

"I guess Gerald and I saw the same guy, or at least the same jacket. The guy I saw on Sunday night wore a jacket that had a tiger face or a wild cat face emblazoned on the back of it."

Jeffrey furrowed his brows. "The guy who reminded you of your first lover?"

"I thought you forgot about my existence ever since you met Rani."

A mischievous smile spread across Jeffrey's face. "Are you jealous?"

"Yes."

In an instant, Jeffrey grabbed Yuul by her arms, pulled her close to him and kissed her on her lips. He then whispered by her ear, "I love you."

"Eew!" Ella cried.

Caleb just shook his head.

"I've been meaning to ask you all about it," Liz said. "Did he look like your trainer?"

"Wild Cat was white, and my trainer was yellow or brown – whatever colour Koreans are supposed to be. So, no. Wild Cat moved like my trainer, an ex-Special Forces Soldier. And the cat wore military-grade boots."

"Are you familiar with military manoeuvres?" Caleb said in interest.

"You remind me of my trainer as well," Yuul said.

Caleb stared at Yuul.

"Isn't she something?" Jeffrey said, laughing.

"What's so funny?" Liz said, tilting her head.

"He's *not* an ex-soldier, but a current one," Jeffrey said.

"You haven't really seen my moves. So, how could you tell?" Caleb asked.

"When we came in, you were by the door standing upright, chin up, chest out, shoulders back and stomach in, just like my trainer when he was not in motion. And, your haircut."

Caleb frowned. "Fair enough. Anyway, I don't like where this story is headed. We're talking about a dirty cop and an ex-military. I sincerely hope it ends well."

"Did you see his face?" Ella said, looking at Yuul.

"Yes, I saw him in the moonlight."

"Have you seen him anywhere else?" Jeffrey wanted to know.

"No, I've never seen him before."

"Could you recognize him if you saw him again?" Jeffrey wanted to know.

"I believe so."

"Good," Jeffrey said.

"If the guy Gerald saw is the same guy Yuul saw, that begs the question. Doesn't it?" Liz said.

"Which is?" Jeffrey asked.

"Why was he at Adam's house on Friday night, November 22nd and why did he come back again on Sunday, December 1st?"

"It was more like early Monday morning," Yuul said.

Jeffrey then knew for sure that Wylie had been involved in setting up Adam Brooks for murder. Wylie had played him like a fiddle and that royally pissed him off. "I don't know why Wild Cat came here on November 22nd but I do know why he came here very early Monday morning on December 2nd. It's because I wanted to search Brook's house to see if we could find the murder weapon, or the clothes and shoes he wore during the murder. Wylie suggested putting it off a day since it was late Sunday evening. Wild Cat came here that night to plant them. We had already detained

Adam Brooks. So, no one was supposed to be there. It would've been a done deal if Yuul hadn't intercepted him."

Looking at Yuul, Caleb said, "What did you do?"

Yuul shrugged.

Jeffrey said, "She saw the guy coming up from the ravine. At the time, she thought that the guy was trying to sneak into our place, so she went out after him."

"You're brave," Caleb said.

Jeffrey shook his head at Caleb. "Do not encourage her."

Liz said, "It means Wylie has another accomplice."

Looking at Caleb, Jeffrey said gloomily, "I'm with you, bro. I don't like where this is going, either"

"Ahem." Liz cleared her throat to get attention. "Once again, why did Wylie care so much about the book?"

Everyone sat there racking their brains for a while until Ella raised her hand excitedly. "I think I know why." She surprised herself that she had remembered it. "The blood on the book, that's why. Do you remember the red stain on the book? Gerald insisted that it was shit, but I clearly saw the red stain."

They all slowly nodded their heads in agreement thinking that the blood could definitely be a good reason for Wylie to want to retrieve the book.

The thought, *only if it was Wylie's blood,* sprang to Liz's mind. "We know one thing for sure. It wasn't Wylie's blood if, in fact, it was blood at all. It was Wild Cat's. The incident occurred more than a week before the murder. Even if Jeffrey had run the DNA test and identified Wild Cat because he had a criminal record, so what? As far as we know, Wild Cat didn't commit a punishable crime that night. He could simply say that he'd lost his way. Instead, Wylie went the extra mile to get his hands on the book and then made sure that it could never be used to acquire any evidence. Why?"

They all fell silent again while they thought it over.

They were all quiet until Ella raised her hand slowly and said, "Maybe… he's… related… to Wylie?"

Everyone gasped.

"Brilliant!" Jeffrey clapped.

Her chin up, Ella said, "Thank you."

"We need to speak to Adam," Jeffrey said. He looked at Caleb. "Who's Adam's lawyer?"

"Harvey Rogen," Caleb said.

Tapping the countertop, Jeffrey looked at Caleb for a moment. After much thought, Jeffrey finally said, "We need Charlie on this case. Do you think you can convince your brother to change his lawyer to Charlie Khoury?"

"As long as it works in his favour, of course, I can and he will. You think he's better than Harvey?" Caleb said.

"I don't know." Jeffrey shrugged. "But under the circumstances, we need a lawyer who can go to Adam whenever we need him to and ask the questions we need answers to, so we can solve this thing. We also need a lawyer who's a devoted KSK fan. Who's better than Charlie?"

"We have the village idiot. Can't you just send him to see Adam if you need anything from him?" Yuul wanted to know.

Liz blushed again.

Jeffrey smiled. "Let's call him the village idiot only when he's not around. Okay sweetie?"

"Okay," Yuul said.

Jeffrey wrapped his arm around Yuul. "Adam is being detained at the Toronto East Detention Centre. While Adam's waiting for his trial, he only gets 2 visits per week from family and friends, and each visit is limited to 20 minutes. Only lawyers get to visit detainees as long as they want and as often as they want."

"Let's ask Charlie if he's available," Ella said.

"Haven't you wrapped him around your little finger yet?" Liz said.

"I have, but I still have to ask."

"Call him and put him on speaker," Jeffrey said. "I want to talk to him as well."

Ella phoned Charlie.

Charlie picked up the call immediately. "Am I forgiven now?"

"You're on speaker," Ella said, almost in a shout, a second behind Charlie.

Everybody gazed at Ella, eyes narrowed.

As if he could see what was going on at Adam's, Charlie said, "Rani."

"Ah-ha," Everybody said in unison except Caleb.

"Who's this Rani I keep hearing about?" Caleb said.

"A goddess," Liz said. "Being single sometimes has its advantages. No reason to be jealous about anyone."

"Why am I on speaker?" Charlie wanted to know.

"Are you following the Adam Brook's case?" Jeffrey asked.

"Yes."

"Ella told us that she's willing to forgive you but only if you accept the job as Adam's defense lawyer," Liz said.

"No, I didn't," Ella protested.

"I'll do anything for her forgiveness except that. Just to remind you again, I am not a criminal lawyer. I'd be worried that it might be considered as a dereliction of duty if I represented Adam in court."

"Ella will explain it later in detail. To make a long story short, our goal is to get the charges dropped against Adam before the trial. I can't work on this case in any kind of official capacity. Adam's brother, Caleb, just hired KSK to investigate Adam's case. They need full access to Adam. It means they need a lawyer who's willing to work with them anytime they want. You're the only one that fits the bill. I need you on this case. If you won't do it for Ella, do it for me. If you do, I'll accept you as her boyfriend," Jeffrey said.

"I'm already her boyfriend."

"Not in our eyes, and remember I'm family. I'll get in your way. Do you really want that? And don't forget I am also a cop."

"I'll sue you."

"That's the spirit."

"Haha. You guys always seem to forget that I already have a full-time job."

"I'll call Al. He owes me," Liz said.

"Only if Ella forgives me. I really wasn't laughing because of Rani. I laughed because of Yuul."

"What did I do?" Yuul said.

"I think I finally can tell when you're angry. Ella, what do you say?"

"You're forgiven for now," Ella said.

"That's great news. If Al okays it and Adam okays it, I'm more than happy to be at your service."

"We'll call you back after talking to Al. I need you to meet Adam first thing Monday morning. I need you to ask him some questions for us."

"Okay, I'll wait by the phone."

Liz called Al. After a lot of yelling, she finally hung up the phone. "Al is cool with it."

• • •

In the southwest corner of the city, people gathered for Madison Cooper's funeral. Tina Preston's husband, Vince Preston had come with their two sons from the United States of America. Ned Cooper's wife, Cindy Cooper had come with their daughter from South America.

Tina stood by her daughter's grave. She couldn't leave her child all alone in the cold. Her heart was so empty but at the same time filled with love, anger and fear. She was wretched. She was beaten. She was hurting. Her father, who wasn't as tall as he used to be, put his arm around her and pulled her to his chest. He patted her head ever so gently, ever so lovingly. Her face buried in his chest, tears dropped, and she cried a silent cry.

Tina couldn't bear the thought that her father was now all alone in this place that was filled with the memory of the dead – his wife first and now his granddaughter. She asked him to go to the States with her. He said no. She begged him. When beseeching didn't work, she guilt-tripped him. He didn't budge. After a lot of yelling and screaming in tears, Tina eventually gave up and asked Birdie to keep an eye on Ed for her.

"Don't worry a thing about him. You go look after those two beautiful boys." Birdie hugged Tina real tight.

• • •

At 10:00 p.m. Birdie, Agnes and Will left Ed's and went home. Birdie and Agnes went straight to their respective sleeping nests. Birdie snored. Agnes snored. The two ladies snored louder than a train whistle, shattering Will's ears.

Will woke up, turned the TV on and upped the volume trying to cancel out one noise with another. While he was jerking and twisting on the uncomfortable couch, he fell off landing on carpeted floor between the couch and the coffee table. While he was mulling over whether or not he should climb back onto the couch, he fell asleep. It had been a long, sad day.

• • •

Adam Doyle parked his 2012 Chevrolet Malibu on the dimly lit street of Culnan Avenue *again* patiently waiting for the city to fall asleep *again*. He couldn't believe how fast the time had flown. It had been only three weeks ago that he'd parked his car right on this same spot for the very first time to carry out his ISTAR practice, although it also felt like that had happened a life time ago.

He couldn't help but feel melancholy while watching Madison's house. He now longed for Madison whom he'd loved and lost. *Or, should I just say the love of my life that I killed?* A grin widened on his face.

His feelings of love for Madison had been very powerful. Knowing that their love could never come to fruition had intensified everything and made her even more desirable to him.

Right before he'd slit her throat, Madison had closed her eyes expecting a kiss from him. *Oooh, her moist, scarlet red lips!* He shivered from an itching desire.

When she'd felt a long, sharp metal blade at her throat instead, she'd abruptly opened her eyes. He'd put his vinyl gloved hand over her lips using light pressure so that he could watch her fear filled eyes for even a second longer. She'd murmured something unintelligible just before she drew her last breath.

With a quick side-glance at the house next to Madison's, he knew that everyone was lost in a deep slumber with no clue that someone was watching over the house.

Ladies and a gentleman! Here comes trouble.

20

SUNDAY, DECEMBER 8

Adam Doyle quietly got out of the car and walked over to the house next door to Madison's. Tonight, his targets were the two oldies and the young man living in this house.

He inserted the lock pick into the front door keyhole and rotated the plug: *click*. The lock released, and he slowly pushed the door open. *A piece of cake*, he thought.

As he entered the house, his body involuntarily tensed up from all the racket. Loud laughter with applause hailed him, and then he heard something else that sounded like a train whistle.

He automatically extended his arms forward and raised his Glock to eye level ready to shoot anyone coming at him Western style.

While he was stealthily going deep behind enemy lines, he scanned and searched the space. No one was coming at him with a gun. That was a relief. There were just lots of noise: a male voice and laughter, and a train whistle…

He then realized what the train whistle was – a very loud snore! When he turned in the direction where the light kept flashing, he solved the other mystery - Tonight Show. Jimmy Fallon was chatting away with his guest while the audience was laughing away.

Oh Jimmy! Adam shook his head. *You almost took my breath away.*

He scanned the room one more time to confirm that no one was lurking in the shadows. Once it was confirmed, he lowered the Glock and proceeded upstairs.

On the second floor, he walked straight to the end of the hallway where the master bedroom was located. This was where he'd been told to start and then kill the rest on his way out.

He opened the door an inch but stopped because the door squeaked loudly. He held the Glock close to his abdomen. When he heard another series of snores, he opened the door wide enough and entered the bedroom.

In this ancient old house, even his light, careful footsteps still made the floor squeak every time he made a step: *Squeak, squeak*. Thankfully, the squeaks were buried by the train whistles.

On his third step, he felt something under his right foot. At first, he thought that he must've stepped on a ball of yarn of some sort. As he put his full weight down on his foot, he heard the squeal, and squeal again of an injured animal followed by the sound of blood gushing out. He slowly lifted his foot and saw a flattened mouse matted to the floor in its own blood.

"*Ahhhhhhhhh!*" he screamed like a little girl. It was so massively gross that it made him jump. As he landed back on the floor away from the flattened mouse, he suddenly saw an alarm clock flying right at him. That knocked him off balance and sent him crashing awkwardly to the ground.

Out of the corner of his eye, he saw target #2 approaching him with her cane raised up. The next thing he knew target #2 was beside him whacking him on his butt with her cane. Even though it felt more like tapping than blows, it hurt just the same, more his pride as a hired killer than anything else.

Around the same time, as if the alarm clock wasn't enough, the main target was now coming at him with a lamp in her hand. He couldn't let that happen, could he? Beaten down by two oldies, that could scar him for the rest of his life. He sprang to his feet ready to shoot them all, but only came to a realization that the gun was no longer in his hand. *Fuck!* He screamed inside. *Fuck! Where did it go?*

Then, he heard the third target call out, "Grandma! Grandma!" as he stomped up the stairs. Adam realized that he was out of options. He had to retreat for now. *The night is still young. I'll shoot you all in the face before this night ends*, he promised himself, looking at the oldies angrily. With that thought, he pushed past the two old ladies and charged the young man in the hallway like a bull knocking him down and with that he ran out of the house.

• • •

Birdie got to her feet just as she heard Will being thumped to the floor. She rushed over to him promising herself that if anything happened to him, she was going to avenge him at any cost. "Will, Will!" Birdie screamed in panic, shaking him. He didn't move. Tears streaked down. "Will, Will!" She slapped his face. "Wake up!"

"You're hurting me, Grandma." Will held Birdie's little, shaky hand with his. "Are you okay, Grandma?"

"I'm okay. Little Susan sacrificed her life for mine," Birdie said, stroking Will's arm.

"Who's Little Susan?" Will asked. Looking all confused.

"A mouse. I named it Little Susan." Birdie curled the corner of her lips upwards in a semi-smile, thinking about how ironic it was. "One day, I saw a mouse running down the stairs. I was going to get a mousetrap, but then somebody killed our Maddie. After that, I just didn't have the heart to do it. Tonight, I think the intruder accidently stepped on her. The sound of squealing and popping woke me up, and luckily took him by surprise. Anyway, while he was screaming, I unplugged the alarm clock and whipped it at him."

"That's unreal!" Will said, eyes widened.

"Look at this," Agnes extended her hand forward, a gun dangling from her index finger.

"That's a gun!" Will cried.

"I'm not blind," Agnes said.

Will placed his right hand over his chest to calm his racing heart down. "A house burglar with a gun?

Liz, the Neighbour

What's happened to Canada while I've been gone? And of all the houses on our street, he picked this place, the house with probably the least valuables." Will shook his head in disgust. "He doesn't even have the basics of burglary 101 down."

"I've noticed that more and more people are bringing a gun to a knife fight these days," Agnes said, waving the gun at him.

"Why did he pick this house?" Birdie said, more to herself than to the others. "He walked straight up to my bedroom with a gun in his hand. Why? Did he come here to kill me?"

"Ha-ha... Why would anyone want to kill you, Grandma?" Will said.

"That's what I'm saying. Why would anyone want to kill such a perfect angel?" Birdie said, still stroking her chin.

Will laughed. "Exactly! It's not *you* he came for. He probably figured that most people keep their valuables in the master bedroom."

Birdie nodded. "You have a point there. Anyway, let's call the police."

• • •

While two uniformed police officers were taking Agnes's and Will's statements, Birdie was transfixed by the gun – a Canadian burglar armed with a gun. By the time the police had put the gun in an evidence bag, Birdie was sure that the burglar wasn't a burglar at all but an assassin who had come here to silence her forever.

After the uniform officers left, Will closed the door behind them.

"We've got to move" Birdie said. "Pack enough for a couple days stay."

"What do you mean? What's going on?" Will wanted to know.

Agnes didn't waste time asking questions. She headed right up the stairs to get packed.

Will didn't move. He just stood in the same spot.

"What are you waiting for?" Birdie said.

"Don't you remember? I'm already living out of my luggage. I'm good to go."

"Good," Birdie said. "Before I pack, I've got to call Ed."

Birdie went upstairs and found her cellphone on her night stand. "Ed, it's me."

Aghast, Ed asked Birdie if she was okay.

"I'm good, but I need you to pack some clothes for a short trip. I'll explain everything once we're on the road. Don't turn on any lights. Just wait by the door. Right now, I just need you to trust me and do exactly as I say." Birdie disconnected the call and started throwing some clothes and toiletries in her suitcase. It took her like 10 minutes, give or take, to pack everything she needed. She then walked over to Agnes's room. "Are you ready, Agnes?"

"Yes," Agnes said, holding her luggage handle.

They made it downstairs to where Will was standing, holding his suitcase handle.

"One sec. I've got to call a taxi," Birdie said.

Will was at a loss. "Are we taking a taxi? Why? Where's your car?"

"It's a long story."

"Grandma!"

Liz, the Neighbour

"Not now. I'll tell you all about it first chance we get, I promise." Birdie took her cellphone out of her jacket pocket.

Will had asked his grandma to join him in Hollywood. Just the warm climate itself should've been a good inducement since she'd been complaining a lot about the weather, especially after she'd hit 70. Surprisingly, she'd given him a firm no. Since she had been so adamant about not moving in with him, he'd bought a new house for her in Toronto. Again, he'd received a firm no. He'd ended up selling the house. The Toronto housing market had been so hot that he'd made a handsome profit, but that wasn't the point. He'd wanted to spoil her. He'd wanted to wrap her up in a blanket of money. Instead of a house, she did ask for a car. She'd always loved cars, especially fast cars. She'd always dreamt of driving a car on the Autobahn. She'd even once told him to put her in a car and send it off a cliff when her time came, like Thelma and Louise. Now this car-enthusiast somehow had no car. *What's going on?*

"You know what?" Birdie said, looking at Agnes.

"What?" Agnes asked.

"Do you have those girls' business card?" Birdie looked at Agnes.

"I do. Let me go get it."

"Who are those girls?" Will asked.

"Private detectives that Agnes's nephew hired to locate her."

"Was she missing?"

"No, she was hiding out here."

"Here," Agnes handed the card to Birdie.

Ring, ring, ring... The call went to voicemail. Birdie tried again, and this time Liz answered.

"Hi Liz, It's Birdie. Do you remember Agnes and her nephew Jonas?"

"Of course I do. How are you?" Liz said, perking up her sleepy voice.

"Good, good. I'm calling to take you up on your offer. I need you to come and pick us up right away. Unless you want me to die, I need you to come here right away. It's a matter of life and death. Do you remember where you dropped us off last time?"

"I do," Liz said, trying to figure out if this was a prank call.

"Good. Uh, I forgot to mention. There're four of us with luggage. When you get here, flash your lights three times. We'll be right out."

. . .

Yuul stared at the monitor, trying to figure out what all the numbers meant when she heard footsteps coming down the stairs. Her first thought was that someone probably needed water, so she ignored it. When she heard the footsteps heading to the living room, she wondered why, so she came out of her office and found Liz putting on her jacket and boots.

"Where are you going?" Yuul asked.

"You're up? Of course, you're up. Do you remember our first client Jonas Fischer? I got a call from his aunt and her friend. They need a ride."

"At this hour?"

Liz shrugged. "She said it's a matter of life and death. She needs me there right away unless I don't

Liz, the Neighbour

mind her being dead. So, yes, I'm going out right now at this late hour."

"I'll go with you."

"No need. It's probably nothing. I'm going there as a part of our after service. More importantly, I don't have room for you in my car. She has three other people with her and luggage."

"Send me the address where you're going. I'll follow you with Jeffrey."

"Don't wake him up. He's too riled up over this Wylie thing. Let's leave him out of this one."

"You're right, but I'm still going with you. Send me the address. I won't wake Jeffrey. I'll hitch a ride."

"Hitch a ride?"

Yuul smiled a lopsided smile, looking over next door.

"I don't think he has a car," Liz said.

"He does. I saw a car parked in the driveway."

21

SUNDAY, DECEMBER 8

Birdie saw the high beams flash three times through a gap between the curtains. They all came out, dragging luggage. Will went over to Ed's house and knocked on the door. Ed came out with his suitcase. Will put all the luggage in the trunk and hopped into the front passenger seat.

"Can you take us to the Colony Hotel on Carlton Street?" Birdie requested from the backseat.

"No problem but while I'm driving, can someone please tell me what on earth is going on?"

"We had a visitor with a gun," Birdie said.

"Oh My God!" Liz cried out in shock. "You should call the police."

"We already did," Birdie said. "They came and left. But I think this thing is bigger than it looks. Someone came to my house tonight to kill me, and that same someone works at Wild Peach Estate."

"What is Wild Peach Estate?" Will asked.

Nobody answered Will.

"Are you sure?" Liz asked in disbelief.

"It took me some time to place him, but I'm sure of it," Birdie said. "I'm trying to figure out how he found me, and why he tried to kill me now. It's been almost 4 months since I got kicked out of Wild Peach, and it's been 2 months since Agnes ran away. Did you ever contact the home again?"

"No, we didn't," Liz said, peeking at Birdie through the rear view. "And we haven't heard from them, either, just in case you're wondering."

"Hmm... We didn't do anything to draw attention to ourselves. Meeting you and Ella was the last venture we did before..." Birdie's voice trailed off, feeling the pain of losing Maddie.

"Did something happen?" Liz asked.

Birdie placed her hand over Ed's and gave a little squeeze. "Maddie, his granddaughter, was murdered last Saturday."

"I'm sorry," Liz said, looking at the poor old man through the rearview mirror. *So many murders... Maddie died on the same day Madison Cooper died. Maddie... Madison... on the same day...* In shock, Liz turned around to see Birdie and lost her grip on the steering wheel. Her car slid over the line, scaring her passengers. Their bodies lurched forward, and in fear they tried to grab onto each other. Just in time, Will turned and quickly righted the steering wheel to bring them back into their lane.

"I'm so sorry," Liz profusely apologized.

"Keep your eyes on the road," Will said sharply.

"I am," Liz said curtly, giving Will the once-over.

"Eyes on the road, lady," Will shouted.

"My eyes are on the road," Liz sparred.

"Your eyes—"

"That's enough, Will!" Birdie scolded. "What is it, Liz?"

"Oh, yes. Are you talking about Madison Cooper who passed away last Saturday?" Liz said.

"Yes," Birdie said quietly. "Do you know Maddie?"

"My brother was one of the detectives who worked on the case."

"We met two. Which one is yours?" Agnes asked.

"Jeffrey Knight."

"Speaking of those detectives," Birdie said, "the last thing we did was talk to his partner over the phone, Wylie. We didn't even go out."

"When was that? What did you talk to him about?"

"When was it, Will?" Birdie said.

"Liz Knight?" Will said slowly, looking at Liz like he'd just seen a ghost.

"Yes, that's her name," Birdie said. "We all know that. Now, when did we talk to—"

"Wednesday, the Wednesday that just passed," Agnes said instead.

"What did you talk to him about?" Liz wanted to know.

No one answered and a silence filled the space.

Liz knew why. They didn't want to upset the man who had just lost his granddaughter. *They called Wylie Wednesday, the day Adam Brooks was charged with murder. Why did they call Wylie? Did they remember something that Madison said about her date? Would that be it?* She had to

Liz, the Neighbour

know. She glanced at Birdie through the rearview mirror. "Did he follow up on the information?"

Birdie stared at Liz thinking, *Clever girl.* "We don't know. We haven't heard from him yet."

Bingo! Liz thought excitedly.

"Liz Knight!" Will's voice jumped an octave. "Will, Will Pemberton," Will said, jabbing his thumb into his chest.

"I know," Liz said.

"Don't tell me she's *the* Liz?" Birdie said.

"Yes, Grandma," Will said, smiling.

"Grandma?" Liz asked in surprise.

"Yes, he's my grandson," Birdie said proudly.

Liz looked at Birdie through the rearview mirror. "Did you hear about me?" She then shook her head. "No, no, don't answer that. We need to just focus on the situation at hand."

"What situation?" Agnes asked.

"The dangerous situation that you guys are in? The Ninja Assassin who just made a visit to your place?"

"Oh that," Agnes shrugged off as if to say no biggie.

"Are you sure that the Ninja Assassin is gone?" Liz asked.

Birdie laughed. "No, we're not sure. How can we be sure? But then again, why would he hang around?"

"We're almost there," Liz said. "This is what I want you to do."

• • •

Caleb watched three retirees getting into Liz's car while a man in his 30s put their luggage into the trunk of her car. After putting the last bag in the trunk, he jumped into the front passenger seat. Caleb then saw Liz's car slowly driving away.

"What are you waiting for?" Yuul asked.

"It's How to Protect Your Asset 101. You've got to give them some leeway."

Just then, they saw a white Chevrolet Malibu that was parked further down come slowly up the street and take off in the direction of Liz's car.

"Did you see anyone come out of a house and get into that car?" Caleb said.

"No," Yuul said.

"You see, How to Protect Your Asset 101." Caleb started the engine and followed the Malibu that was now following Liz's car.

Yuul checked the rear view mirror and side mirrors to see if anyone else was out there following anyone else. If there was, Yuul didn't see it.

The sneaky car tailing came to an end when Liz stopped the car at The Colony Hotel.

Caleb and Yuul parked on the street silently, watching as three people in their 70s and a man in his 30s popped out of Liz's car and walked over to the brightly lit hotel's front entrance. Liz drove off as soon as the oddball group got out of her car.

"Look." Caleb pointed over to the Malibu where a stranger was leisurely getting out and began to follow the pensioners into the hotel. "Get a picture of his license plate. I'll go in and assess the situation." Caleb got out of his car.

Caleb entered the hotel just in time to see the group as they walked right past the front desk located on the left side of the lobby. They continued on walking straight through all the way to the other end. Caleb realized that they were heading right out the back door. He involuntarily smiled. *Not bad for a civilian. I'll wait for you and take you to my place and then I'll take you somewhere else the next day.*

When Caleb spotted the Malibu man about to catch up to them at the back door, Caleb grabbed the man by his arm and said, "Où est la salle de bain?/Where is the bathroom?"

"What the fuck!" The man shouted as he tried to shove Caleb out of his way, but to no avail. "Get out of my way. I don't know what you're talking about."

As Caleb saw everyone get into Liz's car and drive off, Caleb let the man go and said, "Où est la salle de bain?"

"You Moron!" The man shouted with hatred in his eyes and then ran out the door where the pensioners and the young man had walked out only a few minutes ago.

"Monsieur, vous etes tres grossier/you are very rude," Caleb said with a smile. He turned and walked towards the front desk.

"Bonjour. Je cherche les toilettes/Hello, I'm looking for the washroom." Caleb saw out of the corner of his eye the man running back to the front door and gave him an angry look before he exited the hotel.

"Suivez cette voie. C'est sur ton côté gauche/Follow this path. It's on your left side," the front desk clerk said.

"Merci" Caleb walked out the front door, leaving the front desk clerk in puzzlement.

Caleb walked out and saw the Malibu still parked on the street. He quickly stepped into the shadows.

When he finally saw the man drive away, he ran to his car and hopped in.

"Let's go catch the bad guy," Caleb said as he started an ignition.

After a prolonged drive in silence, Caleb finally said to Yuul, "Do you think it'll be a nice day tomorrow?"

"I don't like weather talk."

"What do you want to talk about?"

"Whose car is this?"

"This is Adam's wife's car."

"Where is she?"

"Paris. She's flying back on Monday, actually so are my parents, from Newfoundland. That's where we're from – me and Adam. Have you ever been to Newfoundland?"

"No."

"If you want to see one of the most beautiful places on this planet, you have to go. It's truly a magical place. We're from a small fishing town called Witless Bay, and yes, we are witless."

Yuul said nothing. She just sat there, clicking away on her cellphone.

Caleb shugged. "I guess I'm not as funny as I thought."

No response. Yuul sat, just clicking away.

Caleb finally stopped talking. In his line of work, humour played a very important role in keeping them sane – a good sense of humour, not a sick one. Obviously, this Asian lady didn't need humour to keep her sanity, he figured.

"Hahaha!" Yuul laughed and couldn't stop.

"What is it?"

Liz, the Neighbour

"Dildo? Hahaha!" Yuul laughed, wiping her tears away with her hand. "You guys have a good sense of humour."

"That name stands out for obvious reasons, but my town's name is a lot funnier in a more sophisticated way."

"You're right. I've never seen anything this beautiful in my life. I'll be going as soon as the weather gets warmer," Yuul said.

Caleb liked that. He smiled.

• • •

Liz drove up Yonge Street, thinking hard. She'd originally planned to take her guests to her house, but she was no longer sure if it was such a good idea. She wondered if Birdie might be the last piece that completed the puzzle, and it seemed that way. She knew that somehow Wylie was linked to Rob and Doreen. Now, it looked like Wylie might be involved in the attempt on Birdie's life. She imagined Rob and Doreen laughing an evil laugh while watching every move that they'd made and listening in on their conversations. That image made her shiver. She needed a viable option. She was thinking hard *where* and then an idea came to her. She smiled. She changed lanes and drove faster. She knew where she was going now.

• • •

The man in the white Malibu drove down Wallace Avenue for a while and then slowly turned left on Emerson Avenue.

Caleb turned left very slowly while searching for any signs of danger lurking around the corner with his two watchful eyes. When he completed the turn, the Malibu could no longer be seen on the road. For a brief second, he felt panic, thinking that they'd been made or they'd lost him. As if Yuul read his mind, she pointed slightly up the road to the right. He then saw the tail end of the man disappearing into a house and then light filling its entranceway and main floor.

"Let's go." Yuul unbuckled her seatbelt.

Caleb grabbed Yuul by the arm. "Where to?"

"The house he just went into."

"For what? To torture him to death?"

"Duh!"

Caleb's eyes smiled. "We've got the license plate number and the address. I think it's a pretty good couple of hours of work."

"And his pictures." Yuul showed pictures of the man walking back to his Malibu after the chase in the hotel.

"He looks pissed." Caleb's eyes grinned a little and stopped. "Let's check in on Liz."

Yuul took out her phone and pressed 'Liz'. "Where are you?" A pause. "Okay. Text me the address." Another pause. "He's from Witless Bay. He won't find it. We need the address." Yuul smiled a little. "Swear to God. It's in Newfoundland. It's next to Dildo." Yuul let out a roar of laughter.

"Witless Bay is not next to Dildo," Caleb couldn't believe he said the word out loud.

"This summer, for sure. Now, text me the address. We'll do Google Maps or just end up driving straight forever."

Liz, the Neighbour

• • •

A man sat at a table in the dimly lit kitchen of a coach house on Thirty Road in Grimsby, Ontario having his 10th coffee of the night. He'd been patiently waiting for a call from his ex-subordinate for a debriefing on how the mission had gone down. The mission should've been completed hours ago. He should've already received a call reporting its status. Yet, it hadn't happened. A strain of deep discontent had been brewing for some time underneath his calm demeanour.

When he clicked his cellphone to check the screen for the hundredth time, he finally heard a chirping noise telling him that the wait was over. *5:12 a.m.* He shook his head in irritation.

"Sir, Adam Doyle here."

No codename for this mission? the man thought. "What's the status?"

"Failure to execute, Sir!" Doyle said in his usual boisterous voice.

Feeling the veins in his neck begin to throb, the man said curtly, "Give me the details."

"I parked the car in my favourite spot on Culnan Avenue at twenty-one hundred hours. While waiting for strike time, I was feeling sentimental—"

"Did you infiltrate the enemy line?" the boss said while breathing deeply.

"Yes, Sir!"

"Tell me where it went wrong."

It's a really good question, Doyle thought. He remembered vividly the first domino that had knocked over the rest – the freaking mouse. He told his exsuperior officer who wanted him to address him as Troy now, about everything, starting from the freaking mouse and ending with him losing the targets at the hotel. He told Troy everything except for the part where he'd screamed like a little girl when he'd stepped on the mouse.

While listening to his boss's increasingly rapid and heavy breathing sounds, Doyle quickly wrapped up his report. "I understand that you might feel it's all fucked up, but it's actually not that bad, Sir. Since we're living civilian lives now, let me put it in civilian terms – Situation Unchanged, Still Fucked Up, which can actually be a beautiful thing. Nothing's changed. I just need one more chance to carry out the strike, which I'm more than happy to do."

Troy screamed in his head, *just because you used the words and not the acronym SUSFU, it doesn't make it a civilian term, you shit pump!* Troy wanted to kill Doyle right there and then, if only he knew how to reach out and grab Doyle through the wireless airwaves, he would have. He wanted to smash Doyle's head into a wall repeatedly while choking the life out of him.

"Sir? Sir? I guess I lost—"

"You're right," Troy cut Adam off again. "You should strike again. Give me the plate number of the get-away car."

"Uhh..."

"What do you mean *uhh*?" Troy yelled.

"I didn't bother with it. I just assumed that they Ubered."

When this is over, I will kill you. Troy promised himself. After imagining 10 different ways of ending him, his breathing returned to normal. "Stand by. I'll see if we have anyone at 22 Division to look into the police report filed on tonight's case. Over and out.

22

SUNDAY, DECEMBER 8

Jeffrey was woken up by the chirping phone on his nightstand. Jeffrey looked over at the other side of his bed while reaching for his phone. It was empty. He sincerely hoped that his wife was quietly working away in her office, not chasing off after a bad guy in their backyard.

He checked the caller on the screen - Liz. Mechanically his forehead creased. *Why are you calling me at 6:00 a.m.? You better be locked in your washroom and need me to bring the key.*

"Jeffrey, before you say anything, remember you won't be the only one who's listening in on our conversation," Liz gushed out.

Liz, the Neighbour

Jeffrey didn't like the tone of Liz's voice. She sounded as if she was talking while being chased by a pack of dogs. But he got the gist of what she was saying – *Don't yell.* "What is it?"

"I'm at Mr. Sandhu's with the people who might hold the last missing piece to your puzzle. Come here around 9 with Ella and Charlie. Yuul and Caleb are already here with me."

Despite the many questions that he had, he said under his breath, "Okay."

• • •

Jeffrey knocked on the front door of Mr. Sandhu's house at 9:00 am. Ella stood behind him. The front door slid open in under 3 seconds as if someone was already waiting at the door.

"Good morning," A small white old lady greeted them with a big grin on her face, holding the door open for them. "Small world, isn't it?"

Dumbfounded, Jeffrey stood, transfixed by the old lady. He recognized her right away. How could he not? She'd made such a strong impression on him at their first meeting. However, seeing her here at Mr. Sandhu's left him flabbergasted.

As baffled as Jeffrey, Ella said, "Fancy meeting you here."

Jeffrey turned to Ella. "You know her, too?"

"She's the famous Nancy Drew." Ella smiled.

"Let's talk inside." Birdie waved them in as if she owned the house.

"How are you?' Jeffrey said, following Birdie in.

"How much time do you have?" Birdie said without turning back.

"Uh…"

"Wait in the living room. I'm busy helping Mr. Sandhu with breakfast."

"That's the breakfast that you actually want to drive miles for." Ella said teasingly as she followed Jeffrey in.

Jeffrey turned to Ella and shook his head disapprovingly for a second before he turned left, into the living room, where he found Agnes sitting on the couch. "How are you?"

"My hip hurts like hell. Other than that, I'm peachy," Agnes flashed the most adoring grandmotherly smile at Jeffrey.

Charlie arrived twenty minutes later. He saw Ella at the front door, waiting for him to come in.

She put her arm out towards him, her palm open.

He held her hand in his hand and whispered, "I miss you even when I'm with you."

• • •

Everybody made their plates from the food that was nicely spread out on the dining table and ensconced themselves in the living room with their breakfasts. They started working on their food

"Liz, what is this about?" Jeffrey wanted to know. In his mind, the wait had been long enough and it had to end now. He wanted to know why Ed, Birdie, Agnes and a man in his 30s were here at Mr. Sandhu's.

Liz put her fork down on her plate and pointed over at Agnes. "Let me introduce Agnes Winter to y'all."

Agnes gave a brief nod with a smile.

"Her nephew was our first client who hired us to locate her. Next to Agnes is Birdie Pemberton a.k.a. Nancy Drew, a.k.a. Agnes's homie. Early this morning, I got a call from Birdie asking me to pick them up. Yuul caught me just as I was leaving. She wanted to come, but I had four people to pick up, so I said no."

"And then I said I would wake *Jeffrey* up," Yuul said, nodding her head proudly. "You see? I'm listening to you *all the time*. But Liz told me not to."

"Did you just throw me under the bus?"

Yuul smiled her lopsided smile.

While squinting at Yuul, Liz continued, "This was supposed to be a simple job."

Bamboozled, Birdie said, "A simple job even though I told you it was a matter of life and death?"

Liz scratched her head. "In my defence, you didn't explain anything." Liz turned to Jeffrey. "Plus, I figured that you needed a good night sleep. And then, Yuul told me she would hitch a ride and she went and got Caleb."

Narrowing his eyes at Yuul, Jeffrey said, "Okay, you and I are going to talk about this later. Anyway, then what happened?"

Caleb then explained to Jeffrey what they had seen. "Your wife wanted to walk into the house and torture him, but I said we should call it off."

"Nice!" Liz punched Caleb in the arm.

"Oww," Caleb rubbed his arm. His eyes were ever slightly smiling.

Eyeing Caleb, Yuul said, "You just made it to my list of people I should remember."

"What does that mean?" Caleb wanted to know.

"You should look over your shoulders," Mr. Sandhu chimed in. "She can just touch your shin and make you cry like a baby in his wet diaper."

"I'm military. Nothing scares me," Caleb said sternly, averting Yuul's gaze.

"Are you? My second son is with the Royal Canadian Air Force," Mr. Sandhu said proudly. "You?"

"Army," Caleb said casually but didn't elaborate.

"So, why are we here?" Jeffrey wanted to know.

"Can you guess what triggered all this?" Liz asked.

"What?"

"A phone call that they made to Wylie," Liz said.

"What phone call?" Jeffrey asked, staring Birdie straight in the eye.

Birdie put down her fork and pointed her finger at Will. "That's my grandson Will. He had something that might be helpful to your investigation. So, we called Wylie and told him to follow up on it. We called Wylie because we had his business card, not yours."

Jeffrey recalled the day he'd visited Ed's with Wylie. He clearly remembered the moment where he'd been about to hand out his card, but Wylie had hurriedly given his card to Birdie instead. Jeffrey sucked in a gulp of air. "What information?"

No one answered. A silence fell and filled the space.

"Birdie," Ed said in a hoarse voice, "do you want me to go to the other room? It's not like I'm in a moving vehicle where I can't jump out. If keeping me in the dark would make you feel better, then just do that." Ed put his plate down on the coffee table and stood up.

"Please sit," Birdie said. "You're already in so much pain."

"We all are," Ed said. "Being kept in the dark makes me feel more powerless and angry. If this is not what you want, let me hear it. I want to know."

"Okay," Birdie said. "Please sit."

Ed sat down on the couch. "Birdie?"

"On Wednesday, Will caught the news about Adam the prosecutor being charged for Maddie's murder. He told us about another Adam whom Maddie had met at the Mississauga Hospital. He was the guy that Maddie went out on a date with that night.

"How do you know it wasn't the same Adam?" Ed said looking at Will. His clenched fists were trembling in silence.

Birdie held Ed's trembling hand with her bony hand.

Will said, "Maddie and Adam Brooks, the prosecutor, were long time friends. Maddie was a good friend with Brooks' wife as well. Maddie told me about the Adam that she met at the hospital a couple of weeks ago when she injured her ankle. She told me about the date."

Dropping his shoulders limply, Ed looked at Will. "Are you sure Adam Brooks is not her murderer?"

Will just nodded.

Birdie unleashed her grip from Ed's and gently tapped his hand.

"Go on," Ed said to Birdie.

Birdie gazed into Ed's eyes feeling unsure if she should go on or drop it.

"I want the real killer," Ed said through gritted teeth. "When we catch him, I'll make him suffer."

"I'll help you," Caleb said solemnly.

"Me too," Will said his arm wrapped around Ed's.

While rubbing Will's arm, Ed looked at Caleb. "Who are you?"

"I'm the brother of Adam Brooks – the man who's been wrongly accused of Madison Cooper's murder. We have a common goal – find the real killer and beat him to death."

Ed nodded in approval.

"Jeffrey should tickle him while you beat him to death," Liz said, recalling what Jeffrey had done to Yuul on their honeymoon.

Yuul slowly nodded. "That'll make him go mad before he dies."

"I've never seen this side of you," Will said to Liz in incredulity.

"I hope your future husband isn't ticklish," Agnes said, looking at Liz.

Dang! Will muttered under his breath. He was very ticklish.

Ed showed a little smile for the first time since the death of his beloved granddaughter. "I like it. I approve of this method."

"Birdie, can you please continue?" Jeffrey said.

"Okie-dokie. Down the line, I told Wylie that we were gonna drop by next week and check on their progress."

"But he said, don't trouble yourselves," Agnes chimed in.

"And," Birdie said, "I told him it was no trouble at all since I had to speak to Tim and Sam about the Wild Peach case anyway. Tim Johnson and Sam O'Hara are also detectives."

"They're in my squad," Jeffrey said. "What's the Wild Peach case? I haven't heard about it."

Birdie looked around the room before she went on. "Wild Peach is a retirement home. A few months back, Agnes told me about the place. It's affordable, and they offer good food and lots of fun activities. She told me I should move in. She said that they always have rooms available. I thought to myself if the place is that good, they should've been packed with people and a long waiting list to boot."

Agnes put her plate down on the coffee table. "I said to Birdie, this is a retirement home. Old people die all the time. Maybe, such tasty food speeds up the process a little, but nothing unusual."

"I thought okay that could be it. Then, Agnes dropped a big bomb on me. She said that the home had encouraged them to invite their friends – the ones who were all alone in the world. The people at the home said that they were happy to be the friends and family that these people needed. Friends and family my foot." Birdie's forehead creased in disgust. "Anyway, it was clear to me all they wanted was people with no children and no next of kin. Why? Insurance scam, what else? So, I went there undercover. While staying there, I did see things I shouldn't have, like the suspicious deaths of some of the residents, *and* I also heard rumours of some staff members that had been killed before my time there."

"Why didn't you take it to the police?" Jeffrey wanted to know.

"I did. I went to the police station on College Street. I heard that homicides were normally investigated by detectives from that division. That's how I met such a sweet detective, Tim Johnson, and a not so sweet detective, Sam O'Hara. Tim said he would look into the staff cases, which he did. He actually called me to let me know what he'd found out. One nurse fell, slipping on the staircase resulting in a broken neck. Another nurse is believed to have been murdered by her boyfriend. That case is still ongoing. The third nurse was killed in a random shooting. A two-man-team drove by a shopping mall and shot up the place. The third nurse was one of the people who got shot that day."

"I remember seeing that on TV," Ella said.

"When you said some staff members, are those three nurses you were referring to or is there more?" Jeffrey asked.

"Those three nurses are the only ones I heard about, but there might be more," Birdie said.

Jeffrey said, "What about the suspicious deaths of residents? What leads you to believe there was foul play involved?"

"Like we told Liz and Ella before, they were the picture of health one day and suddenly dead the next."

"Anything else?" Jeffrey asked.

Birdie shook her head. "You're just like them." She shot a dirty look at Liz and then Ella, recalling their reaction when she'd told them. "Anyway, the day after I went to the police station about it, I don't know how, but the home found out about it. That's what got me kicked out of the home. A little after that, another resident, Jason Reindeer, dropped dead. A good friend of Jason's, Tom Bauer, also coincidentally dropped dead right after he caused a stir over Jason's death. They said Tom had a heart attack. Ha, heart attack my

Liz, the Neighbour

FOOT! After that I got Agnes out of there as quick as I could. That was mid September. Once Agnes and I teamed up, we did drive up there a couple of times to see what we could see. That was until my car got totalled."

"Your car was totalled?" Will asked. "Did you get in an accident? Were you hurt? Why didn't you call me?"

"I'm fine." Birdie laid her bony hand assuringly on Will's shoulder trying to soothe his worries. She looked him in the eye and smiled. "Show me a smile."

Will smiled back at his grandma.

"What a handsome boy you are!" Birdie patted on Will's back. "Where was I? Oh, yes. My car was totaled. After that, we had to stop sneaking around. In late September, I saw Maddie and told her all about it. She said that she was going to look into it. Right before she broke her ankle, she told me she was starting to make some headway and wanted to fill me in on it next week. And then…" Birdie looked over at Ed, her eyes moist.

"You called Wylie on Wednesday," Jeffrey said, "and somebody tried to kill you early this morning. If Wylie had anything to do with it, why would he wait until now? Why not Thursday or Friday?"

"Maybe it's because we had guests over at our house," Birdie said. "Maddie's father and his family stayed with us the last two days."

"Hmm…" Jeffrey was positive that Birdie was right on the money. *Why was Madison Cooper murdered? Why was Adam Brooks chosen to take the fall? How long and in what capacity has Wylie been involved in crimes? Who are Rob and Doreen? What are their roles in the crime world? Birdie holds key evidence to Madison's murder. Is this why someone tried to kill her? Wild Peach, a retirement home. People are dead. An insurance scam? Too many pieces to put together. Do I have all pieces to complete the puzzle, or is there more to come?*

"Do you know what else I found out?" Birdie said.

Birdie's voice drew Jeffrey out of his deep thoughts. "What?"

"Wild Peach often took us on field trips down to the States. After we came from those trips, I saw men removing crates from the bus. Today, I saw one of those men in my house trying to kill me."

"What?!" Jeffrey exclaimed.

"Uh-huh." Birdie nodded, a twinkle in her eye.

His jaw dropped open for a quite a spell and it stayed open until Birdie closed it for him. "I need a break." Jeffrey said. "It's gonna be a long day. Let's grab some food."

Will sprang to his feet. "I'll go get lunch for all of us." He pulled at the edge of Liz's red wool sweater. "Come with me."

Liz stood up. "I don't know the area. We should take Tejas with us."

"I'm sure we can manage it," Will said.

Caleb stood up, 6'4" from the ground up, he cast a mighty shadow over the others in the room.

"Where are you going?" Jeffrey looked up at Caleb, stretching his neck as far as he could extend it.

"I'm going with them," Caleb said to Jeffrey. "They need protection."

"We don't need protection. This part of the city is safe from all those bad people," Will protested, glaring at Caleb. He felt small standing next to Caleb. Will didn't like that.

"When Liz picked you up," Caleb said, "you probably thought so, too."

"All of you sit down, now. Nobody is going anywhere. We're ordering in." Jeffrey said in as deep a voice as he could muster, making it known he was the one with the most testosterone.

23

SUNDAY, DECEMBER 8

They all sat around the living room with plates of food and soft drinks. The sound of chewing, chatting and drinking engulfed the room.

After having another big bite of a pineapple, pepperoni ham pizza, Liz dabbed her mouth with a paper napkin. "About Friday, November 22…"

"What about it?" Birdie said.

"That was the night that Gerald saw Wild Cat for the first time, and that was also the date that Maddie met the other Adam at the hospital. We might have 5 culprits instead of 4 – Wylie, Rob, Doreen, Wild Cat and the other Adam. It could be a coincidence, but Madison and Prosecutor Adam both might've had unexpected visitors that day."

"Why is that important?" Caleb wanted to know.

"Suppose, Wild Cat and the other Adam were each sent out – one to kill Adam Brooks and the other Maddie on that day. But they both encountered the unexpected. Madison came out and broke her ankle. She ended up in the hospital. As for Adam Brooks, he had guests over and Gerald happened to see Wild Cat prowling around and threw his book at him. Somehow, Madison and the other Adam struck up a conversation. I'm thinking that's where this elaborate murder scheme was first hatched."

Jeffrey nodded. It finally answered the one thing that had been bothering him the most: *Why did this guy make a point of yelling out his name to Birdie?* Jeffrey slowly clapped his hands in admiration. "It's brilliant."

"Of course, it is. It's your sister's," Agnes teased.

"The supposition makes sense," Charlie said, "but what's the motive? Why did they want to kill Madison and Adam?"

"Wild Peach," Birdie said.

"Only if Brooks is or was somehow involved with Wild Peach, too," Charlie said.

Eyeing Charlie, Jeffrey said, "Find out what he was working on just before his arrest. Ask him about Wild Peach. And also find out when was the last time he saw Maddie or heard from her."

Charlie nodded.

Ella turned to Ed and asked, "Can I have Maddie's laptop?"

Ed nodded.

"I'll go pick it up," Will said.

"I'll escort you," Caleb volunteered.

Will raised his right eyebrow to object but saw Caleb's look of determination. Will nodded instead.

Looking at Jeffrey, Liz said, "We have to check the CCTV from the hospital and compare it with what time Gerald saw Wild Cat. Plus, if we can get a picture of the other Adam, Yuul can tell us if Wild Cat and the other Adam are the same person or not. Can you get us the CCTV footage?"

"I don't think I can convince the hospital to release the CCTV footage without a warrant."

"What do you have to lose?" Ella said. "Just call them up and see what they say. If they say yes, Liz and I go pick it up."

"True enough. I'll make the call and see what they say," Jeffrey said.

"I'll go with Ella," Charlie said. "We could use some alone time."

"Did you already forget that you're going to see Brooks tomorrow?" Jeffrey said.

"No. I can go with her after my visit with Brooks."

"Maybe, I can drive," Ella said in excitement.

"You mean you want to drive *my car*?" Charlie said.

"Yes, I need practice," Ella said.

"She really does need the practice," Liz agreed.

"I'll give you anything you want. Do you need a new heart? No problem. You can take mine. Do you want my wallet? You can have it. Just don't tell me you want to drive my car."

"Okay." Ella's shoulders drooped, her bottom lip jutted out and her eyes darted to the floor.

"Okay?" Charlie carefully studied Ella's face.

"Yes, it's okay." With sadness in her eyes, Ella gave Charlie a weak smile.

"Okay, you can drive but please, please don't hurt my baby."

"Which baby?"

Charlie took a deep breath and said, "Of course, I meant you, baby. What else? I mean who else."

Jeffrey shook his head. "You're worse than me."

Charlie locked Ella's pinky with his. "That's questionable."

"Ahem." Liz cleared her throat. "We've got to find out what time Gerald yelled out Wild Cat on Friday, November 22."

Looking over at Liz, Ella said, "We should ask Gerald tomorrow morning."

Liz nodded. "Just out of curiosity, how easy is it to steal a car?"

"That's actually a great question," Jeffrey said excitedly. "Charlie, ask Brooks if he talked to anyone after he parked his car on the night in question. His baby is a 2019 Audi A6."

Charlie let out an appreciative whistle: *Fweet!* "That's one fine car."

"You don't say," Jeffrey said. "Anyway, a car like that, you can't just break into it. You have to be in close proximity to the car's key fob, so you can jam the signal."

"I know what you mean. I'll ask him about it," Charlie said.

Turning to Caleb, Jeffrey said, "I need you to spy on Wylie. I could send the three amigos, but Wylie already knows their faces."

"Snoopy is my middle name," Caleb winked. "What do you need?"

"I don't even know where he lives. Follow him around and see what you can find out. I think I'll be chained to my desk all day tomorrow. Come to my station tomorrow around 4:00 p.m. and wait in the parking lot. After work, I'll walk out to the parking lot with Wylie. Start from there."

"Will do," Caleb said to Jeffrey. He checked his watch and said, "Can I have everyone's phone numbers?"

"Why don't you give me yours?" Ella said, "I'll make a contact list and send the list to you all."

Jeffrey nodded. "That's a great idea."

"I've got to go to the airport to pick up my parents and then Anya, Adam's wife. If there's anything else I can do, let me know." Caleb turned to Will. "When do you want to pick up the laptop?"

"I guess the earlier, the better." Will looked up at the ceiling, trying to figure out a reasonable time to get up at to get it done. After some thought, he finally made up his mind. "Let's say 12 o'clock."

Caleb narrowed his eyes at Will. "You mean 12 o'clock tonight?"

"No, no!" Will looked at Caleb like he was crazy. "12 o'clock noon tomorrow."

"Hah," Caleb let out a short mocking laugh. "8 o'clock sharp tomorrow morning, I'll pick you up. Where are you going to be?"

"No way! That's way, way too early." Will vehemently shook his head.

"Tsk tsk. Because of you, Canada can't have a bright future that's for sure," Birdie said.

"At least, he's America's problem for now," Agnes said smiling.

Everybody laughed except Yuul. She was with Will on this. She didn't know why people were so obsessed with getting up early. She quietly just shook her head.

Liz, the Neighbour

"It'll be better for all of us if we bring him home to our place tonight," Jeffrey said. "We'll sneak him in and then sneak him out over to your back door tomorrow morning. You can take him from there."

"Send him by 8. We don't want to waste a minute. I want to get Adam out of jail asap."

His eyes narrowed and his lips tightened, Will said, "You should be nicer to the guy who's helping you out."

"Good point. I'll buy you a coffee. I've got to run. Anything else?"

Jeffrey said, "Nothing I can think of right now. If there's anything, we'll contact you."

"Got it," Caleb said, standing up. "Thank you for all your help."

They watched Caleb dash out the door and turned their attention back to each other.

With such tender eyes, Will looked at Birdie, and then Ed and then Agnes. "You should stay at my house in Hollywood until this all blows over."

They thought about it but shook their heads.

Birdie said, "Until this is over, we're sticking close. We'll stay in a hotel."

"You should stay here with us," Mr. Sandhu suggested. "I need someone to babysit Tejas."

"Dad, I'm 17 years old. I don't need a babysitter." Tejas protested.

Will liked the idea of having people around them. At a time like this, it would be good for them to stay with some kind hearted strangers like the Sandhus. More than anything, it would give him some comfort having someone keep an eye on Birdie and Agnes. Will liked the idea a lot. "What about this? If you let them babysit you, I'll take you to Hollywood when all this is over."

Tejas thought about it for a minute and then shook his head. "No, not good enough."

Will knew that he needed to play a big card. What could it be? Who could it be? Of course, it had to be Anissa Walsh – a sensational Canadian songbird who was stealing every young boy's heart in the world right now. Luckily, he knew her on a personal level. "I'll introduce you to Anissa Walsh."

With his eyebrows raised, Tejas put his hand over his heart. "Anissa Walsh?"

"Yes," Will said, smiling.

Tejas nodded aggressively.

"But you have to listen to them," Will said. "And at the same time, you have to keep an eye on them. Make sure they don't sneak out. Can you do that?"

"We're not teenagers," Agnes and Birdie protested.

"You're acting like you are," Will said.

Tejas gestured V-sign fingers first at his eyes and then at Birdie, Agnes and Ed. "I'm watching you."

Everybody laughed.

When the laughter died down, Ella raised her eyebrows. "How are we going to explain Will to our noisy neighbours? Those devils are always listening in on us."

Will smiled an enigmatic smile. "Why don't we stick to the truth? Literally, Liz is my ex-girlfriend who just reappeared into my life in a very strange manner. Let's just build a story based on that." He suddenly but gently held Liz's hand and looked at her. His eyes were dark now, his expression serious.

The room fell in silence. All eyes were on Will as he held his gaze on Liz as if no one else in the room mattered, as if no one else in the world existed.

"Once we re-connected, feeling a desire stronger than ever, Liz takes me home and locks me up in her bedroom because," a pause, "because she doesn't want to let me go ever again," another long pause, "and because she wants to keep me all to herself." Will slowly moved in closing the gap between him and Liz and then stopped an inch away from her.

Everybody's heart pumped expecting a kiss.

After 10 seconds of a wait that seemed much longer, Will turned, gave a slight curtsy to his audience and turned his brilliant simile on them. Turning to Jeffrey, Will said in a casual tone, "That's how I end up in your house and live there happily ever after."

Coming out of the spell that Will had just cast on her, Liz said, "We're just going to change the genre from a thriller to a teen flick. The theme is runaway teens."

"Do you have an idea?" Ella asked.

• • •

Jeffrey left Mr. Sandhu's house with Yuul and Ella at 4:00 p.m. Liz had originally planned to stay at Mr. Sandhu's until 7:00 p.m. In the end, she left at 5:00 p.m. instead, having yielded to Will's whimpering about how dangerous it could be driving late at night.

When they stepped outside, they saw the beautiful city night from the northeast corner of Toronto. The blue moonlight and the streetlights reflected off the snow-covered street and shone back in a variety of colours. The temperature was -2°C but with the wind chill, it felt like -10. It was another typical cold evening in Toronto. Yet, something about the cold street covered by snow on a dimly lit night made Liz feel helplessly romantic.

Wrapped up in her warm jacket, she buried her hands deep in her jacket pockets and carefully walked onto the sidewalk. As she was about to cross the street, she felt a strong grip on her arm.

"What is it?" Liz said casually while looking at the collar of his jacket. She just didn't dare to look him in the eye right now. She was too confused and too dazed. When she'd held his gaze earlier at Mr. Sandhu's, she'd felt something so wonderfully familiar but at the same time oddly strange.

Will put his hand in her jacket pocket and locked her hand in his. "Let's go. It's too cold to stop here."

Just like he said when he held my hand for the first time, Liz froze on the spot. She'd almost convinced herself that that'd actually never happened after going through one too many misfortunate relationships. She'd almost believed that she'd imagined it all.

A light pull on her hand broke the spell. Liz smiled as she crossed the street with Will to where her car was parked.

"You got to let go of my hand," Liz said, standing next to her car.

"Just one more minute."

They stood there on the street, looking each other in the eye silently before they got in the car.

"I guess I've finally grown a pair," Will said, looking at Liz sweetly.

Liz, the Neighbour

Liz gave a quick side-glance at Will as she merged onto the main road.

"Keep your eyes on the road," Will said.

"What do you mean?" Liz wanted to know.

"Back in our university days, it took me over a month just to hold your hand."

"I don't think it was a month. It was more like after a few meals."

Will thought that Liz was cute. She had no idea what it had taken to just have one meal with her. That brought back old memories. How naïve and shy he'd been. After he'd met Liz through their mutual friend Karl at school, he'd walked around the campus just to find her and run into her as if it'd been totally accidental. So many days in the cold, he'd stepped on his foot with his other foot to keep them from going numb.

Will smiled. "If you establish the timeline based on how many meals we had, you could say that. But you have to think about all those days I was lurking around in the shadows waiting for you to show up alone."

Liz laughed. "That makes you a creepy stalker."

"I was, I admit it." Back then, Will had wanted to look cool, and he'd had no idea how to pursue a girl because he'd never had to. With a smile on his face, Will said, "Did you miss me at all?"

Liz just stared at the windshield.

"I did. I imagined many times that I come back into your life and sweep you off your feet." Will smiled a self-deprecating smile. "But I was never able to find the right time to do it. You seemed to always be in a relationship. When I heard from Cheryl that you were accused of murder, I was going to come back to rescue you. But I was in the middle of shooting a new movie. The production company threatened to sue me if I broke my contract with them. So, I had no choice. I had to finish it. I finally finished the project and went to the wrap-up party. I got drunk out of my mind that night. I was so excited about the prospect of seeing you again. That was the night I got the call from my grandma about Maddie." Will stared into the ceiling of the car, trying not to drop tears again. "On the plane here, I wished I could cry on your shoulder." He couldn't hold the tears back anymore. He covered his face, shaking with sobs.

"I'm here. Talk to me," Liz said.

Will told Liz about his little sister, Madison Cooper. How pretty she'd been. How adorable she'd been, and how she'd filled a hole in his heart while growing up. He told Liz about the times Maddie had been mischievous and naughty. He told Liz about the times Maddie had been so upset and agitated during her parents' divorce and one day, at age 12, how she'd left home without telling her parents and had taken the subway and buses all alone just to come to see him. He told Liz about how ineffectual he'd been feeling since Maddie's death. He wanted to console Ed and Tina but he couldn't be a big enough man for them as he himself was sinking deeper into a bottomless pit that he didn't want to swim out of just yet. When Tina had lost her best friend, Will's mother, she hadn't just sat in the dark and cried. She'd consoled and comforted Birdie. She'd made sure that she was a part of their lives and that they'd always been a part of hers.

"I want to be there for her and for Ed but I don't know how," Will said. He felt tired. He felt sleepy.

Liz, the Neighbour

Since the time he'd gotten the call from his grandma about Maddie, he hadn't felt any of that. He'd just felt pain and anger. He'd felt confused, paralyzed and overwhelmed all at once. Now, he felt sad more than anything.

"They know you're there for them," Liz said while making the turn onto York Ridge Road from York Mills Rd. She parked the car on the street and killed the engine.

"Do you think so?" Will asked.

"I don't think. I know it. Like you knew she was there for you, she knows you're there for her and Ed," Liz said, looking at Will's tired eyes

He smiled a weak smile. "Is it show time?"

"If you're up to it." Liz smiled back.

• • •

When they walked in the house, Jeffrey, Yuul and Ella were all in the living room, waiting for them as discussed.

"Where were you?" Jeffrey yelled. He turned to Will. "Who's this?"

"His name is Will. We used to date in university. After graduation, we went our separate ways. Last night, fate brought us together again. We started talking, and it was like we never left each other. It was so magical. All the old feelings washed over me. Our feelings were so strong, so overwhelming that we couldn't bear the thought of being apart again. Once we met, I could hear the fireworks going off in the sky, blasting into beautiful shapes and lighting the brightest light of the darkest sky."

"What is all this gibberish?" Jeffrey said. "You're talking like a crazy woman. And frankly, I don't care about your love life. Don't just disappear on me."

"Don't tell me what to do. You're not my dad. You probably forgot how love makes you feel."

"Are you saying he doesn't love me anymore?" Yuul asked.

"You tell me. Obviously, he doesn't understand how I felt last night."

"Be that as it may, it still doesn't give you the right to just take off without telling anyone," Jeffrey said.

"Sorry about that part."

Jeffrey took a deep breath and blew out. "OK. That's settled. But I still don't know why he's really here."

"Okay, don't get mad. He's just a bit down on his luck and needs a place to stay for a bit."

"Are you saying he's a jobless loser?" Jeffrey said.

"Don't be rude! He happens to be in between jobs. That's all."

"I don't care if he's in between jobs or he's working two jobs. He's not staying here," Jeffrey said.

"Give us until the end of the month. By then, we'll find a place to move to."

Jeffrey didn't know if he should say *yes* now or if he should put up a fight for a little longer.

Silence fell as no one was sure what to say next. It was almost a miracle that they had carried on with the conversation for this long. They realized that they should've had a well-thought-out script although it was definitely too late for regrets now. They just shook their heads at each other, blaming each other for the awkward silence.

Liz, the Neighbour

After a while, Ella finally said, "It's already late. Why don't you just let him stay tonight and you can talk about it tomorrow?"

Jeffrey gave a thumps-up to Ella. "Just make sure he's gone before I come home tomorrow."

24

MONDY, DECEMBER 9

Liz tried to wake Will up at 7:30 a.m. believing it would still give him enough time to get ready for the trip but soon realized that she'd made a mistake. She should've woken him up a lot earlier. When she tried to wake him up, Will just pulled the big fluffy duvet up over his head and rolled himself up tight in the blanket. He looked a lot like a caterpillar in its cocoon. She couldn't help but laugh knowing that sooner or later, he would have to emerge from his cocoon to avoid suffocation, or so she thought. It turned out that she seriously underestimated him. He just made a little bigger gap around his head for breathing and continued to slumber away.

A good thing, I just happen know a drill sergeant, she smiled devilishly and walked out of the room.

Liz, the Neighbour

• • •

Leading Caleb up the stairs, Liz said quietly, "Do your thing."

"Yes, ma'am!"

Here we go again calling me ma'am. Liz wheeled around and pushed him slightly, at least that was what she thought she was doing until she saw Caleb flail his arms around in the air trying to keep his balance so as not to fall back down the stairs. *Gotta grab him!* She reached out quickly to grab him before he fell.

Caleb saw Liz's hands coming at him. He instinctively knew what she had in mind. He knew, too, how it would end when a woman who looked like about 135 lbs with more curves than muscle power tried to save a 220 lbs man built of solid muscle: Both of them crashing down to the bottom of the stairs, and breaking body parts.

He flailed harder trying to move away from her grasp, but she was one heck of a determined lady: Save him. As her hands grabbed his arms, he stopped thinking, instinct and training kicked in and left him with only one thing in his mind: Save her.

By quickly twisting his left wrist, he grabbed her arm and pulled her towards his chest locking her tightly into him, he deftly spun around and made a spectacular leap down to the first landing. It wasn't a perfect 10, but in this case, he really did stick the landing.

Liz saw steam coming out of Caleb's head and ears. She knew what was coming and that she had to stop it. She swiftly put her hand over his mouth and whispered in his ear, "People are listening."

Caleb looked her right in the eye. She'd made him uneasy from the day 1, and she just made him feel inept. With her, he would never know which way she was going to jump next. She was unlike any life form he'd ever encountered on this planet. She was too much. She made him crazy.

Liz removed her hand and proceeded up the stairs once again, and Caleb followed her once again.

When Caleb walked into the room, Liz was already pointing her finger at the duvet. He studied the duvet with his careful eyes and saw the tip of a head poking out. That made him chuckle.

"Is there a bug upstairs?" Caleb whispered to Liz.

Liz shook her head, smiling widely.

Putting a serious look on his face, Caleb said in a typical drill sergeant voice although a slightly-toned-down version, "Rise and shine, soldier. Up and at 'em in three, two—"

"I'm up." The muffled sound came through the duvet when the countdown reached one, but there still wasn't any movement.

Caleb grabbed the duvet. "In three, I'm ripping off the duvet. Three, two—"

"Don't do that," Will said. He extricated himself from the duvet revealing himself fully, well all except for his bikini briefs.

Caleb hurriedly put the duvet back over Will's body. "You've got a lady standing here."

"Don't get me excited," Will turned to see Liz, but she was already gone.

"You have 5 minutes to get showered," Caleb pronounced.

Liz, the Neighbour

"No one can shower in 5 minutes," Will said as he rolled himself back into the duvet.

"4 minutes and 45 seconds."

"What are you going to do if I don't make it in time?"

"I'll take you downstairs in your little underwear and toss you out in the backyard."

"You think I'll let you?"

"You'll see in 4 minutes and 9 seconds."

Will looked Caleb up and down from head to toe and concluded that he must be around 6'4" tall, 220 lbs just in muscle alone. Being 6' tall and 197 lbs of more flab than muscle, Will didn't want to take the chance. He got up and put his pants on and headed for the bathroom.

• • •

Caleb didn't know what to make of Will. One moment, Will was all rich and famous, and then the next moment, he acted like a wounded cat. After all fuss over waking up, Will had been silent for most of the trip. When they turned onto Culnan Avenue, Will looked out the passenger side window.

"Do you think it's gonna be a nice day out today?" Will asked dolefully.

Caleb smiled, recalling the exact same conversation he'd had with Yuul in his car just two nights ago.

"What are you laughing at?" Will asked.

"I asked Yuul the same thing just the other day. You know what she said to me?"

"I don't like playing games."

"Games?"

"You already know that I don't know the answer."

"I don't like weather talk." Caleb chuckled.

"Fine, don't talk about it then," Will said clearly irritated.

"Haha. That's what Yuul said, 'I don't like weather talk.'"

Removing his seatbelt, Will said, "Let's go."

All business now, Caleb grabbed Will by his arm and shook his head. He scoped the area with his sharp eyes. When he was sure the coast was clear, he released his grip on Will's arm and said, "Follow me."

Caleb had Will unlock the front door while he continued to scan the area with his penetrating eyes. When the door was unlocked, Caleb gave Will a hand signal telling him to move off to the side. Caleb walked in first. He quickly searched the main floor to see if anyone was hiding anywhere. No one was, so he walked up the stairs with Will right on his heels. When Will hit the top of the stairs, Caleb made a hand gesture signalling for him to wait there. Caleb quickly but quietly moved around the house like a snake.

As he came out of Ed's bedroom, Caleb declared, "All clear."

Will walked over to Madison's room and slowly opened the door desperately wishing that he would find Maddie sitting at her desk typing away on her laptop. When the door was all the way open, he was once again forced to face reality – Maddie's gone. He walked inside and saw a thigh-high slit, V-neck red dress through a half-open closet.

The memory washed over him. Madison had picked it out when he'd taken her to the shopping district on Rodeo Drive this past summer. When she'd tried it on at the store, everybody had gasped for air. She'd

Liz, the Neighbour

looked so beautiful that she actually shone. People had always assumed that they were lovers. When they told them that they were sister and brother, people had had different reactions, and Maddie and Will had just laughed and laughed.

Will took another step and saw the crisp indigo ocean stripe duvet and held it in his hands. It was his Christmas gift to her last year.

He walked over to the desk and saw their first picture together, taken right after she'd poohed in his arms. Placed next to her laptop was a picture of the two of them at her high school graduation. Every step he took, more memories of Maddie flooded in.

"We have to go," Caleb said in a gentler tone.

"Yes," Will wiped his tears away with the back of his hand.

• • •

Liz and Ella went out the back door, walked through the backyard and knocked on Gerald's back door. No answer. They knocked on the door again. No answer. They banged hard on the door this time, and finally Gabriel toddled to the door.

"What's going on?" Gabriel said, standing there. "Why didn't you come to the front door?"

"We have our reasons," Liz said, smiling mischievously. "Can we come in?"

"Can you be quiet? Gerald is sleeping right now."

"Of course. We won't stay long," Liz said.

Gabriel stepped aside and Liz and Ella walked in and stayed close to the back door.

"How is Gerald doing?" Ella asked.

"He's had better days."

"We have a question for you," Ella said.

"What is it?"

"It's about the first time that Gerald saw Wild Cat, on that Friday, November 22, you said that Adam, his wife and her friend came out back because of the chaos. Do you remember telling us that?" Liz said.

"Yes, of course."

"Do you happen to remember what time it was when that happened?" Liz asked.

"No, not really."

"Tell us about the night. What were you doing before the incident?" Liz said.

"Hmm…" Gabriel stood with hands clasped behind his back, head bobbing. "It was after dinner. So, it was definitely after 7 o'clock. Gerald wanted some tea. His son, Jerry, insists that Gerald has only green tea. He hopes that it will slow down his deterioration. All we can do is hope. Anyway, we had our tea together. After tea, Gerald nodded off on the couch, and Jerry left. I turned the TV on and watched my favourite British crime drama. During the show, I went to the kitchen to make a late night snack and I remember seeing Gerald suddenly stand up and walk out of the living room. I just thought he was going to the washroom. The next thing I knew I heard him yelling away outside."

"What time does the English show come on at?" Ella asked.

"9 o'clock."

"Is it a one-hour show?" Ella asked.

"It's a 90-minute show."

"So, Wild Cat was here between 9 and 10:30 at night," Ella said.

"What about the second time?" Liz asked. "Adam heard Gerald yelling out Wild Cat again sometime between late Friday night, November 29 and early Saturday morning, November 30. It could've been midnight. It was a couple of days before Adam was arrested."

"Ah, I remember. Gerald's yelling got me out of my bed. Yes, it was definitely the middle of the night. It was a couple of days earlier right around midnight like you said."

"Thank you so much for your help," Ella said.

"Can you please not tell Rob and Doreen about our little visit today?" Liz said.

Waggling his eyebrows, Gabriel said, "What are you two up to?"

Liz covered her mouth in an attempt to suppress a burst of laughter. "We suspect that they might be the ones who let Wild Cat loose."

Gabriel pouted. "That's disappointing. They seemed to be nice people."

"Can you please not tell Mike and Abigail as well?" Ella said.

"What's the deal with them?"

"They seem to be very close to Rob and Doreen. You just never know," Ella said.

"That can be done with pleasure. Unless I really need to see how nasty some people can be, I try my best to avoid them."

"I know right?" Ella shook her head recalling the day they'd visited them.

"Do you know anything about Rob and Doreen?" Liz said.

"No, not really." Gabriel suddenly put his index finger over his lips. "Shh."

Liz and Ella heard a series of dry, chronic cough sounds coming from deep inside the house.

"That's my cue," Gabriel said.

"Thank you for everything again," Ella said.

"You might be right about Rob and Doreen." Gabriel said as he opened the door for them.

"What do you mean?" Ella wanted to know.

"I just remembered something. They were very unhelpful when Jerry asked them for some advice about retirement homes. Jerry was quite irked by it."

"What made Jerry ask them about retirement homes?" Ella quizzed.

"I don't know who told him, but Jerry was told that Rob and Doreen own some retirement homes. Anyway, I believe that they didn't even invite him inside their home. That's all."

"Interesting," Liz said, forming a steeple with her long fingers.

25

MONDAY, DECEMBER 9

Charlie Khoury drove along Eglinton Avenue East until he reached Birchmount Road. He turned right and then made another right turn. There it was the Toronto East Detention Centre. After walking through security, Charlie was escorted by a guard to the lawyer's visiting room. It was his first time visiting a prison. He was as nervous as anyone would be but he didn't show it.

He sat down in the chair and placed his briefcase on the table. He slowly took out a notebook and a ballpoint pen and slid the briefcase off to the side. He'd brought the notebook and the ballpoint pen because he didn't know what else he could or he should bring with him.

Fighting the urge to click the ballpoint pen open and closed again and again, he just stared at the pen as if trying to make it levitate like Houdini while he waited for Adam to be sent in.

When the door opened, Charlie raised his head and stood up to meet Adam Brooks expecting to see a Caleb-lookalike. He had never been so wrong! Adam Brooks wasn't anything like he'd expected. Like Caleb, Adam was clean-shaven and had greyish green eyes. They even had the same shade of dark brown hair in a crew cut although Adam's had more volume on top and on the sides than Caleb. The similarities ended there. Adam was 6' tall and slim, and had almost delicate features. In contrast, Caleb was really tall, rugged and hardened with six-pack abs.

They shook hands and sat down across from each other.

Adam Brooks wore a smile on his overall tired looking face. "Trust me we are brothers by blood. I had our DNA tested. Don't tell my brother or my parents. I just had to know for sure."

Charlie looked him in the eye, his right eyebrow ever so slightly raised. "People used to say no one could read me." He cleared his throat as he flipped the notepad open. "I'm Charlie Khoury, your attorney."

"I heard."

"What did Caleb tell you?"

"I just told you everything he told me."

Charlie's eyebrows were narrowing in confusion, but before they narrowed all the way, he got what Adam meant. He let out a chuckle and then re-adjusted his facial expression to a blank.

"Are you a criminal lawyer?" Adam said.

"No, I'm not, but let's not worry about that for now. When push comes to shove, you'll get one. For the time being, I'm the lawyer you need. Your brother agreed. Otherwise, I wouldn't be here today."

Adam bluntly scrutinized Charlie as if he was hiding anything.

After a bout of silent staring, Charlie asked, "Do you trust your brother?"

"Yes, I do." Adam nodded. "Do you know what he does for a living?"

Charlie tilted his head to one side.

Adam smiled. "Are you sure people said that you were hard to read?"

Charlie smiled. "I guess I've loosened up too much. I was told he's in the military."

"He is. Do you know just how big the military is?"

"Not really. No."

"It's *reeeally* big. People don't tend to give the Canadian Military enough credit. But they are fierce. My brother? He's the fiercest of the fierce military men. Don't give him unrealistic hope. He might not take it well if you come up short on your promise."

"You don't think you can be acquitted?"

"Whoever set me up set me up good."

"Can you read my mind now?" A mischievous smile slowly spread across Charlie's face.

"Hmm…"

"Your case is not as cut and dried as the bad people who've set you up had originally hoped. Can I ask you a few questions now?"

Adam stared at Charlie for another long moment and then slowly nodded his head.

"What were you working on prior to your arrest?"

Liz, the Neighbour

"You think this is related to one of my cases?"

"Yes."

"You can't be any more wrong. I prosecute petty crimes. Nobody kills anybody unless it's by accident. The people I deal with don't generally have the time or the brainpower *or* even the inclination to devise an elaborate scheme of this caliber."

"Hmm… That's disappointing." Charlie drummed the table with his fingers. "Does a place by the name of Wild Peach Estate mean anything to you?"

Adam involuntarily adjusted his silver metal framed round eyeglasses with his thumb and index finger.

"I got you. Didn't I? Tell me what you know about the home and how you got involved with them. Obviously, this wasn't one of the cases you were working on at the time of your arrest, was it?"

"Actually, it was, but not officially. I was working on it as a favour to Chris McAvoy, a Member of Parliament/MP. One of his constituents was killed during a drive-by shooting. The victim's name was Derek Sommer. His wife, Fanny Sommer, didn't believe that his death had been random. She was convinced that Derek had been killed by his employer, Wild Peach Estate. She said that before his death, he'd been afraid of his employer. Are you going to write this down?" Adam motioned towards the notepad in front of Charlie with his chin.

"This?" Charlie grinned. "I didn't bring it here to write on."

"Then, why did you bring it with you?" Adam narrowed his eyebrows.

"Haha. It's actually a funny story." Charlie grinned again. "I felt compelled to bring something in here

Liz, the Neighbour

with me, but I didn't know what you're allowed to bring in or not. In the end, I went with a safe choice – a notepad."

Adam just shook his head.

"Continue," Charlie said. "I might write it down if you say something important."

Adam shook his head again but went on. "After her husband's death, Ms. Sommer learnt that two other nursing assistants at Wild Peach Estate had also recently died. So, she filed numerous complaints with the police to try and get them to re-investigate her husband's death as well as the two other suspicious murders. But the police ignored all of her requests."

Charlie wrote 'Police' and then wrote 'BAD' beside and circled it. "You see I'm making notes."

Adam shook his head and went on. "So, she took the case to her MP, Chris McAvoy, who happens to be a family friend of mine. Chris asked me to meet with Ms. Sommer and dig into it for him as a personal favour to him. Chris thought that Ms. Sommer might be able to better accept the reality of it if it came from me, being a prosecutor and all. So, I looked into it. The police report on Derek Sommer's case was a one-liner – Killed in a random shooting. What else could you say about it? Before I checked off the box for completion, I wanted to quickly review Ms. Sommer's complaints and have a quick conversation with the officer assigned to the case if there still was one. You can't leave a job half-done, right?"

"Right." Charlie rolled his eyes. He didn't understand what Adam meant by half-done job.

Adam grinned. "Anyway, I went down to the police station, thinking 30 minutes in and out. My plan changed after going to the police station. There was no record of any complaint ever being filed by Ms. Sommer. Ms. Sommer sounded a little crazy, but I was sure that she wasn't lying about filing all those complaints. It was very odd, I thought. Since there was nothing to look into as far as Mr. Sommer's case, I drove all the way down to the retirement home and started probing the other two cases."

"Now we're talking." Charlie leaned forward. "What did you find out at the home?"

Adam shrugged. "Nothing much. I was able to meet up with the operations manager there. The manager told me what he knew about the other two murders. One nursing assistant was supposedly killed by her boyfriend. The other case involved a nursing assistant who slipped on a staircase, fell and broke her neck. The police came and concluded that it was accidental."

Charlie said, "They don't sound overly suspicious or connected for that matter. So, why did you keep working on them?"

"I don't know why," Adam shrugged, "but I went back and asked for a copy of the murder books for those two cases."

"Did you find anything?" Charlie wanted to know.

"In the domestic homicide case, the nursing assistant's name was Carol Stewart. She was shot by someone that used a Glock, and her boyfriend, Curtis Nutter, found her dead in her home. The police believe she was murdered by Curtis Nutter. Nutter owned guns and was definitely rough around the edges. However, no direct evidence was ever found that could link Curtis to the murder."

Liz, the Neighbour

Charlie furrowed his forehead. "The case doesn't appear to be linked to the home."

"I thought so, too." Adam nodded in agreement. "So, I moved onto the slip and fall case. The victim's name was Dalisay Aquino. According to the police report, there was no CCTV installed in the stairwell. There was no trace of a struggle on the victim's body. It looked like a legitimate case of slip and fall."

"I sense a *but* coming," Charlie said, hoping he guessed right.

"I'm not saying it wasn't. I just don't know why she was in the stairwell to begin with."

Charlie cocked his head to one side in confusion. "People use the stairs for a lot of reasons. Don't they?"

"True, but would you use the stairs if you were 60 years old and severely overweight"

"I'm guessing the answer should be no?"

"If you're 60 and overweight, you're more than likely to have joint pain. People with joint pain don't climb stairs if they can help it. That was why I couldn't stop looking into those murder cases."

"Did you meet the family of the slip and fall victim?" Charlie wanted to know.

"I talked to her husband, Rodrigo Aquino, and he confirmed that she had osteoarthritis. Mr. Aquino said that Ms. Dalisay had been distracted lately and talked about quitting her job shortly before her untimely demise."

"Hmm…" Charlie furrowed his forehead.

"That's what I thought. So, I went back again to the domestic case. I called Nutter and asked him if we could meet up. Understandably, he refused in the beginning but eventually he agreed. He's a third-generation farmer. All of his guns are hunting guns that he inherited from his grandfather. He never used a Glock in his life. The reason that the police didn't arrest him for the murder of Carol Stewart was because he had an alibi. Can you guess what his alibi was?"

"No."

"Opera."

"Opera?" Charlie asked with wide-eyed.

Adam nodded. "At the time of the murder, he was in Toronto attending an opera. He never told to anyone about his love for the opera. Carol was the first person that he confessed his passion for the opera to. They used to drive to Toronto to go to them. They were supposed to attend an opera the day she was murdered. But Carol was way too stressed out to go. He wasn't going to go, either, but she insisted that he go."

Charlie let out a sigh. "It's a lot to take in."

"That's how I felt, too. At the same time, I was exhilarated. I couldn't stop thinking about the cases. I was re-visiting the shopping mall shooting spree prior to my arrest. Ms. Sommer wasn't wrong about the first two cases. Why would she be wrong about her husband's case?"

"What did you find?"

"Nothing because I was arrested" Adam smiled a bitter smile.

Charlie checked his watch. "I was told that you and Maddie were friends. When was the last time you saw or heard from Madison?"

"The last time I saw her was when I met up with Ms. Sommer at the coffee shop. Ms. Sommer was very emotional. She cried a lot. I tried to console her. Maddie saw us from outside the coffee shop and misunderstood the situation. Maddie thought that I was cheating on Anya. She dragged me out of the coffee shop. She shouted and yelled at me. I tried to explain the situation to her, but she wasn't having any of it. Eventually, I told Maddie to butt out. Not long after the incident, Maddie called me and asked to meet up. She said that she had some questions about the woman I was with at the coffee shop. I got really irritated. I told her to give it a rest. It's not what you think and hung up. Maddie called me back a few times, but I didn't pick up. That was the last time I heard from her."

Charlie wrote in the notepad: **Adam bad**.

Adam narrowed his eyes at Charlie. "I'm telling Caleb."

Charlie looked Adam in the eye and slowly crossed it out.

"Smart choice."

Charlie checked his watch and asked, "Do you still have those files?"

"I did, but I'm not sure if I still have them. They're on my laptop, and I'm not sure if the police confiscated it or if it's still on my desk at home. Was Maddie somehow involved in the Wild Peach cases, too?"

"There's reason to believe she was. However, we'll know for sure after we pick up her laptop."

Adam pressed his lips together.

"Now, let's talk about the Friday night you drove your car for the last time before you got arrested. What time did you get home?"

"Around 5:00 p.m."

"Did you meet anyone after you parked the car?"

Adam thought about it and then he shrugged. "No one special."

Charlie clicked his ballpoint pen. "Does that mean you met no one?"

"I ran into my neighbours, Doreen and Rob."

A twinkle flashed in Charlie's eyes.

"Why does that interest you? They're just my neighbours."

"Their names keep popping up. Tell me where you ran into them and what you talked about."

"As I was driving up to my house, I saw them crossing over to my side of the street. We talked a bit about the weather and my wife."

"Why didn't you park the car in the garage?"

"My wife kept her car in the garage."

"This is good." Charlie put his notebook and ballpoint pen back in his briefcase. "I've got to hit one more place before the day ends. I just want you to know that Maddie might be able to help get your charges dropped."

"What do you mean?"

"I'll tell you all about it over drinks."

"You buying?"

"Only if you buy me one first"

• • •

Ella couldn't sit still. Her mind was racing with the detective stuff she was going to do with Charlie. It was exciting and nerve wracking all at once. Nothing on TV interested her. She had no one to talk to. Liz, Will and Yuul had left for Mr. Sandhu's right after they'd interviewed Gabriel about Wild Cat. She tried to hack Maddie's password-protected laptop, but her mind constantly drifted away to her upcoming quest. She knew that there was only one thing she could do to take her mind off things– work out.

She put the dirty dishes in the dishwasher and tidied up the rest of the kitchen. That didn't take too long. She walked upstairs and cleaned the hell out of her bathroom. When everything was squeaky clean, she took off her sweaty clothes and took a long, hot shower. She put on a black dress shirt and grey dress pants. She hoped that she looked just like the experienced, antagonistic detective that she'd once seen on TV. She grabbed a long grey dress coat and went downstairs.

She turned on the TV to make some noise just for Rob and Doreen's benefit. Her cellphone showed 12:47 p.m. when she eventually got a call from Charlie. She turned off the TV.

"Hi Charlie!" She said boisterously. *Get it? It's just a phone call from my boyfriend.*

"Ahaha. I take it you missed me a lot."

Ella swallowed. Charlie went off the script that they'd worked on last night. That threw her off her game. She stared into space and then decided the best thing was to just stick to the script. "Oh My Goodness! Your mom wants to see me. Why?"

Laughing hard, Charlie said, "Because she misses you, too."

"On My! Lebanese food? I don't know anything about it."

Laughing even harder, Charlie said, "What? You don't know anything about Lebanese food?"

Ella did a mental eye-rolling. "I guess I should learn sooner or later."

"Sooner will be good. I want you to feed me, shower me."

Her cheeks flushing at 100°, her heart beating hard, Ella forgot her next line in her script.

"After the shower, I want—"

"Okay, I'll go to your mom's." Ella hurriedly disconnected the call. Touching her cheeks with the back of her hands, Ella tried to think about boring stuff, the stuff that would bring her heart rate down.

What can I think about? Charlie naked… Oh no! No Charlie naked. Oh my! Her cheeks were burning up again. She fanned herself with her hands pacing back and forth.

Anything else but Charlie. Oh, Char… No, no, no, no, no… The front window caught her attention, and even though the curtains were drawn, she knew what was behind the curtains, Doreen and Rob.

That's right, Doreen and Rob!!! Bang, her mind was racing with detective stuff again. Her heart was palpitating with anxious thoughts that she would say something stupid at the hospital and embarrass herself.

Stop, Ella! Ella admonished herself. *Not everyone is mocking you. Let bygones be bygones and make new memories. Make a new past that you'll be happy with tomorrow. All I've got to do is just ask for a copy of the CCTV footage of the parking lot. Be vague about who I am. In the end, I'm not there alone. Charlie will be there. Mmm, Charlie… Naked…* Ella drooled.

26

MONDAY, DECEMBER 9

Ed just sat on the couch. One moment, he wanted to go home. He worried that Maddie would come home and not be able to find him anywhere. It would worry her. He didn't want to worry her. He was sure that this whole thing was one big mistake and that Maddie was still alive. In the next moment, he saw her dying on the bench in the playground. He was sure that he could save her if he rushed down there. In another, he would come back to the reality that Maddie had been taken away from him permanently. Nothing held any meaning for him now except revenge – Find the man who had taken her from him and take his life with his own hands. He imagined shooting the murderer with a machine gun. He imagined the murderer's guts pouring out of his body, blood gushing out everywhere. When the thought that Maddie was waiting for him to come home hit him again, he saw Tejas setting up the PlayStation out of the corner of his eye.

"Do you want to play?" Tejas said, handing the game controller over to Ed.

Looking at Tejas, Ed thought, *Why would he think I have any mind to play a game right now?*

"When my mom was dead, I played it. I mean I played it a lot," Tejas said.

Ed looked at the boy. His heart ached for the boy and for himself.

"Play with me." Tejas jiggled the PlayStation control.

Ed looked at Tejas for a moment and then took the controller from him. While looking at the game playing on the TV blankly, Ed said, his voice trembling, "I want her back."

"Me, too," Tejas said, sadness in his voice.

Not too far away from Ed and Tejas, at the table sat Birdie, Agnes, Liz, Ella, Yuul and Charlie. They watched Ed and Tejas in silence, fighting back tears. A sombre air hung low in the room for a long moment until they re-grouped and went back to the tasks they had assigned themselves. *Ding!* The sound that announced that Ella's second attempt to unlock Madison's password had failed, chimed loudly.

"That's strike two," Charlie said.

Ella pouted her lips. "I know."

"Should we take it to Ajay?" Liz interjected, keeping her eyes on the CCTV playing on her laptop.

"I have a couple of ideas before I wave a white flag." Ella grabbed Maddie's laptop and walked over to Ed. "Ed, can I have your email?"

"What for?" Ed asked while pressing his thumb on the controller and keeping his eyes glued on the game.

"There's a very slim chance that Maddie might have used your email address as her recovery email."

"She did. FirstJournalist@gmail.com, that's my email address." Ed's voice was hoarse.

"Thank you." Ella pranced back to the table.

"First journalist? That sounds super cool," Tejas said, still transfixed on the game.

"Maddie made it for me. I was one of the first black journalists ever hired to work for a major newspaper and the first black journalist to receive the excellence in journalism award."

"Oh wow! That's dope," Tejas said, multitasking. "You know what? You should finish what Maddie started."

"What do you mean?" Ed turned to Tejas.

"You write about Maddie and her investigation on the Home. It's like collaboration between you and Maddie. That way, you can let the world know that she was pure fire," Tejas said, moving his thumb a million times a minute. "Come on, Ed! Start shooting. Our guys are dropping like flies." Tejas felt a shadow towering over him one second and then the next second, he got a tight hug that almost choked him.

"You have the mind of a healer," Ed said almost in a whisper.

The people at the table watched Ed and Tejas again in silence and then turned their attention back to the tasks they had on their hands.

"It has to be this guy," Birdie said, pointing her index finger at a guy on Liz's laptop.

Liz, Agnes and Yuul all nodded in agreement.

"We've got the guy," Liz said, looking at Ella.

"Oh ya?" Ella said without a trace of interest in her voice, her eyes fixed on Maddie's laptop. She didn't even bother to move her head an inch.

They figured whatever Ella and Charlie had found on Maddie's laptop must be really good.

"It's going to be a long night," Birdie said, looking at Ella and Charlie.

"What should we eat for dinner?" Agnes said.

"We should order in," Yuul said.

"We should order—" Liz said.

"This is just too crazy," Ella announced, finally lifting her head.

Everyone looked at Ella.

"I couldn't agree more," Charlie said, shaking his head.

Everyone looked at Charlie.

"We could tell you, but I think we should wait until Jeffrey's here," Charlie said.

Birdie said, "We could drop dead in the blink of an eye right now, never knowing what you two have found out."

Charlie smiled. "I can't let that happen."

• • •

Caleb was in the parking lot, waiting for Wylie to finish his day and go home. He was a patient man. He'd been on numerous missions, and all of them had required patience more than anything else. He could go on like this for days or weeks. On this one, unfortunately, he didn't have the luxury of time – his brother's freedom was hanging by a thin wire.

If it was up to him, he would snatch Wylie and take him to a place totally off the grid and extract everything from him, even things buried so deep that it would drown Wylie dredging them up to the surface. At the end of the day, he was a member of Joint Task Force 2, Canada's premier special operations unit and the country's main counter-terrorism elite.

For whatever reason, he trusted Jeffrey and his crazy sister, even though he had just met them. He remembered his first encounter with Liz – the crazy toothy smile, the booming hello. Then, that image overlapped with the recent one where she'd put her hand over his mouth while whispering in his ear. *Thump, thump, thump.* His heart raced again just like it'd done on that day. *She thought that I was sexy.* A smile curled on his lips. *Damn it! I'm thinking about her again.* Damned woman somehow made him think about her all the time. Yes, it was her fault as far as he was concerned. He was sure that he wouldn't even be thinking about her at all if she wasn't so damn crazy. It bothered him that he wasn't just thinking about the mission 24/7. It was all her damned fault one hundred percent. He'd never blamed anything on anyone. That wasn't his way. But in this case, he was sure it was all on her. He was the guy who fixed things and he was really good at it. You know why? Because he never lost his focus while he was on a mission. Although this was the most important operation of his life, he was losing focus… because of that crazy woman… who also looked so—. *Stop!* He gave himself a loud mental slap.

He shook his head hard trying to shake off his unhealthy obsession with Liz, and told himself once again that for now, he'd go with their plan and protect Liz like she was the Queen of England… He meant, for Adam, not for her sake… He wouldn't have cared about her safety otherwise. Why would he? It wasn't like he knew of her. *Focus.* He shook his head again.

He'd met Harvey Rogen, Adam's original lawyer. That was why he knew if anyone could prove Adam's innocence, it would be Liz and the gang. And he hoped like hell he could get Adam out of prison, in a legal way, for everyone's sake.

He'd assist them in any way he could to expedite the process. If the wait got too long though, he would have to go on a solo mission. One way or another, he had to get his brother out of prison before something happened to him.

He was getting more and more worked up, picturing his brother locked away in jail, when he suddenly spotted Jeffrey and Wylie leaving the building together. *Time for action*, he thought, grinning.

Jeffrey and Wylie stopped to talk for a little bit as if Jeffrey wanted to point out to Caleb that this loser was Wylie, and then Jeffrey got into his car and drove away. Wylie wasted no time. He jumped into his car and headed out as well. Caleb slowly started his car.

Caleb realized it was going to be a long night when he saw Wylie pull into a public car park on Church Street. After parking his car, Wylie crossed the street and headed west towards Yonge Street. When he hit Yonge Street, he slid into a big chain restaurant about a half block or so up the way. Caleb waited for about 5 minutes before following him in.

He didn't bother looking around to try and find Wylie. He went straight to the Wait to Be Seated sign. He didn't need to know where Wylie was sitting. All he had to do was not lose him when he left the restaurant. He asked for a window table at the front and sat down, which gave him an unobstructed view of the exit.

He ordered a Ribeye Streak, baked potato with all the fixings and a Perrier. He really could have used a beer, but this wasn't the day for guilty little pleasures like that. He finished his dinner, dessert and a coffee but still no Wylie.

The longer he waited, the more he was sure that Wylie had made him and somehow managed to give him the slip. After some deliberation, he decided he might as well stay for another 30 minutes. If he had missed Wylie, at this point there was nothing he could do to change that. He would just have to do it all over again tomorrow.

Hang tight, Adam, Caleb prayed.

After sticking it out for the extra 30-minute, he asked for the bill and got ready to leave. It turned out that his patience was well rewarded, as just then he spotted Wylie with a woman on his arm making their exit. He took pictures.

As he drove along Cummings Street, he noticed Wylie's car parked in the driveway of a semi-detached and happened to spot Wylie going in. He just kept driving right on by. He circled around the neighbourhood aimlessly for a while and then finally drove back around, stopping the car across the street from Wylie's place and took some more pictures.

27

MONDAY, DECEMBER 9

Jeffrey arrived at Mr. Sandhu's at 6:30 p.m., bringing the gift of food - boxes of pizza, chicken wings, potato wedges, salads and sodas. Since his home was no longer privacy protected, Mr. Sandhu generously offered them his place to be used as their temporary headquarters.

Passing by the murder board, his arms loaded with all the food, he noticed there was nothing on it. It was just a blank white board.

"Very impressive!" Jeffrey said sarcastically.

"Don't be a smart mouth," Birdie said.

"Sorry," Jeffrey said, placing the food on the dining table by the kitchen.

By 7:00 p.m., everyone had made a plate of their choice and was now sitting around casually in the living room. Birdie, Agnes and Ed sat on the couch while Mr. Sandhu sat in his recliner. Jeffrey, Charlie, Will, Liz, Yuul, Ella and Tejas sat on the floor finishing their plates while shooting the breeze.

At 7:30 p.m., Jeffrey said, "We don't have all day. Tell me what you guys found out today."

"Nothing much," Ella said as she put her plate down on the floor. She saw the disappointed look on Jeffrey's as she was walking over to the murder board. She stood by the murder board and flipped it. "Ta-da!"

There were pictures stuck on the board and notes written below the pictures. Some words were circled in red and some were underscored. The murder board was colourful and well organized.

"That's impressive!" Jeffrey said, suddenly springing to life.

"Are you happy now?" Birdie said.

Jeffrey nodded enthusiastically.

Ella grabbed a red marker from the pen tray and pointed to a picture of a driver's license. It was blown up large but still high quality. "This is the guy who followed Birdie and Agnes to the hotel early Sunday morning. This morning, Jeffrey ran the license plate of his car and got his driver's license and sent me a copy of his driver's license, which you're looking at it right now. As you can see, the car belongs to *Adam Doyle*."

"He's not anything like I thought a criminal would look like," Tejas said. "He's almost movie star good-looking."

"All that is gold does not glitter," Agnes said.

"Now, look at this picture." Ella pointed to a picture of a man entering the emergency room. "As you can see, this man enters the emergency room shortly after Maddie was taken in by the paramedics. Look at the time code on this picture." She paused and waited a minute for everyone to see the time code. "As you can see, it reads 7:37 p.m. on Friday, November 22. Now, look at this picture. Yes, that's Madison leaving the hospital with a man at 11:09 p.m. on the same night. This is the guy who's responsible for Maddie's death."

"I guess we've found other Adam," Jeffrey said.

"Yay!" Everybody cheered.

"Ahem!" Ella cleared her throat. "May I continue?" Everyone gave Ella a nod.

"Since Wild Cat was seen around Adam Brooks' between 9 p.m. and 10:30 p.m. on Friday, November 22, we now know for sure that we have at least five accomplices – Rob, Doreen, Wylie, Wild Cat and Adam Doyle." Ella gave this a minute to sink in before she continued. "There's more."

"Bring it on" Jeffrey said with excitement in his voice.

"Charlie, do you want to take it from here?" Ella said, passing the marker to Charlie.

Charlie told them about Adam Brooks' investigation into the deaths of the three nursing assistants and about the last encounter between him and Madison. He also told them about Brooks' encounter with Rob and Doreen on the night of the murder.

"I'm speechless," Jeffrey said.

"But somehow, you're still talking," Charlie said, grinning. Passing the maker back to Ella. "Why don't you finish it off".

"Gladly. Let's move onto Maddie. Her laptop was, of course, password protected. After a couple of failed attempts, I thought that Maddie may have used her grandfather's email address as her recovery email, and *voila*."

"Look at you," Jeffrey said, "talking like a professional hacker."

"A little bit, right? I'm very happy with myself as well." Ella cleared her throat. "As you already know, Maddie was working on the Home cases as well. She started with a nurse named Carol Stewart, moved onto Dalisay Aquino and then finally Derek Sommer. I believe that she started from Carol Stewart's case because it was on TV and in the newspapers. Since she was a reporter, she probably thought that she could've utilized her connections better on the Stewart's case."

"It's a very good supposition, isn't it?" Charlie said proudly.

Birdie smacked Charlie in the head, "Get a grip."

"Haha! Trust me. I tried." Charlie rubbed the spot on his head where Birdie had just smacked it.

Ella blushed.

"Move on," Liz said.

"Moving on," Ella said. "Maddie came to the same conclusions that Adam Brooks did regarding Carol Stewart and Dalisay Aquino. While Brooks didn't get a chance to go over the Sommer's case, Madison did. She methodically searched images available online and collected anything that might be relevant. Then, she visited the shopping mall and talked to the people that worked there and anyone she could close to there. Doing that, she found even more images. Through her social media accounts, she asked people to contact her with any information related to the shooting. She put everything she had together and discovered two important things. One, Mr. Sommer was the first victim to be shot in the drive-by shooting. Two, that he was in a crowd of people right before he got shot. He stood back against the window of the mall. There were people on his left and right side, and there were people walking by in front of him."

Ella paused and then pointed at another picture on the board with the marker. "As you can see in this picture, after Derek drops to the ground, people are frantically flying out of the bull's eye. Maddie called Fanny Sommer who then told Maddie about Adam Brooks' investigation into these cases. At that point, Maddie tried to contact Adam Brooks. Due to the misunderstanding they had, Adam Brooks didn't take her call. With the help of Fanny Sommers, she obtained the medical examiner's report on Derek. It says that he was shot exactly in the centre of his heart and died instantly. Maddie talked to some gun experts and found out that that kind of shot could only have been made by a very, very skilled marksman."

"Military," Yuul said.

"An ex-military or a want-to-be is also a possibility," Mr. Sandhu added.

Ella cleared her throat. "Based on her findings, Maddie concluded that Derek Sommer was murdered and was, in fact, the intended victim."

"This is incredible!" Jeffrey clapped his hands hard three times before turning to Charlie. "What do you think as a lawyer?"

"It's really good…" Charlie said, his voice slurred a little. "But I don't think that what we have so far will get the charges dropped against him."

"We've got a lot!" Ella said. Her face looked like she was about to cry.

"Yes, you've got a lot," Charlie said, "a lot of circumstantial evidence."

Everyone looked at Charlie in anger.

Charlie held up his palms. "Hey, don't kill the messenger."

"Explain," Jeffrey said.

"First, we have Will's statement about Maddie going out with an Adam whom she'd met in the ER. We have the CCTV to prove that Maddie met Adam in the ER. We can prove that Birdie's attacker is the same Adam whom Maddie met at the ER. We can also prove that Maddie and Adam Brooks both worked on the nurses' cases. They are all good. Unfortunately, none of them prove that Adam Doyle drove Brooks' car, and none of them place Doyle at the murder scene. Yes, we're very sure that Doreen and Rob jammed the signal to Brooks' car, but we can't prove that they were the ones that actually did it. Even if we could, it won't help the case, unless we prove that Doreen and Rob were the ones that gave the car to Adam Doyle."

"What about the gun?" Ella said. "Adam Doyle brought a gun to Birdie's."

"Don't hate me, babe." Charlie gently stroked Ella's head. "What we do have, will definitely help him in court."

Liz, the Neighbour

Liz slowly shook her head. "That's not good enough. We don't want Brooks to have to take his chances in court."

Ding! Ding! Jeffrey looked at his cellphone and found a message from Caleb with a caption reading: **Wylie's Woman**. He squinted at the picture and his face turned white. "This is getting worse by the minute."

"What do you mean?" Ella wanted to know.

"Caleb just sent me a picture of a woman, and he thinks that she's Wylie's woman."

"And?" Liz said.

Jeffrey passed his phone to Yuul who was sitting next to him. "Her name is Keira Scott. She's our duty officer. Sadly, this explains why Fanny Sommer's complaints all went missing."

Looking at Charlie, Ella said, "What about now? Does it change anything?"

Charlie continued to stroke her head. "Not yet, but it says that we're very close."

"Charlie's right," Liz said with conviction. "We'll soon find enough evidence to discover all the dirty secrets Wild Peach buried, and lock up all the bad people, *and* get the charges dropped against Brooks."

Jeffrey looked at Liz and then everyone else in the room and saw their determination. That scared him. "What you guys have accomplished in such a short time is nothing short of incredible. But this is as far as you go. You've seen that these people are willing to kill anybody that gets in their way. It's just too dangerous for you guys to continue on with this investigation."

"We're already neck-deep in this," Yuul said. "There's only one way out for us. We eliminate them before they eliminate us."

Will stared at Yuul. "What do you mean *eliminate them*?" He made a finger gun. "Are you talking about bang-bang?"

Liz put her hand over Will's finger gun and put it down. "Of course not. She means well."

That got some people cocking their heads to the side.

Ignoring the reaction in the room, Jeffrey said, "You're right. We have to go all the way. When I say we, I mean the police. I'll brief my boss on this and we'll investigate the hell out of it."

Ella shook her head. "Jeffrey, do you remember why you made Caleb hire us?"

Jeffrey remembered. He'd been forced to take time off. Supposedly a reward for a job well done. He sighed.

Looking at Jeffrey, Liz said, "Jeffrey's right. We at least need to minimize the risk. Anybody who doesn't work for KSK pips or is a detective or in the military should drop everything and go into hiding"

"What's KSK pips?" Birdie asked.

Ella smiled. "KSK pips is KSK," She pointed to Liz, Yuul and herself, "us, and PIPS stands for Private Investigation and Protection Services"

Agnes nodded in approval. "That's really a good name."

Her eyes hardening, Birdie said, "I'm not going into hiding. If I hadn't asked Maddie to investigate this stupid mess in the first place, she would surely be here today."

"Don't be silly," Ed said in an assertive voice. "It's not the mother's fault who sent her kid out to get milk and the kid never ends up coming home. It's the drunk driver's fault who got behind the wheel when he never should have."

Agnes gently patted Birdie's hand, smiling. "I'm staying as well. I need to see it through."

Ella said, "Charlie's done his part. He's out."

Everybody nodded in agreement.

"I'm not going anywhere without you, babe," Charlie said, locking Ella's eyes with his.

"Okay. We're all staying. Now, we should move to another undisclosed location tonight while we have the three cars," Liz said.

"Why?" Mr. Sandhu asked, narrowing his eyes at Liz sounding a little offended.

"We put you and Tejas in danger by just being here," Liz said, squeezing Tejas' shoulders.

"Danger keeps you young. You stay, and that's that," Mr. Sandhu said matter-of-factly his arms crossed over his chest.

Jeffrey scanned each one of them and said, "Okay, then. It's settled."

"What about me?" Will said. "I haven't said anything."

"Who are you?" Jeffrey asked, cocking his head to the side.

"That's hilarious." Will sneered. "And, of course, I'm in. Let's get the party started."

"He's too Hollywood." Birdie shook her head.

"Grandma!"

Everybody laughed.

When the laughter finally died down, Liz said, "I have an idea, and for this one to work, we've got to go big. I mean Hollywood big in order to get the charges dropped, and so no one can ever bury the story."

"What do you have in mind?" Birdie asked.

"This is how we're gonna do it."

28

TUESDDAY, DECEMBER 10

A red Mazda drove through the Wallace Emerson neighbourhood and came to a complete stop on Emerson Avenue south of Wallace Avenue.

While the neighbourhood had consisted of low-income families many of whom had witnessed and some who had committed serious crimes in their lives, this part of the neighbourhood was slowly being replaced with middle income families in recent years, thanks to the skyrocketing home prices in Toronto.

It was here that a lady in her mid seventies leapt out of the back seat of a black Beamer while her elderly friend basically crawled out the other side. An old man exited the car from the front passenger's seat, murmuring something about the cold weather. When they were all out on the sidewalk, they turned to the left and to the right looking up and down the street to make that they weren't being followed or watched.

They spotted a few pedestrians walking along the sidewalk, their shoulders hunched trying to stay warm, while keeping their eyes glued to the ground concentrating on every step to avoid slipping on any ice. The three seniors were sure that they were just innocent bystanders. The gang of three gave a knowing look to each other and marched on down the street.

If those other pedestrians had only looked around, they would have been in for one big, nice surprise. They were far from Hollywood where you could spot a celebrity around just about any corner although even in Hollywood, it had to be a very lucky day to see a big star trying to catch a bad guy in real life. That was what people on this street were missing out on right now.

The three retirees walked over to the red Mazda and blew out a sigh of relief once they got inside the car.

"What took so long?" Birdie asked.

"It's not even twelve o'clock yet," Will replied, pouting his lips.

Birdie shook her head. "I don't know how you're ever going to make a living with your lax attitude."

Will grinned. "Don't worry. Hollywood doesn't like early-risers."

"You're fibbing," Birdie said.

"Just a little." Will smiled.

"Tsk, tsk" Birdie shook her head.

"Were you waiting long?" Liz asked.

Liz, the Neighbour

"We got here a little after 10:00 a.m. Good thing Caleb was already here. Otherwise, we would've all froze to death by the time you got here."

"Sorry…" Liz said.

Birdie waved her hand dismissively at Liz. "It's okay. We actually had a really good time with Caleb. He's one fine man."

"That's a relief," Liz said, smiling. "Which house?"

Birdie pointed her finger upward and to the right. "The white house in between two red brick ones is where our target lives."

"*Our target?*" Will asked perplexed. "Why are you talking like that?"

"That's how Caleb talks. He's dope," Birdie said nodding in approval.

"Dope?" Will said. "What's gotten into you? Since when did you say 'dope'?"

"From this morning," Birdie said. "Stakeouts are hard on the body, so we have to do arm stretching and a neck roll here and there while keeping our eyes peeled for the target all the time. We don't want to be the guys who lose the target because we blinked for too long, do we?"

"Did Caleb tell you that, too?" Will asked.

"Yes, he did," Agnes said, giggling.

They saw cars driving by now and then, but none stopped at Adam Doyle's house or even stopped nearby his house. They saw pedestrians, too, but everyone passed by Doyle's house without even taking a quick peek at the place.

Two hours into the stakeout, Agnes said, "I've got to go pee."

"Me, too." Birdie raised her right hand up.

Liz, the Neighbour

Liz took out her cellphone and called Caleb. "We've got to go pee. Can you call me if the *target* moves?"

"Copy that. Bring me an empty bottle on your way back."

"What for?"

"If you have to ask that, you haven't watched enough movies."

"Eew!"

Caleb laughed. "Get lunch while you're at it."

Liz thought that that was thoughtful. "Do you want me to pick something up for you or do you want to dine in after we come back?"

"Neither. I brought my lunch with me."

"Okay then. *Over and out?*"

"Out."

They picked an Irish pub that sat right on Bloor Street West. At the restaurant, Birdie, Agnes, Ed, Liz and Will sat down at one of the tables to enjoy a nice lunch together.

Liz said, "I've been thinking about those three nurses. They must've seen something, and whatever it was, it had to be medical related, them being nurses and all. It goes well with Birdie's insurance scam theory. Agnes, you said your friend, Tom, died from a heart attack. Correct?"

Agnes placed her knife and fork down on the table. "Yes. His anger probably got to him."

"Why was he so angry?" Will asked, having another bite of his club sandwich.

"It's a long story," Agnes said. "Anyway, the gist of it is that Tom's good friend at Wild Peach, Jason Reindeer, passed away. Tom got really angry because the home didn't reach out to Jason's son for the funeral. In the home's defence, no one knew that Jason had a son. Jason had himself just found out that he had a son from his college sweetheart shortly before he died. Anyway, Jason told Tom all about his son and how much he was looking forward to meeting his son. Shortly after that, Jason died and Wild Peach rushed to have him cremated. Tom was really upset because he knew that it would've meant a lot to Jason if his son had been there at his funeral. Tom was as healthy as a bull. Yet, right after the outburst, Tom dropped dead from a heart attack. Poor soul, rest in peace now."

"Do you happen to know the official cause of Jason's death?" Liz wanted to know.

"A heart attack," Agnes said.

"Does everyone there die from heart attacks?"

"Oh dear, don't be silly." Agnes gave Liz a dismissive hand-gesture. "Just like anywhere else, people at the home died from all different causes. Only those people who seemed to be lively as a cricket one day and dead the next were the ones who died from a heart attack."

Liz said, "Nobody else suspected anything?"

Agnes said, "I can't speak for anybody else except that Birdie did. I remember vividly the day we met you for the first time. Birdie told you that there were too many suspicious deaths. You said, "Suspicious, how?" Birdie said, "Healthy people just dropped dead.""

Birdie nodded smiling.

After some silence, Liz asked, "How many people would you say died from a heart attack?"

Agnes said, "My memory is not as good as it used to be. During my stay, there were 5 people that died from heart attacks."

"Do you happen to remember their names?"

"Of course."

Another long silence followed.

"Their names...." Liz prompted.

"Do you want me to tell you now?"

"That'd be nice."

"Kim Taylor, Michelle Sauer, Nick Chovinski, Jason Reindeer and Tom Bauer in that order"

"And you said your memory is not as good as it used to be?" Liz said.

"She was once a very famous physicist with an IQ of 150," Birdie said.

"153," Agnes corrected.

"Do you know their birthdates?" Liz said teasingly.

"Of course, Kim Taylor, February 16, 1949. Michelle Sauer, July 14, 1950—"

"You're incredible! Can you text me their names as well as their birthdates? I need them in writing. I can't remember things the way you do."

"Of course."

Liz stood up and walked over to the waitress at the counter. As she was walking over, her cellphone dinged, telling her she had a text message from Agnes. She clicked it and saw the names and their birthdates.

As Liz sat down, she said, "Is there anything you can't do?"

Agnes giggled and said, "Of course, there're a few."

"Can you excuse me? I need to make a call."

· · ·

They drove back and forth three more times between the vantage point and the washroom in the restaurant where they'd had their lunch before they called it a day.

"Holy Guacamole! Stakeouts are no joke," Birdie said, rubbing her butt.

Will turned to back and checked on his grandma. She seemed to be aging even faster than she was 10 years ago. The little woman who had once seemed bigger than a mountain to him now hardly reached his shoulder. The woman had raised a child of her own and lost her. But she had never had time to mourn. She just mopped over the loss, picked herself up and raised her grandson with wit and wisdom.

"Don't be a wimp," Birdie said. "Let's go."

Liz drove through the night with the two ladies asleep in the back seat and the man she had once been madly in love with in the front passenger seat beside her. Bloor Street was lit up from the streetlamps and all the lights streaming through the windows of the many restaurants and bars that lined the street. The street was busy with people walking about, entering and exiting the shops, eateries and other entertainment venues.

Liz was driving past a group of people – their arms interlocked walking and singing together, when she noticed a call from Caleb coming in.

"Stop at the gas station on Sheppard," Caleb said.

"Where are you?" Liz asked.

"I'm right behind you."

"Over and out." Liz disconnected the call.

"What's with all this WWII stuff?" Will asked, smiling a little.

"I'm just following your grandma's lead. She just makes everything more fun. You should try it one day."

"I'm glad you guys are getting along." Will gazed at Liz.

Liz drove to the gas station and Caleb pulled in 10 seconds after.

Caleb walked over beside her car and planted a GPS tracker on the undercarriage and then walked over to the driver's side and gave Liz five ½" thick, 2" in diameter discs through the open window. "GPS trackers, one each. Keep it with you at all times until this is over."

"Thank you," Liz said.

"About your car, it's really not made for Covert Ops. Red leaves too strong an impression. From tomorrow, park it on Bloor Street. That'll be close enough." Caleb saluted and disappeared into the night.

29

TUESDAY, DECEMBER 10

Two middle-aged white men hurriedly walked down Purpledusk Trail, keeping their eyes out for slippery patches on the sidewalk. One man was short and plump and slightly hunched, while the other was stocky and average height. He was the younger of the two men. Soon they came upon a small detached red brick house, they checked the number over the garage and nodded at each other as if to say that they had the right place.

The plump man took his hand out of his jacket pocket, knocked on the door and hurriedly buried his hand back in his pocket.

Loud sounds of chatter and laughter and a waft of food gushed out as the door flung open. "Detective Tim Johnson." A man tipped his head to the hunched man while holding the door open. "Nice to see you again."

"Likewise, Mr. Sandhu," Tim said in his usual croaky voice, inclining his head to Mr. Sandhu.

"Good to see you, Detective Sam O'Hara," Mr. Sandhu said, smiling at the man walking in behind Tim.

"How are things?" Sam followed Tim in, shaking Mr. Sandhu's hand as he entered.

"Thanks for coming on such short notice," Jeffrey said. "As promised, we've got lots of delicious food. Follow me."

"Isn't this my sweet detective Tim?" Birdie said, rushing into the living room with a plate of Chinese.

Everybody looked around the room, searching for Sweet Detective Tim but found only cranky, old Tim in the living room.

"Did you miss me?" Birdie asked.

"You know I did." Tim kissed Birdie's hand.

"Have we met before? You look awfully familiar," Sam said, looking at Will.

"He's Will Pemberton, the actor," Ella said, blushing.

Tim gave Will a once-over. "Has he been in any movies I might've seen?"

"He's not a big shot if that's what you're asking," Birdie said.

"Yes, I am!" Will protested.

"I won't believe you until you get me Clark Gable's autograph."

"For the thousandth time," Will said, "he's dead."

"Frankly, my dear, I don't give a damn," Birdie said, imitating Clark Gable.

"The legend never dies!" Agnes screamed, showing up behind Birdie.

Both ladies giggled like two teenagers being asked on a date with their crush.

"Stop it. You're freaking me out," Will said.

"Frankly," Tim started and Birdie, Agnes and even Sam chimed in, "my dear, I don't give a damn."

"Oh My Gosh! That's Will Pemberton," Rani said, coming in with Ajay.

"Will Pemberton's here?" Ajay said surprised.

"Yes, he's here," Rani said, extending her hand.

Will grabbed her hand and gently shook it.

"I didn't know you're coming," Mr. Sandhu said, looking at Ajay in surprise.

"I called him," Jeffrey said. "I need his help. I hope it's okay with you."

"That depends," Mr. Sandhu said. "If this is going to bring me entertainment into my life, I'll give you permission to use him however you want."

"Thank you," Jeffrey said to Mr. Sandhu. He then turned to Tim and Sam. "Come with me. We've covered all the bases – Indian, Chinese and Italian. Help yourselves."

• • •

Off in the corner of the kitchen, while Tim and Sam were making their plates of food, Jeffrey told them about his neighbours, Rob and Doreen.

When Jeffrey told them about Wylie and the book, Sam put the salad serving set back in the salad bowl and put his plate down on the table.

Tim almost choked on a chicken drumstick when Jeffrey told them about the phone call Birdie had made to Wylie, and the subsequent attempt on Birdie's life.

Sam grabbed a dining chair and sat down when Jeffrey told them about Adam Brooks and Madison Cooper's investigation into the deaths of the three nurses.

Tim sat down too, next to Sam, while Jeffrey told them about Keira Scott and the text he'd received from Liz this afternoon regarding the deaths of the Wild Peach residents.

As Jeffrey finished, Tim was shaking his head in disgust. "This is not good."

"And this is a lot," Sam said.

"I need your help," Jeffrey said.

"Let's hear it," Sam said.

"I need you to look into the deaths of those residents. Can you look them up and see if they had any life insurance on them? If they did, who was the beneficiary?"

"You know all of this is out of our jurisdiction," Sam said.

"I do," Jeffrey said, slumping his shoulders. "You're right. Forget about it."

Tim shook his head disapprovingly. "Tsk, tsk! I don't know why people in the department think you're going places. You throw in the towel way too easy to have a reputation like that. Why do you need to know all this?"

"Right now, I've got no motive to go on. I'm convinced that the nurses and the residents were killed. But why?"

Tim said, "We'll look into it. Can we go eat now?" Tim didn't wait for Jeffrey's answer. He just started walking towards the living room where everyone else was already seated.

"I don't like it. If I lose my pension, I'm coming after you." Sam threatened, waving his fork in Jeffrey's face. He then followed after Tim.

Jeffrey couldn't believe they'd said yes. "Why?" He asked walking behind them. He sat down next to Sam and asked again, "Why?"

"Why what?" Sam said, looking at Jeffrey.

"Why are you helping me? Like you said, you could end up losing everything."

"I'm wondering that myself." Sam turned to Tim who was sitting beside him. "Why are we helping him with the insurance fraud thing?"

Tim smiled at Birdie. "I'd do anything for my fair lady."

"Why do you have to be so young?" Birdie giggled.

"She called you young. How often do you hear that these days?" Sam asked.

"More often than you think," Tim said.

"Don't lie to me, young man. Nobody calls a 58-year-old man young," Sam said.

Everyone laughed and laughed until Jeffrey cleared his throat. "Ajay, do you have anything for me?"

"Of course, I do. Let me start with your partner, Wylie Townsend. He was born in Montreal, Quebec to Heather Townsend and Patrick Townsend. Heather runs a nursing home in Montreal. Patrick works for the city of Montreal. Wylie has one brother, Troy Townsend. Now, try and guess where Troy Townsend used to work?"

"Military," Yuul said.

Ajay stared at Yuul for a moment and said, "How did you know that?"

"I didn't. I just stayed the course."

"I think I know who Wild Cat is," Liz said.

Everyone looked over at Liz.

"Wylie's brother, Troy Townsend," Liz said.

"Why do you think that it's him?" Ella wanted to know.

"We already established that Wild Cat must be related to Wylie. Yuul said before that Wild Cat might be military. Wylie has a brother who's in the military."

"He *was* in the military, but not anymore." Ajay corrected Liz.

"Sorry, he *was* in the military," Liz said.

Ajay said, "He was dishonourably discharged. Can anyone guess who else is ex-soldier military?"

Ella raised her hand. "Adam Doyle?"

"You Are Correct!"

Looking at Ajay, Ella said, "What did they do to get a dishonourable discharge? It must have been something really bad."

"That's classified information. I'll have to hack the military defence system, which I'm planning to do tomorrow."

"Don't," Caleb said almost in a shout. "I'll get the information."

Ajay looked at Caleb pouting. "You're no fun."

"Anything else?" Jeffrey asked.

Ajay said, "Just a fun fact. Adam Doyle's father just happens to be Canada's most infamous serial killer, Donny Doyle. He got caught because of Adam.

Liz, the Neighbour

Apparently, Adam Doyle isn't the sharpest tool in the shed."

Looking at Liz, Ella said, "Do you remember that Gerald saw Wild Cat on the day of Maddie's death? Do you think Troy Townsend killed Madison?"

Birdie interjected, "It has to be Adam Doyle. The man identified himself as Adam and Maddie would've said something to me if it wasn't him."

Ella said, "Maybe, Adam Doyle was wearing a similar, if not the same, jacket as Troy's on the day of the murder.

Looking at Yuul, Jeffrey asked, "Can you describe the jacket Wild Cat was wearing when you saw him?"

"A black jacket," Yuul said.

Jeffrey closed his eyes trying to picture the scene where Maddie and the perp got out of the car before walking over to the playground. There was one distinguishing feature on the perp's jacket. "Did the jacket have a hoodie?"

"No," Yuul said.

"I don't think Adam Doyle wore the same jacket. His jacket was hooded."

Birdie said, "Troy Townsend stole the car and then gave it to Adam Doyle to drive. Doyle gave it back to Troy after the murder to drive back to Adam Brook's place."

"Why would they do that?" Jeffrey asked. "It's way too complicated."

"They might've had their reasons." Birdie shrugged nonchalantly.

"That's definitely a mystery for another day," Liz said. "Ajay, can you run a little more in-depth search on Wylie's family? I really don't like the part of this whole story that the Townsends' mother runs a nursing home."

"Sure thing."

• • •

God truly moves in mysterious ways, Will thought. Here was the woman whom he'd thought he'd probably never see again sitting only a foot away from him, while Maddie whom he'd thought would always be in his life was gone forever.

It had been 10 years since they'd gone their separate ways. In those 10 years, they both had grown older and matured. He could see tiny wrinkles appear around Liz's eyes when she smiled. Yet, she still smiled a smile that made his heart race."

"Stop staring at me, weirdo," Liz said, feeling Will's gaze upon her.

"Weirdo? No way! I'm too handsome to be a weirdo. Stalker? Maybe. Weirdo?, No way." Will said.

"Stalker?" Liz asked, giving Will the side-eye.

Will chuckled, recalling the time when he'd crossed paths with Liz for the first time. "Do you remember the day we met for the first time?"

Liz shrugged as if to say that was an easy question. "Of course. It was our 4th year in university. Karl and I were coming out of class, and there you were in the hallway waiting for Karl."

Will fixed his eyes on her. All this time, she still couldn't remember when it was that they had actually met for the first time. "Wrong." Will curled the corner of his lips upward a little.

"No way! I remember *that* day like it was yesterday," Liz protested.

Liz, the Neighbour

It was still a mystery to Will that she couldn't recall any of the previous times they had crossed paths. He was pretty memorable guy now and he'd been a very memorable guy back then. He hadn't just turned good-looking yesterday.

"You're trying to pull my leg. I'm not falling for it," Liz said.

"The first time was at the Manor on Spadina when we celebrated Karl's birthday. You and Karl were an item at that time. Do you remember?"

Liz thought about it for a long moment but didn't remember seeing him at the party. She shook her head.

"The second time was at the Red Lantern. You must remember that?"

Liz thought about it again. Still, the answer was no. So, she shook her head again.

"You don't remember the Red Lantern? The pub that Karl used to hang out at all the time."

"If course I remember the Lantern. I just don't remember seeing you there."

"What about the time we went bowling together?"

"Okay, now you're just trying to make me feel bad."

"It's working then." Will laughed. "Every time we ran into each other again, you would say, nice to meet you."

Liz rolled her eyes. "No I didn't, did I?"

"I thought maybe it was because you were with Karl. But no, it was still the same, even after Karl *dumped* you for your best friend."

"That's a low blow." Liz shot Will a quick dirty look. It was true that Karl Gunz had dumped her for her best friend Cheryl Bishop. She wouldn't deny it. It had hurt her a lot in the beginning, but she'd soon realized that she'd been the one in the way of their union.

"Haha! I walked around campus all day, every day just so I could run into you. You see? I might've been an unskilled stalker, but I've never been a weirdo."

"Yeah, right," Liz said, a sarcastic expression on her face, while slowly making the turn onto York Ridge Road and there was her new home just waiting for her to come in. She parked the car on the street and killed the engine.

Will said, "We have to get into show mode now."

Liz was a little puzzled by Will's announcement.

"They're probably watching us right now wondering if we're really a couple, you know. We have to show them we're in love."

"How?"

"Take my lead when we get out of the car."

Liz circled around the car and joined Will on the sidewalk. The street lights and Christmas lights softly lit the silent night. The snow was whirling in the air, and Liz's long, blond hair was blowing gently in the wind. Their eyes locked, and Will cupped her cheeks in his hands, slowly lowering his head. When his lips gently touched hers, she didn't move away. He then opened his mouth and kissed her deeply.

30

WEDNESDAY, DECEMBER 11

Adam Doyle was hurt by the tone his boss was taking over the phone. He could hear the annoyance in his boss's voice although his boss himself was basically saying that there was nothing to worry about with the failed mission, the very mission that he'd been sent out on to collect that oldie's life.

His boss told him that the police had concluded that it was a case of a robbery gone wrong. Somebody over at the Homicide Squad was there on guard, just in case the oldie turned up there. So, really there was nothing to worry about, but his boss's tone said something else.

Now that he thought about it, it was ironic that the mission had failed because of a real rat after he had in fact named the mission Rat Extermination. The irony made him chuckle.

"What's so funny?" Troy asked over the phone.

"Nothing, Sir!" Adam said.

Troy sucked in a long, hard gulp of air before he continued. "I need you to be back here before the next Wednesday for the next package delivery."

"Will do, sir! Anyway, did you get a line on the rat? I would love to finish the rat off before I go on the next delivery."

"We're still searching. When we track her down, we'll send in B Team."

"Sir, you have to let me finish the job," Adam said almost pleadingly. He admitted that he didn't always know when to quit and he wasn't particularly good at making or running a risk analysis while considering influencing factors. As far as he was concerned, that was an officer's job. He considered himself as a foot soldier or a field agent. Sometimes, things didn't go as planned in the field. When that had happened, he believed that he'd risen to the challenge of dealing with the unexpected. He wasn't saying that all of his dealings had been successful. *Still, you got to lose some to win some, right?*

"The decision came from the higher-ups," Troy said.

Adam sniffed without saying a word.

Sniffing? Troy just shook his head. Although Adam had always called him *Sir* even after they'd been discharged from the military, Troy knew that there had been some sort of psychological closeness between them. It had been too personal, not too professional. He'd been resentful towards Adam for all the things that had gone wrong in his life. Adam had been acting like he was his spoiled child or battered wife. He couldn't tell which, but he knew one thing clearly now – ADAM MUST DIE. With the decision, he picked D-Day – the day after the next package was delivered. He smiled a very happy smile. "Do not go AWOL on me."

31

TROY & ADAM'S LITTLE SECRETE

Before Adam Doyle was deployed to Iraq, Troy Townsend had applied his military knowledge and skills to stealing weapons and munitions from armouries and selling them on the lucrative black market. Along the way, he'd carved out a very elaborate network to smuggle the stolen merchandise out of the military base and storing them in the 4 corners of the village.

Once that had all been set, he'd arranged a highly choreographed swap, trading his goods for the buyer's cash surreptitiously somewhere. These handoffs had taken place quickly in alleys, on corners, and in houses.

Liz, the Neighbour

His merchandise was known and loved by many for the quality and variety of the arms he dealt. He'd had Browning Hi-Power, Colt Canada C7A2, Colt Canada C8, Diemaco M203A1, M67 Grenades, and many more. He even had managed to 'acquire' Heckler & Koch PSG-1 and FN Herstal P90.

As soon as Troy laid his eyes on Private Adam Doyle, he realized that he could have someone like Adam do all the legwork for him. Adam Doyle never questioned his superior officer's motives. When Corporate said jump, he asked how high. When Corporate told him to hit himself, he asked how hard. He'd never blinked, no matter what the situation had been. So, Troy had let Adam in on his little secret.

Everything had gone very well. They'd been laughing all the way to the bank *until the day it had no longer been funny.*

• • •

On that fateful day, Adam Doyle drove a truck off base. As instructed, he had driven about halfway to one of the caches when he stopped the truck off to the side of a dirt-road and turned off the engine. He scanned his surroundings to be sure there were no cars driving up from behind. He parked there for 5 minutes, watching for any activity that might indicate surveillance. He saw none. Reassured that he hadn't been followed, he drove the rest of the dirt-road to its end.

He entered a mud hut that had already been blown halfway to hell, reached into his pants pocket and pulled out a GPS logger. He peered at the logger's screen to read out the coordinates of where he stood and then moved to his right a few feet and started digging.

When he finally hit metal, he dropped down and swiped the earth off the top of it with his palms. This was it, a metal crate with a 3-digit combo lock. He slowly turned the numbered wheels of the three-digit combination lock and pressed the button: *Pop!*

He quickly checked the contents of the crate. Everything looked right – a duffle bag on top and the merchandise underneath. The duffle bag contained an 8" x 1" strip of black ribbon, a 16-inch-long stick and his salesman's uniform – a long white robe called a *dishdasha* complete with headscarf. He emptied the contents of the duffle bag onto the ground and then transferred the weapons and munitions from the crate into the duffle bag.

An October breeze blew through the roofless hut and made him almost want to sing a song in celebration of the scorching hot summer almost coming to its end. He smiled.

It was time to don his disguise. He put the white robe over his military T-shirt and pants and wrapped the white headscarf around his head to cover most of his face. He then put on his sunglasses.

Now, all he had to do was transport the merchandise to the rendezvous point and wait there with the black ribbon visible. He bent to the ground, expecting to see the ribbon and the stick. When he

Liz, the Neighbour

didn't see the ribbon, his relaxed state of mind quickly gave way to panic.

Shit! Where did it go? It had to be here. He searched. And he searched some more, but it wasn't there. *Don't panic!* he admonished himself.

Today's buyer was the Jihadists. The colour black was their colour and hence was used as a signifier for any handoffs with them. The colour blue was Troy and Adam's, so their buyer would show up with a blue ribbon on a stick.

Think, Adam, think! He sat down and mulled over cancelling the sales call until he remembered he had another piece of black fabric with him.

Black is black, right? He gave himself a pat on the back and started walking to his car with the loaded duffle bag on his shoulder.

When he reached the rendezvous point, he stopped the engine and inhaled a deep breath and held it. While holding his breath, he took the stinking black sock off from his right foot, put it on a stick, then stuck it out the window and only then let out a long exhale. In combat boots, no one's socks smelled like a rose. Somehow though, his feet were a lot sweatier than other people's.

Adam saw a jeep driving up the dirt road through his side-view mirror. The car stopped and an Iraqi man got out of the car, holding a stick tied with a blue ribbon around it in one hand and a C7A2 Automatic Rifle in the other hand. The man didn't carry a bag. That was odd. Adam watched the Iraqi man weirdly.

The Iraqi man closed his eyes long and hard and opened them again, and it was still a sock hanging off a stick. As he approached the truck, he could smell the pungent smell. It was an insult to his religion to even use a sock as the signifier let alone one with such a stinky stench. Hanging the evil-smelling sock out to summon him, it was like the man was spitting on him, and his religion. He would teach this infidel a lesson. He would kill the man by putting 7 bullets in his body – Hellfire. Then he'd take the merchandise for free.

That's only fair, the Iraqi man thought. He wrapped his fingers around the base grip of his weapon.

Adam saw the Iraqi man deftly swing the rifle expertly shouldering the stock in the blink of an eye. He instinctively swung open the door and leapt out of the truck. He landed on the ground and rolled himself down the hill, a trail of gunfire blazed a heartbeat behind.

He lay flat to the ground quickly scanning the area to see if there was any cover. There was very little, just the odd outcropping of rocks – one of which he was now hiding behind. He had only his Browning Hi-Power semi-automatic handgun on him. He was outgunned – a handgun versus a rifle. His chances were next to none.

He acted quickly, expertly removing the white robe and the white headscarf that made him stand like a tall guy at a midget convention in the dirt-filled area. He balled up the robe and tied it together with the

Liz, the Neighbour

headscarf and then with everything he had he launched it as far to the left as he could.

When he heard the gunfire to his left, he darted off to the right. Then it suddenly fell silent, and Adam stopped moving. He heard another barrage of gunfire moving towards his direction as if the gunman knew where Adam was and in which direction he was heading. Although he knew that the gunman would eventually catch up to him, Adam had no choice but to keep on moving.

It didn't take long when he felt the heat of bullets flying by, missing him by a foot.

Three, two, one – Adam closed his eyes, anticipating death.

Then, there was silence. Adam was sure that he was dead, now blanketed in complete silence. After a long silence, he suddenly heard noise again, the noise of footsteps moving away from him.

He quietly opened his eyes, hoping not in any way to disturb the retreating footsteps. He listened a little more until he was sure that the footsteps had moved away from him. When he was sure, he quietly traversed the hill so that he could assess the situation on the road.

By the time he crawled up the hill and had his eyes on the road, the Iraqi man had finished transporting Adam's duffle bag to the backseat of his jeep. At that moment, Adam knew that it was his one chance. It was now or never if he wanted to do anything about it. He crawled up onto the road and stood up.

"Hey yo!" Adam shouted.

As the Iraqi man turned around to his direction in surprise, Adam squeezed the trigger *once… twice… and then thrice.* He heard, *Thump*!

He quickly moved toward the Iraqi man keeping his gun trained on him all the way until he stood beside him. Adam kicked the man's leg to make sure he was really dead. When he saw no movement, he holstered the gun.

Adam took his satellite phone out of his pants pocket and called Troy. As he was briefing Troy, he saw a tactical vehicle coming towards his direction. He quickly put the satellite phone in his pocket and held his gun pointed at the oncoming trucks.

When the trucks stopped, a bunch of Canadian soldiers jumped out of the back guns in hand.
Oh Shit!

Adam Doyle was taken to an interrogation room. Days of interrogation later, he felt positive for the most part, trying his best to stay calm despite feeling waves of panic about being found out. Repeating it to himself over and over again, he stuck to the simplest story he could stick to for the many days coming. He told them that he'd been out enjoying his day off. He'd been in the truck on the road, where they'd found him, enjoying the scenery and a nice October breeze when he'd been confronted by this crazy gunman. From there, Adam told them exactly what had happened except for the part about his duffle bag being filled with weapons and ammunitions.

Liz, the Neighbour

When questioned about the duffle bag full of weapons and ammo, Adam simply replied, "What duffle bag?" Luckily, Adam had had no chance to move his duffle bag or the bag full of cash to his truck by the time the army had found him.

When questioned why he'd called Troy Townsend, he'd called Sergeant Troy Townsend to brief him as he was his superior officer.

• • •

As far as the missing armaments, the military knew that Doyle and Townsend were the culprits, but they had no way of proving it.

Before Doyle and Townsend had a chance to retrieve all their cash and get rid of their remaining stash of arms, they were on a transport headed all the way back to Canada. Immediately after arriving home, they were both dishonourably discharged.

Troy Townsend was furious when he found out what Adam Doyle had done. Using a smelly sock went way beyond just being culturally insensitive. When Adam botched something, he really botched it good. Despite all the anger he'd had, he recruited Doyle for the Wild Peach job. At the end of the day, Doyle had never ratted him out. For that, Troy had given Adam a second chance, but he'd had enough of Adam.

32

WEDNESDAY, DECEMBER 11

After another awkward day at work trying to avoid Wylie and the captain, Jeffrey was happy when the day was finally over and it was time to go home. If Jeffrey had been more wary of his surroundings while he was driving, he would've spotted the SUV following him, but he'd totally missed it. He was too focused and too eager to do real detective work from his new headquarters a.k.a. Mr. Sandhu's house hunting down the real bad guys. He was the hunter in this concrete jungle. For that reason, he never thought that he could be the hunted, leading the big bad wolf back to the three little pigs' house. His attention was fixated on the road ahead.

Jeffrey saw Yuul, Ella and Charlie getting out of Charlie's car as he made the turn onto Purpledusk

Trail in Scarborough. He smiled. He honked to announce his arrival on the street and to tell them to wait for him.

After parking his car, he rushed out to Yuul and hugged her. Charlie and Ella teased him a little, and for that, Jeffrey hugged Yuul even tighter. Their laughs echoed and vibrated up and down the quiet street of Purpledusk Trail.

Mr. Sandhu opened the door and welcomed them in before any neighbour could knock on his door and complain about the noise.

Once they had all disappeared inside Mr. Sandhu's, Purpledusk Trail got quiet again.

Scarborough had the reputation of being one of the rougher parts of the Greater Toronto Area. Yet, just like any other place, it was where people came home to after a long day of work and relaxed with family over dinner and sometimes even had a shouting match with their children or spouses just like any other part of the city.

Soon after Jeffrey's arrival on Purpledusk Trail, two more cars turned up on the street – Liz's car carrying Birdie, Agnes, Ed and Will, and Caleb's car without any passengers in tow. People got out of their cars and disappeared into Mr. Sandhu's house not knowing that they were being photographed.

• • •

Although there were four people in a parked black SUV on Purpledusk Trail, only one man in the front passenger seat was closely watching Mr. Sandhu's house across the street.

The other three in the SUV were rolling their eyes and making faces showing their discontent to their boss for killing the music. It was Scarborough. They all played loud music in their cars, but their boss wasn't letting them. For that, they were being rebellious.

The boss understood his underlings' discontent. Unfortunately, he had a boss, too. His boss got mad if he heard loud noise playing in a car during a stakeout and his boss really scared him. His boss could be or should be the boss of a Mexican cartel, in his humble opinion. That was why he had killed the music.

He'd sent all the pictures of the people who had entered Mr. Sandhu's house since the arrival of the detective named Jeffrey Knight to his boss and was waiting for further instruction. He hoped to hear from his boss that it was a good day's work and that they should call it a day. Just then his phone rang.

"Sir!" he called his boss 'sir' because that was how Adam Doyle had always addressed their boss. Chris Winger wasn't going to be pushed behind the line because he couldn't charm his boss like his colleague, Adam Doyle.

"Anyone else enter the house?" Troy said, annoyance in his voice.

"No, Sir! Personally, I don't think anyone else will come since they've already got all the colours."

"All the colours?" The confusion was evident in Troy's voice.

Chris rolled his eyes at his boss's question missing the most obvious thing. "They got white, black, brown and yellow, all the colours of the rainbow here. What other colour's are there left out there to join this crazy bunch?"

There was a moment of silence until Troy let out a sigh. "Stake out the house. Monitor the comings and goings until I say otherwise."

"Uhh…"

"Speak up."

"We haven't had dinner yet," Chris said. His stomach growled from hunger as did his underlings'.

"Go have dinner and get what you need for the stakeout. When you get back, do not leave the house. If you need to, split the team into two."

"Yessir!"

"The main target is the old woman – the one without the cane. Wherever she goes, you go and report back to me."

"Yessir!"

• • •

Troy Townsend just shook his head slightly as he disconnected the call. He couldn't understand all this 'sir' stuff. Whenever people called him 'sir', it reminded him of his military life – the life that he'd loved so much and that he no longer liked to be reminded of.

Civilians were too spoiled in his opinion. These guys couldn't even skip one meal in the midst of the stakeout.He shook his head again in disbelief. He couldn't stop wondering how the hell all the idiots on earth had ended up on his doorstep and under his command. That was a mystery he would like to solve one day, but not today. Today, he had other fish to fry.

He smiled, sitting in the dimly lit kitchen of the coach house where he lived and worked ever since he'd been discharged from the military. It was big. He might... Oh no... It wasn't him. It was his smart brother, Wylie, who just might have saved all their sorry behinds just in the nick of time.

When Wylie had asked him to send his crew to keep an eye on Jeffrey, neither of them had expected this. Wylie hadn't liked Jeffrey's secretiveness. Jeffrey had been acting weird around Wylie, which set off Wylie's alarm bells. Wylie had believed that Jeffrey had been up to something that could jeopardize his career.

It turned out it wasn't just about jeopardizing Wylie's career, but Jeffrey was also digging a grave that threatened to bury them all.

I gotcha! He smiled. The shit stirrer, the rat, the oldie, the pensioner - whatever his people wanted to call her, he had finally found her. He had the oldie who had stirred up all this mess within his grasp. His smile was getting wider and wider.

Silence her. Silence them all. With that thought in mind, he placed a call to his most favourite aunt, Doreen, and not so favourite uncle, Rob.

• • •

Oblivious to the outside world, the people inside Mr. Sandhu's house were having the time of their lives. Cracking jokes over dinner with the people who made everything good. When they finally cleaned up the kitchen after dinner, they all gathered in the living room to talk some serious business.

Turning her attention to Caleb, Ella asked, "Did you find out about this dishonourable discharge thingy?"

Thingy? Caleb smiled. All the serious stuff came here where it was somehow turned into something light, something cute. "Okay. Let me tell you about this *dishonourable discharge thingy*. It turned out that Troy Townsend and Adam Doyle served at the same military base in Iraq. They were given dishonourable discharges because they were believed to be accomplices in stealing and selling arms. They didn't serve any time in prison because the military failed to find any direct evidence to link them to the said crime."

"That sounds like a movie plot. How did they get caught?" Will said

"A farmer reported hearing gunfire. He said he couldn't count how many shots were fired because there were so many in such a short span of time. So, a tactical truck full of soldiers was sent out to the said location to investigate. There they found Adam Doyle on a satellite phone, a dead Iraqi, a stash of weapons and a big bag of cash. The MPs, and by that, I mean the military police, concluded that Adam Doyle was most likely the seller and the dead Iraqi man the buyer. However, they couldn't figure out what had gone wrong on the deal. Maybe, one of them got greedy. Anyway, the last person Doyle called was Townsend. Their satellite cell phone records revealed that they communicated regularly. There were witnesses that Doyle and Townsend had been close. Based on their security clearances, the military concluded that Townsend had to be the thief who had been stealing weaponry from the armouries and that Doyle was the middleman."

"How ever did you get all that information?" Mr. Sandhu looked at Caleb inquisitively. "That sounds like all classified information to me."

"Are you a high-ranking officer?" Birdie wanted to know.

Caleb smiled. "No, I'm just a foot soldier but I happen to have friends in high places *and* low places."

Birdie smiled. "It means you're either a high-ranking officer or an indispensable foot soldier whose request cannot be simply ignored."

Caleb studied Birdie. This old woman was as sharp as a whip.

Birdie smiled a teasing smile. "You can't tell us who you are, can you?"

That knocked Caleb for a loop.

"I'm on a roll," Birdie said. "You're not with CSIS since I don't think you lied to us about you being military. It can mean only one thing."

"Be careful, I might have to kill you if you get it right," Caleb warned. Although he meant it as a joke, it came out deadpan.

"You can tell us behind his back," Liz said. "Caleb, can you get us… some water… No, no water. Can you make us…"

"What about beef bourguignon?" Ella said. "I don't know why, but all of the sudden, I have a craving for beef bourguignon."

"Cravings are no good," Yuul said, squinting at Ella. "Are you pregnant?"

"Hick, hick, hick" Ella hiccupped. Her cheeks blushed.

Liz, the Neighbour

"Is she?" Yuul gave Charlie a death stare.

Charlie pleasingly waved his hand. "No, she's not. We haven't slept together yet."

Jeffrey squinted at Charlie. "Don't tell me you're a virgin."

"Maybe, he doesn't know how it works," Will said.

"We shouldn't tease him. He may have problems with you-know-what," Birdie said.

"I know the guy who knows the guy who can fix that problem," Mr. Sandhu chimed in.

"I can explain to you how it works just like I did for Will," Ed said. He turned his attention to Will. "You're all good in that department, right?"

"I think so," Will grinned at Liz.

Charlie put his arm around Ella whose cheeks couldn't go any redder. "You see, babe? You make people doubt my manhood and my skills."

"You guys got to stop before she burns to ashes," Liz said. "Birdie, tell us who Caleb really is."

"Joint Task Force II," Birdie exclaimed. "And if you want to kill me, get in line."

Caleb stared at Birdie shaking his head.

"So, you weren't kidding about a prison break." Jeffrey said in awe.

"I wasn't," Caleb said. He then turned his attention to Birdie. "You can't tell anyone."

"Your secret is safe with me. Zip the mouth, lock it and throw away the key. Here you go." Birdie dusted off her hands. "Remember though. I'm not the only one who knows your secret," Birdie said, pointing her eyes over at Liz.

They all laughed.

When the laughter died down a little, Caleb cleared his throat. "There's one more thing. Birdie might be right about Troy Townsend stealing the car for Doyle. We are taught automotive skills as part of our training, just in case. You never know what might come in handy when you're in a war zone. Doyle was incredibly bad at it while he was excellent at long range shooting. They were actually training him to be a sniper right before he got caught."

"I *really* hope that Doyle moves his lazy buttocks tomorrow," Birdie said.

33

THURSDAY, DECEMBER 12

Although the team had taken turns, watching for the old lady in the red brick house, all four of them had fallen asleep at three. Whatever it was, either a nagging feeling or body aches coming from sleeping in an uncomfortable position, something made Chris open his eyes. Exactly right at that moment, he spotted the three oldies getting into a car.

"Get up!" Chris yelled, slapping Burt Reed's arm.

"What is it?" Burt said, rubbing his eyes.

"Drive!" Chris yelled.

"Uh, okay." Burt started the engine, following orders. "Where to?"

"Didn't you see that white Toyota Camry?"

Burt looked around and found the one his boss was talking about. "Got it!"

Liz, the Neighbour

"What time is it?" Hugh Shannon asked from the back seat, yawning like a hippo.

"It's 9 o'clock," Chris said.

• • •

Birdie, Agnes and Ed exited the white Toyota Camry, their Uber, and walked over to the Red Mazda parked on Bloor Street West just off of Emerson Avenue. They hurriedly hopped into the Mazda, closing the door fast so as not to let any cold air in.

"Good morning, ladies and a gentleman," Liz greeted them with a bright smile.

Everyone mumbled *good morning* to Liz as they settled in.

"I don't think we need to start this early," Will said. His eyes were closed. "Everybody says that no evil does its deeds in the morning."

"Who's everybody?" Birdie asked while trying to find the most comfortable way to sit.

"I forgot their names." Will shrugged.

"When you remember them, be sure to send me their names and phone numbers," Birdie said.

"Will do."

"Did you guys sleep okay?" Liz asked, looking at them through the rear-view mirror.

"It's not like home, but it's pretty good," Ed said. "Tejas is a dear lamb, and he's being very helpful with all the computer stuff. He's showing me some tricks on Word software."

"It's nice to see you working as a journalist again," Birdie chimed in.

"I don't know if any newspaper will let me publish the work, but as Tejas said, it really feels like I'm

Liz, the Neighbour

collaborating with Maddie. That's good enough for now."

Will said, "Maddie talked about it a lot – her collaborating with you. She'd be very happy if you finish what she started."

• • •

At 11:00 a.m., the Irish pub they'd been using for the last couple of days finally opened its doors to patrons, and they were the first ones in. They were about to be seated when Liz got an incoming call from Caleb.

"Good morning, my friend," Liz said cheerfully.

Caleb repeated *my friend* in his head. Just something about the word pained him. *What do you want her to call you then?* Caleb asked himself. *Hmm…* He would've liked it a lot more if she'd called him something… like… Love… *What the heck!* Caleb shook his head vehemently. *Remember what you thought of her when you met her for the first time – Crazy woman.* He cleared his throat and said, "The target is on the move."

"Are you serious?" Liz said as she snapped her fingers to get everyone's attention and pointed her finger at the door.

"As serious as a heart attack," Caleb said. "He's driving south as we speak."

Liz hurriedly followed her crew to outside and walked over to her car. "I just saw your car go by."

"It's show time, babe." Caleb almost lost his grip on the wheel. He did not know why he'd just called her *babe*. He wanted to smack his own mouth.

"What did you say?" Liz said, stopping dead in her tracks.

"It's a military thing," Caleb said.

"I don't think so," Liz said, getting into her car.

"It's a Joint Task Forces thing, I swear." Caleb said.

"Really?" Liz said as she connected her phone to Bluetooth.

"Yes. I can ask my team members to vouch for me. But then, they'd have to kill you after they tell you, you know? I don't want you to die."

"Okay," Liz said.

"Okay?" Caleb couldn't believe she'd actually bought this shit.

"Yes. Truth be known, I'm ready to die. Let me have a talk with your team members on FaceTime."

"Sure thing, as soon as the weather gets warmer. I can't let them dig your grave in this cold weather."

"Where are you? I just lost you," Liz said.

"Turn right. I guess we're going grocery shopping."

"Okay, babe," Liz said.

Caleb almost rear-ended a parked car. He adjusted the wheel and drove around the car. She was definitely crazy... who almost always... made his heart race like a Generation 6 NASCAR.

Will frowned, giving Liz a sidelong glance.

"It's a Joint Task Force joke," Liz said, feeling Will's stare.

Will narrowed his eyes at Liz. "I don't like it."

Liz eyed Will. He looked *so* cute. He was, indeed, edible cute. She blushed as an image of her kissing him, tasting him, popped into her head. She vigorously shook off the image.

Will smiled, seeing her seeing him with longing eyes. He had a pretty good idea what she was thinking, and he liked it. He liked it *a lot*.

"He's inside," Caleb said.

Liz, the Neighbour

That's a really inappropriate thing to say, Liz thought. She drove up to the main entrance and stopped the car. "Are you ready?" Liz asked, looking at her passengers in the backseat through the rear-view mirror.

"Babe, I was born ready," Birdie said as she hopped out.

"Me, too, babe," Agnes said as she hopped out.

"Let's do it, babe," Ed said as he got out.

"Showtime, babe," Will said.

Liz scanned the parking lot. For most people, it was too early to shop. Still, a lot of the parking spaces were occupied. The more, the merrier. They would have enough of an audience, Liz thought. She parked her car close to the entrance and got off the car to go join her crew.

She saw Caleb standing by the entrance. As she walked by Caleb, she put her hand out at her waistline, and Caleb gave her a low-five.

Without too much trouble, Liz found her crew. Ed was the first one in line, pushing his shopping cart, walking around at a pretty fast pace. Behind him was Birdie pushing her shopping cart, followed by Agnes walking with her cane. Next to Agnes was Will strolling along slowly in his cool sunglasses. Liz walked behind Will, holding her cellphone tightly in her hand. She could hear Caleb's heavy footsteps right behind her.

After she'd made a few more strides, Liz saw Ed stop. Birdie and everyone else rushed towards Ed. Everyone arrived almost at the same time. Agnes was last as usual.

Birdie took one look at the young man who was leisurely taking a box of pasta off the shelf. She gave Ed the nod, silent confirmation – *That's the bastard that took Maddie away from us.*

Ed started pushing his cart in the young man's direction. He was only a few feet away when the young man slowly turned. Before the young man realized what was happening, Ed charged him with his shopping cart and hit him as hard as he could.

"Oww!" Adam Doyle cried.

"Oh My Goodness! Did I hit you?" Ed said, hurling his cart into Adam as hard as he could again.

"What the…" Adam angrily grabbed Ed's cart.

"Let go. I'm just a poor old man who can't see well." Ed shook his cart, trying to get it out of Adam's powerful grip.

"You let go. A blind man should never be trusted." Adam yanked the cart away from Ed. "Where to?"

"Right behind you would be perfect," Ed said, rubbing his hands.

"You mean *right there*?" Adam pointed a foot away from him.

Ed nodded.

"No problem." Adam thrust the cart forward, dusting off his hands. "There you go."

The cart glided through until it hit the meat display.

With a devilish grin on his face, Adam gave Ed the wave through gesture. "Off you go."

Ed gave Adam a nod as he passed by. "Oh, I almost forgot. I've got something to show you."

Adam heard the old man's voice from behind him. He turned around, feeling something strangely familiar about the old man. Staring at this odd, old man, recognition finally came. He flashed a grin. "I know you."

"Do you?" Ed said returning Adam's smile suddenly throwing a punch right in his face.

"You crazy old man," Adam snarled. He was just about to show Ed what a real punch feels like, when he felt another shopping cart smash into him from behind. Adam turned around and got smacked in the back of his head again.

"What the fuck!" Adam turned around and saw Ed still smiling. He was about to choke the life out of Ed with his two bare hands, when he felt a tap, tap, tap on his shoulder from his back. He whipped around, his face all red in anger. "What?" He snapped. He didn't know what to make of it when he saw that it was a man around his age standing there not more than a foot away from him. He narrowed his eyes to the man. "Do I know..."

"You son of a gun!" Will threw a punch landing it hard into Adam's stomach.

"Oww!" Adam grabbed his stomach. The power that the punch delivered threw him off. The stranger didn't look like much of anything. Yet, to Adam's surprise, he had delivered one hell of a power punch – the kind that could burst internal organs.

Will knew he had just enough time to throw one more punch. He had to make it count. In a furious rage, he punched Adam again with the roll of quarters still tightly held in his fist, thinking about poor Maddie dying on a park bench in agony next to this worthless piece of garbage: *Bam!*

"Aaargh!" Adam saw a big flash of light as the stranger's fist made contact again, this time striking the right side of Doyle's abdomen right to his liver. He slowly collapsed onto the floor hugging his stomach with both hands.

Will sprung on top of Adam and whispered in his ear, "This is just the beginning."

Beginning of what? Adam wondered. Lying on the ground, he just looked up at the stranger. *Where have I seen him before?* Adam wondered. He knew this guy. He was sure of it. He then heard light footsteps, and an old woman with a smirk on her face came into view. It hit him who she was – *the rat.*

"Oh My God! Will Pemberton!" Birdie yelled out while smiling at Adam. "You got the killer!"

"The killer?" Agnes said, emerging from behind Birdie. She started hitting Adam's legs with her cane: *Dab dab dab!.* "You naughty boy!" *Dab dab dab.*

Dumbfounded, Adam Doyle just stared at the ceiling. Although he couldn't see who was hitting him, he had a pretty good idea who that might be. He didn't even bother to thrash around to get his legs out of striking range of the cane because it wasn't actually hurting him much, although the humiliation of it all was more than he could bear. He just lay there trying to figure out what was happening to him.

"Grandma!" Will cried. "He's the killer, right?"

"Yees!" Birdie squeaked. She turned to Adam grinning down at him.

Who's he? Will Pemberton... That's what the rat called him. He knew the name. He thought about it for a moment and then it came to him – *the movie star.* The realization made him even more confused. He couldn't figure out why the hell this big-time movie star was in this store throwing punches at him. All and all, it had become a very confusing day for him. He just closed his eyes and wished that his superior officer was here to sort this out.

• • •

People were abandoning their shopping carts to get an up close and personal look at all the commotion and goings on in the pasta and sauce aisle. Others leaned on their shopping carts from a distance and poked their heads down the aisle. The store staff, who were working that day, walked over to check out the fun scene that was going on, hoping for something big that would entertain them for a change. The store manager hurriedly came out of the back and headed to the spot where all the spectators had already gathered.

"Aren't you Will Pemberton?" a young pregnant woman at the front of the crowd screamed with joy. "You played Morgan in The Playboy."

As if that was a cue, everyone took out their cellphones and started recording.

"Yes, I am." Will flashed a bright smile, still sitting on top of Adam Doyle.

"My favourite is you as Joe in Two Brothers," a young man with acne said. Standing 5'6" tall with his pimply face.

"Bobby in October Surprise was the best," a man wearing a cheap suit in his early 50s chimed in.

"Thank you, thank you," Will said, giving a slight bow to the people delivered earnestly from Adam's chest.

"Uh…" The pregnant woman pointed her finger at Adam as if she just realized that Will was sitting on a man. "Why are you sitting on that man?"

Liz, the Neighbour

"Are we on some kind of hidden camera prank show?" the young man with acne said excitedly, looking around the store, trying to spot the hidden camera.

"No, unfortunately, this is not a hidden camera show. This is as real as you can get. Can anyone please call 9-1-1? This man here tried to kill my grandmother."

"Your grandmother!?" The pregnant woman said, eyes wide.

"Yes, that's my grandmother." Will motioned with his head to Birdie.

"Oh My God! That man," the pregnant woman pointed her index finger at Adam again, "tried to kill your poor old grandma?"

"I'm not *that* old," Birdie said.

"Sorry," the pregnant woman apologized.

"That's okay," Birdie said. "I don't think the store lighting is very flattering."

"Grandma, about this awful man…" Will said gently, prodding Birdie to deliver her next line.

"Oh yes!" Birdie nodded. "That man tried to kill me last Saturday. I don't know why he wanted to kill me though. Everybody calls me an angel."

"There's got to be a reason," a black man with a thin build in his 60s piped up.

"No, not a clue," Birdie slowly shook her head. After a moment of silence, she snapped her fingers. "I don't know for sure, but it might have something to do with a retirement home that I've been investigating for insurance fraud and murder."

"What? Murder?" a young mother with a toddler in her arm squeaked.

"Why don't we just ask him?" a teenager in baggy pants said dispassionately, tilting his head in Adam's direction.

"That's a great idea," the young man with the acne said. He looked at Adam and said, "Why did you try to kill her?"

Adam kept his eyes closed.

"It's so disturbing, especially at a time like this," Will said.

"What do you mean by *time like this*?" an old man standing next to an old woman who was probably his wife asked.

"I just lost my dear, dear sister."

"I didn't think Will Pemberton had a sister," a young girl in a green hoodie said.

"She wasn't my sister by blood. She was my sister by heart." Will took out his cellphone, showing everyone a picture of Maddie. "That's my sister, Madison Cooper." He extended his arm out to the spectators so they could see Madison's picture.

"She was so young," the pregnant woman said, taking the phone and passing it to the young man with acne in the red hoodie.

"She was *so* beautiful," the young man blew out a whistle.

Everybody moved closer to the acne man to have a better look at the picture.

"We grew up together. Her grandparents and my grandma have been living next door to each other forever. Her mother and my mother were best friends. Madison Cooper was taken from us on Friday, November 29. Losing Maddie has been unbearably painful. On top of that, this man here tried to take my grandma away from me. I want to know why. I want to get to the bottom of all this."

• • •

Four men in a black SUV watched in total bewilderment as Adam Doyle was dragged out of the Miser superstore and put into the back of a cop car.

In the front passenger seat was B-Team leader Chris Winger. He didn't know exactly what was happening but he did know one thing – He was definitely moving up the corporate ladder. Although Adam Doyle and he were somewhat equals in the chain of command, there was a bond between Doyle and the boss he couldn't seem to bridge. Whatever happened from this day forward, Chris was sure that things between Doyle and the boss would never be the same again. With a grin on his face, he clicked 'Sir' on his cellphone.

"It looks like Adam has been arrested," Chris said.

"Adam who?" Troy was at a loss.

"Adam Doyle… Our Adam… The guy with strawberry blond… The guy…" Chris almost wanted to add, *the guy you prefer over me*, but he stopped himself just in time. He wondered if the boss had amnesia. Otherwise, it didn't make any sense to him. *Adam Who? What the hell*, he thought.

"Where are you? Why aren't you watching the pensioner?" Troy snapped.

"Uh sir, we have been watching her."

"Then, how do you know that Adam was arrested?"

"We followed the oldie to the Miser superstore on Dufferin Street. While we were waiting in the parking lot for the oldie to finish her grocery shopping, we saw

Adam being dragged out by a couple of uniformed cops and stuffed into the back of a cruiser."

Troy knew it was bad. He was no rocket scientist but he knew this was very bad. The oldie resided on Culnan Avenue in the southwest corner of the city. She'd stayed in the east end of Scarborough all last night, then *boom*, out of the blue she pops up all the way downtown on Dufferin Street to go grocery shopping. Why would she do that? The Miser had great prices on everything, that was a given, but there were Miser superstores everywhere.

"Uh Sir?"

"I'm here," Troy said in a clipped voice. "Whatever you do, do not let that woman out of your sight. Send Hugh and Giovanni to get the guns." Troy paused for a moment and then added, "Tell them to bring out the big guns. Tonight, she's going down. Everybody and anybody that gets in the way, blow their heads off as well. I don't care how you do it. Just get it done. When you're all geared up, call me back."

"Yessir!" Chris tapped his left palm with his cellphone, mulling over what all this meant for him. From what the boss said and by the tone of his voice, whatever it was, it was bad… *for Adam*. It was definitely an opportunity for his career advancement if he got it right tonight. Why wouldn't he? What could stop him? Nothing! He grinned to himself then turned to the backseat.

"Go to the warehouse and get the big guns. I'll text you the location of the surprise party as soon as I know it."

Hugh Shannon and Giovanni Spatola nodded away in their seats but still hadn't moved their asses an inch.

"What are you waiting for? Go!" Chris yelled.

"Now?" Hugh asked as if the order was something beyond his comprehension.

"No, no," Chris nonchalantly said, grinning. "Next year will be just fine."

"Okay." Hugh and Giovanni slouched back into their seats.

"Yes Now!" Chris yelled. Spit flying in all directions.

"Okay boss," Giovanni said, still sitting there on his fat ass.

"What now?" Chris asked.

"We're ready, Boss," Giovanni said. "Burt, let's roll."

Chris rolled his eyes until he got too dizzy to do it anymore. This was why his team was called the B-Team. None of the other teams had a team name except for his. They'd come up with a name just for them to distinguish his team from the rest of the teams.

"Get a taxi. Get an Uber. Get Lyft," Chris yelled. "Get out now! Get yourselves down to the warehouse, grab the gear, load the SUV and be ready to roll in an hour."

"Got it." Hugh and Giovanni got out, still wiping the spit off their faces.

34

THURSDAY, DECEMBER 12

All four members of the B-Team sat in their respective seats in the black SUV parked on Purpledusk Trail, waiting for the right time to go in guns ablazing, literally and figuratively.

The first soldier Hugh Shannon and the second soldier Giovanni Spatola had played the "Are We There Yet?" game for the last hour or so, and now they had moved on to "I Spy".

"I spy with my little eye something starting with S," Hugh said.

"S…" Giovanni scanned the area and saw no object that started with S. "Hmm…" He kept searching. "I don't know. Hmm… What words starting with S? Saw… Switchblade… Stiletto… Shotgun… Yes, shotgun!"

"Where do you see a shotgun?" Hugh said contemptuously.

"Here." Giovanni pointed at the gun lying across his lap.

"These aren't shotguns, you moron," Hugh scorned.

"What did you call me?" Giovanni grabbed his assault rifle.

"That's enough!" Chris yelled.

After a moment of silence, Giovanni said, "Tell me what your *little* eye spied starting with S? You saw shit!"

Hugh smiled. "Ding ding ding!"

Giovanni frowned, pointing his gun at Hugh again.

"Put it down, Giovanni!" Chris yelled, glaring at him.

Giovanni stared right back at Chris for a long moment and slowly put the gun back down on his lap.

"Look!" Hugh pointed at a pile lying on the sidewalk.

"Bullshit! That's not shit!" Giovanni challenged Hugh.

"Go check it out and see for yourself." Hugh accepted the challenge, opening the car door.

"Stay inside," Chris hissed, emitting a thousand volts of angry.

Hugh closed the door slowly in a pout.

Chris let out a sigh. It had been almost 15 minutes since all the lights had gone out in the red brick house. Ideally, he wanted to wait at least another 30 minutes just to make sure everyone had fallen asleep. Yet, if they waited any longer in here, he wouldn't have anyone left alive to go and kill the oldie or anyone else in that house. He scanned the street quickly. He liked what he saw – *Nothing!* The street was totally dead.

"Ready?" Chris said, admiring the array of lethal firepower that the team members were armed with. As instructed, they brought out the big guns - modified semi-automatic assault rifles that fired almost as fast as the fully automatic ones.

Everyone held their guns a little higher except for Burt. Since he was the driver, his hands were still on the wheel.

Chris said, "Giovanni, you stay on the main floor and shoot anything that moves. Hugh, you'll come upstairs with me. You wait by the first door you see until I make it to the last door. Once we're in position, we start shooting. Got it?"

"Yessir!" Hugh and Giovanni said in unison.

"It's go time," Chris said.

They all moved stealthily in the dark and piled up at the front door of the red brick house, silently waiting for Chris Winger to unlock the door. Chris jiggled his pick a little: *Click!* He quietly turned the doorknob, which glided all the way. He smiled as he pushed the door in. The three formed a line, Chris in the lead with Giovanni bringing up the rear. They quickly entered the dark house, eyes straight ahead.

Click-clack, click-clack. As their feet fell on the wooden floor, the house creaked and squeaked. As Chris was frowning at the annoying creaking sounds, he felt something around his ankle.

Trip wire! Fuck! He was already falling by the time he recognized what it was: *Fa-thud!* On his way down, his gun sprung out of his hands and flew across the floor.

Walking right behind Chris, Hugh was the next one to go down: *Fa-thud!* As he was going down, his finger accidently squeezed the trigger, and a shot was fired. Stunned by his own accidental gunfire, he landed right on top of Chris, his mouth wide open.

As Giovanni quietly closed the door behind him, he heard the first *Fa-thud!* Before he blinked his eyes, he heard the second *Fa-thud!* Before he could let out a laugh over Hugh's misfortune, the place suddenly light up brighter than the brightest sunny day in July. Although the sudden burst of light temporarily blinded him, he was still able to hear the creaking sound of a door opening and then *Wham!* Somebody whacked him in the back of his head.

"Get off of me!" Chris yelled, trying to crawl out from under Hugh.

Hugh rolled off to the side, holding his gun in his right hand.

Chris lunged for his weapon, but before he could reach it, a foot appeared and kicked it away off to the far right. He stretched his neck up and saw an Asian woman who stood in front of him smiling a lopsided smile. He grinned. *It's only a girl.*

As Chris jumped to his feet, the Asian woman lifted her right knee while turning her left foot and body in a semicircular motion, extending her leg and landing a full strike on his left knee joint with the instep of her foot.

"Oww!" Chris howled. He jumped around on his right foot, hugging his left leg with his hands. It hurt like hell. Still, being kicked by a girl, it wasn't game over. Besides, he wasn't going to be put down by a woman, no matter what. It would be way too humiliating. Just as he was trying to get back on both feet again, the woman was already raising her right leg in the cocked position, her knee pointing at him. Then, in the blink of his eyes, she had whipped the leg into an arc striking him in the head with the blade of her foot.

Fa-thud! Chris collapsed in a heap on the floor.

In the meantime, when Hugh Shannon rolled off to the side, he heard running footsteps and then just caught a glimpse of a middle-aged Indian man holding some kind of round black object above his head. In a swift move, before he even realized that the black object was a cast iron frying pan, the pan had already hit him with almighty power: *Bang!* As his head hit the ground, he lost his grip on his rifle.

"Welcome," the Indian man said. "We've been waiting for you." He circled around Hugh and picked up the gun. He raised it up for inspection. He'd never used this type of gun before, but they were all the same to him. A gun was a gun. It had been a while since he had held a gun in his hands. A grin spread across his face.

Caleb swooped in and expertly bound Hugh's hands together with a white zip tie. "Good job, Mr. Sandhu."

"MmHmm," Mr. Sandhu said perfunctorily totally engrossed in the gun, the wide grin plastered on his face

Caleb gaped at Mr. Sandhu. "I don't like the way you're looking at that gun."

"MmHmm." Mr. Sandhu just nodded his head.

• • •

Liz, the Neighbour

The wheelman Burt had been intensely watching the entrance door of the red brick house ever since his comrades had left the SUV to pop the people inside the house. He'd only heard one gunshot though, and that was it. After that, silence. He knew for a fact that there was more than one person in that house. He twisted his body to the right for a better view.

Insistent tapping on the driver's side window quickly made him turn his attention to see what it was. He turned to his left and found a blonde standing right there outside of his car. She was pretty, but not really his type. "What's up?" Burt said, rolling the window down.

"Hello," the blonde said, flashing a smile. "I'm just wondering if you're out here, stalking me."

"What?" Burt frowned in confusion.

"You can drop the act. I saw you following me for most of the day."

"I don't know what you're talking about." Burt stared angrily at the blonde hoping to scare her off.

"I guess you're dumber than I thought," the blonde said.

"You crazy bitch!"

"You think?" the blonde waved a screwdriver in her hand.

"What the f…"

Next thing he knew, the blonde was going all stabby like on his tire with the screwdriver.

Burt jumped out of his SUV, his face burning red with anger. He was going to teach her a lesson.

The blonde swiftly turned on him with the screwdriver pointed threateningly. "You're under arrest."

"What?"

"Jeffrey?" the blonde yelled. "I need the handcuffs."

"Too bad," Jeffrey said, emerging from the dark. "I'll take it from here. And Liz, put away the screwdriver."

• • •

After Jeffrey left with the cops who took the four goons away in their patrol cars, everybody gathered together in Mr. Sandhu's living room. More than anyone, Tejas seemed to be very excited.

"You seem to be terribly excited in spite of our current state of affairs," Mr. Sandhu said with a hint of concern in his voice.

"Dad, I've just decided what I want to do when I grow up."

"What future have you chosen?" Mr. Sandhu said.

"I want to be a soldier," Tejas said with a big proud grin on his face, "just like you've always wanted."

"Boy, you've never wanted that. What finally made you see the light?"

"When I saw you guys take on these badass mother—"

"Watch your language, young man," Mr. Sandhu said sternly.

"Sorry, dad," Tejas said, showing such a sweet smile that would melt anyone's heart.

"You're *good*," Will said with admiration in his eyes. "Maybe, you should be an actor like me."

Tejas took a minute and said, "Maybe later fam, when I get really old like you."

"What? Me old? No Anissa Walsh for you, young man."

"Being an actor like you, well of course, it's dope," Tejas said, giving a thumbs-up to Will.

"Too late," Will grumbled with a twinkle in his eye.

"Go on," Mr. Sandhu encouraged Tejas to continue.

"All I'm saying is that what you guys showed me tonight was just downright fire. I want that. I'm gonna join the military and learn how to kick some a… I mean butts."

"If you become an actor," Will said, "the best part is, you don't actually have to do any of the butt-kicking yourself. Stuntmen do it for you. Wouldn't that be so much better?"

"Let it go," Liz said, patting Will on the back. "You can't win."

Will laid his head on Liz's shoulder and made a sobbing sound.

Everyone laughed.

When the laughter died down a little, Caleb said, "Today, I realized that these people aren't going to stop until they kill *you*, Birdie, and now probably everyone else, too. All of you need to go into hiding until Jeffrey puts all these…" Caleb paused and rolled his eyes for a moment. "Hmm…" He scratched his head for another moment and then finally said, "For a lack of better words, I'll go with *bad people*. Until Jeffrey puts all these *bad people* behind bars, you all should go into hiding."

Agnes yawned. "That's getting old."

Birdie shook her head. "No, no. He has a point." Looking Caleb in the eye, Birdie said, "You should

Liz, the Neighbour

take your own advice and go into hiding. After we clear house, we'll call you."

"You have a target on your back," Caleb said, looking at Will for his support.

"If you can make her go into hiding, I'll give you everything I have. I'm talking about right down to my tighty whities if ya want."

Caleb shook his head in disgust. "Why the hell would I want your gotchies?" He scanned the room, trying to spot a supporter for his cause. When his eyes lingered on Ella for a few more seconds longer than the others, Charlie himself threw a block on Caleb's line of site to Ella.

"Caleb has a point," Yuul said straight to the point. "Mr. Sandhu's place has been exposed. We either go into hiding now or we purge them before they do us."

"Purge them? You mean as in kill them?" Will asked, staring at Yuul. His eyes wide.

"Of course, she doesn't mean that," Liz interjected. "She means… Umm…" She snapped. "We put them behind bars *permanently*, that's what she meant."

"Yeah, right," Will said.

"Actually, there's a way to do just that," Birdie said.

"How?" Caleb wanted to know.

"We can run my play one more time," Birdie said.

Will jumped in, "What did you get up to, grandma? What are you talking about?"

"Me and Agnes is what I'm talking about. Our plan didn't work before because we lacked human resources. Now that we have musclemen, wheelmen, and insiders, I think we can pull it off this time."

"What did you do?" Caleb wanted to know.

Birdie said, "Actually, it's a funny story. As you know, after my visit to the police, I got kicked out of the home. So, I decided to follow them on one of their trips down to the States in my car. After they dropped the residents off at the shopping mall, they drove off. I figured that they were driving to their pick-up spot. So, I kept following them. Unfortunately, I lost them somewhere along the way and lost my way back to the border. My eyes get drier as I get older. Nowadays, it takes me a whole minute to blink once. I think that's why I lost them every time."

"I know the feeling," Ed said, nodding. "Since I hit 70, even with drops, mine are as dry as the Sahara."

"That's it?" Will asked in disappointment.

Birdie squinted at Will shaking her head. "Now I know how little you think of your grandma. Of course, that's not it. After Agnes ran away from the home, we worked together. Based on my earlier experiences, we came up with a new plan. Actually, we revived an old trick, the flat tire scam. We knew what route they were going to take. So, we drove ahead and parked the car on a street we figured we'd be able to flag them down on. Agnes was going to wave the bus driver down and ask for help to change a flat tire. While Agnes kept him occupied, I was going to search the hold on the bus. On that fatal day, while I was hiding around the corner, Agnes was on the street waiting for the bus to come. Some truck rear-ended my car and totalled it."

"Oh My God!" Will exclaimed, startled for a moment from a shock that paralyzed his brain. "That's how your car got totalled."

"In retrospect, the idea wasn't a good one. I'll admit that. At the time the way I envisioned how it was all gonna go down, it looked like a beautiful thing."

Liz said, "What do you want to give another try? Following them down to the States or trying to wave the bus down?"

"I want to follow them down. I know half the way they take to get to their pick-up location. And I know when. According to my source, they're going on the "shopping trip" this coming Wednesday. When they travel to the States, they'll split into two teams – one team guards the coach house at Wild Peach, and the other team is on the bus. Since they already lost 5 men, they'll be spread pretty thin now. We follow them to the States and find out what they're selling or buying. Whatever is going down in the States, I guarantee it's illegal. I'd bet my life on it! We could catch them at the border red-handed."

"Why are they guarding the coach house?" Liz wanted to know.

"I think that's where they keep the stuff. I saw them move the crates from the bus to the coach house."

"Don't you think that Adam Doyle and the 4 goons in custody will talk?" Ella said.

"Absolutely they'll rat out everyone," Liz said. She paused for a minute and said, "If they haven't by Tuesday, then we'll make the trip to the States on Wednesday."

"Either way," Caleb said, "whether those guys talk or we go down to the States, you guys still need to disappear until that happens."

"Hmm…" Mr. Sandhu said in seriousness. "From a tactical point of view, it's too risky to send men to the same location twice. If they get caught again, it'd be too hard to say it was a robbery-gone-wrong again. Besides, Tejas has to go to school. I'll take a week off from work, so that I don't have anywhere to go but to take Tejas to and from school. It might be safer to stay here on high alert. At least we know the terrain."

Caleb took his time, considering the options and eventually nodded. "I'll take Tejas to school and pick him up after school."

"In your Beamer?" Tejas said, his face lighting up brightly.

"Of course," Caleb said.

"Then, can I sit in the backseat?"

"Of course, and I'll even open the door for you."

Tejas tilted his head in thought for a moment and then smiled a foolish smile. "Can Liz do that?"

"Of course, I can," Liz said.

Ella shook her head. "No, you don't want that. Take my word for it. She'll be in her pajamas and her hair will be…" Ella shivered as recalling the time when Liz had taken her to work when she'd been undercover last summer.

"It wasn't that bad," Liz said, defending her honour.

Looking at Tejas, Ella said, "Her words were, "You'll live.""

"Hmm… Maybe, I'll just stick with Caleb."

"I'll get all dolled up. What time do you have to be at school for?"

"7:30"

Liz, the Neighbour

"Caleb, it is then." Liz put her hands up in the air in surrender.

Birdie looked at Liz shaking her head. "Maybe you and Will are a match made in heaven after all."

Will rested his head on Liz's shoulder and smiled.

I can sleep in, too, Caleb thought.

• • •

Although it was way past their bedtime, Rob and Doreen were wide awake in their basement – the basement that they had turned into their haven that was totally sound-proof complete with radio frequency jamming devices and more. After the gigantic failure to exterminate the rat and her followers, it was understandable they couldn't sleep.

Rob paced back and forth in his basement. Every now and then, he stopped pacing and stomped on the carpeted floor. The carpet absorbed any noise that might have been created and just left Rob with aching feet. That was annoying. When he stomped, he expected to hear the stomping noise or at least something. But there was none. In frustration, he started pacing again. After a while, he stopped, and gave the stomping another shot. Still not hearing any of the satisfactory sounds that might mollify his anger, he doubled up stomping harder and harder. Eventually he resigned himself back to packing because he'd really hurt his feet.

Rob couldn't recall the last time he'd felt such a strong urge to whack someone upside the head. The angry inferno that was raging inside threatened to consume him and he knew it wasn't just going to extinguish itself. "Why aren't they dying?" he screamed. "Die! Die! Die!" he stomped.

"You'll break your bones if you keep doing that," Doreen said in her usual calm and soft voice.

"Since when, did it become so hard to kill people? And we are talking about old people here."

"Never," Doreen agreed while knitting on the couch by the fireplace.

"What are we going to do, Doreen?"

Doreen couldn't help but smile when she saw this 67-year-old man acting like a 5-year-old boy asking his mommy to solve all of life's challenges for him. To her, he would always be that adorable 5-year-old boy. "We'll find a way to keep the lid closed."

"How?" Rob stomped again. "You heard what that Hollywood punk said. He won't rest until he finds out who really killed Madison."

"That's exactly what we'll do." Doreen had a serene smile.

"If we do that, it'll create more problems for us, and I'm talking serious problems. First off, Adam Brooks will be released and then guaranteed he'll resume his investigation into the home."

"No doubt about that. That's why I'm saying, he needs to go."

"How?"

"We go back to our original plan and take him out."

"Even if we succeed in killing him, Jeffrey will pick up where Adam left off."

"We'll off him, too."

Rob let out a sigh. "Doreen, aren't you forgetting something?"

Liz, the Neighbour

Doreen stopped knitting and looked up at Rob. "What is that?"

"Don't you remember we already tried that? It's not for lack of trying that they're still breathing."

"We'll succeed this time," Doreen said confidently.

"Even if we do, the real killer will rat us out to cut a deal," Rob said grimly, recalling his own experience. Back home in Chicago, he'd been a big time dealer. He'd bought drugs from Central America and sold them on the streets of America. He'd bought weapons from his fellow Americans and sold them down in Central America. It had been a very lucrative business up until the FBI finally caught up with him. He did what he had to do when he was arrested. He ratted out everyone he'd ever dealt with and in turn they gave him a shot at a new life on the condition that he never set foot in America again. So, he fled to Canada. Ever since, he'd kept very low profile to hide away from all those who wanted to settle scores with him.

Doreen put her knitting needles down on the coffee table.

"What?" Rob asked.

"Let's call Troy."

Eyes wide open, Rob said, "Why? We already talked to him."

"Yes, but that was him reporting to us on B-Team's failed mission. Right now, I have questions that I need answers to."

"What questions?" Rob asked flabbergasted.

His look made her laugh. "Where were you when I was young enough to bear your child?"

"I was hiding until you couldn't bear children. I could never share you even with my own child."

Doreen shook her head, her eyes dancing. "You always know just the right thing to say."

"Admit it. You just like whatever I say," Rob said, taking his cellphone out of his pocket. He pressed 'Troy' and put him on speaker.

"Troy? Did I wake you?" Doreen said.

"Aunt Doreen?" Troy said. "No, I'm awake. How could I sleep after making such a mess?"

"Don't lose sleep over trivial things, my little darling. As you said, the B-Team will stick to the robbery story. Things didn't get any better for us, but more importantly they didn't get any worse, either. Now, tell me about Adam Doyle."

Adam? Troy was taken aback. *Why?* He wondered. It was the furthest thing away from what he thought his aunt and uncle would be interested in at this point. "What do you want to know?"

"What does he know about our operation?"

"He's pretty much in the loop on everything," Troy said.

"Obviously, he knows about your involvement in Wild Peach. What about the others? What about Wylie or us for that matter?"

"He doesn't know anything about you guys, just the people he works with at Wild Peach."

"Is he solid or is he the type that's gonna rat you out to save his own skin?"

Troy thought about the question. Considering what went down in Iraq, he was sure that Doyle wouldn't. "He's solid, I trust him."

"Good! That's what I needed to hear," Doreen said. "We're going to send him a lawyer first thing in the morning. The lawyer will tell him to confess to the murder of Madison Cooper. Do you foresee any problems with this plan?"

With just a little encouragement, Troy was sure that Doyle would do as he was told. "No, he'll do it. I know the right buttons to push to get him there."

"It's settled then. It won't be a bad thing for your friend, either. He's only gonna do time for one murder. Before he knows it, he'll be out."

"Aunt Doreen, you don't think they'll stop the investigation just because they've put Doyle behind bars, do you?" Troy was baffled. He'd never taken his aunt for a fool.

"No, I don't, but it will give us enough time to clean all this mess up."

"How?" Troy wanted to know.

"Just like we planned, we'll shoot Adam Brooks, the oldie who brought us all this trouble and anybody else standing in our way."

"Tell me more," Troy said.

Doreen told Troy and Rob about her plan.

"I love it," Troy said with a devilish grin on his face. "I'll get everything ready. Have a good night!"

"You, too, sweetie," Doreen said.

Rob disconnected the call and put his cellphone back in his pants pocket.

"What's wrong, Rob? You don't look too happy. You don't like my plan?" Doreen asked.

Rob said, "You know I do. I'm just thinking we need a contingency plan. Lately, for whatever reason, things haven't been working out the way they should."

"What's your Plan B?" Doreen asked, picking up her knitting needles.

"Just tell me, if things don't work out, are you willing to sacrifice Troy or Wylie, or both?"

"Darling, we don't sacrifice family members, unless of course it comes down to us or them, and we're not there yet."

"Oh, I love you, my darling." Rob cupped Doreen's face and kissed her on the lips.

35

FRIDAY, DECEMBER 13

Earbuds in, Jeffrey watched 'TBC's Morning with Cindy' on his phone while sitting at his desk in the homicide unit. Although it was just a little after 9:00 a.m., the unit had already half-emptied. His partner, Wylie Townsend, was sitting at his desk, looking like he was minding his own business. Wary of each other, neither cracked jokes. None of the regular casual chit-chat or office banter.

Tim and Sam sat together at Tim's desk. Their heads were buried in paperwork, which they were taking great care to keep guarded from prying eyes.

Jeffrey gave a quick glance over to the captain's office just to make sure that she was still there. After he caught a glimpse of her, he let out a sigh of relief inwardly. Not even the most gifted fortuneteller could foresee who would be where on Fridays at the homicide squad. He turned his attention back to the television interview.

As usual, the show's host Cindy Woods was sitting in her comfortable chair, interviewing her guest. Unlike other days, today she was dressed provocatively, wearing a tight fitting red dress that really showed off her incredible figure.

She gently touched her guest's arm while he talked about Madison Cooper, and her untimely death. Cindy leaned in closer to her guest when he talked about a guy named "Adam". Cindy's jaw dropped in shock as Jeffrey talked about Madison's date and the revelation of who she had gone out with on the night she was murdered. Cindy shook her head in disbelief as he gave her the rundown on the call he and his grandmother had made to Detective Wylie Townsend.

"Will, can you share any of the details from when Detective Wylie Townsend called you back?" Cindy leaned in, giving Will her full attention.

"I wish I could, but we never did hear back from Detective Townsend. All we know at this point is that the police never bothered to follow up on it at all. Don't you think that's odd? Why wouldn't they?"

"Yes, it's absolutely odd," Cindy enthusiastically nodded her head.

"You know what's even more odd, Cindy?" Will fixed his eyes on Cindy.

"What?" Cindy said, placing her hand on her chest.

"A few days after the phone call to Detective Wylie, we got a visitor. My grandmother was woken up at gunpoint." Will paused.

"Oh no!" Cindy placed her hand over her mouth.

The camera zoomed in and got a close-up shot of Will as he looked out into the audience at Birdie with love and concern, then zoomed in on Birdie looking back at Will with such a tender heart.

Will continued on recalling the part where Birdie had called KSK pips for help that night. He praised the work the agency had done.

"Obviously, this guy couldn't take *no* for an answer. Or, should I say he couldn't take failure well? He lurked around in the shadows for another chance to kill my grandmother. It's a good thing, the agency sent out more than just one team. So, while we were being transferred to a safe house, the other team followed the attacker and was able to get his home address and license plate number." Will flashed a mischievous smile at Cindy. "Can you guess the name of the attacker?"

Cindy bit her bottom lip for a moment. She then said, her voice unsure, "Adam?"

"Yes!" Will said. "KSK PIPs figured out that this Adam guy, who tried to kill my grandmother a few nights ago was the very same guy that Madison met at the hospital and ended up going out on a date with that fatal night. I've got to say God really works in mysterious ways. Yesterday, we just happened to run into this Adam guy at the Miser superstore and were able to catch the man. That's what you saw on social media. Someone recorded the whole thing and posted it online." Will paused again and let out a long sigh.

"What's wrong? You caught the guy. It's a happy ending, isn't it?" Cindy asked.

"Unfortunately, it's not. Last night, four people showed up at our safe house with semi-automatic weapons and *once again* tried to kill my grandma." Will looked at Birdie in the audience again. He then looked Cindy squarely in the eye. "When this Adam guy showed up at my grandma's pointing his gun at her, we thought that it was a cover-up for the murder of Madison. But now, we're not so sure. It's started to look like something else entirely."

"Are you suggesting there's more to this than just Madison's murder?" the host wanted to know.

"My grandma has had some suspicions about a retirement home that include insurance fraud and a bunch of other awful things. I didn't believe her in the beginning, but it's really starting to look like she might have been right all along. We'll keep digging. We want to help the police put the real killer behind bars." Will stopped and then in a plea to the camera he continued. "Detective Wylie, if you're listening, we've got more gifts for you. All you have to do is open them this time."

• • •

Tick-tock, tick-tock. The time on his cellphone had just changed from 9:59 a.m. to 10:00 a.m. proving to Jeffrey that time hadn't stopped ticking. He used his phone to go online to see if people had started talking about Will's morning show interview on any of the social media platforms. Yes, the numbers were growing with more and more posts. Still though, none of the phones in his unit were ringing off the wall. Everything was just as quiet as it had been 30 minutes ago.

Will had put out just the right amount of information to make the bad people give up on Adam

Liz, the Neighbour

Doyle and he'd laid it all out in such a way that it pushed the police into re-opening the case. And most importantly, they now had to look into the goings-on of one of their own – Wylie Townsend. Individually they were all highly explosive, but all together it should create a supersonic explosion. Yet, so far it hadn't.

Be patient, Jeffrey kept telling himself. Word had to get out and circulate before shit hit the fan. He was about to click *Search* on his phone again when out of the corner of his eye, he saw Wylie spring out of his chair, his cellphone glued to his ear. Jeffrey noticed the veins in Wylie's hands and neck had started protruding and bulging. *Is he mad? I hope he is.*

And then finally, there it was, the phones on all the desks started ringing off the hook. He gave a sidelong glance over to the captain's office.

Holy Shoot! She's on the phone, too. Is she mad? Is she yelling? All of the above. It got him excited. He quickly scanned across the unit. Whoever was there was now either taking calls as they checked their computer monitors, all except for Phil Lee. Phil Lee was just meandering about. He was the proverbial office slacker in his unit, and every unit had one.

"Jeffrey!" the captain's voice reverberated through the unit.

Jeffrey wiped off his grin before he got up. The captain was standing at her office door, beckoning him over. Jeffrey innocently pointed to himself as if to say, "Who me?" When he saw the captain nodding, he slowly walked over to the captain's office. "What's up?" Jeffrey said, closing the door behind him.

The captain angrily took her phone off the hook and sat down. "Where's Wylie?"

Jeffrey shrugged. "I don't know."

The captain glared at Jeffrey, her nostrils flaring. "Did you see the TV interview?"

"Yes."

"Why the hell didn't you tell me about this Adam guy?"

"Wylie never said a word to me about any of it."

"Don't lie to me." The captain bellowed.

"Why would I lie to you about that?" Jeffrey shot back. "Look, I'm not an 'I told you so' kind of guy, but when I did tell you that there was more to investigate, what did you do?" Jeffrey paused for an answer, but none came. "You put me and Wylie on vacation."

The captain glared at him ratcheting up the tension using her eyes.

"You were so eager to take me off the case. When did we ever get a reward for putting a suspect in custody?"

The captain dropped the stare and let out a sigh. "He wasn't just a suspect. All the evidence pointed to him."

"Look, all I'm saying is that even if he was the real killer, I've never been put on vacation as a reward like that before. Sure, we had the guy in custody, but he hadn't even been convicted yet. So, why the sudden holiday?"

"The Chief wanted to boost up the unit's morale. Right now, we're facing more crime than ever, and every case gets worse. Our job has become more dangerous than ever. The Chief had good intentions."

Jeffrey studied the captain. "Why was I assigned to this case?"

"What?" the captain furrowed her brow.

"Don't get me wrong. I am sincerely grateful that I was your first choice as the lead on this one even though I was already booked off. But now I'm wondering if I really was your first choice?"

The captain let out a sigh of exasperation. "I definitely would have assigned the case to you even if the Chief hadn't told me to."

"The Chief?"

"Believe me. I was just as surprised as you are now. It is after all my decision to make. Somehow, he got wind of it and told me to put our best guy on the case and then he specifically requested you. That's exactly what he said. You should be flattered."

"You mean Wylie should be flattered."

"Why? I meant you. He named you."

"Then, why did you call Wylie first?"

The captain arched her eyebrows in a questioning look. "Where are you driving at? What's with all the questions?"

"Something doesn't add up here. That's why. The Chief asked for me, but you called Wylie first. It's a simple matter of chain of command, and yes it did piss me off."

"Okay, first of all, you're confusing me. Why are you accusing me of something I didn't do? I didn't call Wylie."

"Then, who did?"

"How the hell do I know? And why does it even matter?" the captain snarled.

Jeffrey fixed his gaze at the captain studying her one more time before he put his career and his life in her hands. *We all eventually have to trust somebody, right?*

With that thought, he started talking about what he had so far found out.

The captain sat still and listened to what Jeffrey had to say. She didn't stop him. She didn't say a word while he laid it all out to her. When he was done, she closed her eyes for a spell. Opening her eyes, the captain said, "This is bad."

"As bad as it gets."

"If you're wrong, or if nothing comes out of it, I'll be running so fast in the other direction, it'll make your head spin. You'll be left behind for the vultures to prey on your carcass."

"Me, too. I'll rat you out and tell them it was all your idea."

"Since we understand the rules of the game, let's call in Tim and Sam and see what they've got. If we're going down, let's take everybody else down with us." The captain smiled.

"I like it."

• • •

While Jeffrey was in the captain's office listening to Tim and Sam about the insurance scam, Doyle got a visit from a lawyer who didn't even bother to tell him his name or give him his card. The lawyer wasn't there to discuss the case. He was just there to relay the order – do the time for the murder.

Doyle shook his head. "No way, I won't do it. Why should I? The police can't prove that I was the one who stole the car. You know why?" He paused, waiting for any snappy wisecrack from the lawyer. When none came, he continued. "It's because I didn't

Liz, the Neighbour

steal the car. Without that, how are they going to tie me to the crime?"

"If you don't, they'll start looking into other matters."

Doyle thought about it and shrugged. "So?"

"If things come out, you won't be going down for just one murder."

This gave Doyle pause. He thought on the matter some more and then shrugged again. "I'll take my chances."

The lawyer bluntly showed his frustration. "Your superior officer told me to tell you that if you take this hit, you'll be forgiven, whatever that means."

His forgiveness... Doyle liked that a lot. He needed order. Like the military, prison would provide that. Plus, with his aptitude and skills, he might even thrive in prison. "Tell my superior officer, I would appreciate that very much."

The lawyer finally relaxed a little. "Will do."

"What's next?" Doyle said.

"You sit back and relax. I'll let the detective know that you want to confess."

"Alright, alright."

"From here on in, you have to request my presence whenever you're being questioned," the lawyer said resolutely, staring at Doyle.

Doyle returned the stare. "Why? Are you saying he doesn't trust me anymore?"

"This isn't coming from him."

"Then who?"

The lawyer said nothing.

36

FRIDAY, DECEMBER 13

At 4:00 p.m., Caleb was with his usual crew – Birdie, Agnes, Ed, Mr. Sandhu, Tejas, Will, Liz, Ella and Yuul – at Mr. Sandhu's house on Purpledusk Trail. Since Will's TV appearance early this morning, Caleb had been anxiously waiting for Jeffrey's call. He knew that something had to squeak, crack and give, but he'd heard nothing so far. He'd checked his cellphone every five minutes or so, but it had been deadly quiet. Just as he was about to give up on hearing from Jeffrey, his phone rang and almost made everyone's heart stop. He put Jeffrey on speakerphone right away as he knew that no one wanted to wait to hear the news not even for another second.

"So," Birdie said right away, "what's the verdict?"

"Adam Doyle confessed—" Jeffrey was stopped by enthusiastic celebratory screams.

"Fantastic!" Charlie hailed and hugged Ella.

"Hurrah!" Birdie, Agnes and Ed put their arms in the air as they cheered.

"Cheers!" Mr. Sandhu and Tejas responded enthusiastically.

"Yeah baby," Will put his hand up for a high-five and got a big one from Liz.

"*Preet!*" Yuul whistled, grabbing everyone's attention.

Everybody stopped cheering and fell quiet.

"Go ahead, Jeffrey," Yuul said.

"Good job, everyone! They're going to release Adam Brooks tomorrow."

Everyone cheered again but louder this time. Their cheers even buried Yuul's whistle.

Caleb had expected this, nothing less than a confession. Liz had told him it would all go down like this, and he'd trusted her. Still, it hit him like a daydream. His jaw dropped but not even one celebratory word came out.

Looking at awestruck Caleb, Liz jumped on him.

Startled, Caleb dropped his cellphone. He could've caught the phone before it hit the ground but couldn't be bothered to do so. Instead, he just hugged Liz squeezing her bones out. "Thank you, thank you."

Liz said, "Okay, you've got to let me go, buddy, before you crush my bones to dust."

"Sorry," Caleb said, unlocking his arms.

"That was a little over-dramatic," Will said, looking at Liz sourly.

Liz laughed. "I know I'm a bit of a drama-queen." She placed a kiss on Will's cheek. "He reminds me of Jeffrey so much. Jeffrey was like that when I was accused of murder."

Caleb felt a cold, dry wind whirl through his body when he'd seen Liz kiss Will's cheek. *She's with him…* Disappointment hammered his heart. *Do something! Do anything before anyone sees through you.* He turned his attention to Will and smiled. "Who's next?"

Will waved Caleb off. "No thanks. I need all my bones intact."

"*Preet!*" Yuul whistled once again, and this time she succeeded in grabbing everyone's attention. "Go ahead, Jeffrey," Yuul said, passing the phone back to Caleb.

"That's all for now folks. Enjoy the party," Jeffrey said.

"What about the other stuff with Wild Peach?" Birdie asked.

Jeffrey said, "I'm going back in to investigate the hell out of that place until something gives."

"Does that mean you got nothing?" Birdie asked.

"Uh… Yes…" Jeffrey slurred. He cleared his throat and said, "I'm not a magician. I need some time to torture the hell out of them."

"Okay then," Agnes said and pressed the end button on Caleb's phone.

Everyone looked at Agnes in silence for a moment and howled with laughter.

"Without food, this cannot be called a celebration," Liz declared. "Let's order some up and celebrate the heaven out of it."

"Oh-kay, then. Let's parrr-ty," Will said.

"Here, here!" everybody cheered while wiping away the tears of joy from the corners of their eyes.

They all moved about clearing up space for the food to be delivered and making places to sit. Ed stood watching all these young people chatting and cheering and thought of Maddie. She could be one of them. She should be one of them but she wasn't. He missed her laugh. He turned around to remove himself from this happy scene that Maddie couldn't be part of when he saw Tejas standing next to him with two plates of food in his hands.

"Whenever I saw a boy my age walking down the street with his mother, it made me think about my mother, too. It felt like I should've had that moment just like the other boy. It felt like God had robbed the moment from me."

Ed took one plate off Tejas' hand.

"You know what a wise man once said to me?" Tejas said.

"What?" Ed asked, his voice choked up with tears.

"It is true that all the happy and sad moments I should've shared with my mom were robbed from me. But I can't rob all the happy and sad moments from the people who want to share them with me."

"Cheers to the wise man," Ed said, holding up a drumstick in his hand.

"Cheers to the wise man." Tejas grabbed his drumstick off his plate and hit Ed's with his.

"You have to put down your plate now," Caleb said, looking at Ed.

The gravity in Caleb's voice startled both Ed and Tejas and made them wonder what was coming.

Caleb took Ed's plate and placed it on the table, then so unexpectedly, he gently hugged Ed. "I am so sorry for your loss."

"Hey, keep your hands off my pops," Will said, pushing Caleb aside. "He's my father and my grandfather all rolled into one. He's my pops, not yours."

Caleb frowned. "You know that's one really messed-up family line, right?"

Will let out a long sigh. "I know." He turned his attention to Tejas and tousled his hair. "You're the smartest kid I've ever met."

"And you know smart is so sexy?" Liz said, locking arms with Tejas.

"Aha! I knew you loved me for more than just my pretty face," Will said.

LOVE? Liz froze in her tracks.

• • •

Jeffrey Knight parked his car on Purpledusk Trail and sat there for a long 5 minutes darting glances at his rear-view mirror. He wasn't going to lead the big bad wolves back to little red riding hood's house again. He didn't see any suspicious movements on the street, so he got out of his car and stood there on the sidewalk, looking up and down the street and checking out the parked cars for anything out of the ordinary. When he was sure there wasn't any, he crossed the street and looked around one last time before disappearing into the red brick house.

As Jeffrey walked into the living room, the people inside the house gave him a big welcome-home-hurray. "Ya, ya, whatever," Jeffrey brushed off their teasing greet and gave Yuul a peck on her cheek and disappeared into the kitchen.

While Jeffrey was chowing down on his dinner, Caleb stood guard at the window, surveiling the street through a tiny gap in the front window curtains. He spotted a man hurriedly walking along the sidewalk, his shoulders hunched. Caleb said, "Ajay's here."

"I'll get the door," Liz said as she scrambled down the hallway

"I'll go make him a plate," Mr. Sandhu said, standing up.

They all heard the door creak open and then the sound of footsteps approaching the living room.

Emerging from the hallway, Ajay said, "I heard you guys had one hell of a time last night, kicking butts and guns blazing and all."

"Did we ever," Tejas said, feeling the thrill and excitement tingling up his back all over again. "Did we ever," Tejas said, feeling the thrill and excitement tingling up his back all over again.

"Where's Rani?" Ella said, looking past Ajay down the hallway.

"She's still at work."

"Here, eat up." Mr. Sandhu handed Ajay his dinner. "Okay, now everybody's here. Let's hear it."

Everyone turned and looked straight at Jeffrey, who was still busy filling his face.

Jeffrey paused and put his plate down. He sighed as he looked off into space for a minute. "Surprisingly, no one is talking. Adam Doyle admits to killing Maddie, but it stops there, and those 4 goons are all sticking to their robbery-gone-bad story."

"What about Tim and Sam? They must have found out something by now?" Charlie asked.

"This is the thing." Jeffrey let out a frustrated sigh. "Tim and Sam now know for sure that Wild Peach is running an insurance scam, but they can't prove it because all those people that died from a heart attack are gone. What I mean by that is dead people can still talk to us through their flesh and bones and DNA they leave behind, but unfortunately, all these people were cremated leaving us with nada."

"You should talk to Lilibeth," Liz suggested.

"Who's Lilibeth?" Jeffrey asked.

"She's the nurse at Wild Peach. If those three nurses saw what was going on, then Lilibeth must've seen it by now as well."

"That's a good idea," Jeffrey said, making a mental note to contact Lilibeth asap.

"She's such a sweetie and a hard-working woman," Birdie said.

"She is," Agnes chimed in. "She works all the time."

"Do you think she might be working right now?" Liz asked.

"Not one hundred per cent sure but the probabilities are pretty high," Agnes said. "I saw her at night a lot."

"Do you think we should call her right now?" Ella said.

"Yes, she might need to be rescued right away," Birdie said excitedly.

"Let's give it a try then," Liz said, taking her cellphone out.

"No, no, no," Jeffrey said, shaking his head. "Let the police do the real detective work from here on in."

Ella said, "We won't do anything. We're just gonna call her to make sure she's still alive. If she is, you guys can take over from there."

"Yes, that's all we're doing," Liz said while pressing the phone number for Wild Peach saved in her cellphone. When the phone started ringing, she put it on speaker.

"Hi, can I please speak with nurse Lilibeth?" Liz asked when the phone was answered.

"Speaking," the woman on the other end said.

"Hi, I don't know if you remember me. I'm Liz Knight. I was there a few weeks ago, trying to find Agnes Winter."

"Oh yes. How are you, dear? Did you find her?"

Liz looked at Birdie and Agnes and got a nod from them.

"Yes, we did."

"That's wonderful news."

"Yes. The thing is they told us about some unfortunate deaths of nurses who used to work there."

"They? Who are they?"

"Agnes Winter and her friend *Nancy Drew*," Liz said, smiling at Birdie.

The line got quiet. Lilibeth said nothing. Liz checked her phone to see if the call had inadvertently been disconnected but it hadn't.

"Are you there?" Liz asked.

"Oh sorry. I've got to go. Somebody's started a commotion in the kitchen. Can I call you back on this number?"

"Yes, of course." Before Liz even finished the last word, Lilibeth was gone.

Liz shrugged. "Now we know she's alive."

Agnes blew out a long but weak sigh. "What a relief!"

Birdie furrowed her brow. "Who starts a riot at 7 o'clock in the evening?"

"Arthur McMillan, maybe?" Agnes suggested.

Birdie gave it thought for a brief moment. "Hmm… In the kitchen at 7 at night? But then again, we are talking about Wild Peach here. With that place, it's very much anything goes."

"Ahem," Ajay cleared his throat. Once all eyes were on him, he said, "Since all the boring stuff is taken care of, I want to tell you some exciting stuff. Drum roll, please."

There were stares but no drum rolls.

Ajay shook his head in disappointment. "You guys gotta learn how to enjoy life a little. Okay then. Let me start with a question. Guess what your neighbours and the Townsend brothers have in common?"

"Hmm… That's a tough one," Ella said.

"Can you just spill it?" Birdie said. "Some of us might kick the bucket before you're done playing your little game."

"Sorry." Ajay flashed an apologetic but not-so-apologetic smile. "Okay, I'll give you a clue. The Townsend brothers have a mother whose maiden name is Pelletier. Guess who else has the same maiden name?" Ajay stopped for dramatic effect.

Everyone gave Ajay another death stare instead.

Ajay pouted as if to say, *Why don't you play along with me?* Still, he was met with nothing but death stares.

Liz, the Neighbour

Ajay sniffed. "Seriously you guys are no fun. Your neighbour, Doreen, she used to be Doreen Pelletier."

"That's huge," Liz said.

"I told you so," Ajay said triumphantly.

"Whatever is going on at Wild Peach might be going on at the Montreal home as well," Liz said.

"You're so smart," Ajay said to Liz.

"Thank you." Liz curtsied.

"You're welcome." Ajay curtsied back and then continued. "Almost all the residents' deaths at the Montreal home have been from heart attacks crazy, if I may exaggerate a little."

Liz turned to Jeffrey. "This does sound like it calls for real police work. Don't you think?"

"Absolutely," Jeffrey said, nodding his head. "I made a mental note – tell Tim and Sam."

"Hahaha," Everybody laughed in unison.

Liz turned back to Ajay. "What about Rob? Did you find out anything about him?"

"That's where things get really interesting. He's an American who came to Canada about 15 years ago. That's all I've got. He's like a ghost."

"That's disappointing," Liz said.

"Don't be," Ajay said. "I'll find more. It's just a matter of time."

"I trust you," Liz said as she stared at her chirping phone. "A call from Wild Peach."

"Put it on speakerphone," Ella requested.

"Of course," Liz said as she pressed the icon.

"Hello Lilibeth," Liz said pleasantly.

"Liz Knight?" Lilibeth asked.

"Yes, it's Liz. Did you put down the insurrection?"

"What?"

"Haha. I was talking about the riot."

"What riot?"

"Uh… Didn't you say that there was a commotion in the kitchen?"

"Oh, yes!" Lilibeth whooped. "It was a false alarm. Hahaha! I got in a car accident a year ago. Ever since, I forget things all the time, although the damned insurance company doesn't believe me. Anyhow, about what you were saying earlier, what were you saying?"

"Since those nurses' deaths don't look accidental, I was wondering how you're doing and all," Liz said.

"Can we talk in person?"

"Yes, of course."

"I actually wanted to talk to somebody about something," Lilibeth said almost in a whisper. "I couldn't take it to the police because I'm still not sure what I think is happening here is really what is happening. Or, if I'm just being paranoid like Nancy and Agnes."

"You're not being paranoid over nothing," Liz assured Lilibeth.

"That's a relief." Lilibeth let out an audible sigh. "I'd like to meet you and possibly Nancy and Agnes as well."

Liz looked at Agnes and Birdie and got a nod from both of them.

"Okay. When and where?"

"Tomorrow at 10 at your house? I can't think of any other place safer than yours."

Liz rolled her eyes. She wanted to say any other place would be safer than Mr. Sandhu's at this point. Yet, she couldn't think of any other place to have a talk with Lilibeth about all this secretive and deadly stuff. "That sounds…" Liz paused, looking over at Yuul shaking her head.

"What about 12?" Liz suggested.

"That'll work, too," Lilibeth said delightfully.

"Can I bring my husband with me?" Lilibeth asked.

"Of course."

"See you tomorrow then," Lilibeth said cheerfully.

"Hey, hey!" Liz yelled.

"Yees?" Lilibeth said perplexed about Liz's hurried shout-out.

"Aren't you forgetting something?"

"I don't think so," Lilibeth said, sounding unsure.

"My address," Liz said.

"Oh My!" Lilibeth smacked her forehead. "You've got to talk to my insurance company for me. I really can't carry out my daily activities. Maybe, that's why I couldn't put things together as to what's been happening here earlier."

"Do you have a pen and paper with you?" Liz asked, re-directing Lilibeth's attention back to the matter at hand.

"Oh yes. Go ahead."

After giving the address, Liz disconnected the call and looked over at Jeffrey. "Now that's how you get the job done." She dusted off her hands.

"Good Job!" Jeffrey agreed.

"It's like we do all the hard work, and the police just walk in and scoop up all the credit," Ella chimed in.

"Exactly!" Liz exclaimed. "The police can gloriously march into Wild Peach in their shining armour and play the hero for solving the biggest insurance scam in Canadian history and all the murders of those poor residents."

"This is not the biggest insurance scam in Canadian history," Jeffrey said.

"What was the biggest scam in our history then?" Ella asked.

"I don't know off the top of my head but I'm very sure this one isn't it."

"Until you prove otherwise, this one is the biggest," Ella declared.

"And tomorrow we might even be able to hand you the key evidence to the insurance scam on a silver platter," Liz said.

"Anything's possible," Jeffrey said.

37

SATURDAY, DECEMBER 14

The first thing Adam Brooks saw when he walked out the gate of the Toronto East Detention Centre, was Caleb and Anya waiting there for him. He marched straight over to Caleb and gave him a big hug.

Caleb lifted Adam up.

"Put me down," Adam shouted. "You're embarrassing me in front of my girl."

"That's what brothers are for," Caleb said and put Adam down. "You've lost weight."

Adam put his arms around Caleb's waistline and interlaced his fingers. He then gave it everything he had and tried to lift him off the ground. After a few seconds of trying, he finally let Caleb go. "You lost weight, too. I lifted up the heels of your feet this time."

"Only the heel of one foot," Caleb said. "Go. Don't make your girl wait too long."

As Adam laid his eyes on Anya, tears welled up. He ran to her and hugged her very tight. Tears ran down his cheeks and dropped on her pastel pink dress coat, making the same sound of light summer rain hitting the roof. He promised himself that he would never, ever let her go again. As he rested his head on her shoulder, he finally felt complete again. He felt strong again.

"We should get going," Anya said, untying Adam's fingers. "Your mom has been up since God knows when, cooking up a storm."

Adam crossed his arms over his chest. "I won't move a muscle until you promise you'll never ever leave me again."

"I promise," Anya said.

Adam got lost in her eyes as he moved in to kiss her.

Anya hurriedly put her hand over his mouth. "If you kiss me, I won't be able to stop. We don't want any hanky-panky here in front of your brother, do we?"

Adam locked his hand with hers. "Hurry up and let's go home then."

· · ·

They all got into the Beamer. As Caleb slowly drove out onto Civic Road, he noticed a couple of black SUVs following him out – SUVs just like the one that had been parked on Purpledusk Trail a couple of nights ago. Glancing through the rear-view mirror, he saw a man in the passenger seat of the SUV holding a rifle. He had no doubt the other SUV had its own shooter as well. Seeing no one in the back seat, he thought, *Not the sharpest tool in the shed*. He hoped that the second SUV had the same arrangement.

"Listen to me carefully," Caleb said, giving Adam and Anya a quick once-over through the rear-view mirror.

"From here on in, I need you to do what I say without question. Got it?" Caleb saw their frowned faces in the rear-view. They looked frightened but he was just happy that they hadn't asked any questions and were doing what he had told them to do.

"We've got a tail. Not a biggie. I need you to trust me right now. I want both of you to hold on to the grab handles above your doors and hang on for dear life."

Adam and Anya looked to the ceiling and then held on tight with both hands to the handles.

Warden Road was coming up fast with only a few meters or so to go, Caleb tried to time the oncoming cars, looking for an opening to merge into.

"Ready, set, go!" Caleb hit the gas and made a sharp right turn. The car slid and skipped, just before it rolled, Caleb regained control with a firm grip on the road and pried his way in between two small cars in the far-left lane.

"Hang on!" Approaching Eglinton Avenue, Caleb swerved from the left lane to the right lane just in time to make an outrageous right turn. He sped along Eglinton Avenue, darting glances at the rear-view mirror. He saw no black SUVs, at least for now. He knew these guys would catch up to him sooner or later.

"Anya, do you have your cellphone handy?"

"Yes."

"I need to find a safe place where no one else will get hurt if bullets start flying."

"That's a tough one," Anya said.

"You've got a couple of minutes."

"There's a storage rental place nearby. Will that work for you?" Anya said.

"It's as good as we're gonna get," Caleb said. "Where is it?"

Anya said, "It's on the northeast corner of Bertand Avenue and Warden. It's just north of where we were before you turned onto Eglinton. We're too far away now, I'll find another place."

"That place will work just fine. Anya, can you get an Uber?" Caleb asked.

"Yes," Anya said.

"Good. I will drop you guys off somewhere safe. When I stop the car, you're going to have to jump out and hide somewhere until your ride gets there. Go to a hotel. Go anywhere but home. Got it?"

Adam and Anya both nodded.

"Good. As soon as you get there, you call me."

Caleb checked the mirror and spotted the two black SUVs closing the distance between them. "In one more turn get ready to jump out," Caleb said approaching Kennedy Road. After he made the left, he spotted a pharmacy on the right. "Run to that pharmacy over there." He stopped the car abruptly.

Adam and Anya jumped out of the car and started running to the pharmacy hand in hand. He drove off as soon as they were out, but not too fast this time. He needed to make sure that the two SUVs were following him, not Adam and Anya. Within a few seconds, he saw the two SUVs fly onto Kennedy Road to come after him. He finally was able to let out a smile, hoping that he didn't miss this storage rental place Anya was talking about.

He turned off Kennedy onto Landseer Road. When he hit the dead end, he went right on Ionview Road. All he knew was that he had to get back to Warden Avenue as soon as possible. He made another left turn and drove west on Bertand Avenue. He saw the big sign indicating the storage rental place. He slowed down and placed a call.

"Jeffrey, it's Caleb."

"What's up?"

"I'm being chased by four morons with rifles. I'll be in the parking lot of Bertand Storage Rentals at Warden and Bertand. Send some cops before I kill them all."

"Roger that." Jeffrey disconnected the call.

Caleb glanced in the rear-view mirror one last time. When they got close enough, he pulled in and parked the car in the middle of the lot and hopped out. He ran to the corner of the storage facility and watched the two SUVs pulling in. All he had to do was grab one moron with a gun and take it – *Walk in the park*.

The four morons got out of the SUVs and looked around trying to spot their targets. They held their guns as if they were ready to shoot on sight. One guy gave an order to the others to spread out and get operational.

Definitely ringleader, Caleb thought, grinning. He saw the ringleader slowly moving in his direction. *My lucky day*, he smiled. *Knock over the lead domino and the rest will follow.* As the ringleader got closer to him, he moved out from the corner as far as the shadows allowed him to. He counted the ringleader's footsteps. One more step towards him and the ringleader would be turning his gun towards Caleb as he swept the area. When the last footstep fell, Caleb saw the gun muzzle peeking at him. As the ringleader turned, Caleb grabbed the gun with both hands, and then pulled the gun and its owner inward. Moving the end of the rifle upward with his left hand, he jabbed the ringleader in his neck with his right – just hard enough to make him lose his grip on the gun. Still holding the rifle in his left hand, Caleb punched him in the face so hard that he almost smashed the ringleader's head right through the wall: *Fa-thud!* In less than five seconds, the game was over.

Caleb trained the muzzle of the gun on the ringleader's head and walked him out into the open. The other three morons were walking around still acting like they were the hunters hunting their prey.

"Drop your weapons!" Caleb yelled.

The three morons all turned around at the same time shocked to see the bloodied beaten face of their leader with a gun to his head.

"I'll give you something to think about. Which part of your body do you think you won't miss the most when it's gone?"

The three morons looked at their leader and then looked at Caleb as if they weren't too sure what to do.

"Which part?" Caleb asked the commander.

Liz, the Neighbour

"What?" the commander cried back letting out an involuntary shiver.

"Pinky, right? That's what most people pick. Are you one of those average Joes who picks the pinky?"

The ringleader shoved his hands down his pants pockets.

"I'll still hit the bullseye. The only problem with using a rifle like this is that it tends to cause a lot of collateral damage." Caleb saw the three morons all straining their tiny pea-sized brains trying to figure out what to do next. "I'll make it easy for you. I'll shoot him first," Caleb said, pointing at the commander, "and then you," Caleb pointed at the short, skinny man standing on the far-right, "and then you," Caleb pointed out the man standing in the middle, "and then you. How does that sound? Who knows maybe you get lucky and one of you puts a bullet in me before I take you all out but it's highly unlikely. I know I'm bragging a little but if you've been sent to all the nasty little parts of the world like I have because you're the best and the baddest, it's hard not to brag about it. I'll give you three seconds to drop your weapons or I'm gonna start taking you apart piece by piece starting with your commander. Three…"

"Drop your guns!" the ringleader screamed. "Do as he says and drop them!"

The three morons were about to test their luck when they heard the sirens.

Caleb said, "If anyone moves, I'm shooting. Be smart about it. So far, you've done nothing wrong. If you say the right things, you might even get rewarded for your honesty."

The three morons dropped their guns and got down on the ground just as the police cars started pouring into the parking lot.

38

SATURDAY, DECEMBER 14

At 7:30 a.m., Birdie and Agnes marched around the house waking the rest of the residents of the red brick house on Purpledusk Trail with their persistent squealing and shouting while Ed enjoyed a morning tea with Mr. Sandhu at the kitchen table. Ed and Mr. Sandhu heard grumbling voices in defiance and then the thumping noise of people falling onto the floor. They loved the noise while appreciating the fresh tea.

By 8:00 a.m., the young people were hustling about, putting the house in order while the old people bustled about the kitchen, preparing food to welcome their very special guests. Tejas was spared from any labour as they all considered him as their little baby and he had final exams to prepare for.

Liz, the Neighbour

At 8:30 a.m., Caleb who had escaped doing any household chores under the excuse of picking up Anya before heading to the Toronto East Detention Centre, bid good luck to all the suckers who had been forced into the spring cleaning. He was out the door and gone before anyone had a chance to give him a dirty look.

By 10:00 a.m., the house was spotless.

By 11:30 a.m., the people in the house had all cleaned themselves up nicely and put on the best clothes they had in their luggage and for some lucky ones, from their closets. The house was filled with the aroma of fresh baked cookies.

At 12:00 p.m., Birdie waited by the door while Liz, Ella and Will were bringing the cookies and teas over to the coffee table in the living room.

"Welcome!" Birdie announced the arrival of their guests in her cheerful voice.

"Oh My Goodness! What a nice surprise to see you again!" Lilibeth exclaimed in joy.

Birdie said, "You took the words right out of my mouth. Come on in."

Lilibeth walked in.

"Go on ahead," a middle-aged gentleman said, looking at Birdie in the hallway. "I'll get the door."

"Ok but please make sure you lock it," Birdie requested.

"Of course," the gentleman said.

"Come with me," Lilibeth said. Holding Birdie's hand, Lilibeth lead Birdie inside. "How have you been, dear?"

"It's been crazy, to say the least," Birdie said.

"Oh My Goodness! Agnes!" Lilibeth ran over to Agnes and hugged her. "You gave us a lot of grief."

Liz, the Neighbour

"My bad," Agnes said.

"It's okay now that I understand what was going on in your head." Lilibeth looked around and met the many pairs of curious eyes. "You've got an army of people here."

Birdie said, "To fight an army of people, you need an army of people."

"Where's your husband?" Agnes asked.

"Hoho!" Lilibeth laughed. "He's probably struggling to bring in our small gifts that we brought for you. Don't move. We want it to be a surprise." Lilibeth rose up. "Sweetie, do you need help?"

"No, no. We're good," the gentleman said.

"We?" Birdie muttered.

They all heard heavy footsteps approaching, and then two armed men entered the room with their guns drawn.

"Anyone moves, everyone dies," the middle-aged gentleman yelled. "Here, sweetie." He handed a pistol over to Lilibeth.

"Thank you," Lilibeth said delightfully.

And just like that, the residents of the red brick house were cornered with nowhere to run.

"You," Liz pointed at a man standing next to the middle-aged gentleman. "Troy Townsend!"

"You know me?" Troy said. "I'm honoured."

"I don't understand," Agnes said, looking lost.

"Then, you're not as smart as some people might want to give you credit for," Lilibeth sneered.

Liz caught Tejas's head poking through the staircase railing upstairs.

Thank God you're there, Liz thought. Turning her full attention back to Lilibeth, Liz said, "Obviously, you're not as smart as your people might think, either."

"How is that?" Lilibeth asked leisurely.

"If you shoot us all here, somebody will *call the police*," Liz yelled.

"Don't worry. Before the cops respond to your neighbour's call, we'll be long gone. Besides, do you see this here," Lilibeth pointed at the extension attached to her pistol. "This is called a silencer. It won't kill all the noise but it does a pretty good job."

Liz saw from the corner of her eye Tejas quietly retreating. She let out an inaudible sigh of relief while thinking to herself that she needed to keep them talking for the next 10 minutes. "Out of curiosity, is one of them really your husband? Or, is that a lie, too?"

"It's gotta be a lie," Birdie said as she pointed at the middle-aged gentleman, "I recognize you now. You're the operations manager at Wild Peach."

"Hoho!" Lilibeth laughed. "So, how does it make me a liar?"

Birdie sniggered. "Are you saying you're married to him?"

"Yes, that's exactly what I'm saying. What's so unbelievable about that?"

"Huh, I guess that's one of my shortcomings," Birdie pouted her mouth. "I never saw that coming. I never saw you two as a couple let alone in cahoots together."

"Enough!" Troy said, fixing his gun on Birdie. "I'll start with her. Let's—"

Liz, the Neighbour

"Before you kill us," Liz hurriedly interjected, "can you tell me just one thing? That's all I'm asking for. I'm just too curious."

"What is it?" Lilibeth said, pointing the silencer at Liz.

"How did those three nurses find out what you were up to? Did they see you killing the seniors? You seem to have created a pretty elaborate system to kill residents and collect the insurance money. It's my dying wish. How did they figure it out?"

"First of all, they were not nurses. They were nursing *assistants*. There's a huge difference." Lilitbeth sneered.

"Sorry?" Liz rolled her eyes.

Lilibeth frowned. "Seriously, it's insult to me after all the time and money I put in to become a *real* nurse." She paused and glanced over to Troy. "I'm a Catholic. Let me fulfill her last wish and then we'll kill them all."

Troy looked annoyed but gave her the green-light, knowing that it wouldn't even take 10 seconds to kill them all.

"I told you about the car accident, right?"

Everyone nodded.

"That is true, and the fact that I've become forgetful is also true. As instructed by the insurance company, I went to see a psychologist to get a full assessment of my mental state after the accident. During the assessment, the psychologist gave me some tips on ways to cope with my mental deficits. One of them was to write down all the important things I have to do. So, I made a to-do list and hid it in the beginning. The problem with that though, I could never remember where I'd hidden the lists, so I messed up with when-to-kill and when-to-order more potassium cyanide that kind of thing. It also turns out that I killed too many people in too short an interval. That's a big no-no in this business. So, I started keeping the list in my drawer at the nursing station. The list had just names of the people I should inject with and when. That's all. It's not like I wrote 'kill so-on, so-on, on what dates next to the names. So, I thought that it would be safe to keep it in the drawer. It turns out those three nursing *assistants* figured out what it meant."

"You wrote it down on the paper and kept it in the drawer?" Troy hissed. He couldn't believe what he was hearing. *She wrote it down on paper...* His anger was boiling up and it took everything he had to fight the urge to just turn his body a little to where Lilibeth was standing and shoot her first. He placed his left hand underneath his gun to keep it at Birdie, not Lilibeth.

"I know I said one question—" Liz stopped in her tracks as she heard Charlie's voice coming from the front door.

"Guys, the front door is not—"

• • •

Yuul saw Troy turn his attention to the hallway. This was the moment she'd been waiting for. Yuul had been sitting on the floor when the gunmen had barged in. Her hands were already placed slightly behind her, on the floor, to help support the weight of her body. In the blink of an eye, she swiftly spun her leg counter-clockwise almost to 45 degrees given the limited space, and then quickly rotated it at full speed, kicking Troy in the side of his knee with the ball of her foot as hard as she could.

"Oww!" Troy screamed out of surprise and out of pain. He jumped off to the side, knocking the officer manager Rodrigo out of commission.

Before Troy's scream had time to hit the walls of the house, Yuul had double-quickly repositioned her body, using her arms and legs to propel herself as high as she could while her knees rose up to her chest all in one fluid motion, she fired out a well-placed kick striking Troy in his solar plexus knocking the wind right out of him.

As Troy doubled over in pain, trying to catch his breath, Will punched him in the face as hard as he could. And then Will jumped around, holding his right hand with his left from the shooting pain he'd inflicted on himself from punching Troy.

Rodrigo caught only a blurry image of the Asian woman as she spun and kicked him hard into the right side of his ribcage just as he was squeezing of a shot. A bullet was indeed fired which luckily flew harmlessly into the ceiling. Despite the pain he was feeling, he held onto his gun when he fell to the floor. In anger, he fired off another shot, aiming the gun at no one in particular. Before he had time to squeeze the trigger for a third time, he was suddenly assailed by an Indian man who had launched himself at him. The next thing he knew, he had been knocked to the ground sans gun and was being smacked by a cane. He then felt wet. He thought that maybe he had wet himself. He wanted to put a bullet in his own head. It would just be way too embarrassing to have to live with afterwards. He didn't think Lilibeth would ever want to have sex with him again. As he was slowly moving his arm to his head, he looked over in time to realize that Birdie had just emptied a tea pot on him. *Of course, I didn't wet myself.* That was the last thought he had before a bullet struck his leg and he passed out cold.

After hearing Troy scream in agony and the gunshot fired by her husband, Lilibeth raised her gun to shoot anyone she could just to get the house back in order but didn't know where to aim. The scream was hurting her ears. The commotion made it hard for her to have a clear shot at anyone. She didn't want to shoot her husband in any case, and she didn't want to shoot Troy if she could help it. Then, she saw Liz. All of the sudden, she had a clear shot at Liz. She aimed her gun, smiling. As she was pulling the trigger on Liz, somebody from behind wacked her in the back of the head. It messed up her aim and the bullet flew off through the air and lodged itself into her husband's leg.

Liz screamed, "Awesome Power!"

Ella screamed the next, "Awesome Power United!"

Liz and Ella catapulted their bodies over to Lilibeth and they all ended up rolling around on the floor together. Ella pulling on Lilibeth's hair while Liz was busy pinning Lilibeth down for the count.

Charlie couldn't believe he'd just wacked a *woman*. He just stood there in shock next to Ella and Liz when he heard the sirens wailing up to the house.

39

SATURDAY, DECEMBER 14

As the B-Team was being marshaled into an interview room, they passed by the four members of the other team who had been defeated single-handedly by Caleb. The other team sat leisurely around a desk, eating burgers and drinking pops. Two middle-aged detectives sat on the other side of the desk chatting away with them like they were old buddies.

What the hell is going on? Chris Winger wondered as he was ushered into the interview room with his team.

The two officers who had marshaled them into the interview room closed the door behind them once they had all sat down around the table inside.

As soon as the door was shut, Hugh looked at Chris. "Why are they here? Why do they look happy?

Don't you think Nicholas and his team looked almost giddy?"

"Yeah totally," Giovanni chimed in. He wrinkled every inch of his face as he stared at Chris. "Boss, you saw what we saw and you know it means only one thing."

"What would that be?" Chris asked half-heartedly. As far as he was concerned, Giovanni almost never said anything worth listening to. Giovanni and Hugh were the two reasons for his team being named the B-Team. Chris wouldn't have had them for any other reason than the lack of human interest in being a gangster these days.

"Isn't it obvious, Boss?" Giovanni said. "They're snitches."

Chris put his hand up and was about to mechanically give Giovanni a dismissive wave when Hugh interjected.

"Gotta be!" Hugh said. "Think about it, Boss. That night, they were expecting us. The Indian man said it himself. How could they, unless someone had told them about the order to attack them in advance."

"I know!" Chris couldn't believe his two idiot foot soldiers had figured it out before him. He wasn't going to admit that to the men who needed to follow his orders.

"What're we gonna do?" Giovanni asked, jittering his hands.

Chris thought hard. What hadn't been said that he could say to the cops – that was the question he asked himself. He wanted to make a deal, the best deal he could make for himself. While racking his brain, he saw the door swing open.

At the door stood the plainclothes police officer who had apprehended them at the red brick house on Purpledusk Trail on Thursday night.

• • •

Jeffrey Knight walked into the interview room. He placed some notepads and pens on the table. "You're going to write about the night you broke into the house on Purpledusk Trail. You're going to write why you were there and who gave you your marching orders and I want it in detail. When you're done, write down everything you know about Wild Peach, and every crime you and your colleagues have ever committed. If you lie about it, it'll go against you. If you give us more than what those guys," Jeffrey pointed his finger at the door, "gave us, you'll win brownie points. Good luck!" He walked out of the room and over to the kitchenette, smiling all the way.

Tim and Sam were already waiting for him there.

"I can only guess it worked beautifully," Sam said.

"Yup, that lot is about as solid as a soup sandwich. You guys are pure genius," Jeffrey declared.

"If you've done this job as long as we have," Tim said, "you're bound to pick up a few tricks along the way."

"Are you okay?" Jeffrey said, studying Tim's face with concern.

"Everything's peachy except your stare," Tim growled.

"You worry me," Jeffrey said. "You're not as cranky as you used to. You're sometimes even sweet. Seriously, is everything okay?"

"You'd better tell him," Sam said.

"Tell me what?" Jeffrey said.

Tim shrugged. "Darlene and I are talking about giving co-habitation a try. I think that might have made me happy a little."

"Oh Man! Congrats!" Jeffrey punched Tim in his arm.

"We're just talking," Tim said, smiling.

"It's still weird to see him smiling like that," Sam said, looking at Jeffrey.

"Is that a smile?" Jeffrey said, faking surprise.

"Okay boys, let's get back to work," Tim said. "I don't have all day. I promised Darlene a wonderful night."

"Okay, let's move along," Jeffrey said. "What about your guys? Did they talk?"

Sam said, "As soon as they saw your guys walking by, they all folded like a cheap lawn chair. I'll wager that our guys'll write at least two more pages than your guys."

"How much?" Jeffrey said in confidence, remembering how fast his guys had started writing before he'd even entirely left the room.

"10 dollars a guy," Sam called.

"You're on!" Jeffrey called.

"Go get your friend. He looked really pissed last time when I checked on him," Sam said.

"Before he blows up the building, let me send him home," Jeffrey said.

• • •

Jeffrey opened a grey door next to a plaque that read "Interview Room #4".

"Hey buddy," Jeffrey said, sitting down on a chair. "Let me see what you wrote." He pulled a yellow notepad and studied it. "Hmm… This is all you got? I can't say I'm not disappointed."

The notepad had a big 'X' drawn on it.

"Did they talk?" Caleb asked.

Jeffrey squinted and rubbed his temples.

"I knew it! I'm taking them to an undisclosed place and torture the hell out of them."

Jeffrey couldn't hold back any longer. He burst into laughter.

Caleb looked at Jeffrey, lost for a minute, and then he got it. The corners of his eyes moved upward. "No way!"

"Yes way!" Jeffrey said.

Caleb rose to his feet, marched over to Jeffrey and laid one of his famous bear hugs on him.

"Okay, man, you gotta let me go. Do you hear the phone ringing?" Jeffrey said. As Caleb released his grip, Jeffrey connected the call. "What's up, Liz?"

Liz? Caleb wondered why she would be calling Jeffrey at this time. He then saw Jeffrey's face all wrinkle up in anger. Caleb could only think about one thing: *Save her!* "Where is she? I'll go." Jeffrey just gave him the hand telling him to be quiet. Caleb waited in frustration. When he finally saw Jeffrey putting his phone back in his pants pocket, he asked again, "Where is she?"

"She's okay," Jeffrey said. He told Caleb what had happened at Mr. Sandhu's while they'd been here.

Jeffrey punched Caleb in his arm. "It's over."

"It surely does look that way."

40

SUNDAY, DECEMBER 15

Liz opened her eyes and saw the bright sunlight coming through the curtains of her window. She yawned while stretching. It felt good. She rolled her head around in a semi-circular motion, and that eased the tension around her neck. It was so nice to sleep in and especially in her own bed. She'd missed it. She rolled around on her bed, enjoying the scent of her duvet. She looked around and found a new love for everything she had, and everything she didn't have. *Grr!* Her stomach growled from hunger.

In the midst of this poetic moment, your stomach clock goes off like clockwork. This is why you can't lose weight. Liz gave herself a mental slap. She slowly climbed to her feet and headed downstairs to the kitchen.

Liz, the Neighbour

The house was engulfed in silence. She figured even Jeffrey was sleeping in for a change. She could only imagine how stressful it had been for him. After placing slices of bacon on a heated pan, she washed tomatoes and lettuce in running water. Everything felt therapeutic. She understood why Ella cooked when she was stressed out. While slicing the tomatoes on a cutting board, she heard a knock on the back door. She wiped her hands on the dish towel that was draped over her shoulder and walked over to the door to see who it might be. She hoped it was Caleb and crossed her fingers.

She flashed her mega volt smile as she opened the door. "Good morning, Caleb." She placed a peck on his cheek.

Caleb stopped in his tracks. His heart raced faster than a NASCAR on a racing track. His eyes fixed on her, and he couldn't blink. He couldn't breathe. His heart desired more, more than a peck on his cheek. Looking her in the eye, he wanted to tell her that he wanted more.

"*Shooooot!*" Liz screamed while rushing to the kitchen. "*My bacon!*" Smog was floating in the air and getting thicker.

Caleb opened the door wide while Liz quickly removed the pan off the stove top and turned it off.

Liz couldn't quite figure out why she'd pecked him on his cheek. Looking at Caleb's reaction, she'd felt embarrassed and wanted to run into a mouse hole and hide herself away until Caleb went back to wherever he'd been before his brother's misfortune. *Think before you act!* She scorned herself. "My bacon," Liz moped while dumping the burnt bacon onto a plate.

"I'll cook the bacon," Caleb said, dumping the rest of bacon from the package into the pan. "You toast the bagel."

"How did you know I was going to have bagel?"

"Because I can read your mind, even the deepest, dirtiest secret in your mind," Caleb said, passing a bag of bagels that was sitting on the kitchen countertop to her.

"You better not," Liz said. "What's up?"

"Uh?"

"Is there a special reason for your early visit? Or, is it just to have breakfast with me?" Liz gave herself another mental slap. She didn't know why she kept saying things like this to him.

Caleb looked at her. He had to ask her. *Now or never.* "Are you with—"

"What did you do, Liz?" Jeffrey said, covering his mouth with the sleeve of his shirt without knowing that he had just interrupted a big moment for Caleb.

"It's Caleb," Liz said. "I told him not to but he insisted that he would make breakfast for us." Liz shook her head indignantly.

Caleb looked at her in disbelief.

"You'd better learn how to throw people under the bus before the other guy does it to you, if you want to survive in this family," Ella said, walking into the kitchen.

"I don't want him in this family," Jeffrey declared.

"Why not?" Caleb asked, feeling hurt.

"As you know, I'm already taken, although I did find you pretty interesting," Jeffrey said. "Yuul and Ella are taken as well. So, that leaves Liz. That's why."

"You wouldn't like me as Liz's boyfriend?" Caleb wanted to know. *Boyfriend... Mm...*

"Let's say, you guys are seeing each other. And then, what happens?" Jeffrey looked at Caleb.

"I'll make her so happy," Caleb said confidently and with style.

"And then?" Jeffrey asked again.

"And then what? You tell me," Caleb said.

"You'll be sent to God knows where for God knows how long. Where is she going to be while you're gone? Here, with us moping. I don't want to see that."

"She can be in our own home, raising our children," Caleb said.

Jeffrey narrowed his eyes at Caleb.

"Yes, I'll open the door," Yuul said, coming out of her room.

"What?" Ella said, her eyes following Yuul.

"It's Will," Yuul said, walking over to the kitchen.

"How are you, Yuul?" Will said to Yuul's back.

Without turning to Will, Yuul said, "Good. You?"

"Good," Will walked over to Liz and pecked her on her cheek. "How are you?"

"It's been interesting," Liz said, placing a peck on his cheek.

"What did I miss?" Will said, sitting next to Yuul.

"Why are you here?" Jeffrey asked Will. "Isn't it a little too early for you to be up and about?"

"I want to go over the bill I received from your wife last night."

"What bill?" Liz wanted to know.

"His bill for room and board and the other services we provided," Yuul said.

"Room and board?" Ella tilted her head to one side.

"We stayed at Mr. Sandhu's, eating his food and using his household items. We have to pay. Since Will is the money man, I invoiced him for that."

"Still, that was one big bill for the stay, don't you think?" Will protested.

"Don't complain. I applied the family discount," Yuul said.

"No, no!" Jeffrey said. "No family discount, no one's raising anyone's children!"

"Who's raising whose children?" Will wanted to know.

"Caleb wants Liz to raise their children in their own house," Ella said.

Will frowned. "Liz?"

"Never mind. *In this family*," Liz smirked at Jeffrey, "people start a conversation at A and then somehow end up close to Z."

"I still don't like it," Will said.

"Did you go over the bill?" Yuul asked, looking at Caleb.

"I did and forwarded it to Adam," Caleb smiled.

"I don't care who pays but I want it before you leave," Yuul said.

"Are you leaving?" Will said as his face lit up.

"I'm not telling you," Caleb said.

"AhhHaHha!" Will laughed whole heartedly. "You don't have to. You've already said enough."

"Don't you have a movie to make?" Caleb said. "Or, no one wants you anymore?"

"Can we continue this conversation over breakfast?" Yuul asked, looking at Jeffrey.

"Of course," Jeffrey said. He walked into the kitchen followed by Ella, Liz and then Caleb and Will.

"Everybody, get out!" Jeffrey yelled. "I don't have enough space for you all,"

They all walked out of the kitchen and sat around the table.

"How are your parents?" Liz asked, looking at Caleb.

"Oh My God!" Caleb said. "I forgot all about them. They're the reason why I came here. They want to invite you all over for dinner except for Will."

"I'm coming if Liz is," Will crossed his hands over his chest. "When are you leaving?"

"I'm not telling you," Caleb said.

"Are you really leaving?" Ella asked.

"Hmm... Yes, this Wednesday, I have to leave," Caleb said.

"This Wednesday?" Will said, frowning.

"What's wrong with this Wednesday?" Ella asked, looking at Will. "Did you plan something special for you and him this Wednesday?"

"Of course not," Will said, pouting his mouth. "I'm leaving on that day as well. I have to go on a tour to promote the film I worked on. The movie producers have patiently waited for me to finish this. They booked the ticket." Will looked over at Caleb. "Don't tell me we're taking the same plane?"

"I'm special," Caleb said. "I don't take civilian airplanes. I have a fearless military airplane."

"I know which one you're talking about." Will grinned. "The one that's super uncomfortable to ride on, right? Some of them don't even have seats."

"I'm going on a plane that has seats."

"So, everyone is leaving," Ella said. "That's depressing."

"I'll be back," Caleb said.

"I'll be back before you," Will said.

"You want to bet?" Caleb said.

"Okay, you both need to go," Yuul said. "I can't have breakfast in the midst of a pissing match."

"I'll stop if he stops," Caleb said.

"I'll stop if you stop first," Will said.

"Three, two…" Before Yuul hit 'one', they both stopped.

Liz said, "We'll all go to Caleb's for dinner tonight. It means we have to go to Mr. Sandhu's tomorrow or the day after tomorrow. He wants to throw a party."

That put a smile on everyone's face.

"Let's do it tomorrow," Caleb said. "I have to be at Trenton on Tuesday."

"Tomorrow is good for me as well," Will said. "I have a meeting with a producer of a TV show on Tuesday. They're interested in Maddie and Ed's story and their investigation on Wild Peach."

"Tomorrow, it is then," Ella said. "I already miss them."

"Me, too," Jeffrey said.

"I'll be right back," Liz said, getting to her feet. "I left my cellphone upstairs." She walked up the stairs, thinking about Will and Caleb. She hadn't thought about them leaving. She hadn't thought about *him* leaving. *He'll be back*, she thought. She hoped. She then laughed at her wishful thought. The chances of seeing him again would be slim, she knew. She then accepted that it was what it was. She knew that she would miss him. She would miss both of them. Yet, she would survive just like she always did.

41

MONDAY, DECEMBER 16

Inside Mr. Sandhu's on Purpledusk Trail, people were gathered around in the living room busy eating and listening to the man who had just come in to join them after a long day at work.

"How did it go?" Birdie said, looking at Jeffrey.

"It went well," Jeffrey said, placing a slice of pizza he'd been enjoying back on his plate. "I don't know what Ms. Sommer was told over the phone about Keira Scott before she came down to the station. But when she got to the station, she threw herself over the front desk at Keira Scott. By looking at her, you would never have guessed how light and agile she was as she leapt across that desk like a puma. It was almost like watching Yuul in action." Jeffrey turned to Yuul and smiled.

Yuul smiled a lopsided smile back to Jeffrey.

"Ms. Sommer pulled Keira Scott's hair. She scratched Keira's face really good. By the time one of the police officers in the lobby rushed over and broke it up, Ms. Sommer was holding a big chunk of hair in her hands."

"Where were you when all this was happening?" Agnes asked.

Jeffrey looked off into space, grinning. "Umm… I was there but not in a close enough proximity to stop her. Anyway, you wouldn't have believed the venom that poured out of Ms. Sommer as she was putting the finger on Keira Scott for taking down all those reports she made that never got filed. She was really awesome." Jeffrey flashed a thumbs-up. "Once we took Scott in for questioning, she wanted to cut a deal right away. When we showed no interest, she talked anyway." Jeffrey covered his mouth to stifle a laugh, but eventually broke into a fit of laughter. Spit was flying through his fingers and in all different directions.

"Oh man, you're so disgusting," Will put his plate down on the floor and wiped his face.

"Eww!" Liz and Ella screamed in unison.

Charlie turned to Ella and wiped the spit off her face with the sleeve of his shirt.

"Eww!" Tejas yelled at Charlie.

"Don't be jealous, my baby brother," Ajay went after Tejas pulling his sleeve all the way down ready to wipe whatever was on Tejas' face with it.

"Get away from me!" Tejas ran to Mr. Sandhu hiding behind his back.

"What's so funny? Share," Liz demanded.

"It's really nothing," Jeffrey said, trying to hold it in but broke into another fit of laughter.

"Spit it out!" Liz felt all eyes turn on her. "Oops! No pun intended."

"It's really nothing. As soon as Keira Scott realized she was in big trouble, she sold him out so fast calling him names and everything. At one point, she even called him Wile E. Coyote. Do you remember the TV cartoon, Wile E. Coyote and the Road Runner?"

They all nodded.

"She said that we might as well call him Wile E. Coyote. He thinks he is always hatching these cunning and sly plans, but nothing ever works out because he's the Wile E. Slimy Coyote, Wily the Idiot Coyote, Wily the Dimwit Coyote, Wily the Pig-Ignorant Knuckleheaded Coyote. She went on with the Wile E. Coyote thing for like a good solid 15 minutes."

Liz shook her head in disappointment. "Is that it?"

"You're not getting it. You never did appreciate those cartoons like I did," Jeffrey protested.

Liz just shook her head disapprovingly.

"Tell us what they were loading up on down in the States?" Birdie wanted to know.

"Guns," Jeffrey said.

"Guns?" Everybody said in unison.

"Rob and Doreen were running an organized crime syndicate with revenues probably in the millions of dollars. They made Troy Townsend their Underboss when he joined in on the family venture. The ex-Underboss objected to the decision, and Troy had Adam Doyle kill him. Although as the Underboss, Troy ran and oversaw the day-to-day responsibilities of the whole operation, Lilibeth and Rodrigo Valentia were given a wide berth to make their own decisions about certain goings-on at the home. The organization's main focus was running guns across the border. They bought guns in bulk in the States and sold them here in Canada for 10 times the price. Let's say, they paid $300 for a gun in the States they'd turn around and sell it for $3,000 here. It was a very lucrative business. Troy took over the business and expanded their operation. He turned the coach house into a warehouse equipped with underground bunkers and hired platoons of foot soldiers who were willing to do anything for a dollar."

"What about Rob and Doreen?" Birdie wanted to know.

"Rob and Doreen left the country. We got a visual of them at Pearson Airport from last Saturday, not long after Troy was apprehended. We're tracking them down and we will get them sooner or later. I promise you that. One last thing, it turned out that Grayson, the Police Chief, was also on Rob and Doreen's payroll. He's being investigated by the Internal Affairs Unit as we speak. These Internal Affairs guys are like pit bulls. Once they bite, they never let their suspect go, at least without taking a big chunk of flesh out of their suspects. I'd say it's just a matter of time before Grayson's all washed up."

"So, this is not over," Liz said.

"It is over in a big way," Jeffrey protested.

"Rob and Doreen still have their money. They could hire assassins to kill us from anywhere," Liz said.

Jeffrey grinned. "Don't worry. With the help of Ajay, we tracked down their offshore accounts, and we froze them. They can't withdraw a penny from their accounts."

"They might have lots of cash," Birdie said. "I don't believe they put all their eggs in one online basket."

"They probably do have some cash, but the question is how much cash can you really take with you overseas? The answer is not that much."

"There still might be some offshore accounts that Ajay didn't find," Agnes said.

They all got sombre and nodded in agreement.

"We'll worry about it when it comes to it," Mr. Sandhu said cheerfully. "Right now, let's just enjoy the day we have!" He put his glass up.

"He's right!" Jeffrey seconded it. "Let's enjoy the party!" He put his glass up.

Raising his glass, Ed said, "I want to thank Mr. Sandhu and his family for everything and that includes the wonderful hospitality they've shown us during our stay."

"Cheers!" everybody raised their glasses.

42

TWO MONTHS AFTER

1:00 a.m. – A Town in the Sierra Madre Mountains Far away from Canada, alarms went off quietly in the seven suites of a privately-owned, luxury hotel. The seven men occupying those suites each heard their alarm and as if by previous agreement, they all got up and entered their bathrooms to shower and prepare themselves for their upcoming mission.

The hotel had 24 suites, of which only 7 were occupied. At the client's special request, the hotel hadn't received any more guests. This client had paid double the going rate for all 24 suites and had even promised a very generous tip on their last day if the seven were properly served. The hotel manager was very sure that they would get that tip.

The hotel had offered the best food prepared by their very best chef and served by charming waiters and waitresses. Bartenders were always ready to pour tequila or whatever they wanted anytime of the day, any day of the week. The seven rooms had been professionally cleaned while those men had been served breakfast in the dining room, and any dirty clothes on the floor had been picked up, laundered, and then dropped off back to their rooms during their lunch.

The hotel manager was very happy with his guests as well as the agreement. Those 7 men had been just marvelous. They were polite and charming in their own right. Most importantly, since the hotel was perched on a hilltop above an old mining town and even though it was nestled in the foothills of the magnificent Sierra Madre Mountains, very few tourists ever passed through the village, unlike the beach towns nearby.

The old mining town, just like its residents, had run its natural cycle arriving almost at the end of its journey. The town had seen some tourists wander in and enjoy the flora and canyons, but no one ever stayed for more than a day or two before going back to their beachside hotels or resorts as they'd found the town too quiet to even meditate.

There'd been no new residents to the town for almost half a century up until two months ago, and the newcomers had lowered the average age in town. Before the newcomers, the youngest resident had turned 70 years old, and that was a few years back.

The newcomers lived in a Mexican Colonial style ranch that was nestled at the far edge of the mining town, 30 minutes east of the hotel by foot. The property was fenced in by stucco retaining walls with one wooden main gate that connected the ranch to the mining town's only street. The rest of the property was surrounded by oak trees and shrubs.

• • •

A tall man came down to the lobby first, his cellphone to his ear.

"It's all set in motion," the tall man said.

"It's been a long wait. I wish I were there to watch everything go down with my own eyes," a man on the other end of the line said excitedly.

"Will, you're too famous to be seen here," the tall man said.

Will sighed. "I know. Sometimes, being gigantically famous has its downsides. I sometimes envy you, Caleb. You can go on with your life forever without ever being watched by a curious pair of eyes."

"I know you're bragging, but I'll let it slide only this time since you're financing this operation."

"Money talks." Will laughed. "Do you need anything else?"

"You bought me everything I've ever wanted," Caleb squeaked.

"Ahahah!"

"The mission will begin at zero three hundred hours Zulu. The package will be dropped off at zero seven hundred hours."

"Okay. Call me back when you're up in the air. Please don't make me look up a military dictionary and please talk like a normal person."

Caleb cracked up. "Understood!"

Will let out a long sigh. "And don't forget the deal."

"You don't forget the deal!" Caleb exclaimed.

"If you tell Liz about your heroics, I'll tell her I was more heroic than you ever were."

Caleb let out a laugh again. "I don't want that. This'll be our little secret."

"I'll make sure Jeffrey finds our little gift for him," Will said. "There's a super bug going around right now, and countries are starting to shut down. Be safe wherever you get stationed next."

"Thanks, you, too" Caleb said, looking at his men gathering in the lobby – 4 gunmen, 1 wheelman and 1 pilot. He would finally remove the risk from his loved ones' lives forever.

• • •

Five men passed through the oak trees and everything else that grew between the hotel and the ranch. There was only a lone moon awake that dimly lit the whole mining town. Those five men moved swiftly, like it was daytime. With the help of their night vision goggles, they reached their operation field in no time. They went up and over the fence as if it weren't even there.

The four men moved separately and silently taking up their positions while Caleb scaled the outer wall of the house. After he had made it to the roof, on cue, each of the four men pulled their triggers taking out the armed guards that were stationed there to protect the occupants of the ranch.

One of the guards on the roof saw Caleb when he came up but wasn't really sure what he was seeing. As the guard was squinting his eyes to improve his vision,

Caleb pulled the trigger, shooting him in the shoulder. Then he immediately turned 30 degrees to his right and squeezed the trigger again. The two men dropped their guns jumping to the sky in agony. Caleb moved in fast, grabbed their AR-15s, released the magazines from their rifles and after he pocketed them, he descended to the ground.

By the time Caleb had landed safely, his four men had already broken into two two-man teams positioned on either side of the front door. Caleb had almost rejoined the team when the front door suddenly flung open, shots were fired, and a hail of bullets burst out.

Caleb reacted, launching himself through the air, he fired off a salvo through the opening as he flew across the doorway. Caleb landed on the other side of the door rolling in behind his team members. No more bullets flew straight out at them, but shots were still being fired out from the flanks.

His men timed their attack perfectly in between the barrage of bullets. They quickly subdued the enemy. In less than a minute after making it inside the house, the guns were silenced. They swept through the house and found eight men on the ground holding their wounded limbs to stop the bleeding while crying their eyes out.

Caleb's men moved expertly and bound the combatants, using zip ties while Caleb kept them in place with his gun. After the men had been neutralized, Caleb walked up the stairs with two of his men while the other two stayed behind, securing the main floor.

Caleb and his team quickly moved to the master bedroom and flung open the door. Seeing no one,

Liz, the Neighbour

Caleb kept moving to the next door, which was supposed to lead to a bathroom based on the blueprints Will had sent him. He kicked the door open while the other two men trained their guns on the doorway ready to shoot anything that moved.

As the door flew off its hinges, Caleb saw Rob and Doreen hiding inside the bathtub, terrified. His men entered. They pulled out their tranquilizer pistols from their gun holsters and fired – one Ketamine dart for Rob and the other for Doreen. They snatched Rob and Doreen out of the tub and whisked them out to the main gate where their wheelman was waiting.

They abandoned their getaway car on the tarmac, leaving a duffle bag full of cash on the passenger seat as they'd promised for the local cops.

Two men carried Rob and Doreen over their shoulders, following their pilot to the private jet parked out on the tarmac while the others guarded their backs. Although they had paid off the local cops for their safety and were leaving more money behind, one thing all these men knew for sure was to never ever trust corrupt officials.

Once the three men had boarded the private jet, the next two ran to the jet while the other two guarded them, and then followed by the final pair.

• • •

Rob and Doreen had the sweetest dreams throughout their entire flight and only woke up after hearing the sound of wailing police sirens coming to greet them on Toronto's Centre Island. Still in a daze, they heard a male voice say, "Welcome home." They both just thought that the voice was so much like that of the annoying detective Jeffrey Knight.

BOOKS BY THIS AUTHOR

Liz, the Accused: The Liz Knight Trilogy #1
Finding herself as a wrongly accused murder suspect, Liz Knight decides to find the real killer with the help of a law-abiding cop, a crazy rich psychopath, an orphaned ex-drug addict and a heartless lawyer. The murder that brought them together takes them to an unexpected place where other murders and the mysteries of human hearts have been waiting to be solved.
Can the heartless lawyer afford to have the heart? Can the orphaned ex-drug Addict have a shot at a happy ending? Can the crazy rich psychopath do right by the law-abiding cop until the end? Can the law-abiding cop follow the law no matter what? Will Liz win it all?
Part 1 tells the story about how their pasts shaped them to become the persons that they are now, how their paths

have crossed in the past, what brought them together and who is at the centre of it all.

Liz, the Neighbour: The Liz Knight Trilogy #2
It all started when the bad guys tried to get clever in covering their tracks. Things get complicated.
Now a Special Forces operator, a Hollywood star, ex-soldiers, gangsters and cops are all lurking in the shadows, trying to catch one another and to purge the other team before they do them.
Liz and the gang get caught in the middle after accepting a seemingly straight forward case - locate a 75-year old missing aunt.
In this book, Liz and the gang team up with 3 retirees and a whole host of other colourful characters, to solve mysteries that revolve around a retirement home and the murder of a news reporter.
Who will survive?
Who will end up behind bars?
Will Liz find love again?

Made in United States
Orlando, FL
28 March 2022